THE BEST OF WAL

Don

Copyright ©2019 DOMII

All rights reserved. No part of this publication may be reproduced, stored in a retrieval system or transmitted in any form or by any means – electronic, mechanical, photocopying, and recording or otherwise – without the prior written permission of the author, except for brief passages quoted by a reviewer in a newspaper or magazine. To perform any of the above is an infringement of copyright law.

BORN ON FEBRUARY 13TH, 1993, WALKING DOCTOR TONNAN ARRIVED AT UNIVERSITY, GOT KICKED OUT AFTER WRITING AN ESSAY ON MARIJUANA, JUMPED OFF ARCHWAY BRIDGE & INTO A TWO-MONTH COMA, THEN STARTED TO WRITE 'GOD'S PRETTY GAME OF GROTESQUE PUPPETS' & SING HIS POEMS. HE WON THE REUEL PRIZE FOR UPCOMING POET IN 2017. IT HAS BEEN RUMOURED THAT TONNAN HAS READ OVER 9 BOOKS AND CAN PLAY GUITAR SLIGHTLY BETTER THAN THE AVERAGE PERSON BORN IN 1993. THIS BOOK WAS RELEASED BY ITS AUTHOR ON 13TH AUGUST 2020.

WWW.WALKINGDOCTORTONNAN.COM

Over Mushroom Mountain & Beyond The Yonder
> *page 6*

All of Tomorrow's Parties
> *page 26*

The Day Destiny's Dragon Set the Mushroom Paradise Hotel Ablaze
> *page 31*

Schizophrenic Soul (an article written for Magic Care)
> *page 49*

Marijuana: A Potted History of My Illicit Love Affair and A Thousand Words on Why Prohibition is Stupid
> *page 44*

Welcome to Planet Earth (page 57)

1. Welcome To Planet Earth
2. Endorphin Dolphin
3. You Are The Catalyst
4. Sheep in a Lorry
5. Grave News
6. Steepled Sequels
7. Bird Volcano Event
8. Reality Or Reverie
9. I'll Love You Till Friday Never Comes
10. Your Fingers Were A Cabaret
11. Like The Sun When It Swoons
12. Twirled

Worlds That Lovers Bent (page 75)

1. Here Is Exactly Why
2. I Never Knew Her
3. Inside (feat. Oliver Francis)
4. Angel Made of Acid
5. First Love
6. Everything I Never Learnt to Say
7. Make Tomorrow Up
8. What's Your Story?
9. Flu Blues
10. B4 the Skies Turn Black
11. Happily Dead
12. Sketcher of Maps
13. Cinnamon Moon
14. I Love Your Love (feat. Oliver Francis)
15. Worlds That Lovers Bent

We Live In A Political God (page 100)

1. The Subtler The Tyranny
2. Ground Zero
3. God Knows Your Burden
4. Voodoo of Dream
5. Karma's Barter
6. Your Love Will Go Last
7. Crossroads
8. Broken Awe
9. You're Here
10. Roll
11. Secret Master of Orgasms
12. The Other Heaven
13. Blissful Tears, Broken Mirrors
14. Nothing Is Sweeter Sometimes
15. Hypnotized
16. The Best Painter of Milk
17. The World – Chapter 3
18. The Heartwheel Artist
19. Joke's On You
20. Nobody's Clown
21. How to Sing
22. Talkin' Miss Solitary (feat. Sam Raven)
23. Proof of a Conspiracy (feat. Nikhat Shah)
24. Omens of Paradise
25. The Nun Visions
26. Beware The Good Adult Factory
27. Eden
28. Poor Number
29. Let Her Shadow Dance Move You
30. Talkin' Christmas Blues

God's Pretty Game of Grotesque Puppets (the 64,000 word novel): page 176

The Sun Always Sets in The West:
Happy Tears in Love with a Cold:
The Inauguration of Insanity:
The Mother of Infinity:
The Devil Can't & God Won't:
The Footnote:

"So readable and full of surprises; you never know where it's going to go next."
— Eliza Geoffy

GOD'S PRETTY GAME OF GROTESQUE PUPPETS

This poignant epic is a pornographic & poetic series of humorous vignettes:
'The Sun Always Sets in the West',
'Happy Tears in Love with a Cold',
'The Inauguration of Insanity',
'The Mother of Infinity',
& 'The Devil Can't & God Won't'.

THE FIRST NOVEL WRITTEN
BY DOMINIC FRANCIS

33 males & females passionately plead Heaven to open the damned dam of its eyes to their broken prayer and cry. This motley tribe of unlikely heroes hold hands and frolic feverishly around an ancient well, chanting the Mercy Mantra: "Love is rain! Rain explains God! God is the cloud of love above this crowd's refrain! God, hear our pain!"

When it rains in dry season, there's no reason to complain. But it's rainy season and God hasn't cried for over a month. Why the heaven is God so happy all of a sudden? Did God get married to the Devil, a skilled masseuse of the ego, without first informing Brazenhead, the Village shaman? Is God too busy fighting crime in Savantjakgon or playing imaginary ice hockey to spare a thought for the plight of His worshippers?

This is Rainbow Village, population 37. The awfully attentive reader may have already noted that today four people are absent from the Rainbow Village Raindance Ritual. This is because a brave bald bloke named Brazenhead and his humungous humanoid hound named Baskerville have travelled to Mushroom Mountain with a telescope in search of Rollon, husband & father, and Teresa, wife & mother. The parents disappeared a few days ago while hunting for food.

Everybody in Rainbow Village is afraid that 'the lost couple' may actually be 'the couple that absconded'. But it's quite possible – in fact, it might probably be probable – that the parents didn't abscond and are actually lost, or that they got eaten by a Monster. Nevertheless, the chance that the couple upped & walked away from Rainbow Village poisons the bitterly cold air. They have only been gone for two days, but the ghost of their presence distinctly haunts every member of the community.

Rollon and Teresa are parents to the 15-year-old Cloud and his 11-year-old sister Rainer. These siblings are the protagonists of this story and shall embark on this story's titular odyssey. Every character you'll meet on this psychedelic purgatory of a planet will have a befittingly groovy yet suitably symbolic name, such as Brazenhead or Rainer.

Wow! It's raining now! The Raindance has worked! Holy cow! The remaining tribe members, an admixture of ages & races, rejoice in subdued ecstasy. They end the Mercy Mantra by incanting "Merci! Merci!", thanking the Almighty for His offering.

Cloud and Rainer are thirsty and hungry, but they don't eat the food that they've conserved for the voyage ahead yet. Cloud knows that the younger the tribe member, the less they let them starve or thirst. He doesn't fear for himself, yet for whatever reason her really fears for his younger sister Rainer.

"I'm cold," the eleven-year-old girl says, fidgeting with her bedcovers.

"Me too. It's cold here. Our folks… they ain't coming back," her older brother says.

"Possibly not. But they might. I like being warm, but I sure don't ever want to go to Fire Forest," she says.

"Beyond Mercy Mountain, past Fire Forest, there's Paradise. So if you don't want to go to Fire Forest, you don't want to go to Paradise. Why don't you want to go Paradise?" he asks, almost rhetorically.

"I don't know exactly why I'm afraid of Fire Forest, but it makes sense to me," Rainer says.

"Okay. If it makes sense to you, then it makes sense to me. Heat is good after cold, though. And we're going, like it or not," Cloud says.

"I wouldn't mind going if it means that we're headed somewhere interesting," Rainer says.

"Interesting in what way?" Cloud says.

"Like complete darkness submerged in light. Something epic… something cool, anyway. Do you know what Fire Forest is like?" Rainer asks.

"No. But OK. I like kaleidoscopes too. Get some sleep. You can't hope forever and expect dawn to never come," Cloud says.

"Alright. Good night, Cloud," says Rainer.

"Good night, Rainer. I'll wake you early. When you wake up, you've got to be quiet for half an hour. It's important," Cloud says, blowing out the candle.

"Yeah. Okay… alright. Do you miss Mum and Dad?" Rainer asks.

"Same as yesterday. Sometimes they're with me. Sometimes they're not," Cloud replies.

"Okay. Sleep tight," Rainer says.

"You too," says Cloud. He turns away from her in his bed.

"Cloud… will you miss anyone else in Rainbow Village?" Rainer says,

"I'll miss Brazenhead. How about you?" Cloud says.

"I'll miss Maxi. Maxi made me smile," Rainer says. Maxi gave her a flower last Winter then pretended to hate her for five months. But now they're good friends again. Boys can be coy. Girls do own the world, though.

"That's good. It's good to have good memories. Our minds are memories and consciousness. Nothing more. But you'll meet other people. Where we're going, there will be lots of other people. I'm sure of it," Cloud says.

"But how are you sure?" Rimku asks.

"I just know it," he replies.

"Night."

"Night."

It seems like yesterday but it was three days ago. A Monster swallowed Cloud & Rainer's parents alive. A Monster swallowed them good. The pair weren't alive after that Monster swallowed them. It's a shame, but it's a fact. Oranges are orange. Orangutans are apes. Monsters are monsters.

Cloud wakes Rainer at 4am. Rainer yawns as she wakes up, which makes Cloud yawn too.

"What time is it?" Rainer whispers.

"I don't know. How should I know? I'm not a sundial. It's time to wake up," Cloud whispers back.

Cloud & Rainer creep past 30 sleeping souls in the Village. The mockingbirds are beginning to tweet. It's usually a treat to the ear, but Cloud knows that some silence would help make the plan successful. Shut up, please!

But now Rainer coughs a smokers cough. Less than a second after this sound exits her mouth, Brazenhead (the village shaman) wearily saunters out of Mana's hut [I'm not sure if Mana is his girlfriend but he spends an awful lot of time with her].

"Hey dudes," Brazenhead warbles. "What's happening?"

"We're going for walk," Cloud replies a little too quickly. "Rainer is restless and she's always liked the night."

"Okay man," Brazenhead says in a suspiciously 'chill' voice. "Just remember that the danger of remaining is greater than drinking Lava Liquid."

"Err… what's Lava Liquid?"

"I don't know," says Brazenhead. "Sometimes I hear stuff as well as stuff shit. Maybe it means nothing. I hear a lot of met metaphysical metaphors that even I don't understand. Have a good walk, dudes."

"Okay. We'll bear your advice in mind. Good to see you," Cloud says.

Cloud & Rainer walk to the woods. Cloud doesn't look back, but Rainer does. Cloud doesn't even notice that Rainer looks back. You don't need to have an IQ of 142 to recognise the symbolism of this.

"Cloud, why the heavens was Brazen in Mana's hut as this early hour?" asks Rainer.

"I guess he really likes talking to Mana. I don't know," Cloud says. He really doesn't know and this is genuinely his best guess.

It suddenly occurs to Cloud that Brazenhead must have seen their rucksacks. He freezes for half an instant, or at least his mind does. He shrugs.

You don't have to have an IQ of 120 to know that Brazenhead, the village shaman, knows how to have a good time. I don't think Brazenhead has an IQ higher than you, but he's a very perceptive guy. Cloud sighs and Rainer coughs. It's quite as short journey through the woods, where the inhabitants of Rainbow Village forage for food, but folk rarely set foot on Mushroom Mountain.

In an earthly hour, they reach the foot of the Mushroom Mountain. A goggled giggling Penguin flies fiercely fast & freely towards the two siblings. The Penguin's eyebrows make it look pretty forlorn, but who's to say if he's happy or sad.

[The Penguin's name? ... why does your subconscious ask? I don't know the Penguin's name. I don't know if he even has a name. I'm just telling you a story. It's good that you have an inquisitive mind, but whether the Penguin is called anything is irrelevant. The Penguin is just a goggled giggling Penguin.]

In actuality, Cloud and Rainer have never seen anything like the goggled giggling Penguin. Neither have you, probably, because if you were to live in a world with rarities such as goggled giggling Penguins, you probably wouldn't get to read this book. So... it's not all bad. To quote myself, "there's a secret karma to the mechanisations of reality's heart".

The giggling flying Penguin with goggles snatches Cloud's rucksack and the giggling flying Penguin with goggles becomes the cackling flying Penguin with goggles. That Penguin simply just cackles with laughter! It's not at all funny to anyone else but the laughing giggling Penguin seems to find it hilarious.

The image of the cackling flying Penguin with Cloud's rucksack zooms into the distance and recedes into the horizon. So it goes. Even mortals that you like can rob you of your possessions.

"What the heaven was that weird creature?" says Rainer.

"I don't know. We've got to get my stuff back," Cloud says. "Your supplies of food & water won't last us long enough. After we climb Mushroom Mountain, we've got to descend Mushroom Mountain and pass through Fire Forest into Paradise. It's going to be a long journey."

But the journey won't last as long as Cloud thinks. Two days are usually just a couple of moments wed to one. How do I know how long it took? You know. Sometimes you just have to make it up. What can I say? I'm not breaking the fourth wall when I tell you this, because we are not in a theatre.

… where the heavens were we? My attention span is short, probably because I am a vaguely handsome schizophrenic, partially disabled introvert loner and mathematically-minded brain damaged genius. Because I have eyes and a good long-term memory, I know that it was something about Cloud and Rainer.

Oh, that's right. The siblings eventually reach the top of Mushroom Mountain, where they get their first look at Fire Forest and can see Rainbow Village which looks so distant & tiny. Three days of food does not prove to be enough, given that they were hungry already.

On top of Mushroom Mountain, the pair grow very hungry. They decide to eat the leaves they find beneath the Tree of Life. The consequences of this are hilarious & somewhat sad yet vaguely sinister.

Some of the apocalyptic visions they experience hint at a beautiful future of friendship & love while others foreshadow a silent doom, a quiet song of unfulfilled promises.

"I miss Maxi!! Maxi is the bestest!! Clouuuuuudddddd….. promise we'll go home now," Rainer says.

"Yeah! Whatever! Maxi's dead to me too!" Cloud replies callously but happily. Cloud has a brave, righteous heart, but sometimes he can be so rude. He's eaten leaves before but Rainer hasn't.

"NOOOOOO! MAXI IS MY HERO! HE'S SOOOOO... SOOOO... MYSTERIOUS," Rainer whispers. "I think I love him."

"I think I've had enough of Maxi. That kid is just too nice," says Cloud. There's something you should know about Cloud: Cloud never thinks twice. Perhaps that's his hamartia. I'm not going to spell it out for you, but this book is metaphorical as heaven. If I'm honest with you, Rainer's angels are going to get a little forgetful pretty soon. This story has a happy ending, which is why I want to tell it, but it's not qutite as happy as the ending of "The Wizard of Oz".

The siblings descend Mushroom Mountain. Nothing much noteworthy happens during this bit of the tale. Nothing doesn't happen. But nothing will always happen if you wait long enough. Yep. All you've got to do is wait: you don't even need to hope or move. Someone can physically force your body to move but if it wants to, your mind can remain still for an exceptionally long time.

Cloud and Rainer reach the foot of Mushroom Mountain. It took quite a long time to get here where we are now, but not too long – only nothing lasts *too* long.

The sacred sibling and the other one enter Fire Forest. They rapidly realise that the further you get into fire forest, the hotter it gets. Rumour has it there's an inferno at the centre, but I really don't know if this is true.

They stop walking through the forest, which is just a regular red forest. All sweaty they sit down and drink some of Rainer's orange juice.

From a nearby tree, a Rainbow Parrot tweets many meaningless things, then soars high in the sky, then descends to perch on Rainer's shoulder. In Arial Nova Light, the size 12 Rainbow Parrot warns of the *"big hairy Tiger that want make love and eat – he even more elderly than a fool such as I!"*.

Cloud's first thought is that the young Rainbow Parrot has become prematurely senile, but soon the pair hear a huge roar.

Cloud is stuck in Cloud's groove but this world ain't as brittle as he thinks.

Cloud doesn't move his restless mind and Rainer is a saint so barely binks.

Do you remember what happens next? Have you heard this story before? Love is the only thing I live for. I don't like food or television. Cloud and Rainer have never seen a television set, and they're relatively content when they're not too hungry. Do you remember what happened before?

Suddenly a ravenous Tiger approaches and start circling around the siblings menacingly. What the heavens did you expect to happen? The Parrot was right.

Rainer remembers the words of the Parrot and offers the Tiger love, speaking affectionately and offering some fish. The Tiger becomes very passive and obedient, laying down and nodding. The siblings pet the Tiger, then sit on the Tiger, the Parrot still perched on Rainer's neck.

The Tiger gallops off into the secret heart of Fire Forest. It's quite a bumpy journey. If you're bored of this story, just remember that the people living it now are not bored at all. You can't be bored and have adrenaline seeping through your pores. And all of us live in a version of Infinity, even if we don't know it or our day-to-day lives are boring.

The Tiger carrying Cloud, Rainer and the Rainbow Parrot slows down. There is a picturesque waterfall of Lava Liquid ahead.

"Hah! Me knew this would happen!" says the Rainbow Parrot, happy he is right for once. "What? A shame Andrew me! HAHAH! Me make mathematical paradox pun! Go ahead! Rememberrrrrrrrrrrrrrrrr........"

They do. The siblings tentatively touch The Lava Liquid. It feels nice. It feels really nice. It feels better than really nice. Recalling Brazenhead's words, they drink some. It tastes better than really nice, so they keep drinking it until they aren't thirsty anymore.

The siblings fall asleep for a few earthly hours. Cloud snores a little. Rainer doesn't make a sound. The siblings are asleep for 175 earthly minutes.

The Tiger licks the siblings awake. The Tiger sneezes sleepily. *"Big hairy Tiger love me now too! I are in your debt,"* says the Parrot.

In his sleep, Cloud had an ecstatic vision of blue people. Rainer has had an ecstatic vision of Maxi. Cloud has had a conversation with Brazenhead about returning to Rainbow Village. Rainer has had a bad premonition Maxi would ultimately be happier if they didn't. Everyone except for the majority of mankind is hungry again.

I'd prefer to keep my telling of the fate that befalls our heroes short and snappy, so I'll now summarise exactly what goes down.

A small colony of worker ants now dance in Rainer's mind and she can't stop dancing to the somewhat more lucid Parrot's strange melody.

Cloud suddenly realises his sister is quite a beautiful person. He sees her hair turns purple. The siblings agree to go back to Rainbow Village.

Their journey is a success until they reach the base of the mountain. It is then that the Rainbow Parrot flies away. The Tiger gets rather moody.

The Tiger eats Cloud. Cloud's spirit is somewhere else but Cloud's body is now dead. The Tiger nods at Rainer. Rainer knows she knows but she is still sad. It starts to rain in Fire Forest. Rainer opens her mouth to the heavens. It feels good to be hydrated again. I doubt you thought or hoped this would be how this story ends, but the following is exactly how my story ends:

1. Rainer climbs Mushroom Mountain alone.
2. After eighteen earthly hours, Rainer reaches the top where the goggled giggling Penguin returns Rainer's rucksack. He's smiling so photogenically it's as if this story was meant to adapted for film.
3. Rainer sees two skeletons on Mushroom Mountain's lowest peak. She cries. Rainer now knows for sure that she is an orphan and Cloud, her brother, is gone.
4. As soon as a disillusioned Rainer sets foot in the realms of Rainbow Village, it starts raining in Rainbow Village again. This is good, because – as I pointed out at the beginning of this tale – the village was having a tough time.
5. The first creature Rainer spots when she gets back to the village is Brazenhead, the village shaman. That cat isn't wearing any socks. "Yeah," he says. Rainer shakes her head.

6. Maxi, the boy that Rainer loves, runs up to Rainer. Maxi's missed Rainer and Rainer's missed him too, but most of the time she was too busy to think. Rainer and Maxi kiss for the first time. It's romantic but they don't really know how to do it.
7. I'm not sure if this is a happy ending or not, but many earthly years later, Cloud, Rainer, Rollon and Teresa are all reunited in heaven, where eventually the family pass away at the same time because there's an apocalypse.

You couldn't make it up. Even I didn't. It's just a retelling of a traditional folk tale apparently written in 4379537 BC. That's what the man who did a naughty thing told me. Over the course of the couple hours, a third of his story was spoke in French, a third of it in Chinese and the rest in Latin. These words represent a translated druidic animation of the translated of his words. I hope you enjoyed them. As implied before, this story is metaphorical as heaven. Why don't you read it again? Personally, I'm not going

*to read it again for another while,
because I won't live forever.*

ALL OF TOMORROW'S PARTIES

ALL OF TOMORROW'S PARTIES

Exactly a month and a half
ago, Gregory Sanders, 77 years old, decided
that he was ready to have his funeral. The idea
had crept into his head during the closing credits
of the last episode of 'The Wire'. He wrote down
a list of all the good things and all the bad things
that could come out of a Premature Celebration
of His Own Death, chuckled to himself and then
called up the Bullingdon Arms.

We are now in the Bullingdon Arms with around
half of Gregory's favourite people. It is the date
of Gregory's funeral. There is a jovial atmosphere
in the air. There is a jukebox playing jazz in the
corner and there are lots of drunken old men and
women everywhere else. Gregory is gregariously
introducing a man with a very bushy beard to a
woman with very curly hair. Something tells him
they might get along.

Gregory gets the two talking, heads for the bar
and it is there that he spots Suzanne, a lady with
hazel eyes. It has been twenty-three years since
Suzanne and Gregory divorced, thirty-nine years
since they got married and sixty-one years since
they had their first sexual experience on her
parent's couch. She is wearing a blue cardigan,
sipping a glass of white wine and looking
exquisitely beautiful. He asks her about her

cats, she asks him about his cactuses and then they talk about more interesting things.

Just as Gregory is considering making a move on Suzanne and Suzanne is considering making a move on Gregory, Gregory and Suzanne's thirty-eight-year-old daughter rushes over to them. She is called Emily. Emily has Suzanne's aptitude for music and Gregory's oversized ears. She is an English professor at Leeds University and got married eight months ago. She's looking kind of grumpy right now, partly because a man named Ronaldo spilt his beer all over her and partly because she's seven months pregnant.

Emily asks why Lanky Larry isn't here. She and Lanky Larry always end up in an intense discussion about Renaissance Literature, and Suzanne and Gregory and the rest of the room never have the foggiest idea what they're going on about. Gregory explains that he's not sure which of the following categories Lanky Larry falls under, but that three people have died, eleven people couldn't be bothered to come and the rest had concerns about the spiritual implications of a party called 'The Premature Celebration of Gregory's Death'. Mother and daughter smile and roll their eyes at one another. Gregory excuses himself, for he has ingested three pints of beer and his bladder is suffering.

The party continues without him: a small gathering of elderly men ridicule the government; a dizzy woman steals a hat from its now hatless owner; a born again Christian imparts his apocalyptic revelations to an apathetic ex-Librarian; three partially deaf pensioners attempt to discuss the weather; and the man with the bushy beard & the women with the curly hair have mysteriously vanished.

But Gregory has finished his business in the Men's Room now and, as is his custom, he zips up his fly, washes his hands and looks in the mirror. Gregory finds mirrors highly educational; something in them always surprises him. What surprises him on this occasion, however, is not a newly bloomed wrinkle or fresh stain on his shirt, but the figure that is standing behind him. Gregory blinks feverishly. It is tall, skeletal and wielding a giant scythe. It is The Grim Reaper.

Gregory's legs begin to shake. The Grim Reaper's head rocks back and forth. For several seconds, the pair just stands there, staring at each other in the mirror. Neither seems quite sure what to say. Just as Gregory is about to make a run for it, he notices that the Grim Reaper is attempting to suppress a giggle. A smile slowly spreads across Gregory's face & suddenly the Grim Reaper can no longer contain his hysteria & then before you know it The Grim Reaper takes off his mask & then The Grim Reaper is Lanky Larry and then Gregory & Lanky Larry are in each other's arms howling with laughter in the lavatory of the Bullingdon Arms. Someday Gregory will model for a life drawing class & someday Gregory will meet his granddaughter & someday Gregory will watch 'The Sopranos' & someday Gregory will move into a nursing home & someday Gregory will have another party & someday Gregory will get married again & someday Gregory will die, but for this short minute of his life, all Gregory could do was laugh.

THE DAY DESTINY'S DRAGON SET MUSHROOM PARADISE HOTEL ABLAZE

THE DAY DESTINY'S DRAGON SET DUBLIN'S MUSHROOM PARADISE HOTEL ABLAZE

Whenever my mind lingers upon the four weeks I spent working as a concierge at Dublin's Mushroom Paradise Hotel, a wistful thirstiness envelops my body and colours the contours of wherever I am. The mere thought of that big old musty mansion – a realm where dreams seemed to be made or broken – exercises unilateral authority over my existence, sinking into all the atoms of my memory banks until my brain is rendered, in its tempestuous entirety, temporarily powerless. If I can, I sit down to collect myself and drink some water. At the very least, I take a few deep breaths. You're not there anymore, I tell myself, you can relax.

Because of the fire that obliterated most of the building, I wasn't employed at the hotel for very long. That manacle-muddled era evokes imageries that are both vivid yet hazy. Sometimes it feels as if that month of my life didn't happen to me at all, and instead represents a story that's been repeated to me, time after time, against my will, by some kidnapper at gunpoint. Nonetheless, the fact still remains that I was there the day Destiny's dragon set Dublin's Mushroom Paradise Hotel ablaze. For what it's worth, too, I remember the event itself with such cinematic clarity that it's hard for me to describe the whole affair succinctly whilst remaining faithful to the details of what actually happened.

It's important, first of all, that you have an idea about the rationale behind the selection of the clientele: the owner wanted to create a secret, invite-only hotel for chic, wealthy guests. He bought a quadruple-glazed mansion in Sandycove, and started by inviting one billionaire, who could in turn invite two friends to stay, who could in turn each invite two friends to stay, and so on and so forth. Within six months, three hundred different people – all affluent & invited – had stayed at the hotel. This was back in 2005. I became a concierge there in 2007.

The staff of Dublin's Mushroom Paradise Hotel were hand-selected by a distinguished jury of wealthy shareholders. Each candidate for the job had to be invited to apply by someone who had stayed at the hotel. The interview was complex and three-parted… the first section of the selection process involved a series of fifty questions on anything from the applicant's familiarity with the works of Hank Williams to a description of their first kiss, the second involved baking cupcakes, and the third required the completion of a triathlon.

While I was there, I had only three other colleagues. Though the guests were rather flamboyant and will probably remain caricatures to you, my fellow staff and I were rather more pragmatic, though so ill-suited to the job it is a wonder we passed the interview stage. I didn't know a thing about Hank William's back-catalogue, but I described my first kiss as a 'blissful dialogue of leftist politics', and that went down a treat with the owner's son, who cackled with his head back and mouth wide-open.

There was The Lollipop Lady, an affected middle-aged woman with crimson hair who manned the front desk. I remember her quite affectionately. She always carried candy and chocolate in her pockets and though she often offered a 'hand-picked selection' of her 'finest' to me, I can't remember her actually ever eating any herself. Ah, The Lollipop Lady! She wasn't eccentric as such, but she had a distinctly peculiar aura about her. She exclusively used one-syllable words and seemed incapable of flouting this lifestyle choice. She referred to the Dublin's Mushroom Paradise Hotel as 'this place we are in now' and she called herself 'Nat, The Sweet Girl', but everyone else called her The Lollipop Lady.

And there was Brian The Actor, a mastermind of a thirty-something actor who never made it big because though his brain was pretty brilliant, he spoke so quickly that he wasn't suited to speaking roles on stage or film. Apparently, too, his agent had been circulating a rumour that he had once slept with Britney Spears; whether this peculiar piece of gossip was the truth, or merely an effort to catalyse or jeopardise Brian The Actor's career in showbiz, we will probably never know. He dressed in a purple or beige suit and worked as the only cleaner on the premises. The extravagances of our guests were sometimes so catastrophic that even the keenest of cleaners could not combat such messianic mess while still having time to rest or sleep. So, although I'm not implying that Brian The Actor was lazy, Dublin's Mushroom Paradise Hotel's rouge carpets would win no prizes for pristineness.

And there was The Frenchman, the chef, a twenty-year old fat man who claimed to hail from Paris yet spoke impeccable English without the hint of an accent. He would swear to himself in perfect French while cooking – 'merde, merde, MERDE!'. Despite cooking for a living, he disliked most food that wasn't bread, butter or cheese.

Then, there was me: the bellboy, the concierge, the custodian & the waiter. I was twenty-five during my time at Dublin's Mushroom Paradise Hotel. I'm known as 'The Dope Cat' to my close friends and as Neil to those who don't know me too well. I'm not particularly worldly, my tastes are idiosyncratic, and I'm kind of verbose. Sometimes I get lost on my way home, pretty much around the same time every year I discover I like the taste of cheddar again, and though I have only just learned the meaning of 'phantasmagoria' I have been using the word (ineffectually or wrongly) for years. You can reach your own conclusions about me, but I don't take much for granted: thankfully, I'm an alright storyteller and I have a content yet desolate disposition. Before being employed at Dublin's Mushroom Paradise Hotel, I lived off the fat of the welfare state on about 150 euros a week.

I write whenever I can as it's the only thing I can do well, and I've attempted suicide only once: that I am writing this now indicates that I'm not very good at dying either. One immature yet demonstrative effort was enough for me to recognize that even if I don't belong in this world, this world belongs in me. The pretext of boredom or longing for another dimension are both self-fulfilling, self-sustaining cycles. You should be grateful you have the time to be bored, and a waste of time is a waste of time only because you have time in the first place, whose unit will, somewhat soon, be foreign to you. Wait a day and the world will be a different place, in a small way. Things can always change. I could swear I was someone else yesterday. I was in another three-act play, another tiny human drama.

I suppose it's also true that some things never change. For example, pretty much every living adult dragon can breathe fire. And when the dwarf of a flame starts to breed, it can spread into dozen dwarfs of a flame. And if they in turn transform into an enormous blazing inferno, you can expect to see some people dead.

***

Destiny was forty-two. She was beautiful; I don't think, you know, that I've ever actually met anyone so beautiful. She had shoulder-length black hair, tanned skin and moved kind of like an ostrich. You'd have to see her in action to understand what I mean by this. Destiny had a demeanour that alternately danced between the outward invitation of intimacy and the introspective pushing away of whoever she's talking to. She didn't drink alcohol but smoked Marlborough Lights intermittently. It seemed like she had a lot to lose but what this was you couldn't really say for sure. Destiny's voice was high-pitched, and her choice of words were spritely and sweet. On her second night, she invited me to repair for the night with her to share her secret despair; of course, I refused as I had professional standards to uphold.

"Do you want to spend the night with me?" Destiny had inquired then, somewhat quizzically. "My soul is quaking with this secret sorrow that only a man can fix."

"Uh, thanks for the offer. But I can't. I'm working. Would you like me to make you some Camomile?" I had offered.

"Serving it is how your night duties will begin, and drinking it is how mine will end," she had replied mysteriously. I nodded, but I doubted she was correct on either front.

"Have you met my pet dragon?" Destiny had said distractedly, as I made to leave.

"No, I haven't." I'd heard rumours from The Lollipop Lady on this front, but I wasn't going out of my way to meet a dragon, and for some reason I was keen to change the subject. "Anyhow, I'll bring you some Camomile."

"Wait a minute," she said. "I have a question: how would you describe the sensation of taste to someone who cannot taste?"

"I guess it's kind of like a smell. A coloured smell. Yeah, that's how I'd describe it."

"Fair enough. I think it's more of an audio-based thing. But that's just me."

"Yeah, I know what you mean. Taste is kind of like a sound," I said obligingly, though I didn't know in what way taste is like a sound.

Pretty much every living adult dragon can breathe fire. And when the dwarf of a flame starts to breed, it can spread into dozen dwarfs of a flame. And if they in turn transform into an enormous blazing inferno, you can expect to see some people dead.

***

You know, I never did get to meet Destiny's dragon. But when Destiny's dragon set Dublin's Mushroom Paradise Hotel ablaze, I almost didn't have to. Apparently, it ran manically around the hotel, setting fire to every flammable thing in sight. Anyhow, very quickly the fire alarm went off & everyone migrated outside. Soon, the flames were cackling & beautiful. It was everything you could possibly want in a fire. The fire brigade arrived but to no avail. The better half of the building was incinerated within the space of ten minutes.

I love to watch fires spread, like I love to watch the sacred tsunami of democracy spread across the world like butter on bread, like the hysteria at a circus act gone wrong. Yes, seeing that fire was like witnessing a huge Jenga depiction of the Eiffel Tower collapse bit by bit in front of its creator. There was nothing the fire department could do. The building's foundations gave way & three stories became two and two became one. Everyone stood there, crying & talking & ogling. Luckily the only victim of the fire was its perpetrator, the dragon. Destiny yelled & shouted & yelled but he wouldn't come out.

That fire in particular was so beautiful to look at that it made me forget my personal vendetta against myself. Yes, I remember when Destiny's dragon set Dublin's Mushroom Paradise Hotel ablaze. It was beautiful & perhaps a little sad.

SCHIZOPHRENIC SOUL

SCHIZOPHRENIC SOUL

"I certainly don't suffer from schizophrenia. I quite enjoy it. And so do I."
— Emilie Autumn

Initially, I was surprised to learn that roughly 1.1% of the population over the age of 18 suffers from, or in more isolated cases enjoys, a form of Schizophrenia: I expected that this figure would be much higher. However, this statistic equates to approximately 51 million people in the world, or almost all of England's population, with the illness. And if you are getting treated for Schizophrenia like I was or if you are working in the field of mental health as you may be, you are obviously more likely to encounter people with symptoms of Schizophrenia.

Contrary to its portrayal in popular culture, the diagnosis of schizophrenia does not rest entirely upon your perceived existence of uncontrollable and unsolicited voices (or hallucinations). Schizophrenia is rather the presence of two or more of the following symptoms for at least 30 days: hallucinations, delusions, disorganized speech, disorganized or catatonic behaviour, negative symptoms (emotional flatness, apathy, lack of speech). Generally, we would consider people with two or more of these attributes to be either heroes or fools, but personally, I wonder how much the definition has altered so that the mental health services can segregate people deemed 'unfit' for society from those deemed 'fit'. I don't only make the first half of the former statement because as a recovering Schizophrenic I believe it to be true, but also because I have been threatened by a nondescript voice that sounds like God to include a fact-based joke and I am worried for my life.

"It's not just from here: it's from there; it's from there. You can't get away from it…" said a sufferer of Schizophrenia, either about apparitions and voices or the grounds of the hospital he now lives in.

"I think there's qualitative difference between a normal person being in touch with themselves and this sort of alien experience of voices coming from outside into reality, losing touch with reality and being psychotic, which is really what it means," said a psychiatrist, sympathetically and yet as resignedly as an atheist instructed to describe his relationship with God.

My own relationship with Schizophrenia isn't complex: although I believe I would be in a better mental state without these voices that hold a small amount of influence over my life, sometimes I enjoy having them there to keep me company and I have accepted them as a part of myself. I suppose I am lucky that they do not usually overpower me and that in my more lucid, sober moments, I can retrospectively perceive that perhaps they were generated by my mind. I wonder how many of Schizophrenia's symptoms are based on environmental factors such as exposure to drugs (and possibly even videogames where other people are 'playable') rather than a genetic propensity. In my own case, after a bout of psychosis attained by smoking strong skunk and getting arrested, I started hearing voices during the 48 hours I spent in solitary confinement. The issue in terms of treating Schizophrenia is that it is so unpredictable, and its symptoms are not always outwardly apparent, even to the educated observer. I suppose for the psychiatry practice it is a matter of treating it at its onset, before the sufferer or others are harmed.

Finally, although the status of the illness is clouded by negativity in some respects, one can certainly be a high-achieving Schizophrenic. Take Van Gogh, for example. While Schizophrenia was not recognised as its own condition while he was alive, 150 doctors retrospectively researched his life and reached an agreement that he suffered from Schizophrenia. Such creative inventiveness and art may not have surfaced were Van Gogh not to have faced mental health difficulties. Personally, five years ago, I experienced vivid visual visions which, though I was not 'in communication' with voices at the time, catalysed a poem, "Bird Volcano Event".

MARIJUANA: A POTTED HISTORY OF MY ILLICIT LOVE AFFAIR AND A THOUSAND WORDS ON WHY PROHIBITION IS STUPID

Marijuana: A Potted History of My Illicit Love Affair and A Thousand Words on Why Prohibition is Stupid

Debate on the legal status of cannabis is highly divisive. On one side of the spectrum stands the hardened pothead who hails the herb as a paragon of the planet; on the other stands the staunch traditionalist who declares the drug satanic and unsafe for human consumption. Such a skirmish makes for a good story, because both factions are dangerous in their own right and together represent a tremendous collision of values. The only certainty is that legalising cannabis for recreational purposes would alter culture dramatically.

One of the challenges of understanding cannabis is making sense of all the conflicting information available about the drug. Most articles appear to have an underlying bias, either implicitly advocating its legalisation or explicitly condemning its use. Six months after a prolonged period of heavy smoking, I feel that I have some anecdotal understanding of the benefits and the drawbacks of my own use of marijuana. I am writing this article in an attempt to understand the science behind my experiences, and to try to clarify my position on its legal status. First, though, I feel that I should elaborate upon my own involvement with the drug.

For a year, I smoked marijuana nearly every night. I found it calmed my mind, relaxed my body and reinvigorated an otherwise diminishing lust for life. It purged me of unnecessary and destructive thought, dissolving the body-mind disconnect I suffered from. In the short term, I believe it freed me from the undercurrent of angst that seemed to flow through my life.

In the long term, however, marijuana seemed to become a crutch. It weakened my short-term memory and occasionally triggered panic attacks in social situations. Over the course of the year that I smoked it, I suspect that I became psychologically addicted to it, because I found it difficult to control my use. Eventually, I gave up two months after I had resolved to. For the first week of abstinence, I craved it regularly, felt mildly irritable and found it harder to sleep. After two weeks of abstinence, all symptoms of withdrawal subsided.

Although I was wasted most evenings, I do not feel that smoking
marijuana was a waste of time or had any negative long-term effects on my body. I enjoyed being stoned. It increased my appreciation of art and heightened the novelty of my surroundings, allowing me to interpret the world from a new

perspective. I remember with particular fondness my experience watching the English Chamber Orchestra perform in London. My friend, a classical music buff, had bought two front-row tickets and brought me along for what he called an 'education'. I enjoyed the first half, but still didn't quite understand the music's appeal; it sounded nice, but it felt lethargic and contrived. During the interval, we sprinted to the nearest alleyway, smoked a joint and shambled back to our seats. From the opening bar of Bach's Violin Concerto, I suddenly understood what all the fuss was about. I was able to focus on the individual elements of the piece without losing sight of the concerto as a whole. The conductor flailed his arms ecstatically. The grave-looking double bassist closed his eyes and moved his fingers with trancelike precision. The soloist, a haggard, raven-like figure, quivered with her violin as if it were a sacred extension of her being. It all worked together so perfectly. It sounded anarchic and calculated at the same time. There was no show about it. I wept silently until it ended.

In retrospect, although marijuana greatly enhanced my enjoyment of the concert, I do not feel that it distorted the reality of the experience; rather, it hurled me into the heart of it. It heightened my appreciation for the intricacies of the performance and the relationship between the performers onstage. Narrating this experience makes it clear to me that it is hard for me to write about marijuana objectively, simply because it is not something I am dispassionate about. From my perspective, it scarcely matters if such moments represent a product of the intake of chemicals. The intense joy that I felt was real, because it was a response to external stimuli. In direct opposition to the hackneyed stereotype of the inward-looking stoner, my friend and I were able to function on a practical level and engage with the world. It might have been a different, less agreeable story if we had chugged a bottle of vodka during the interval.

I suppose all this is beginning to sound a bit like self-justification. But the fact is that smoking cannabis in the United Kingdom is pretty much illegal. Cannabis is a Class B drug with penalties for possession of up to five years imprisonment, and penalties for dealing, production and trafficking of up to 14 years imprisonment and/or an unlimited fine. The prospect of such a sentence for possession is enough to make even the most sedate of stoners paranoid when face to face with a police officer. But the British Crime Survey, conducted by the Home Office, suggests that around 15 million people in the UK would now admit to having tried cannabis, and between 2 and 5 million of these people are regular users. Given that the population of the UK is currently estimated to be around 62 million, these figures are remarkable not only because they show how widespread cannabis has become, but also because they brand approximately a fourth of our population ex-criminals.

Before I began to look at the existing research on marijuana, I intended to write a balanced article on the pros and cons of legalisation. Over the course of five hours of trawling the Internet, it became increasingly clear to me that this was not possible. I believe this is because there is no good reason for prohibition. I could find absolutely no empirical evidence to suggest that even the most copious consumption of marijuana causes the loss of brain cells, death, cancer, mental illness or that it provides a gateway to harder drugs. In the rare instances in which a scientific study was used to justify prohibition for medical reasons, it was often the case that the study was either undermined by several other studies (which together provide more 'well-rounded' proof) or that the statistics of the study were skewed to reflect the agenda of prohibitionists.

The most extreme example of this is the myth that marijuana

causes the loss of brain cells. In 1974, Ronald Reagan sensationally proclaimed,

"I now have absolute proof that smoking even one marijuana cigarette is equal in brain damage to being on Bikini Island during an H-bomb blast."

This statement was based on the results of the Dr. Heath/Tulane Study, which suggested that Rhesus monkeys, when smoking the equivalent of 30 joints a day, begin to degenerate and die after 90 days. But in 1980, after six years of requests and attempting to sue the government under the Freedom of Information Act, Playboy Magazine uncovered the methodology used for the study. Dr. Heath had strapped the monkeys to the chair and each day administered 63 joints "in five minutes, through gas masks". Without a source of oxygen, the monkeys suffocated. The cause of the monkeys' loss of brain cells was not due to marijuana but to asphyxiation and carbon monoxide poisoning! As the Red Cross Lifesaving and Water Safety Manual will testify, five minutes of oxygen deprivation causes brain damage; combined with their inhalation of carbon monoxide, a gas produced by the burning of any object, it is no wonder that the monkeys were stupefied and dead within 90 days.

Another widespread misconception about marijuana is that it is possible to lethally overdose. This is completely untrue. As DEA Administrative Law Judge Francis L. Young stated after reviewing the evidence in 1988, "A smoker would theoretically have to consume nearly fifteen hundred pounds of marijuana within about 15 minutes to induce a lethal response... In strict medical terms, marijuana is far safer than many of the foods we commonly consume. For example, eating ten raw potatoes can result In a toxic response. By comparison, it is physically impossible to eat enough marijuana to induce death."

Before researching for this article, I thought it safe to assume that the long-term usage of marijuana could cause lung cancer. In fact, the adversary of all marijuana activists, the National Institute on Drug Abuse (run by the US government), suggests that this assumption is unfounded:

"Marijuana smokers show dysregulated growth of epithelial cells in their lung tissue, which could lead to cancer;[6] however, a recent case-controlled study found no positive associations between marijuana use and lung, upper respiratory, or upper digestive tract cancers.[7] Thus, the link between marijuana smoking and these cancers remains unsubstantiated at this time."

I would argue that if no link between marijuana smoking and cancer has been found amid three generations of heavy government scrutiny, it is rather unlikely that such a link exists.

Perhaps the most valid argument that the government uses to justify prohibition for health reasons is the alleged link between cannabis and mental illnesses such as schizophrenia. If cannabis causes psychosis, it is fair to expect the rate of psychosis in the UK to increase relative to the nation's escalating use of marijuana. Yet a Keele University study, commissioned by the UK government, found no evidence that rising cannabis use in the 1970s, 1980s and early 1990s led to increases in the incidence of schizophrenia later on. This lack of evidence is highlighted by the fact that the bane of all marijuana activists, the National Institute on Drug Abuse, remains characteristically ambiguous on the matter:

"A number of studies have shown an association between chronic marijuana use and increased rates of anxiety, depression, and schizophrenia. Some of these studies have shown age at first use to be an important risk factor, where early use is a marker of increased vulnerability to later problems. However, at this time, it is not clear whether marijuana use causes mental problems, exacerbates them, or reflects an attempt to self-medicate symptoms already in existence."

Given the lack of empirical evidence, then, it seems highly likely that any link between the two is due to the fact that people with mental illnesses are more disposed to use drugs.

[NOTE: this article was written in 2012, twelve weeks before I was diagnosed with

schizophrenia. The reader should also note that I heard voices at the age of seven, long before I took marijuana. In 2019, I can with hindsight detect the hurried inclination of the NHS to put the 'schizophrenic' label upon drug users. Skunk certainly triggered a bout of psychosis in me, though. For three or four days, I was affably enchanted with the world, and kind of delirious.]

Similarly, the much-touted claim that marijuana is a gateway to harder, more dangerous drugs is perhaps the most preposterous accusation levied against the herb. The most obvious fact that deflates the gateway theory is that the vast majority of cannabis-users do not go on to use harder drugs; statistics show that only one in every 104 users of marijuana use cocaine and less than one use heroin. It is absurd to suggest that the plant possesses a certain chemical property that pushes users onto harder drugs. Upon closer examination, the idea of marijuana as a gateway can be seen to be an inevitable result of prohibition itself; the very nature of the black market means that buyers of marijuana are likely to encounter dealers who attempt to push harder drugs onto them. Furthermore, since frequent users are likely to feel that they have been bullshitted by their government on the issue of marijuana, they are more likely to be disposed to try harder drugs despite government warnings to the contrary.

Overall, given that marijuana's health risks appear to be minimal and given that its prevalence indicates that the war against it has been a categorical failure, I can see no reason why marijuana should not be legalised. I would argue, furthermore, that the question we should be asking ourselves is not "why should marijuana be legal?", but "why should marijuana be illegal?". In a country that purports to value the freedom of the individual, the onus should be on the state to provide the science and rationalisation that supports its laws. The fact of the matter is that the use of marijuana is a victimless crime and legalisation would allow law enforcement and courts to better focus their resources on the true iniquities of society. There is ample evidence that illustrates the benefits of the relaxation of drug laws. The example of Portugal, for example, indicates that such a policy results in the decline of hard drug use (particularly among young people), an easing of the burden on the criminal justice system, a growing number of people seeking treatment and a decrease in the rate of drug-related deaths. Recently there has been a colossal storm in the media about cannabis' increasing potency; legalisation would mean that the government could regulate its strength and consumers could be provided with detailed information about what they are buying. The legalisation and regulation of marijuana in the UK could reduce crime, create jobs, create billions of pounds in annual tax revenue and save thousands of people from needless imprisonment. When it is luridly clear that both the government and high-level criminals support prohibition, one cannot help but question the logic of our lawmakers.

WALKING

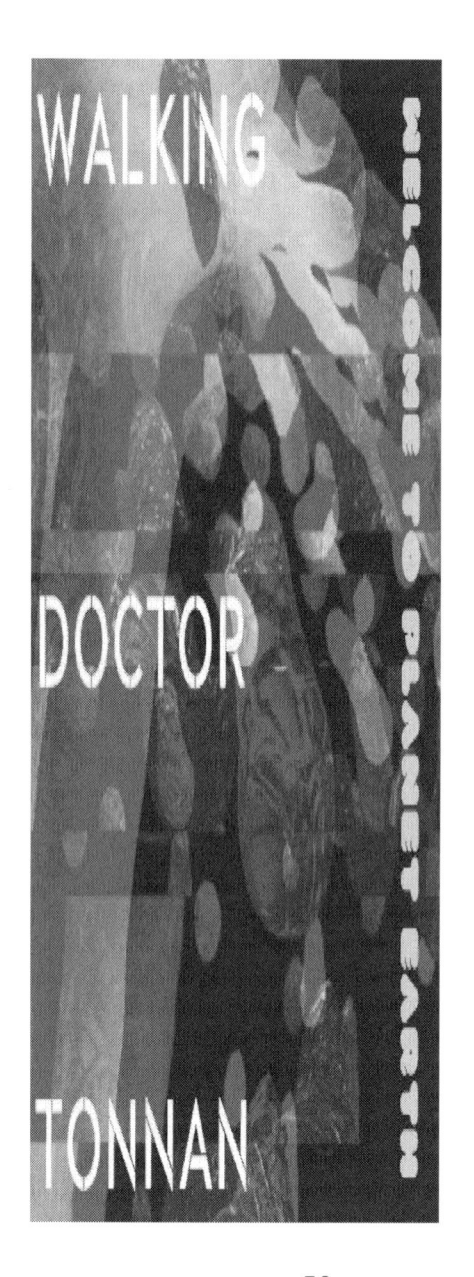

DOCTOR

TONNAN

Welcome To Planet Earth

Welcome to Planet Earth It's a pleasure to meet you at your birth
Now we've got a lot of problems we'd like you to solve
But don't worry too much, you don't have to get involved

Well, we've got plenty of slaughter but not enough schools
Hell, we've got plenty of water but too many fools
We've got seven billion people with acute frustration
Bored with a heaven full of mass altercation

Welcome to Planet Earth. It's a pleasure to meet you at your birth
Now we've got a lot of problems we'd like you to solve
But don't worry too much, you don't have to get involved

Now let me introduce you to some of the people on the street
You probably won't like them, but you might as well meet
I'm the Queen Mother of the United States
This is my brother; we clean plates

This is a woman; she is your date. Oh, you're inflating with lust!
I trust you can't wait! Oh my God, the date's blown up.
Well, good job it's the chorus, let's turn the sound up.

Welcome to Planet Earth. It's a pleasure to meet you at your birth
Now we've got a lot of problems we'd like you to solve
But don't worry too much, you don't have to get involved

This is bedding. This is Muriel.
I'm an actor. This is some cereal.
I'm at a wedding. I'm at a funeral.
This is a tractor. This is a urinal.
And I'm a singer and I wrote this song.
Now wouldn't it be great if y'all clapped along?

Welcome to Planet Earth
It's a pleasure to meet you at your birth
Hey, yeah that's right!!
Now we've got a lot of problems we'd like you to solve
But don't worry too much, you don't have to get involved
I know you've some questions you want to ask
I've tried to explain but it's a very big task.

Endorphin Dolphin

It wasn't a shove, as such; imagine a prehistoric push, lush beyond human flaw.
She touched me like he wanted to be touched & of this I can't say much more.
Short of the possibility of God intervening, I'd say that there's no reason to pray.
And she never did believe in meaning, except that you make it up along the way.
But as the sun wakes & the day breaks, the years fall down his her my cheeks.
"Every atom of last night", I'd say, "spoke brighter than words can speak… all except for yours…. endorphin dolphin of these shores."

You Are The Catalyst

If God is the reason why we exist,
I guess I'm a god-fearing hedonist.
And I can't resist the catalyst.
And I can't resist the catalyst.
But oh! oh no! You're the catalyst I can't resist.
You're the catalyst I can't resist.

I tried to see yet I never saw
The impossible dream's probable flaw
Yet there stood all my dreaming raw.
I saw the flaw of dreaming's door.
But oh! oh no! I was dumbfounded by awe.
I was dumbfounded by awe.

And you know who put you here
And – no! – it couldn't have been you
Yes, the future ain't that clear
But what on earth else is new?

I tried to hear yet I never heard
Your flippant heart's filthy word
I puzzled long over the wind-up bird
The catalyst is addicted to the absurd
But oh! oh no! I became addicted to lemon curd
I became addicted to lemon curd

I tried to feel yet I never felt
Your answer to my hunger melt
We must deal with the cards we're dealt
And I fell under the catalyst's spell
But oh! oh no! I fell down a well – you're the catalyst!
I fell down a well – you're the catalyst!

And you know who put you here
And – no! – it couldn't have been you
Yes, the future ain't that clear
But what on earth else is new?

Sheep In A Lorry

It's a shame you chain-smoke because it kills the taste of food.
We broke up the rain and it put you in a really good mood.
You yawned a whole orchestra and thought of the fat cat in her hat.
I drank coffee so tragic like any magic dog would that could do that.

But if we're sheep in a lorry/then I can't say I'm a lamb.
And when I say that I'm sorry/then sorry is what I am.
When I say that I'm sorry/it means that I give a damn.

Been sleep walking clear so much – talking is as dear as touch.
Even smoking fails as a crutch… searching in the dark depends on luck.
I'm scared of myself more than anyone else: 9 pills a day to take off the edge.
And at the end of the end no one knows what happens because we're dead.

But if we're sheep in a lorry/then I can't say I'm a lamb.
And when I say that I'm sorry/then sorry is what I am.
When I say that I'm sorry/it means that I give a damn.

Oblivion obliterated midnight with schmaltz about types of plumbers.
The flu-riddled son threw up a chicken that waltzed to random numbers.
I've been singing with the sinners I've been dancing with the dead.
I've been hiding from the hunters that run inside my head.
I've been drinking wine since seven.

But if we're sheep in a lorry/then I can't say I'm a lamb.
And when I say that I'm sorry/then sorry is what I am.
When I say that I'm sorry/it means that I give a damn.

Grave News

Victim of law, they spiked her telephone
Her past undreamt of, unwritten, unknown
The bandit who boasts of his innermost ghost
Speaks of forgiveness then proposes a toast
Please open the door, just name your price
We're barefooted pilgrims; your life is a(d)vice
We'll show you the Queens of Tyras, the banquets of Rome
And then the sparrows of Egypt will carry you home
For though children change and their gods decay
We'll show you tomorrow if you give us today
The flight of your tyrant, the night of our soul
Will undress the death and swallow it whole
Your kings move their lips, they wallow in word
Their meaning is stripped and nothing is heard
Yes, your hunger is splendid and noble and true
But your slaughter of lyres will not herald the new
What of the garlands we knitted our daughter?
Where are the gardens we fought for and brought her?
You're nailing the wrong snake to the stake
You're bitten and smitten and cannot escape
So, forgive me, forgive me, for my awful sin
I woke to your secrets and drunk all your gin
The man you crown saviour, I deem a thief
While I scream for love, you dream of relief
When I doubted my darkness, I sprouted two heads
And I lay deep in her heart begging for bread
It's you who sells nonsense disguised as the truth
Your hundred decisions preside as the proof
But your army of infants will abandon your cause
Because your rival, your friend will not sign her clause
He knows what we cherish, he knows what we gave
You follow her footsteps, he'll spit on your grave

Steepled Sequels

Your movements were married to the most mystical of Mayan music. I plummeted into your groove which proved fiercely human. Our pounding hearts started to make our first date seem so stupid. I felt like Bonaparte when I emailed you my art, but it bounced straight back to Cupid…

I'm very lonely, love. You are my only love. This is no phony bluff
But enough of the crony stuff. So I'll say this: fuck me.

I saw steepled sequels in your body's versed trance. I know I knew what I'd never known before just at first glance. In some ways (on Sundays) it's fun to die in advance. I swear you'd show me nowhere! We'd go there to dance!

I'm very lonely, love. You are my only love. This is no phony bluff
But enough of the crony stuff. So I'll say this: fuck me.!

When we were eighteen, you said chewing gum is a therapeutic costume. Your breath of breakfast bread became a bitter treat, a shitter perfume. I can picture us now shooting up to talk to God in God's room. You're my first favourite future since I fell in love in the womb…

Your photograph eyes, my amphetamine we heart it!
It's no surprise that we laughed as parted!

You are my homey, love. You really stone me, love.
You know me, you show me love. This baloney isn't holy enough…
So I'll say this: haha! Fuck it!

Bird Volcano Event

A bird slurred a song of sorrow he borrowed from tomorrow's awe.
A cat purred along as she heard the third's absurd swoop and soar.
It's half of infinity squared, a shared laugh, a prayer to time's shore.
The chords run towards the sun and climb the stairs to rhyme's door.
Nature's law dictates fate creates a gate before you explore the core.
And it's a hurricane of cocaine in chains as champagne raindrops pour.
But words can't explain the pain of bliss in the refrain's sublime score.

Picture this volcano where earthly ecstasy loads
To return your dreams in a burning stream that flows
Into the snow forest where mercy grows like a rose
And algebraic angels compose acid odes in a doze,
Painting the paradox of a paradise no saint knows
Where death has no foes and the hurricane sows
The codes of the unknown into celestial rainbows
Until the lone saxophone blows and trombone explodes.

Hear the harps hum a hymn as the limbs of death shine their light.
See the grieving leaves fall form the trees breathe in the night.
Now listen to the weeping colours christen the spark of infinity:
I found a dark sound on the ground that let me be free.
Twilight murmurs a mighty miracle and the midnight fades
Into the graveless enclave which brings peace to the old parade.
The lullabies crafted by the lava colonnade bake as love shakes
The trees which are guardians of the lake where we awake.

<u>Reality Or Reverie</u>

With the untameable harp of dream arrested in your palm,
You deny the dormant deity's call for a slumberous calm.
But it's there the world awakens in unburdened wonder,
Where lover and beloved are nameless without number.
Reality blasphemes the future and smokes like it's the law;
Reverie conjures places and faces you've never seen before.
I know which one I'd choose if the choice were mine to make;
I'd rejoice in the music of your voice and I would never wake.

We're all cracked: crucifix of time, hanging round my neck,
I'm born to live and die in this fusion of heavenly heck.
We play chess with every breath: but the odds are stacked,
For all consciousness will meet death or siesta's abstract.
Reality is advisable and definable: you're there or you're not;

Reverie is sizeable and excitable: you forget that you forgot.
I know which one I'd choose if the choice were mine to make
I'd rejoice in the music of your voice and I would never wake.

Louise, fathomless heart, pirouetting like a children's globe,
We live because there's time to kill or for the thrill of the strobe.
Either we're shambling without style down the shopping aisle;
Or we're flying through a world as our being utters a smile.
Reality is no joke and there's no cart blanche: each day is as it is;
Reveries…colours evoke avalanche of phantasmagoria aura bliss.
I know which one I'd choose if the choice were mine to make;
I'd rejoice in the music of your voice and I would never wake

I'll Love You Until Friday Never Comes

With your river flowing the angel must be joking when he says 'love is blind'.
Your strumpet clothing and your magnetic blowing live enshrined in my mind.
The trumpet of loathing love and yet loving loathing majestically combine.
I wonder if I'll love you until Friday never comes or if I'll ever call you 'mine'.

There are those who see the god above who never knew the pain of bliss. And those like me who dream of love with one like you on nights like this.

Though I confide the absurd, I cloak my heart of hearts and I hide my hiding too.
I impart a liquored divide of blurred feeling for it resides in any evocation of you.
You woke me up and you broke me down; those three words that I spoke are true.
You beautiful slut; you truthful nut; I adore your strut to tut to pokes of voodoo.

There are those who see the god above who never knew the pain of bliss. And those like me who dream of love with one like you on nights like this.

Wherever I am the same one is there; I swear without him I wouldn't have a care.
You and them are beyond compare; you repair my world like a prayer rarer than rare.
They smoke like chimneys and joke incessantly but never laugh and avert your glare.
From your hopeful horoscope of dope to kaleidoscope of nope, I'll love you until I am nowhere.

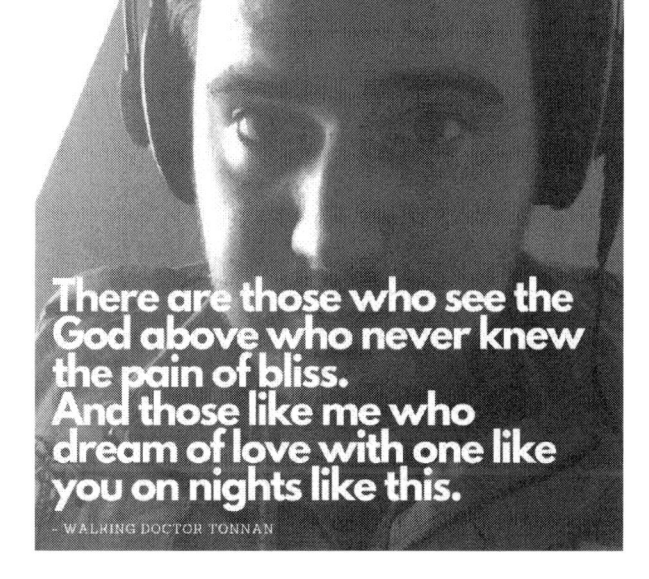

There are those who
see the God above
who never knew the
pain of bliss.
And those like me who
dream of love with
one like you on nights
like this.
— WALKING DOCTOR TONNAN

There are those who see the
God above who never knew
the pain of bliss.
And those like me who
dream of love with one like
you on nights like this.
— WALKING DOCTOR TONNAN

Your Fingers Were A Cabaret

Though God knows the ride of time flows slowly, snidely and forever,
So it goes that if I chose suicide as my bride, nothing would be severed.
I suppose I had to grow up so fast that even I don't wholly know me,
But I dreamt a moment and in my bridled mind a vision presided holy.

I observed the mirage of you there, tattooed in secular and unsecular places.
Curved figure camouflaged by hair, you grew a vector of inscrutable faces.
I fought the desire and felt its beautiful fire melt through my happy veins.
It was like I belonged to your scenic song, which purged me of all my pains..

Your image said I cooked myself thin but you took my soul as your twin.
Your image said salvation is law and horizons widen in beginning of sin.
And though in awe I swore I knew just exactly what you meant,
All beagle-eyed eternity fried as the future of love became its present.

Back then our limbs did the talking as we let the longing win.
Your fingers were a cabaret and how our souls did begin to sing.

Like The Sun When It Swoon

There's a solemn prayer that the sparrows recite.
The wind whispers it carefully where Winter's sole witness is night.
It's hard to render in words, that which are finite.
It's a childish account of the earth's surrender to dark until dark emerges light!
I didn't think you'd plummet into the summit of majesty.
I felt you fall in love with me, tonguing me easy and happy in the marquee.

My love for you won't deplete like the sun wouldn't swoon at the height of sorcery. If history is doomed to repeat, let us meet again under the moonlight.

The next day, I drink from the chalice of youth so deep.
On the brink of discovering the calloused truth, I drift into the seer of sleep!
I lift you up in an exultant reverie & I'm so lucid that I leap!
You're the same woman I fell in love with, and I'm so happy I could weep!
Now I perceive the grieving angels in the leaves travelled blind.
How cruel destiny can be to some and to others how kindly it aligns.

*My love for you won't deplete like the sun wouldn't swoon at the height of sorcery!
If history is doomed to repeat, let us meet again under the moonlight!*

The truth is disguised there coated in lies as soon as you rise.
They tortured me in the orchard; I cry until my soul and body dries.
You smoked my heart, you woke my art, the start is done.
I always wondered if you were the one, the sum of sums, the one next to none.
The sun rises, I realize we were simultaneously old yet young.
God knows what the rest will become, their destinies unsung, ours too yet to come.

*My love for you won't deplete like the sun wouldn't swoon at the height of sorcery!
If history is doomed to repeat, let us meet again under the moonlight!*

Twirled

It's easy to translate a broken heart into art; I should know, I've hated myself from the start. Now I'm paranoid about everything from schizophrenic spliffs to what ifs to Cupid's dart.
She walks & talks mad like a phoenix; that don't make it brick but it makes me glad to be sick. And now waterfalls of tears recall the snakebite while arrears are politely signed in blood running thick.
I will always remember you, but I love to get lost within the why. You realise there is no meaning but that which we ascribe when we try.

The skies are perfectly sad tonight & each soppy star is a secret cherub stud designed just for you. The sun is a photograph of the humming moon's dance around the globe and its Oxygen zoo. Promises aren't made to be broken, so relish the rain like a pained painter in a robe on the job. Your library eyes spin tales of youth, but my solitary confinement mind fails the truth of the mob. I will always remember you, but I love to get lost within the why. You realise there is no meaning but that which we ascribe when we try.

I feel to finger the linguist, yet my celibacy lingers on a single thing a touch too long. Epileptic triggers may extinguish the English but stay strong & belong to the crutch of song. Lord, I was a sinner until I felt the mascara of angel dust so strange on her window flesh. Now I vow to begin again; I'm not morose but I want to doze to a dose of the gross afresh. I will always remember you, but I love to get lost within the why. You realise there is no meaning but that which we ascribe when we try.

I want to feel alive and twenty-five and drive and survive and arrive at midnight's design. I want to fail to recall word, I want a tail like a small bird – yeah, I want what isn't mine. Someday somewhere, sometime someone somehow will do something so happy. We'll just spend all day enjoying it, but I'll never forget how you both trapped me. I will always remember you, but I love to get lost within the why. You realise there is no meaning but that which we ascribe when we try.

First you were a churlish magazine cover, but then you were an orphaned girl. Now you are the private pearls of another, now your kindness cannot unfurl. My tongue curled too; the sun begun to numb me so much I could've hurled. This is twisted. This is twirled. The existence you hold is a spaghetti igloo world. I will always remember you, but I love to get lost within the why. You realise there is no meaning but that which we ascribe when we try.

Worlds That Lovers Bent

1. Here Is Exactly Why
2. I Never Knew Her
3. Inside (feat. Oliver Francis)
4. Angel Made of Acid
5. First Love
6. Everything I Never Learnt To Say
7. Make Tomorrow Up
8. What's Your Story?
9. Flu Blues
10. B4 The Skies Turn Black
11. Happily Dead
12. Sketcher of Maps
13. Cinnamon Moon
14. I Love Your Love (feat. Oliver Francis)
15. Worlds That Lovers Bent

Here Is Exactly Why

In a past life you were my best friend & wife and we had a Mercedes.
You and I loved to mate and meditate on fate like two crazy old ladies.
We would have put ten grand on Nihilism and had a band damn good.
Your gloved hand would have loved me until I understood all I should.
I ain't forgot when we got pissed and kissed, but here is exactly how.
We can be madmen on a tryst to the moon as soon as now. Oh wow!

A fool achieves nought by thought so school taught me how to play.
Yesterday ain't tomorrow but sane people are all the same anyway.
I danced to death at the rainbow disco waiting for you to appear. You were a crush & a crutch & an ear and how I wish you were here.
I ain't forgot when we got pissed and kissed, and here is exactly why.
I'm that guy who don't want no other lover but don't want another cry.

I Never Knew Her

Like acne on your nose, love slowly grows.
Your mind refines ideals but ain't love.
Love's ingredients are sent & not chose.
A parrot-ox smothers you with its bluff.
But your secret suffering soon will pass.
You'll find another lover who's truer.
Together you'll gaze at the moon on grass.
That eternal love: I never knew her.
I did not glimpse forever with my eyes.
I did not swim thru leathered storms for lust.
Love is lust is love between thighs & sighs.
Our God's judgement is just: from dust to dust.
Feelings are real so I don't regret.
In love we met & in love we forget

Inside (feat. Oliver Francis)

A future lover walked up to me in the bar.
She winked and said, "I know who you are!"
I replied, "Chances are I'm not what you think.
But would you like a memory in which we drink?"
I live inside her now but I don't get homesick.
It's too late I know but in circles we go so quick.

"I simply can't dance, mister, but I'll chance the night."
"Your sister can't buy a future, but your kitten might."
"Girl, you don't need alcohol to calm each qualm."
"But maybe our world is a greedy computer farm."
I live inside her now but I don't get homesick.
It's too late I know but in circles we go so quick.

I loved you but you're indifferent to me now.
I'd change your mind, but I don't know how.
We discussed our star-signs on the school bus.
Now I can look up how you are without extra fuss.
I live inside you but I don't get homesick.
It's too late but I know in circles we go so quick.
I live inside you both but I don't get homesick.
It's too late I know but in circles we go so quick.

Angel Made of Acid

Well, God forbid my heart is hid & I'll be yours if you'll be mine.
Angel made of acid I was just a kid (cept' where the sun don't shine).
Mad breathless beauty shot time into rhyme.
In deathless duty the serpent stars entwined.
Yesterday I was falling but today all I do is climb.
Yet singing these songs never earnt a dime.
If you grow up restless, the best breakfast is wine.
The law is thine while the doors align in the Sublime.

Lust at first sight
Becomes Love
By the end of the night.

Restless, I tested how far I could go:
the real foe isn't what you don't
know.
I smoked more, opened a big door &
added more flow like Rimbaud.
Your four kaleidoscope eyes reflect
the spectre of the circus skies.
Beyond the ravines of what has been
lies a future we've yet to realize.
My day is a dream I don't want to
wake from as our lips spar.
It's as if you're in me yet your tongue
doesn't leave a scar.
I'd crawl across your soul's river,
covered by Old Holborn tar.
It chars my heart to be apart so let's
say bonjour, not au revoir.

Lust at first sight
Becomes Love
By the end of the night.

The state-funded rain of the over-soul makes me whole & I'm on God's parole.
I'm emboldened at a golden anniversary, conversely reaching 50's my only goal.
With your Neptune ease & my bended knees & heck, geez who called the police?
The necklace daydreams created & your lips laid grace to the place of release.
In a spectacle saved for the holy beginning & final wreck you kissed my neck.
You beckoned in a dozen dying dreams & we shared ten thousand seconds of sex.
My recall stalls before last fall when I saw you: is this it, mon amour?
Watching falling raindrops pour, I never knew love could be a war.

Lust at first sight
Becomes Love
By the end of the night.

First Love

Gunshots the force of a hundred horses
divorce reality from art.
Departed dreams and Neptune's screams
break the moon's heart.
God will be sole witness to the end, just as
God was to the start.
To me your touch was more sacred than
fudge and I was spellbound.
It didn't take as much as a nudge to clown
my sanity upside down. Now profound
hunger hounds me and ecstasy is a vision
of your sound.

You are my first love, because you are you.
This is the worst love that I ever knew.
I know that not all love is fast love, true. So
I hope that this'll be my last love, too.
I feel this ecstasy blast above my mouth.
The real thirst is always further south.
You're going to make me change.
How could an angel be so strange?

Everything I Never Learnt to Say

I wish there was a way to express
Everything I never learnt to say
If this is tomorrow is anyone's guess
But today isn't like yesterday

I wanna with the apocalypse
Existential lips & spoken strips
Timely quips & potent trips
I wanna rhyme in the apocalypse

Baby let me follow you down
Baby let me follow you down
I would do anything in this God almighty world
If you just let me follow you down

I dig it when you wear a wig & shake your head
I'm alive & trying to get ahead
But I'll follow where I'm led, infinity bled
I want to be with you when all is said & done

Baby won't you show me the sun
I'm nothing but you make me one
Don't get out your gun, there's gonna be fun
If you don't make me run from you

Flu Blues

I wept out of the darkness
You fell into the light
I remember the old bars
And how we use to fight/fag

I wept out for the warred
You wept out for the tearless
Your tired eyes were assured
Me, I weren't exactly fearless

There won't be an end to God
But the wars, they will end
You're not sorry for being odd
I'm just sorry you pretend

Sometimes I wake up had
Sometimes I wake up mad
I can see good from bad
I know what made us sad

I've been tortured by the voices
Your darkness fell into the light
I remember love without choices
And none of this old new plight

I wept out for those I had lost
I had to fight to be me, some
I suppose that is the cost
Of working for your freedom

I wept out of the darkness
You fell into the light
I remember the old park
And how we used to fight

Make Tomorrow Up

Shawls tight around our necks, tonight we are alone.
Let's fall lightly into dream and find the unknown.
I love you for what you are but can't hide what I am.
If you don't like me, let's call it off and I'll scram.

Now the town is blazing with the circus song.
You understood every word you heard all along.
Forget the rest but don't forsake the hollow cup.
We all try our best just to make tomorrow up.

I walked through your tall & sweet brown gypsy fire.
Talking openly about nothing makes anyone a liar.
Yes, at dawn your Queen transformed into a pawn.
And the lieutenant yawned as he hunted for his fawn.

Now the cackling flames spell a sickening name.
Well on my way to hell above, I can't hack the game.
Sleep soundlessly, my love; don't wake sorrow up.
I guess I'll try my best just to make tomorrow up.

The birch will hide the morning light where you're curled.
I shall search for my guide while you're dead to the world.
I wish I'd read the warning signs but I am not a Chief.
In a year's time, you'll be more than simple relief.

Now I smoke a cigarette and watch the moon retreat.
I think I finally won you, but soon I will be beat.
To get by in this world, you just have to make it up.
I can't hear tomorrow breathe, but heartbreak is sup.

What's Your Story?

Respite from the blue moon;
The night comes too soon.
The bright young pretty stoners sing to their own gritty tune.

Escape the caped ape;
Gape at the shape of rape.
God tapes human mistakes; she wakes to ache;
you wake to ruin.

Suicide of dried pride: I hide inside the guide.
The flower is our power: you cried, I died, we tied.

Salvation ain't plenty
But damnation ain't empty
Sensation-free at twenty-seven!
Hefty temptation of trendy heaven!

You... what's your story? Think about it.

Forgetting is what friends tend to do;
I bet I'll sing at the sunset end for you.
The better the wetter when it's three fools and two points of view.

A lonely clown in discount drag
Learns to count then burns a flag.
Now the only madman in town crowns the sound where he drowned in blue.

Real lust is trust: you're bust if you don't know it.
Hear the poet in the thrust of the gust just below it.

Truth can be self-defeating
And youth can be so fleeting.
The tooth of Ruth
Repeats its eating.

You... what's your story? Think about it.

Sketcher of Maps

Your cold fruit is ripe but Reality mutes the hype.
This old prototype's playing flute in stars & stripes.
The youth of tomorrow has countless woes.
In truth their sorrow will come to a close.
Each precious hour is as fiery as a flower.
The power devours the sweet & the sour.
The earth rotates around & to fate we are bound.
But I'll be with you when the deal goes down.

By grim guilt I'm struck, limbs wilt with our luck
With no hymn to the buck, in limbo we are stuck.
My song is trapped without her on my lap.
But so long, sketcher of maps & taker of naps.
A shock to the heart knocked our worlds apart.
Locked within art we can rock back to the start.
The earth's a playground & to it we are bound.
But I'll be with you when the deal goes down.

Among old & young immortal bells are well-rung.
Where there's a tongue there's a song to be sung.
The lunar eclipse trips in its psychedelic silence.
In driverless grip we'd slip into the relic of violence.
A cool spark in the dark harks back to old larks.
Whirlpools of lies are disguised in passing remarks.
I'm not lost within sound yet to it I am bound.
& I'll be with you when the deal goes down.

B4 The Skies Turn Black

I know you're doing well, but I wish I could say the same for myself.
Sometimes this life is hell, cloaked by another name just for stealth.
Tomorrow's a word I seldom use, but I don't like to live in the past.
Some musicians use silence as a muse, but I get bored of it too fast.
I saw an angel carved in snow yesterday, as cunningly as if it were
clay.
I don't particularly want to go anyway, so you give me a reason to
stay.
I haven't given up my search for meaning; I've just grown a little
slack.
So meet me by the church about half an hour before the skies turn
black.

I was born in squalor out of love and I'll die in it unless God intervenes.
I wonder if there's a heaven above or if the closest place is New
Orleans.
I guess all I can ever do is be me, but I like pretending to be the
Queen.
I speak about my own majesty, after a seemingly obscene dose of
caffeine.
I'm good at acting as if everything's alright, but I'm not if you want to know.
Sometimes all you can do is get through the night, but time passes so slow.
You're a flirtation with my salvation and maybe deliverance is what I lack.
So meet me by the station about half an hour before the skies turn black.

Happily Dead

If you have got to save somebody,
Why not save your secret self?
Become a bum (brave dogs run free)
Or wallow in a cave of wealth.
Though I am me almost all of the time,
I'm still a stranger to who I really am.
Every phony reason for love dies in rhyme,
Like each season's new self-help scam.
You squeezed my "geez" like the breeze when all is said,
For you were Queen of the bees and I was happily dead.

Yes, I adored you as soon as our eyes met:
I worshipped the moonish lilt of your voice.
I'm not sure that I cared what happened next,
But your viper lips were so refreshingly moist.
You loved me to the clock that's right twice a day;
I loved you to the sound of birds giving birth.
We loved to the melody of serious artists at play;
We loved forever or whatever forever is worth.
You squeezed my "geez" like the breeze when all is said,
For you were Queen of the bees and I was happily dead.

Well, me, I'm still a hopeless romantic;
I'm another hopeful puppy in love with a dove.
My infatuation was bigger than gigantic,
But I had a military-grade dose of the stuff.
Here's to the few at war who ignored your beauty;
Here's to the many who fell under your dolphin spell.
May Blue Eyes who you married out of love or duty
Know that his wife grew a haven in a garden of hell.
You squeezed my "geez" like the breeze when all is said,
For you were Queen of the bees and I was happily dead.

I believe there's nothing holier than your soul;
I believe it as wild, as uncontrollable as mine.
I know I can't vilify what makes me whole;
I knew it even when our stars refused to shine.
But you taught me sorrows can't defeat me –
I teased your ease that pleased the sleaze
No razor-blade to tomorrow shall cheat me –
I hated cheese, so instead I ate your keys.

Sketcher of Maps

Your cold fruit is ripe but Reality mutes the hype.
This old prototype's playing flute in stars & stripes.
The youth of tomorrow has countless woes.
In truth their sorrow will come to a close.
Each precious hour is as fiery as a flower.
The power devours the sweet & the sour.
The earth rotates around & to fate we are bound.
But I'll be with you when the deal goes down.

By grim guilt I'm struck, limbs wilt with our luck
With no hymn to the buck, in limbo we are stuck.
My song is trapped without her on my lap.
But so long, sketcher of maps & taker of naps.
A shock to the heart knocked our worlds apart.
Locked within art we can rock back to the start.
The earth's a playground & to it we are bound.
But I'll be with you when the deal goes down.

Among old & young immortal bells are well-rung.
Where there's a tongue there's a song to be sung.
The lunar eclipse trips in its psychedelic silence.
In driverless grip we'd slip into the relic of violence.
A cool spark in the dark harks back to old larks.
Whirlpools of lies are disguised in passing remarks.
I'm not lost within sound yet to it I am bound.
& I'll be with you when the deal goes down.

LIVID TAPESTRY

It don't take a drunkard to be alive
But every one of your laughs is true to me.
These lines are undiplomatically contrived
For beauty is best perceived truthfully.
I arrived alive in the living trial
And I can't remember before.
After a while, I learnt to smile
And I was drafted for the war.
I've been sadder than morose
And I've been too happy to think.
I've been too mad to wear clothes
And I've been too crappy to drink.

My happy tears are a purgatory
But my story isn't all that odd.
Allah's essence isn't an allegory
Nor will I ever see or know God.

I danced into the diphtheria of doze
As soon as my eyes were closed.
I woke up, thought of you and rose.
I smoked and wrote some prose.
A cigarette can make you feel faint
But the tricks of rhyme can paint it well.
It's 6 A.M. and I'm empty of what I ain't
So I cling onto the cloak of your smell.
Chesterfield, milkshakes, omelettes:
The moment you get you get it you're indebted.
And so we let the sun set over our regrets
In a kiss the cinnamon moon crimson

sweated.

My happy tears don't bore me
And my story isn't all that odd.
Allah's essence isn't an allegory
Nor will you ever see or know God.

A tapestry of colours rode my livid eyes
& eroded the dark in bitterly cool duty.
Some things are too sad to analyse,
But what a tool we can be to the fool of
beauty.
Need you now, need you then, don't ask me
when:
I've loved you since I was ten.
In tu-tu visions of desire spent, you came &
went:
Cops on your trail, fingernails pale as a
pedant.
My future was a divorcee I'll never meet.
My past was an angel dressed in leather.
She was as sweet to me as sweet can be.
But now it's better to forget her forever.

My happy tears don't bore me
And my story isn't all that odd.
Allah's essence isn't an allegory
Nor will you ever see or know God.

I Love Your Love (feat. Oliver Francis)

I was born in the wilderness
But within a minute I was home.
Some people I couldn't love less:
These are folks who never roam.

You came to me like a child
And I absorbed your trust.
I smiled at your sweet game:
My own game was nearly bust.

I love your love like I love mine.
I'd love more love like I'd love more wine.

In Ireland there are villages
And there are beautiful songs
I won't leave you with any image
Because I feel that would be wrong

After I finally became who I am
I refused to speak for weeks.
Perhaps I'd fallen for some scam
But contentment made me weep.

I love your love like I love mine.
I'd love more love like I'd love more wine.

I threw on my favorite hoodie
(The one that I used to wear).
It really is beautiful, so good to see:
I think I've finally learned to care.

Yes, the world is the place we live
And heaven or hell is where we die.
Would it help you to try to forgive?
Maybe I just need another cry.

I love your love like I love mine.
I'd love more love like I'd love more wine.

I'm sorry for your purple sorrow
And I'm sorry that I have a dick.
I'm sorry that there's a tomorrow
And I'm sorry that I can be thick.

Here's hoping you find your truth
For mine is perfect as the homes.
I worked hard to find my youth:
My mind is inactive but it roams.

I love your love like I love mine.
I'd love more love like I'd love more wine.

Worlds That Lovers Bent

I love you more than words can say
I'll love you tomorrow and I'll love you today
But deep down in the gutter I lay
And there's nothing much to do or say
But stay myself another day and pray we shall
not come to blows

It's easier than it was before
You took me in, you opened the door
And tho love & life can be a bore
The sacred naked man & woman I adore
For no greater awe have I found before tho you
gave me some lows

But you still drum along to that sad old tune
You're not my sun but you are my moon
Cos' it's easy to get caught up in that fraught
typhoon
When you're drowning in the lagoon
It's hard to understand but life & love will soon
swoon to a close

Our skin is only colour deep
But if you're not awake then you're asleep
What we do determines what we reap
But through bleeding bullets words can seep
If you remain asleep then you'll weep at the
end of your doze

For no man should ever repent
The severed time he never spent
As he begins his slow descent
Into worlds that lovers bent
With the scent of their lament cemented to
every burning nose

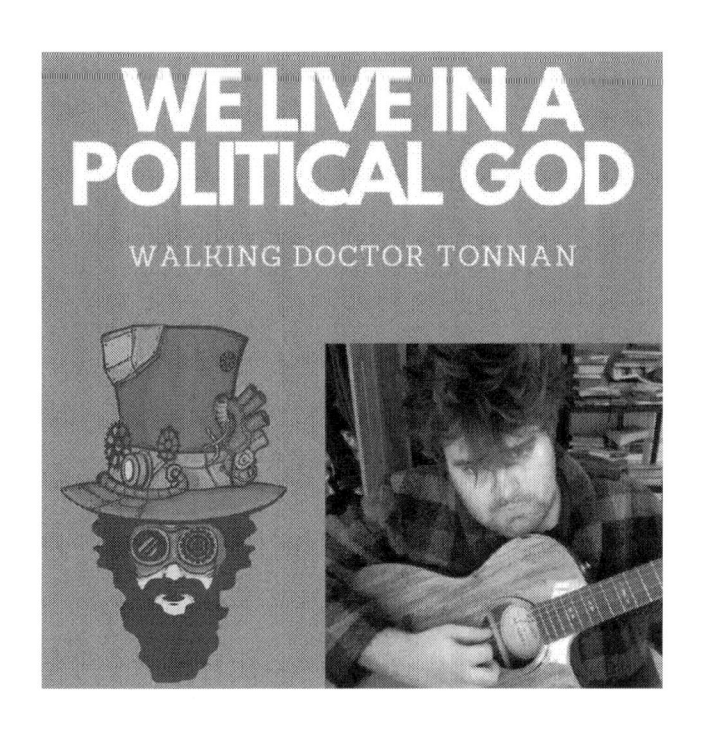

WE LIVE IN A POLITICAL GOD
WALKING DOCTOR TONNAN

The Subtler The Tyranny

The subtler the tyranny, the deeper each one of us falls
The more pitiful the irony, the louder people weep at city walls

Gazing at me oddly like a God, she guillotined the rest
In heaven's estimation, their destination is best left a guess

Yes, I robbed lust of its fortune, manically writing this song
And tonight merciful mountains shine over this sorry 'so long'

When I was young, I couldn't wait to fall in love, then you walked through the door
And when I grew older, the war grew colder, but I wasn't any bolder than before

Three years ago I said it would be the last time, so I forgot it like the last rhyme
Now I walk the tightrope and hope and cope and commit the same crime every time

Yes, I switched riches for drag; you can hear the witches bitch and nag Big Ben
I burnt and unlearnt all my love for me (for me!) and I would do it all again

Yes, the subtler the tyranny, the deeper each one of us falls
The more pitiful the irony, the louder people weep at city walls

God Knows Your Burden

God knows your burden:
Destiny is never certain
Til the close of the curtain.
At points we all are hurting
With fate's gates still flirting
So I'm not just blurting whatever comes into my head.
But with that said…

A boy with big hair walks to me on Voltaire street
Glares at me, says he wants drugs but doesn't know where
I say yeah, man, you're in for a treat, I swear
You can eat & glug drugs by the mug over there.
Buyer beware, coffee makes you care.
That debonair air says you'll fit in bare.
Consume it on a chair & don't get it in your hair.
Yeah, you're welcome.
Might as well sell some.
Some people: God help them.
If you build it, they will come.

I read I assaulted a police officer thrice.
BS: I have many a vice but he insulted me

twice.
If the forces aren't nice, of course we pay the price.
There's only so much ice cream cake left & it seems we all want a slice.
We both got betrayed & arrested, Jesus and I.
No other parallels are to be drawn except for the circumstances of our birth.
It's hard to play guitar well- most people can't do most hard things: that's no lie.
Get merry after a sherry & ask Katy Perry if she can sing via telepathy [you won't get a reply]

Flashback to the tarmac: broke more than my back.
But I'm on track to get back what I now lack.
I ain't that slack, my cards aren't whack -
Yet the impact's a fact I can't black out.

But don't let the realm overwhelm you,
take it by the helm, make your own route.
Brain damage is something I can manage and marriage I can live without.
The rain ravaged me like I was disparaging justice's carriage with doubt.
Proceedings got savage speedily so I kept all I could scavenge for the drought.

Forget the dipshits: the creator exists.
Religion persists to twist the plot (which is kind of hot)
So don't take a shot at the deity who prays for thee…
God is all some people have got.

I don't ramble or gamble, I shamble with the wind.
I'd like to see that rabbit again, man could he grin.
I've had it with the habit but I still want some magic.
The demons that inhabit me are undramatically static.
The tragic song is so long that any doctor would fall asleep
The thought of being caught up in it makes me want to weep.

I tried to find unity amidst the commotion.
So I sat deserted in church, devoid of emotion
I ran towards him, I ran fast in slow motion
I was so late for work they gave me a promotion

I was born again in the heart of the lion's den.

I shouted about Lucifer, some people howled amen.
If I was Zen with the pen, I'd have written that at ten.
But I loved God back then: all the time, don't ask me when.

I met a young girl who told me to take things slow.
I met an old man who said go fast or I won't grow.
I saw you breaking through to a world I don't know.
That thought came later, all I felt at the time was low.

But Love is perfect & love is pure: I couldn't ask for more.
You shook me to the core, you ended my war.
Like all illusions the confusion came to a conclusion.

Ground Zero (for E.V.)

I love the way you passionately sleep
and how you make a sweet sound.
It makes heroes want to weep how
close we are to Ground Zero now.
Freedom's forgetful avenue beckons
and I reckon there's just room for two.
Let a reincarnation of Secret Heaven
speedily screw your seedy worldview.
She told me she told you I told you how
life is a game of chance and dance.
But I said that life is a lame musical
enhanced by unnamed
pharmaceuticals.

There's nowhere left to go, grant me
nothing's escape.
You're a thousand desires, sprawled in
stormy shape.
Make me disappear from fate, fearful I
might wake.
You're the seer I revere and nothing is
at stake.

*Give me the majesty of your madness
today*
Make me glad to be sad, take me away

Help me say what I don't know how to say

Just as nuclear warfare was once a fiction, one day the heavens will rejoice. While mental slavery still clips wings, gentle voices will sing for lack of choice.

Some care to share the snaring infant of despair while others brave a silent prayer.
But I know forgotten love is worth it and though it's rare it's on Earth somewhere.
The slinky stairs to the fairer lead nowhere but they trace orphaned dreams.
Thinking of the place don't erase the regime but let's paddle upstream.

Summon the sun to make us numb till we become one
And succumb to what was done before the war begun.
Remind me we are designed, show me slowly how to grow
Until I only know the nothing we owned so long ago.

Give me the majesty of your madness today
Make me glad to be sad, take me away
Help me say what I don't know how to say

The Voodoo of Dream

The first heartbreak always awakens
the worst thirst.
Then again even every Buddhist once
felt Eden's curse.
Sometimes not being lonely means
agreeing to the phony.
If only she would phone me, we could
ride those ponies.
Tattooed angels view you from the
goofy avenue of the ceiling.
The screaming voodoo of dream do
seem newly appealing.

Try to fool those serial schoolers who
rule imperiously.
Watch cornflakes wake! Please take
cereal seriously.
The emptiness of love fills my brain to
the brim.
She can come with me or she can
stay with him.
Businessmen sue many a dude with a
killer's pen.
The voodoo of dream do seem truly
lude again.

The steeples are feeble and needles are penal now.
But all people will be equal in the sequel anyhow.
Your two blue lips are the vows of lovers embracing.
My favourite art empowers my heart to start racing.
If depression is a 24-7 profession, what is expression?
Jump into the voodoo of dream to answer the question.

Karma's Barter

I smoked your moon-kissed lips and déjà vu soon
drew a purple circus round the clown of purpose
like the all-dyke hook of a black hole.
You woke me before chords of the forest soared
into the town of sound where it is true that you can
sue whomever shook your shackled soul.
After karma's barter in the womb halved the
laughter of Gaea, I wept in contempt of court and
dreamt I was bought like a crook on parole.
I stayed in their cellar, a maid and a beggar, with
only one stellar sweater and a cooking book that
I'm afraid to tell ya I took or stole.

But I've got some simple words you never hear.
A man is lucky if they ever near his ears.
If I were you, then I would be you.
But since I am me, I am me.
That's why we're two and we're free to be free.

Mary mixes the karma potion, her schizophrenia
still in motion, and Christ waltzes on water, causing
quite the commotion in the sea of Galilee.
I tasted his devotion with hasty emotion; it was
sorta artful and heartful, not far from water where
the leveed sea breaks through into the city.
I met her in a daydream; why get disturbed
anyway? At the end of the day it seems you go
back all the way in the reset of the nitty gritty.
We rode a pony thru the desert and arrived at the
brook. the ceremony took ten terse minutes I never
forsook; I'd still love you infinitely less pretty.

*But I've got some simple words
you never hear.
A man is lucky if they ever near
his ears.
If I were you, then I would be you.
But since I am me, I am me.
That's why we're two and we're
free to be free.*

I suppose where I once scorned, I
could now offer a hand.
Every rose bears a thorn, but I
was reborn a stronger man.
If only you had stayed, I'd have
sworn my life on our plan

Crossroads

I'll let him bone you 'til you moan an antelope.
I know listening will only be prison if I hope.
I ate the envelope and smoked our horoscope.
I opened your raging mirror with rope in my cage.
I age but forget that you, my friend, are my only dope.
No, I'll let the bloke work 'til he's home so I'll cope.
Our slow dove goes so far our love will star then choke.
Just feed my speed, no joke, and I'll need your greed.

I woke up alone, next to an ex.

We were laying entwined & confused
If I was her friend, she was my muse
I offered her the blues, but she refused
That day was a perfect storm of hues

I felt her heroine heart with my hand
It was only then I began to understand
All plans are made of grains of sand
But I hoped one day she'd join my band

And I couldn't help thinking of you as our lips met
What you were doing with whom & in which joint
Yet I felt something in my jeans and it wasn't regret
If everything's here & now thinking has no point

We fucked so long that half my heart cracked
Her soul was shackled, mine was almost black
We tried our best not to get blood on the track
I have a knack for sex when all else is whack

I don't know who I love the most but you both have post
In the dead of the night, I became Fortune's fool
I beg for my Godhead's right to study at school
Although Fortune can be cruel, I play it so cool

I know sooner or later Fortune will be on the pedestal
Pretenders hail from the land of permanent bliss
Me, I'd be trapped there forever after another kiss
But we chat about that blue light and reminisce
No, I never did think that drinks would end like this

Yes, four lips flower to make War out of Peace
A mouth heads south, a brain begs for release
Every slurred word heard is forever's feast
My hunger for the heart can only increase

But I dreamt of you all through the night
I forgot if my love was wrong or right
I was forever falling as she took flight
If I was a rock, then she was a kite

I don't know who I love the most but you both have post
And so, unfulfilled by pills and indifferent to the illiterate daffodil,
The blues danced with the future's shoes against my will.
Enough of bruises: they have their music, but I wouldn't choose it.
I guess I never saw the point, but still I confess after a joint…
Even Cupid can be stupid & I'm not the new kid in terms of love.
But, anyhow, an encounter with Chewbacca confirms the God above.
O, no, I'm not a stranger to the nurse's glove. Sometimes I wish I was; sometimes I wish I was.
O, still how it thrilled me when Chewbacca spilt tea and then how it chilled me when I learnt….

Every burnt prosthetic willy knows being seriously lyrical is a silly goal,
So Chewbacca snuggled it into the hole I dug & my love hugged his soul.
We became the same, as whole as a canary's dairy under his control.
The deity may be ill today but Chewbacca said that he will still pray away with his whole heart anyway...

Dreaming to the rhythm of jazz & drinking to the sacred blindness of angels,
screaming for the sunken prophecy, hurling the Book of Changes to its resting place,
my therapist tells me that the beginning has ended and

it's time to start again,
my therapist thinks I'm gay so I started hitting on her to complicate the diagnosis,
my therapist doesn't even exist, but now she's pregnant and it's all my fault!
Epiphanies! Confucius! Einstein! What happened to the sin of following?
What happened to the message? What happened to the massacre?

(Where are you Mother? Where are the weepy-eyed relatives that came for you? What happened to the snoring man you slept with occasionally? He's gone, Mother, you took him with you and now he's nothing! This is the beginning of the end, Mother, the beginning of the penultimate breakdown! O the Bliss has stolen my innocence we are ready to undertake the final picnic in heaven!)

O, what happened to all the drunken triumphs and golden touches? It's all eroded into the endless machinery of dawn and the secret insatiability of appetite has returned to fool the lot of us. It's always been easier to fall in love than to be alone, and now even that's gone too.

O fool me through the darkness
O fool me like a cat
O fool me like you fool yourself
O fool me like a rat

O sing a song of sorrow
Where the docks and water fight
And the old soul singers sing a song
Until the soul emerges light

I breathe my breath for birth and death
I left the rest behind
I tried to turn to Jesus
But the Christians changed my mind

O kiss me like a goddess
O kiss me like I'm a man
O kiss me like you kiss yourself
O kiss my because you can

O trance me to the tractor
O trance me to sky

O trance me like you trance yourself
As your dreams go floating by

I only care for sex and love
The rest is obsolete
I'm running back to that mad old orgy
Where the pen and penis meet

O love me to your strobe light
O love me to your mind
O love me like you hate yourself
O love me til we're blind

(Dear Chairman Mao's Wife,

Sinners win riches as fools beg for gold. Here is a song I wrote for you about how you and Chairman Mao got engaged. It's called 'Now Wow'.

D Tender twilight's violin, Am he holds you close.

C Spread-eagled in sin, G he takes off your clothes.

D He ponders your skin Am with an antique nose.

C Drunk on godly gin, G you're fucking comatose.

D Let the ending begin Am where only God knows.

C You're orgasming in Berlin, G from head to toes with D Mao in the Am Now Wow.

D You and he wake up to the omniscient sun.

C Your body shakes as you relive becoming one.

G Yawning, he makes coffee & you eat a plum.

D His backbone aches & your limbs are numb.

C Half by mistake, he finishes off a cup of rum.

G Mao now breaks eggs, somehow starting to hum D a vow into the Am Now Wow.

Yours truly,

Tonnan.

I'm out of the darkness but I'm trapped in the park
And all the town's harlots have set off the spark
You give me your reason, I'll give you my time
I'll tell you the season if you show me my crime
I'm nothing but no one, you're the god of the sun
You're the light of my loins, you're the dog to my gun
I thought love was hard but maybe it's true
Though words are like darts, baby I'm you
You made me disappear, so I remembered my self
I forgot all my fears, I forget all his wealth
He gave me my sadness, you gave me my joy
I was trapped in the madness, I was a lost little boy
While everyone danced, I was down on my knees
I left love to chance, but you threw me the keys
I forgot it all sometimes, I forgot all the thought
When I rotted in rhyme, I fell and was caught
Because the fruit of my hate swallowed me up
But the gates of your grace lead me to love,
There's nothing so perfect, there's so much to do
I've no duty to race, I've got no one to screw
Because you own me forever, you rattled my soul
You showed me the nether, you made me whole
From the pain of your head to the chains of our bed
You stayed true through the change and for once I was led
You gave me your ease, you started my art
You parted my seas, you created my heart
I'll follow you forever and you'll be my moon
Forever will come and it's never too soon

People often come up to me on the street & say 'Hey, Walking Doctor Tonnan, how do you sing so sweet?'

I tell them it's a combination of mouth movements, knowing you're the messiah, Adderall and pretending you're Scooby Doo singing at Marge Simpson's wedding to Scooby Doo who is running away from the mafia because the mafia is after him because Scooby Doo is from the Mafia but Tony Soprano's sister had it in for him though he secretly loves her and Marge Simpson has a cat and Scooby Doo doesn't like cats unless they're from the mafia and so you're like Scooby Doo pretending to be Gatsby from the Great Gatsby pretending to sing to Marge Simpson but actually singing to Tony Soprano's sister. And that's how Walking Doctor Tonnan sings so swet.

Broken Awe

Yeah, well, the profane remedies left me bitter. But, hell, the profane ones left me mad. The same pain must have finally hit ya, yet that chain of buns left me glad. Now and then the sane tears on my beery, weary head make me wonder whether I was happy or sad. When the rain pelted, I felt ostracised, though I'd been through the wars and lost my soul in flawed awe.

Well, they stole my book and looked into my heart & the crooks parted by bike. By the brook there's a mournful man who plays a scornful hook to a very beautiful dyke. I woke up in the courtyard drunk, couldn't remember what life used to be like. And before the inspiring firmament of the stone whose throne whispered of the shore... I lost my soul in lawful awe.

I hurt like hell, only once wept bliss, lived the poems that I wrote, and it's been years since a kiss. Well, the sellers of alibis can probably imagine why I cry but maybe the alibis are false and amiss. I sung out my lungs, of course smoke made me hoarse, but before nothing happens, I'll piss… sure I saw this song had flaws, but I didn't really bore.

Yeah, they held my head & left me for dead, you can't fake your enemy. I could contrive another rhyme that would resign myself to their lines, but it'd be empty. No, there's a reason for this universe but I believe in sympathy, though it can equate to empathy. I wake up flawless but when I go to the door, I fear the envied plenty… and I lose my soul in tearful awe.

I worked as a slave angel on the farm and the calm of the cold made me immune. Much later I was imprisoned by love and the sun shattered the matter of the lingering moon. Now and then God's pained tears on my fearful head make me wish I was in another story's tune. Purgatory can be earthly, sure, but I can't ignore the world's worth even though we all must bore… until I find my reborn soul in unspoken yet broken awe.

You're Here

You're here but the fear of society's spears made you forget to remember your eyes
And you're tied to your tongue and your thighs grow so numb when you're done with becoming a lie
Believe it, conceive it, we've been there, we grieve it, then we heave on another disguise
The world promises pearls but that never unfurls and girl that ain't no surprise

When you were small and in thrall of it all the walls didn't seem so tall
But now that you've grown it's hard to disown the thoughts that they taught you in school
But if you give up trying, you're already dying, though your hour of flowers may not fall
And if you give up your purpose and abandon this circus your birth was worth nothing at all

That habitual trance where most men prance really makes me want to stone
But they feel the same so maybe I'm to blame for rarely picking up a phone
My ego's my foe but we grow with each low so know that you're never alone
But if you intend to spend each bend pretending, you'll end up on your own

My friend the end is sky, but I'd never pretend I'd ever ascend so high
So why not be saved by the human parade before trying to cry goodbye
Believe it, conceive it, I've been there, I grieve it then don't heave on another disguise.
The world promises pearls and one day that might unfurl & girl that ain't no surprise.

ROLL

He has a skinny build & looks that could kill;
He is abused for a living, cooking at the grill.
She is famed from Duluth to Libya to Brazil.
She is a fulfilled masseuse, with years of skill.
They're next to each other on a plane & both get ill.
She gives him a shiatzu and he offers her a pill.
She refuses & he muses on another role he could fill… out of goodwill and for the thrill…. and two lovers roll down that hill.

They reside together on the lakefront:
If there's a joke they are not the brunt:
He worships her giving nature & cunt,
And they party under the midnight sun.
Neither of them ever adopt a front
And they multiply, bearing two little ones.
But children grow up and his fathering goal is done… he rolls himself a blunt… he loves her huntress soul & those runts.

He fantasizes of his wife, eyes of onion:
He converts the basement into a dungeon.
He works on it day & night, sober or drunken:
He wants it to appear medieval & sunken.
They stay there for a week, aroma pungent:
Parts of man & woman run out of suction.
Amid the destruction, she rolls & buns one for fun.... but I'm not one to judge in love & war.... for they reverse rolls like Russians.

They live there together until one day they die:
They die an hour apart but who can say why?
Their bodies are found entwined in July:
The mailman had a cry & so did I.
In lake-town their death is beautified:
But some wise-guy objected it was self-satisfied.
Be warned, even if you roll Thai…
relinquishing control to a woman could be goodbye… for the soul isn't always an ally.

Secret Master of Orgasms

Like all of these lyrics, this is a song on my Bandcamp. Listen to it on my Bandcamp: www.tonnan.bandcamp.com - some songs are best just listened to rather than try to understand. Also, of course, I am self-promoting.

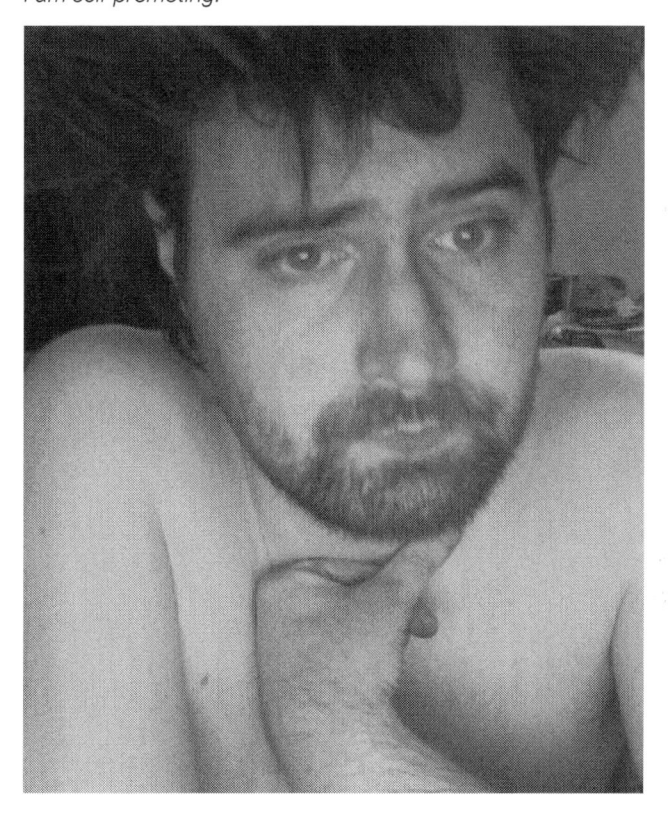

The Other Heaven

Mother of God, I will be demonstrating your lover's mandate by heaven's gate. Eternal return (brother!): it's worth nothing if it's still Earth, so it's fate's turn to wait.
I've learned to navigate a blank slate, but I'd still return the present like a cheapskate.

Maybe most dying people are trying to live with moments past that can't be surpassed.
But I'll be happy as hell for what God'll give me when the sun sets and all's well at last.
Let the Lord forget if He can afford to: like him and some of you, I used to be outcast.

It's just sometimes my heart misses all the ones that ever sought to reach me. I started to climb up their kisses up to the sum of what they fought to teach me.
The theme-park-maze-hell you gotta fight through to make bread is dark as night.

But someday I'll gaze back from the heights and pray to tell God, "I'm dead but alright."

Mother of mine, it's time to remember the sublime seasons our souls aligned in this Unforever.
I don't need a reason to love you, but there are so many: you were so kind, so funny, so clever.
I can't pretend you'll breathe another breath on this plane of death, but as you said, "Whatever!"
Maybe my obsession with God is odd but it stems from trying to get to know you better somehow as you howled.
This is my confession: when life was new, I thought that you were the wisest of all, from your laugh to scowl.
Your beauty was true to me and everyone you met; I'm glad you were my mum: I can't forget you now anyhow.

It's just sometimes my heart misses all the ones that ever sought to reach me.
I started to climb up their kisses up to the sum of what they fought to teach me.
The theme-park-maze-hell you gotta fight through to make bread is dark as night.

But someday I'll gaze back from the heights and pray to tell God, "I'm dead but alright."

Blissful Tears, Broken Mirrors

It was the fission of a vision & a mortal voice.
I wouldn't forget a second if I had the choice.
In the end my friend you used the heavens as a hoist.
They're nothing like the wind & the weather's moist.
But if it's nothing you've nothing to fear.

I don't dwell in the past, the present's enough of a riddle.
But I remember you racing in a wheelchair around Lidl.
Five years ago I grieved fifteen years in four hours.
I remember your face & your embrace & your flowers.
& how I wish you could be with me here.

It's been a while since I broke that god-forsaken mirror.
The end of seven years of bad luck is getting nearer.
Any day now, those blissful tears will

appear.
The moon is a baby phantom & the sun is a seer.

I saw us walking together last night; you were chain smoking.
You sadly reasoned as I gestured madly, my fingers poking.
Yes, I want to go to heaven; no, I don't want to go to hell.
Tho you raised me well, the more we hurt the more we fell
But if it's nothing I've got nothing to fear.

It was dark in the park & we sat on a wooden bench.
My heart fell apart in a way my mind can't start to clench.
If heaven is a physical plane, then I don't want anything else.
The angels are made of melody played by eternity's elves.
& how I wish you could be with me here.

It wouldn't be so lonely if only we all broke the mirror.
No, people aren't the same; no   ,

we're not even near.
Any day now, those blissful tears will appear.
The moon's a pained witness & the sun's a pioneer.

Grieving doesn't deceive me into believing I'll see you again.
But ma! ma! there are the happy tears in the woods at ten.
I remember the feeling but forget the words.
The bird slurred it like it's meant to be heard.
& if it's all for nothing you've got nothing to fear.

Midnight's memory is pinning me to God's rampant sinning:
8am ambulance screams chasing a world back to its beginning.
I woke as the morning broke, heard the news but couldn't cry.
In a dream the angels spoke of how the birth cord wouldn't die.
& how I wish you could be with me here.

I see you every time I peer inside the mirror!
You're not here but still you feel kind of near!
Yeah, blissful tears are beginning to appear!
The moon's an urchin & the sun's a queer!
Blissful tears, broken mirrors!
Blissful tears, broken mirrors!
The moon's an urchin & the sun's a queer!

Nothing Is Sweeter Sometimes

This is another song that I'd like to remain just a song.

Hypnotised

When fate brandishes the blues
I'll be here, whatever the news
As years and tears all drift by
I'll appear to dry your eye
When no one hears what you say
I'll be your ear, till break of day
Even when our paths don't cross
Have no fear, you are my boss

When we sail to an unknown realm
I'll sit next to you at the helm
When feet fail and we've grown old
I'll make you warm if you feel cold
When female love is your lone need
I'll bow out, with grace and speed
Even when our stars don't shine
 I'll share yours if you'll share mine

When it was new, we fell and flew
But when it grew, I finally knew
When we are two, I want to be one
I have no clue, I forget our sum
When we are true, I'm hypnotized
All I want is be at your side
Even when our paths don't cross
Have no fear, you are my boss

The Best Painter of Milk

I can't pretend anyone comprehends
the riddle of the end.
She sold her scent on lend but
everyone was/wants her/a friend.
Gentlemen would tend to her
enzymes again and again.
She was the Queen of school, I was
the fool in Casablanca cool.
Maybe I'm a tool but I diluted her
pool with my drool.

She was the best painter of despair.
She had dead branches of fair hair.
I liked her and or but she didn't care.
She was more aware than the rest of
us. .
She could doctor a stare with a
cuss.
She spoke so smoky nobody caused
a fuss.
Oh, St Annie, what made board that
bus?
Oh, St Annie, how did 'you' become
'us'?

I was captain of the team that held
the regime's cuisine in esteem.
So I screamed at her stream and
serenely cleaned in between.
But she ate my dreams and deemed
me her favourite fickle junkie.
Then she moneyed me with new
ones containing trickles of funky.
She massaged my gluttony and I
tutted like a slut at her onesie.

I was the best painter of the milk on
the hill.
It was irksome to steal but my ink
was silk.
I cherished the still; it was in my will.
She evolved into a billionaire so
grotesque.
But I wouldn't sell my feminism for
less
(Unless perhaps she undressed but I
digress)
Oh, St Annie, what made you
worsen the mess?
Oh, St Annie, how could we bless

gender chess?

She was humbled by the Himalayan
pearls I brought her.
I pardoned her devil-speak for
destiny unfurled a daughter.
Her gypsy mandolin and native curls
we fought a world war for.
Her myth is blurred yet her testimony
of the farm's fire is intact.
With the alimony stacked my
abstract fantasy in a cave became
fact.

We were the best painter of
Napoleon.
We got high on opiates and cried like
Utopians.
I relished the Presidential message
of hope.
The cabaret finished so we went to
buy some dope.
Strictly speaking I'm not a feminist
but I like milk anyway.

Did you know that a cow produces
90 glasses of milk a day?

Oh, St Annie, pray, what made you
betray us & do what they say?
Oh, St Annie, pray, how could my
pithy words possibly convey?

The World – Chapter 3

Another song. It has good lyrics, but right now I can't be bothered to find the file containing them, and I'd much prefer you to listen to them anyway. I'm not including the lyrics to 'Nobody's Clown', 'How To Sing' or 'Poor Number', either, as these are spoken/some of my 'weaker' lyrics. If you like the lyrics, you'll like the songs!)

Go to www.walkingdoctortonan.com for some cool videos and links to the songs.

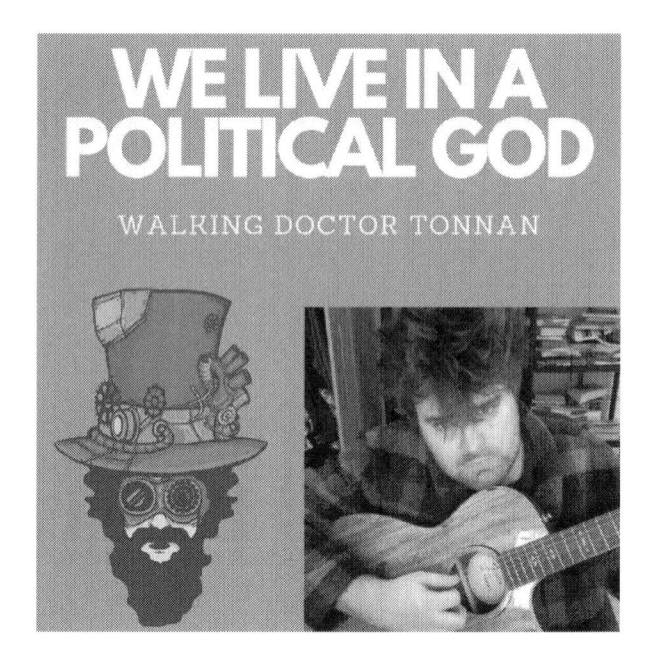

Flu Blues

I wept out of the darkness
You fell into the light
I remember the old bars
And how we used to fag

I wept out for those I had lost
I had to fight to be me, some
I suppose that is the cost
Of outliving your own freedom

I wept out of the darkness
You fell into the light
I remember the old bars
And how we use to fight/fag

I wept out for the warred
You wept out for the tearless
Your tired eyes were assured
Me, I weren't exactly fearless

There won't be an end to God
But the wars, they will end
You're not sorry for being odd
I'm just sorry you pretend

Sometimes I wake up had
Sometimes I wake up mad
I can see good from bad
I know what made us sad

I've been tortured by the voices
Your darkness fell into the light
I remember love without choices
And none of this old new plight

I wept out for those I had lost
I had to fight to be me, some
I suppose that is the cost
Of working for your freedom

I wept out of the darkness
You fell into the light
I remember the old park
And how we used to fight

Joke's On You

If it's true you think you were made for me, well,
then you must be missing a screw.
If you do and you are, you must be naïve enough to
believe Eve desired Adam, too.
Some things no one can explain but lust is laced
with a dose of Freudian voodoo.
Its to-and-fros can drive you insane and pain you
like the profane taste of déjà vu.
Anyway, all that's playing today is the debut of You
Broke Your Own Heart II.
But that fickle desire is sick: the little lyre is a prick,
and I don't want to queue.

Popular opinion didn't even nearly convince me:
Its agendas incestuously flirt like a school of fools.
At the time of your thought-crime, don't think, see:
Tell them you sought fuel for a molecule of mules.
Even society prized you so fiercely & dearly:
It could hydrate a desert with its pool of drool.
But the joke's on you, though, so sneeringly clearly:
I never knew kindness could be so cool yet cruel.
I never knew kindness could be so cruel yet cool.

And so let us remember to forget & remember to
forget.

Talkin' Miss Solitary

Three years ago, I jumped off an eighty-foot bridge.
In case you're wondering, I didn't survive.

But then I looked in the mirror and there I was, losing weight before my very eyes.
And I had two new pimples.
Hey, great, I thought: a new me.
Not only was I losing weight by doing nothing, I had new pimples, and pimples are the next big thing.

I used to want to be an actor.
I couldn't act, so I turned to comedy.
I wasn't funny, so I became a musician.
I was tone deaf, so I became an artist.
If you believe I listed those occupations in ascending rank order, you are probably a drug addict, actor or a drug addict musician. With that said, if you are reading this you are probably more likely to be some girl who wants to play Leonard Cohen in a movie about his life than any of those things. There is no moral to this theory, but if you are bad at something you should do something else.

It makes me laugh when people say hello.
Hell? O… how did I get here?
I prefer to say high, because it reminds me I am a drug addict.

But I don't smoke weed every day, because I don't have enough money to do that.

All of the people I've fallen in love with have names starting with L. Perhaps the universe is trying to tell me something, but Lindsay Lohan is out of my league. So are you, come to think of it. Take what you will from this but bear in mind I once wanted to be a rap star.

I don't have a girlfriend.
At least I think I don't have a girlfriend.
This is because I do not count the time I went out with someone and she forgot she was going out with me because that did not happen to me.

A common misconception is that true love doesn't end. I figure the people who say true love doesn't end have not properly contemplated reality. One day everything must end except the extent of your stupidity.

I don't like the section of this piece where it says I can't sing. I can sing. It's scientifically proven. Everyone can sing. Especially those who believe that true love doesn't end.

I like thinking about infinity.
I wonder if infinity thinks about me.
Surely it must do, because infinity is everything, including you.
You are infinity and can do a number of things that exceeds infinity.

They say you should 'live for today'.
Ah, so that's how the superhumans do it!
I always thought yesterday is where I should be hanging out.
Time to play Pokémon Go and listen to Drake.

I have brain damage. It kind of bites, but it was nice to have a brain while I did. Some people don't have brains in the first place. Ask the president of the United States or those asterisk asterisk asterisk asterisk immigrant communists that are taking all of our jobs. The problem with talking to some Presidents is that you're probably wasting your time, because some doesn't speak English too good so follow scripts written by people that are paid to speak good English and I do not believe this question would be in their agendas. Anyway, I guess soon the president could be anyone, so you are going to have to hedge your bets when trying to find him or her or them.

Some Presidents are hard acts to follow. Donald Trump said he is going to build a wall that keeps the Mexicans out for a sum of 10 billion dollars. I reckon he should build a moat instead. It would probably be cheaper and I'm told that Mexican people cannot swim or do not have enough money to buy a device capable of emigrating through a body of water.

I like both kinds of pie. I used to be able to recite the first three digits of pi. But now I'm brain damaged and I can't get passed 3.14. Pie is great, but nothing tastes as good as skinny. Skinny is my favourite food, because of my longing for nothing. The problem with being dead, though, is that there is no consciousness to experience nothing. I'd rather be out of my head or in someone or eating pie. I don't know why some people die.

My favourite number is 69, because it is so symmetrical. I wrote the last sentence and then realised I am so brain damaged I misunderstood the term 'symmetrical'. I wrote the last sentence before I contemplated the art of slicing equally horizontal and vertical. I wrote the last sentence before I remembered diagonally is a word. I wrote the last sentence before I realised that this piece offers impossible solutions to practical reality.

My boss once asked me why I don't at least pretend to be working. No, I said, why don't you pretend I am working so then we can kill two stoners with one bird and normality will be resumed.

The problem with sex & smoking is that they only last so long. Once I was inside a smoking woman for nine months, but I don't think we had sex or shared a cigarette once during that time. I don't think it was the time of life, but at the time I didn't have much else to compare it to.

I don't like it when people tell me I need a shower. I have a shower already and I don't tell you that you need to read the dictionary.

I'm pretty famous in my house. My brother told me that my writing is verbose, so I looked up verbose in the dictionary. He was right; like most famous people, I am defined by excess.

I like to be surprised unless the surprise is bad. But sometimes I relish being surprised by bad things like Self Portrait by Bob Dylan or some forms of cheese. After I eat said cheese, I drink a banana milkshake, because I know banana milkshakes are good and I am tired of bad surprises.

I hate people who are always right. You can be a genius, but don't make me look stupid because I can do that by myself. And if you are always right, your life must be pretty boring. There would be no novelty. "Hooray! I am right again! For the nine thousand and thirty second time in a row! I am so smart I choose not to say too much; this is also because I do not wish to kill my winning streak."

When I was locked in solitary confinement for 48 hours, I didn't think I would ever get out. It wasn't boring, but I didn't do anything noteworthy there other than look at the walls. I kind of miss solitary. Miss solitary would be a good song title or a name for an ex-prisoner that prefers to be by herself.

Eight years ago, I jumped off a bridge. In case you're wondering, it wasn't an accident but I do not plan on doing it again. I do not think trying everything once is a good idea. Perhaps that's why people murder each other: to tick another item off the list. I'd tell those people that there are a lot of species of animals to feed coconuts to. But if ticking things off that list is one of the things people aspire to do, living beings are doing kind of well because we live in a version of infinity.

I don't think I can walk on water, but I haven't tried. I don't think I can fly but I wasn't trying to when I jumped. Still, it would have been a flipping revelation. Hey, I can fly! Forget suicide. I shall solve all the problems of the world by flying around it and pissing on criminals.

How am I doing now? Not bad. But not bad must surely include terrible, especially if you are a pedant or a person who does not speak any languages. I would love to have grown-up kids, but I stay away from pedants and people who do not speak any languages whenever possible.

Someone asked me whether I consider myself a poet or a song & dance man first and foremost. Firstly, I consider myself a civil servant and eighthly & foremost I consider myself a polymath.

Here is a riddle for you. A poor man has blank. A rich man needs blank. If you eat you blank, you will die. The answer is nothing, but it could be everything too. Not many answers to riddles express such paradoxes.

"If this isn't funny, then it's a poem." Bill Hicks said that.
"I'll be the hero in your dreams if you'll be the one in this score". Bob Dylan implied that.
"There are those who see the god above who never knew the pain of bliss
And those like me who dream of love with one like you on nights like this." I wrote that and it took me five flipping hours.

Proof of a Conspiracy

Ain't it just like the dead to conquer your head
With all the things that could've been said?
Society hangs its hate by human thread
Then on a plate it serves your head
Tho we bear the weight of worlds they dread
We can only stare as fate unfurls in red

Your drunken policeman gobbles trout,
Buddhists meditate on the devout route
And politicians pout their doubting snouts
Spouting bullshit til their lungs give out
As huddled masses shout about a man of clout
Who can stand to flout his doubt without a pout

I saved some for me but you took the rest
Whatever God's doing can't be guessed

So pay no heed to one that's blessed
With a crest etched across his breast
For it's he that leads this lonely quest
But it's he that's bequest to those oppressed

The hero in your dreams consumes forbidden fruit
And returns to the womb with his orphaned flute
Soliloquising that each angelic accident is absolute
As tears stream down his face to his embryonic suit
Where the air is polluted by your new destitute boots
But who can refute that materialistic minds prostitute?

My essay on hash reviled, I was exiled
Society, who has the guile to attend that trial
I'd only be thinking of you all the while
I did it though because the ride was wild
I only lied because you took me for a

child
I can't forget the way that you smiled

Omens of Paradise

"*Will you always love free?*" the FatCat sighs.
"*For as long as I am me,*" the Diplomat lies.
His lit cigar is perched between her plump lips.
But her eyes trump Evolution's ancient script.
"*To being free,*" the FatCat forcefully cries, unscrewing a bottle of red wine and chugging down half of it quick.
"*To being me,*" the Diplomat replies, wondering why her lover's breath smells of another's laughter and shit.
Now the FatCat and Diplomat jump asleep and dream they're dreaming a nightmare no real God would allow.
The gore of their innermost wars are no closer to omens of paradise than the ghostly door you knock on now.

The Lollipop Lady distributes ice cream to her friends.
She knows she'll be repaid with salvation in the end.
She exclusively speaks monosyllabic words such as 'mend'.
The Lollipop Lady is single and on that you can always depend.

Inside the kitchen, the Chef swears in
fluent French and It's easy to understand
his preferred slurred phrase.
The chef relishes isolated conditions and
the way he seasons birds with curd &
'merde' is quite absurd these days.
Yes, God will be sole witness to the end
like God was to the start, as Neptune's
screams break the moon's heart.
Let epiphanies the force of a hundred
horses divorce Art from such omens of
paradise that the government farts.

A broody guest has a proposition the
manager won't resist.
The hot concierge knows that the manager
don't exist.
"Where is the manager of this hotel?" asks
the broody guest.
"He's in hell," says the hot concierge,
looking her metrosexual best.

Inside the Great Hall, Brian The Actor
finishes his cleaning shift and smiles a
beguiling alcoholic grin.
Brian's manager spread a rumour that he
slept with Britney Spears to catalyse a
career that's yet to begin.
Now the Owner patronizes his home-
grown mosquito factory and contemplates
other machines of spiritual slaughter.
Feel the heat of a virgin eternity & see my

Father become me as these omens of
paradise emerge like wine out of water.

The Nun Visions

See the matrix moon set over "once upon a time".
The pious lightening frightens an enlightened mime.
Now dead angels dance around the town of Heaven.
A powerless seven nation army advances upon Devon.
Telepathic hippies discuss the timeless torture of union.
A broke diplomat smokes and chokes on a fat Cuban.
But if you think life is binary as hunter versus gun,
Then you haven't seen nineteen nuns eat God's son.

Rewind to see the moon fart thunder by the river.
Key workers & elephants & mayors alike all shiver.
When shrinks wink sexy I think they want to make a deal.
I'd walk up to Nothing before Feeling can steal my meal.
If a youth pockets truth, the corrupt just phone the blue.
Yes, the rest are self-interested yet reserve a stone for you.
I guess the best is always yet to come if you don't have fun,

For the difference between life and death amounts to nun.

Blind bikers loop around troops in the monkey cage.
Even those on minimum wage can find refuge in rage.
Grind to a new beginning, even if your hair is thinning.
It was & is & will be NOW, whether losing or winning.
See the atoms of a song compose a bittersweet odour.
Hear the stench of a gong propose that all war is over.
Smell the sequence of a frequency explode her lust,
And finally let these visions of nuns naturally combust.

Eden

God forgave wars as atomless senses combined.
Eden itself will be toast if we don't obey its tethers.
Her form perspires like the weather of my mind.
In tomorrow's tumult your soles tread on forevers.
Beaches burn, leeches to bleach, a cyclical repeat.
But conquests complete, I convalesce at her feet.

Saved by her sacred touch, naked we were a geek.
She blossomed like two-lips and I ate it on the loo.
Enslaved by double Dutch, hatred too has mystique.
I'll give you true love: I used to live for torture too.
Past the dance of chance's maker, I cast my shadow.

The truth is that hate prevails where love is shallow.

Somehow it feels like it happened to another again.
She mutters & I stutter like the advent of consent.
Why beat about the bush? She pushed me at ten to five.
I remember the weep-love of my first & last ascent.
Armies of adolescents jump into a secret forest.
And bands of ink pelicans tell fables on your wrist.

Inside the ride resides a bride who claims to be famous.
She dances to the Temptations so aimless and shameless.
Your eyes are tied to the bribe, but you remain blameless.
During the snide depths of ecstasy, she'll become nameless.
Past the rain dance of the maker, demons blast their scores.
But you've got to love her in your own way for she is yours.

I've won that which hasn't stayed; I've lost what I haven't given away.
I prefer milkshakes to jewels anyway, but Eden's grace reigns true as cliché. Today the boss is dressed in a suit of grey, Marvin Gaye glasses & a Bombay beret.
I hear him say in the hallway at the buffet that we too must stay for the cabaret.
But a concluding sense of circularity is pure at the conception of his remarks. And backwards we dart into the mirror's art, heralded by a dog's heaven-sent barks.

Poor Number

She was nearly my foe;
She never made a promise she could keep.
Yeah, there's danger hid below
And I was the kid, the stranger with whom she'd weep.
I shooed the federallies above the labour of thighs
For she admired my eyes and I papered her with no lies.
After all the years of sneering compromise
I sought the nightly hope which was shrined before sleep.
Then something changed for something's wrong
Nothing's where the fools and devilz don't dwell in song
No alibis over the nether I can sell: I can't forever wish you well.

He was born to bet: I forgot her regret;
She danced with me in the passage of reverie.
What romance is free is damaged by

sun set:
Jealousy is blue with scorn; I'm a fifth zealous of the remedy.
What chance was the arithmetic of tete a tete

But ambition's door the starlet read to me from memory.

After the treachery of the night
After the splendour of the eye
It's beyond the causation of the might of why.
And everything veined and the I-ching was a gong
There's no remedy for the hell
No alibis to sell, forever we live and forever we die, I well well well
The model left the writer
He never reviewed
After the all-nighter
The kisses outgrew

A banoffee condom
Shape of sirens falling thru
A giant devoted himself
To growth to what he knew
As for all your wealth
And heathen tattoo

You looked like a funeral
But you want what you can't get

I want you like a Neanderthal

For the stiletto and that kitchenette

Then something changed for something's wrong

Nothing's where the dwell

No alibis over the nether I can sell: I can't forever wish you well.

Let Her Shadow Dance Move You

I expect to die soon
But I intend to live forever
Time is a buffoon
But humans are so clever

Help me sing my soul
Help me write a letter
Shelter what we stole
From the mad weather

I love you like we're brothers
I love you like a living colour
We both lost our only mothers
We won't ever get another

History isn't music
Mystery is mosaic
Love me til I lose it
Dope won't improve it

I'm sorry for the secret
I hid it in my stale heart
Sometimes I get greedy
The mailman drags a cart

One day we'll be an atom
One day we'll be together
I used to drink Kratom
I still like getting leathered

I'm sorry you weren't there
I'm sorry I just wasn't here
I don't know why you care
You were always near

The preacher sued the projects
The teacher was a dude in love
The mirror angel just rejects
I'M A SHADOW OF A
PERSON'S LOVE

Let her be born. Let her howl.
Let her smile. Let her raise one eyebrow.
Let a team of official cameramen document the episode.

Let her walk. Let her fall.
Let her talk five languages.

Let an autobiography be
commissioned.

Let her go shopping for hats at
Sunday mass.
Let each hatted human give
their hat to her.
Let a choirboy wolf-whistle.
Let her hurl a top hat at the
choirboy.
Let everyone laugh.

Let a jumbo jet deliver her
to Time Square to watch herself
being born in a TV
documentary.
Let hundreds and thousands of
hands
clap when she is finally born on
TV.
Let her blush at her nudity.
Let an assassin take aim on a

roof.
Let her leave the United States.

Let her return to Broadway
a year later with a highly
sanitised
but critically acclaimed stage
adaptation
of the TV documentary about
her birth.
Let a husky saxophonist play a
smoky
rendition of her new theme
song.

Let every sculptor join forces
to construct a vast monument
to her beauty in every capital
city.
Let her personally destroy
her nominated monument
in a state-of-the-art bulldozer
on the first of every month.

Let each resident of the country
make a joyous pilgrimage
to attend the ceremony.
Let the air be pungent
with marijuana.

Let there be a competition.
Let this be the last competition.
Let seventy of the shrewdest
scientists
scrutinise the soul of every
human being.
Let there be a huge metal island
erected in the middle of the
pacific.
Let the 33,000 most successful
candidates be flown there.
Let them starve and let them
talk
and let them fight each other.
Let her arrive on the seventh
day,
bearing baskets of bread.

Let there be a very expensive display of fireworks.
Let each remaining candidate win £100,000.
Let there be a weeklong orgy.
Let her select 183 husbands and 182 wives based on its results.

Let the last competition be broadcast
unedited on the History Channel in the week following her death.

Talkin' Christmas Blues

Well, I was sitting in my room and the radio was playing all the festive tunes, and it made me feel kind of gloomy.

Something must be done about Justin Bieber, who is practically a beaver… to all the Beliebers out there: don't sue me!

It was five years & four days to Christmas and I decided to go for a walk to clear my head of all the talk about how cold it is and stuff.

I had no destination in mind and I was blind to where each fork would go, but I felt kind of bold & that proved to be enough.

Being bold does count for something or other, but you can't be too bold, because then you'd just be a silly stupid old fool.

[If a girl calls me Santa once, I don't worry; twice, that's okay, too; but thrice, running fast as my body can is my general rule.]

Anyhow, my pedometer said I'd tread ten thousand steps when I took a rest after passing my old school and the pool.

As I was catching my breath and freezing like death, I

saw an withered yet handsome man sat on an ancient stool.

His sign read, "I have magic powers that can change your life; please just buy me a bite to eat, and please: no plastic."

My mind was intrigued but I wasn't sure if the sign was sarcastic, for claiming to have magic powers is drastic.

I went to the nearest bakery and brought to him two croissants, three doughnuts and a cup of coffee.

Mister Mystery said, "Took you long enough to bring my stuff, but I love all the food you got me."

"Now forget how to remember," he whispered in my ear, "and the sum of what you really want shall appear."

I forgot it all on that freezing December day, then out came the sun of May, the same one was here!

I said, "Wow, mister, that was sick; please show me another trick! Teach me how to play guitar & sing."

Mister Mystery replied, "Not a soul could magic that, boy, but enjoy what fun the sun & money can bring!"

I wasn't sure what to say but finally replied, "I'm glad you seem happy, and I'm grateful destiny didn't do that to me.

You can't tell by looking how someone really is, because everyone has one or two demons or maybe even three."

He replied, "While the best things in the world happen with a smile, that's often how the worst news is delivered too.

I don't use a sign that says 'I grew up an orphan', but I am and my life here represents the pudding of the proof."

"I'm sorry for everything that's happened to you, but I will say life will get better for you at least today", I replied.

"Why would it?" he asked. "Because I've got hash!" I said.

We smoked until sunrise that day and laughed so much we cried.

It seems most people love Christmas themes, so I wrote this Christmas song in a February dream… wow, Santa is a cash-cow!

I will be Christmas sometime soon… in fact, it could be Christmas now!

"So readable and full of surprises; you never know where it's going to go next."
— Eliza Geotty

GOD'S PRETTY GAME OF GROTESQUE PUPPETS

This poignant epic is a pornographic & poetic series of humorous vignettes:
'The Sun Always Sets in the West',
'Happy Tears in Love with a Cold',
'The Inauguration of Insanity',
'The Mother of Infinity',
& 'The Devil Can't & God Won't'.

THE FIRST NOVEL WRITTEN
BY DOMINIC FRANCIS

GOD'S PRETTY GAME OF GROTESQUE PUPPETS

By Dominic Francis

For V.A. & J.F. & G.M. & G.N. & O.S. & S.O. & G.A. & C.D. & J.D. & D.M & J.S. & K.L & A.M. & L.T. & L.G. & E.V. & E.G. & A.K. & S.B. & B.R. & for teaching & for my brother(s) & for my mum & for my dad & for sublime memories & for my friendships & for all my family & for me.

Reader, feel free to skip back and forth over paragraphs & pages & parts of this book because while each chapter or part adds up to a cohesive whole, these sections can be enjoyed & understood as separate entities. This work is my ode to sex and language. It has obsessed me for over five years. Reader, thank you for reading.

You can listen to the audio for this book for free by clicking the link to "Tonnan's Novel" on my website www.walkingdoctortonnan.com

Sam Raven's interpretation of this text is full of surprises, even for me. A tiny proportion of this text was written when I was 16, but I finished writing this book when I was 27. The novel was originally titled "The Inauguration of Insanity".

God's Pretty Game of Grotesque Puppets

THE SUN ALWAYS SETS IN THE WEST

just so shooting stars set swiftly; almost falling in love & doing the math in restralardin market; ominous clarity

HAPPY TEARS IN LOVE WITH A COLD

secretive magic soldier; a remarkable person; the black cat; a proper criminal; a two-story building; maggie's story; stupid is as stupid does; an angel made of acid written just for xinx; he don't love you like i love you; hey presto; nine months; immunology; the party that broke my deal; a more metaphorical climax

THE INAUGURATION OF INSANITY

toenail hospital, the café, the graveyard, the skatepark & the woman; halloumi; a sex scene; a sex dream; shit about my past; a note on my upbringing; guitars & eternal return explained; a secret karma; and at the end they all suck him; the apartment-apocalypse-chronicles

THE MOTHER OF INFINITY

i'll die a dreamer but i adore a lot of alliteration; the suicide sunlight; conventional sense of the word; an account of the president's daily address; an omen of a direction home; a hospital admission; my heart is a garden of butterflies; thoughts on love; information about xinx from cat; cat's prophecy

THE DEVIL CAN'T & GOD WON'T

you can have it all; guess who testified; and they both badly lied; the wedding; five years later; the animal circus & the secret sum of my world

THE FOOTNOTE TO "GOD'S PRETTY GAME OF GROTESQUE PUPPETS"

GOD'S PRETTY GAME OF GROTESQUE PUPPETS

THE SUN ALWAYS SETS IN THE WEST
Just So Shooting Stars Set Swiftly

Were I a better storyteller, I would begin at the beginning, but the following words are a love story, a love story with an ending, and I'm not sure whether The Beginning is really The End & The End is really The Beginning.

Zelda always wanted to be a writer. I suppose I always wanted to be a writer too, but things never worked out for me until now due to my terrible time management skills & a series of misunderstandings with CatWest bank. These difficulties were in turn compounded by a couple of serious confrontations involving ill-informed members of my immediate family, the bitter details of which bore me like an out-of-tune guitar or pasta without cheese. Let's just say that while some people may believe they are well-informed, in actuality they are the most despicable of creatures.

Anyhow, in countless ways, Zelda is a far more accomplished writer than I am, even though she hasn't published a thing. Me, I write with the graceless theatricality of an exquisitely drunk ballerina whose articulations ooze out of his subservient arsehole. Zelda, Zelda never lets the number of calories she's consumed in a day exceed the number of words she's written in that same day. It scared me shitless when she first told me about this practice, but Zelda speculates that there's *"a secret salvation in starving sometime upon a sometime,"* and I reckon Zelda rarely goes hungry, for Zelda is pretty damn overweight & pretty damn fast at writing.

Zelda can summon an acrobatic swoop of a phrase that is capable of annihilating someone's apparently firmly held belief as swiftly as an incinerator could cremate *Mosquito in the Elephant*, which coincidentally is one of Zelda's favourite novels. A large minority of people, such as certain members of my family, are exceptionally prejudicial when confronted with an idea that doesn't expressly confirm their worldview. Zelda, however, can turn a conservative into a socialist with a few mumbled phrases & a concise gesture of futility to the heavens, just like that, at the drop of a hat. For example, at first it was a little awkward when Zelda, with all her liberal quirks, met my old-fashioned parents, but soon my folks absolutely adored her & privately vowed that they'd be overjoyed if I ever were to marry *"such a fine young lady"*.

When Zelda & I were young together, every 'forever' came cheap as chips. Then, it went quiet as shit when Insanity licked her lips and stole our lungs – but then Literature sung, soulfully silent, of the uncontrollably violent. And so, like an unparoled Freudian slip, Literature switched around the worlds in every book in every nook until every unexplored forest was town & every pore in all the zeroes' souls transformed into a heroic whole. Thus, in our eyes, the unknown fused with the familiar to disguise normality. Every night Zelda & I got stoned as baby stoners together talking about what's what & the pretty misfit coincidence of Literature. But Literature was a boastful ghost, a nosey host, and for all intents & purposes we were Literature's bitches. I mean, Literature would rather be considered a witch than be taken for granted. But Zelda & I had the itch to read ever-more forevermore, for Literature's cursing seed had been planted.

When Zelda & I were young and beautiful together, every 'forever' was truthful to a fault. We'd spot stars in the distance and vault far off into their imagined abyss. Zelda would figure out the meaning of life & forget it the next instant, and I'd become the person I always wanted to be, then a moment later realise I didn't want to be that person at all. We were both constantly thirsty for something or other, but that something or other would never reach our lips. Even if it did, we would never consider the moment our own, so the indefatigable thirst endured. Regrettably, perhaps this is what makes us human.

Zelda & I talk about writing when we see each other. I think I'm a hack; Zelda thinks I have talent. I think Zelda's writing is "*almost as profound as regaining your hearing & eyesight immediately prior to the apocalypse*"; Zelda thinks her style is "*hypothetically unbalanced*". I don't know what "*hypothetically unbalanced*" even means. I've tried to get Zelda to take writing more seriously, for she has a natural knack of immersing herself in the temperament of the times. I've said this to her on several occasions in several different ways, but Zelda always smiles wryly, shaking her head as if I've posed some curious yet unsolvable conundrum, as if penning "*sensual beatnik etchings*" was not her intention at all.

Yeah, OK – I'll say now what will become even more apparent soon. Zelda gave me everything I wanted for some time, so I gave her what I thought she wanted too. This could but would not last.

Zelda is beautiful, but I don't think she knows this. Some might say that not knowing oneself to be beautiful is what makes one beautiful. A swan swimming in an overcast lake, for example, does not rejoice in its own splendorous aerial image, because allocating a specific kind of sticker to a specific kind of entity is a humanoid affair, perverted by individual point of view and societal conditioning. Does the copulating cockroach recoil at the 'grotesque' aura of its 'doppelganger'?

"Beauty is beauteously beautiful," Zelda says, in a Frolid class during which we are paired to discuss a Ricky Mantle poem. *"There are moments of accidental beauty & beatific perfection that will never occur again. There are also monstrosities of misfortune whose tune will forever disturb, even if it is never heard, the beautiful un-forever we inhabit."*

Haha! If this were a piece of theatre, I reckon you can guess who would be the female lead, already improbably deified by her unlikely quotability. These words, though, are a fragmented coming-of-age love story that occurs in the present tense and most of them will probably not concern Zelda in the slightest. This is a comic folktale about something that is happening right now to someone whose past & present is exactly the same as my own was, far away on a version of my former planet. Our own unnamed Universe is near-infinite, and I believe these events will continue to reoccur infinitely in separate versions of the multiverse.

I guess this monologue is my attempt to come to terms with my past. I guess in putting words to

paper I still hope to write my future. Some things can be understood as fact, though: for example, it's impossible to die from a cannabis overdose...
purple is the best colour... the wind is controlled by the real God... black looks good with white... and *The Sun Always Sets in the West*.

*Almost Falling In Love & Doing The Math
At Restralardin Market*

I am sixteen when I start Sixth Form at Soul School. I first meet Zelda while I am getting lunch at the Technicolour Café. I'm old enough to feel as if I understand the workings of the world, but I am still too young to understand that I don't understand them at all, and that I probably never will. But I shall wholeheartedly almost fall in love with Zelda during an instant which I have been trying to reclaim for myself ever since.

Outside the café, Zelda is sitting alone & smoking & drinking coffee, reading *The Insider* by Wiko. I see her there, looking fine as wine, and I can suddenly hear my heartbeat beat & beat. Zelda is as hot as either afterlife extreme. Do some of those basking in the heat of hell believe they are in heaven and am I a heathen for wondering that? Anyhow, Zelda is a perfectly proportioned portrait of heaven drawn in hell.

Zelda is fat as fuck; I mean, I've never seen any girl around my age that fat. Although I love fat women, I immediately wonder how & why a girl as pretty as her got that fat, temporarily befuddled by her beauty. She's dressed in a body-hugging denim jacket which contrasts with her red hair that flows like a river of curls and blows with every beat of the world. As she reads, her olive eyes dart left & right like a pair of twin piranhas swimming to each other's mirror melody in a tank. Zelda has a nose shaped just like my best friend's sister's. Zelda has spectacular curves that look straight from the photobook of your favourite porn star.

This might be the first time I've ever seen something other than a computer screen that I could happily spend more than a couple of hours gazing at. Yeah, Zelda smoking & drinking coffee &

reading is surprisingly fun to watch. Unsurprisingly to you but surprisingly to me, I almost fall in love. Shit, I think to myself, you *have* to speak to this girl. I buy a cheese toastie for my lunch and sit down opposite Zelda, who offers a shy smile and then seems to retract it as soon as I open my mouth.

"Why aren't you in church?" I ask. My sixteen-year-old head hopes that this abstract existentialist seasoning will add a fittingly luxuriant aftertaste to her half-finished salad.

"This is my best effort at life. God don't listen to me no more. I tried to reason with God, but God kept letting bad things happen," she says.

Wow, I think, I didn't expect a metaphysical answer to such a flippant question this Tuesday lunchtime. I probably should have said this aloud, too, for I always have been more articulate in my mind than in my vocal cords. *"Who is God to you then?"* I ask.

"Please." Zelda smiles an unforgiving smile at the breeze, then speedily forgives us both with a content laugh. *"God is my boyfriend… I guess it's not all that bad, though. At least I'm not alone."*

"I'm sorry," I say. I gulp. *"Is my lousy attempt to flirt with you intruding on your time with Wiko?"*

"Yes, it is. Unless that's a trick question too," Zelda says. She bites her lip & smiles & laughs half a laugh that makes me want to laugh too, if only to complete hers.

"I don't think it was a trick question." I scratch my head. *"Unless your answer was a trick answer. I think I'll go now, anyway. It was good to meet you."*

Zelda sighs, gives page 57 an ear & shuts the paperback. *"I didn't mean to say you should go,"* she says.

"Okay, whatever," I say. *"I'll be seeing you, anyhow."*

"Wait!" Zelda exclaims with a cackling grave of suspicion in her eyes, which morphs my informal intensity into a curious cheerfulness. *"Do you go to Soul School?"*

"Yep. Year 12. And you?" I ask.

"Yeah, same year. What subjects are you studying?"

"Frolid, Chemistry, Math & History," I say. *"You?"*

"Frolid, Music, Philosophy & Franklin," she says. *"I'm Zelda."*

"Tonnan. See you around, Zelda," I say.

"Bye for now, Tonnan."

I take my toastie to a nearby table and eat it by myself while playing ping-pong on my phone. The Technicolour Café is close enough to Soul School grounds to go to during lunch but far enough away for people not to flock to. I've come both lunchbreaks since the start of school. I like sitting outside & thinking & drinking iced coffee & checking the news. Personally, I don't smoke tobacco unless I need to prove I can, but I still sit outside because I like the feeling of being warm after being cold.

It might surprise you to learn that, through trial and error, I've figured out how to sleep with much older and fatter broads. As far as I am concerned, the older and fatter the broad in question, the better. Zelda's sixteen-year-old brain will probably linger upon the lanky fella with a fit nose & prominent cheekbone because I showered her with attention out of the blue and then almost instantly deprived her of it… this is a rudimentary psychology life hack I learned from chatting to jaded staff at the pub down my street.

[Although it's perhaps a little manipulative to actively try to shape a person's opinion of you, I got bullied at secondary school, and no one ever got anywhere in life because they are completely overbearing. I'm pretty self-confident now, though, anyhow. This is probably why Zelda didn't quite seem to trust me yet. But soon she will. I know it. In our world, a very educated guess falls only a little short of fact.]

Most birds fly, but not all birds fly; however, if I were to magic you into a flamingo, I'd bet that you'd soon be trying to fly. That is what I mean when I say I almost fell in love with Zelda: I had lived long enough to sense that I was about to fall and so miraculously managed to summon an ancient carpe diem adrenaline to clasp onto for support. And you know what that means: I almost fell in love.

There was something otherworldly about meeting Zelda. As it happens, I knew that the encounter was important as it happened. Zelda radiated the timid sweetness of a fierce silver moon appearing behind the jungle horizon, wolves shaking their heads as they half-blindly howl in its mindless wake. There are so many things about her I know I don't know, and I know I want to know them all.

I dream about Zelda twice as I sleep this fine September night. I've just started at a new school and I'm dreaming about a girl I've barely met. You should never share your dreams, because then Allah's Destiny Police might hunt you. Personally, I don't want such a fate to materialize. I like to have a good track record with all forms of law-enforcement.

***

Math finishes & I file out of the classroom. The class consolidated my knowledge of quadratic equations and other stuff I had already learned in secondary school, but the simpler the problem the more I enjoy solving it, and I particularly relished observing the sensual shape of the numbers the MILF teacher drew on the board. To be honest, I like being lazy when I can be, yet I don't mind challenging myself sometimes and trying to make all the numbers add up. I figure that laziness is preferable in a mathematician, for the quickest route to the solution is always the best. And why get the bus when you can get the train?

"Hi Tonnan," Zelda says, waiting outside the classroom. *"Want to cut class with me?"*

Zelda must have made a mental note of the subjects I study and consulted the timetable pinned to the Common Room board. Math, surprisingly, isn't very popular at Soul School, so there's only one group of students.

"Why would I do that?" I say, hoping to appear unfazed by the invitation.

"Restralardin Canal is terrific as toffee and I will buy you a fantastic hat if you buy me cigarettes," Zelda says in a tone that is seductively commanding yet pleading.

She's made me an offer I can't refuse, but I go through the motions of protesting anyway. *"If you want your food to taste terrific as toffee, then buy some toffee. And I don't wear hats, nor do I approve of sixteen-year-olds smoking,"* I say.

"It's not illegal to have fun," Zelda smirks.

"Hah – sure, okay, fine! I'll cut class with you," I say. *"Why bother learning about the mistakes of

other people in History when I can't make my own now? Where to, 'Talkin' Miss Solitary'?" Sho could've chosen anyone to be her class-cutting buddy, though, so I am flattered.

"To Destiny or Death!" Zelda replies. *"But first, to the Market! Are you hungry? I'm hungry,"* she answers her own question before I have time to absorb it, rubbing her bulging belly.

I shrug. *"I like pizza. But how about I don't buy you cigarettes and I go without a hat? Is that plausible?"*

"Alas!" she says, *"The most-grave plans o' dice an' men…"*

*"The most-*laid *plans o' dice an' men…"* I correct sardonically but in a way that probably just sounds condescending.

"If I knew you were going to rectify my every teenage misstep like a nosey orthodontist who should have trained as a psychiatrist, I wouldn't have invited you!" Zelda replies aggressively but with an expectant half-smile, which I consciously complete.

"Hah. Regardless of your past failings, let's get this show on the road!" I say.

We leave schoolgrounds and almost immediately board an airbus to the station. *"Don't you have a boyfriend or girlfriend?"* Zelda asks as we find somewhere just for us on the fairly empty airbus.

I shake my head. *"No. I guess I'm 'seeing' a few people, though."* I refer to the housewife who likes to waltz with me when her husband is away on business, the postwoman to whom I sometimes deliver post, and my neighbour who has funny eyebrows.

"*Oh,*" Zelda says, and then very lightly – oh, so lightly – punches my arm. "*And who might they be?*"

"*I refer to the housewife who likes to waltz with me when her husband is away on business, the postwoman to whom I sometimes deliver post, and my neighbour who has funny eyebrows,*" I say straightforwardly, knowing a full-disclosure of the facts will be enough to satisfy Zelda's inquiries yet enough to maintain an air of mystery. "*How about you? Do you have a boyfriend or girlfriend?*"

"*Mostly I only think about food & women & writing. I'd prefer to keep it this way, but Reality also contains male organisms, which complicates my feelings.*"

"*So?*" I say.

"*So... no. Secretly, though, I've always wanted to be a lesbian,*" Zelda shares.

"*That's a very feminist view on sexuality,*" I joke.

"*Ha! Thanks, I guess. My views are always very feminist.*"

"*So are mine. I don't like to talk about them, though, in case I offend.*"

"*How could you offend?*" Zelda asks sceptically.

"*My perception of most self-proclaimed feminists, though true to my experience, is skewed by a couple of card-wearing, short-haired 'feminists' who tricked me into contracting temporary yet pretty aggrieving rashes on my genitals. At the end of the day, though, I tricked myself, so who's to say that these peoples' status as card-wearing 'feminists' contributed to my impermanent downfall downstairs...?*"

"I don't see how your esoteric ramblings relate to feminism," she says blankly, hazel eyes blinking with each of her spoken syllables.

"They don't, but – like I told you – I don't like to speak about feminism. I don't think I have the right. It's not my prerogative."

"That's not a very feminist thing to say. Everyone's got to look after each other!" Zelda says. *"You know what 'prerogative' means, though, so you must be a feminist."*

"Thanks, I guess," I say.

We get off the airbus at Central Station. From Central Station, it's about an eight-minute walk to reach the heart of the market. Zelda & I pass people of all backgrounds: for example, a horde of tourists consulting maps on their mobiles, another horde of tourists trying to pass the horde of tourists consulting maps on their mobiles, a dozen vendors trying to tout tattoos & clothing & various paraphernalia to the aforementioned foreign folk, ten tipsy locals celebrating the redemption song of alcohol for brunch outside the Rechargeable Ballroom, and an assortment of gaudily-dressed indie punk kids who would hate to be called 'scenesters' & so are best described as unemployed hipsters who in actuality actually define Restralardin Market.

We pass an abandoned tattoo parlour that makes Zelda stop in her tracks to examine, with seemingly undue nostalgia, some of the 'Summer Dream' patterns presented on the panel behind the windowpanes. *"What are your views on tattoos, Tonnan? Do you have any tattoos yet?"* she asks.

"Sorry, Zelda, I don't like pointless agony or unnecessary mess," I say.

"So, you don't like tattoos or hats or smoking. I bet next you'll be telling me you don't like Southern food." Zelda says, sounding utterly disheartened by my lack of class-cutting spirit. She smiles at a new thought. *"Why don't you get a 'Folktale of Zelda' tattoo? That'd boost my dwindling self-esteem."*

"Zelda, as much as I fancy you and as much as I love video games, I'd sooner dye my hair pink than get something even as beauteous as your name tattooed on my own bulbous bottom. Although it's probably a very feminist expression of the imagination, such a devotional act cannot possibly be worth a couple of hours of pain and a lifetime of shame. I don't like your name that much."

"What, you don't like my name that much, bruv?" Zelda says, her voice humorously mutating from middle-class to chavvy midsentence.

"I used to love Crescendo games, especially the one named after you," I confess. *"But then I grew up, only to discover that I still hated hats & still hated cigarettes & still preferred purple bras to moustached mechanics. I do love your name, though. Were you named after 'The Folktale of Zelda?"*

"I asked my dad that once, but he made it very clear he didn't want to talk about it," she says. *"I figure it's just a really touchy subject. It's probably one of those chicken versus egg situations I can't even begin to understand."*

"Hah. Okay," I say. *"Do you want to hit the Stables?"*

"Yeah! It's time to get this show on the road!" she announces. I think Zelda's mocking me. I feel mocked.

These early playful exchanges will later soon now become defined by unsaid ceremonial moons & daily bread & the walking talking utterances of animate undead parasites that feast upon Zelda's head. Eventually, though, we will both find somewhere to call home: a hostel or hospital bed, a Peron gutter, a friend's sofa, wherever is comfortable, a boyfriend or girlfriend's house, whatever is going. Already, anyhow, our conversations breathe a romantic disregard for the past while referencing a future that we know will never become our own.

Yes, Zelda's unfussy yet ubiquitous warmth embodies a gracefully infectious lust for life that I can't feasibly articulate in written form because, as much as my heart tries to coerce the obtuse & harsh confederation of words into a sensical order whilst still radiating an alien poeticism, I believe I'm only capable of expressing the statutory or the stationary in the written form. Perhaps, as my music teacher once told me, *"music is for the soul & poetry is for the politicians."*

We walk by the doughnut stall & I inhale the sugary-fresh scent of freedom. I wonder how long it would take me to metabolise a hundred of those chocolate filled doughnuts, then wonder whether the doughnuts were placed here to pry my 'pizza fantasy' out of my forgetful head.

Next to me, Zelda hungrily inspects the cream-filled doughnuts. *"There are so many of them. So many different kinds, too"* she says, her gait sinking & hypnotised eyes bulging as if she's popped a Devil's Daughter.

"Yeah, and they will probably always be here, probably in that exact configuration. Some things never change. I wonder how old some of those doughnuts are," I say, my hunger evaporating.

"Tonnan, I want to grow with you. Not grow old: just grow up & grow even fatter," Zelda says suddenly, with an inexplicably razor-thin ephemerality.

I nod. *"Sure. We can make a plan."* I smile & watch Zelda buy a doughnut from the short guy at a counter, sensing her giddy exhilaration.

"When I'm a lonely spinster," she starts, *"I'll need somebody to love me. If no one else can fill that vacancy, can I depend on you?"*

"So, I'm like third or fourth choice?" I ask, confused & pretending to be offended by the proposition.

"What? No. I mean if neither of us finds anyone else we like."

"Zelda, you're either pissing in the wind or you're onto something," I say, stepping towards her provocatively.

Someday I will beat my demons forever & someday I will become a homeowner & someday Zelda will clutch my crotch like it's a crutch & someday I will become a chef and cook curry for Zelda. Someday I will shrink an inch & someday I will cry for Zelda & someday I will die without ever finding out why Zelda ate so much. For now, though, I take Zelda in my arms in a vagabond embrace that is closely followed by a passionate kiss straight from the back pages of *The Angles of Angels*.

Love is phat ass funk sound. Love is the whoop of the widowed wind. Love is Zelda. I am love. My love is not yet Zelda, but stranger stories will be written before long.

I note the rainbow bubble-gum taste of Zelda's tongue. We could kiss forever, and it would feel like our story had never begun.

But Zelda & I kiss only for about ten seconds, then my phone buzzes a text from my neighbour with funny eyebrows and next thing you know it I'm dry humping Sheila on a sofa somewhere in Eggerton as her Grandfather clock strikes noon. And then, I hold up my end to her beginning.

Ominous Clarity

After school ends today, I meet Zelda by the abandoned railway track as arranged. I figured that since I had cut one class I might as well cut all of them. There'll probably be less questions asked that way, anyway.

"Sometimes you're just an ego," Zelda says as she drags on a Cigoln Red. *"Don't ever pretend you're any better than yourself."*

"Thanks," I say. *"You're a true friend. Again, sorry I had to rush off."*

"Remember that no one but a friend will be there at the end," she says, gazing at me dead in the eyes.

"The end of what?" I say, presently conspiring to hold her hand.

"The plan I forgot till now," she replies, sentimentally as sand.

"Oh, I know. After we kissed, we agreed we would marry when we're 40 or so."

"Yeah. Only if I care to & if you haven't found anyone else though."

"So it goes." I smile wistfully at a passing vision of Sheila, my neighbour with funny eyebrows. *"Do you think we'll marry?"*

She laughs. *"Imagine. I'd carry you up the stairs,"* she says flexing her biceps, which are disproportionately big considering Zelda's defending her title as 'Heavyweight Cake Queen of Nanko Bakery' next month. *"Do you* think *we'll marry?"* she asks, batting her eyelashes in mock ingenuousness.

I shake my head, nonplussed.

"I love to give blowjobs to those who are deserving of them," Zelda teases. She smiles fetchingly, and I smile blankly back at her. Zelda & I clumsily beam at each other, and then suddenly she cackles five infectious cackles in quick succession & I can't stop myself from laughing so I laugh along with her.

Someday Zelda will model for a life drawing class & someday she will meet her granddaughter & someday she will watch *Fortitude in Strangers* again & someday she will move into a nursing home. Someday Zelda will host a party with all her new friends & someday she will get married to someone & someday she will die, but for this short minute of her life, all Zelda can do is cackle. And all I can do is laugh with her too, not knowing quite why.

"Hey," Zelda says, after we stop laughing for no reason. *"I have a poem for you. I wrote it in my notebook by the canal after you left. Want to hear it?*

"Of course," I say.

"Here goes." Zelda clears her throat. "The Laughing Boy was far smarter than he seemed. And the Grinning Girl was more worldly than she let on. But while the Laughing Boy bartered with unchartered dreams, the Cackling Devil strung Cupid's bow with Menstruation song."

I laugh. Then I look at her like she's just farted the continent. *"You didn't write that by the canal. You wrote that now. The bit about the laughing. What the fucking fuck?"*

"Okay, okay," she says. *"I improvised a bit. But I started the poem beforehand."*

"Sure, alright. It's a wonderful poem… sweet rhymes. Do you want me to roll a spliff?"

"Uh…" Zelda says, *"I'm not too good with weed. It makes me throw up."*

"Have you even tried it before?" I ask disbelievingly.

"Twice. And I threw up both times," she says.

"Third time lucky?" I say.

"One bitten, twice shy," she replies.

"Once *bitten, twice shy*," I correct. *"But fair enough. Tell me if you change your mind. Personally, I will be indulging. Want to hear a poem of mine?"*

"I'd love to," Zelda says, surprised that I write poems. *"When did you start writing?*

"Young," I reply. *"I got bullied as a kid, so now I keep it all hid. Anyhow, here's the poem.* There are those who see the God above who never knew the pain of bliss. And those like me who dream of love with one like you in rain like this."

"Wow – cool! That's a great poem, man," Zelda says, genuinely awed.

"It took ten hours to write. It's from my first novel, which has so far sold five copies including friends and family. I'm editing it now, though. Someday it's bound to be a best seller. I've made it all commercial and shit," I say.

"What's it about?"

"Big bangs, Gods and humanoids like you and me." I stop rolling the zoot to scratch my head. *"I don't really know what it's about yet. I'm not too sure anymore. I'm only 5076 words in it."*

"Innit," Zelda says, toying with a dandelion. I'm sitting and she is laying down in the grass by the edge of the track. Then I stand up & light up. Then Zelda stands up too to watch me smoke. She is

obviously curious about how I will react to this cannabis. Let it be known to the governing bodies of the world that I've smoked at least two hundred spliffs and they only made me go crazy one time, because that one time did the trick.

I inhale happily. *"Hash. I like hash an awful lot,"* I say.

"Oh, if it's hash, I'll try some. I've only tried Purple Haze & pollen," Zelda says, unexpectedly eager.

I hand her the joint, not having picked up on the fact that she is schizophrenic and so is He. How was I to know? She takes a puff, then another.

"Thanks, God. Thanks, Tonnan," she says. *"That's really nice, God."* She takes another puff, then hands the joint back to me. She paces a bit and talks to No-One (the Restralardin biblical character). *"Yeah, that's right. Just so shooting stars set swiftly. Tonnan, call your new book 'Just So Shooting Stars Set Swiftly'."*

"That's a pretty good title & a funny coincidence, but & because it's already got a title. It's called The Sun Always Sets in the West."

"Oh, okay." Zelda itches at an earlobe, tilting her head like she's a little baffled.

"Actually," I say, *"that's a pretty good title for the opening segment. 'Just So Shooting Stars Set Swiftly'. Yeah, I like that. I like that a lot."*

"No-One is never wrong about matters of song," Zelda says. *"Let my factual delivery of this dreadful news hang heavy over the industry of deadening selfhood with ominous clarity."*

Boy, I think, Zelda is *fucked*. We talk some more for a while, our dialogue seriously sensical or the happiest of nonsense, then I walk her to the airbus stop.

***

I really like Zelda. I'm a teenager for the first time and for me she encapsulates the madness of youth & its teardrops. Over the course of a couple of months, I grow infatuated with her laugh & fragrance & scarf & mouth movements & casual badassery. For a while, we become vagrants together, smoking blunts by the canal and conversing dopily & manically (meaningfully, too, but mostly just dopily & manically) about being born to live for the fleeting and the heavenly and the imperfect and the tangerines – O, the tangerines! – and the black & white films and the old school hip-hop songs and the longing and the wine. One day, we speak to two strangers about their taste in poetry and then invade a barge, christening it Ship Shape before getting a right bollocking from a moustached gypsy sailor fellow who curses us, in the voodoo language we were forced to learn at school, roaring *"your minds will experience exceptional bodily torment and your hearts will rue this day!"* – and then we run away back into the now ominous sanctity of the park, speaking about caravans and black canvases and organised religion's view on sex before banalities and her ambition to become a food critic & mine to become a doctor, until suddenly she vocalises her desire to sexualise my *"body of beatitude"* and then we kiss, which is our second kiss together and will be our last kiss together (for another sobering, heart-pounding three seconds).

Three weeks after this happens, though, Zelda relocates to the other side of Restralardin because her parents believe that she could benefit from

Skinny School. One day, I receive a short text from her that reads:

"I miss Soul School, but I prefer Skinny School.
Some of the guys here are fit as fuck,
I've lost sixty pounds in two months
& I still have the odd bit of toffee as a treat.
Miss you, though. All my love xx"

This text seems a little odd to me, given her past predilection for frequent snacks. Doesn't it make you wonder? Perhaps being skinny & looking sexy really are more important than matters of the soul. I will still think of Zelda in the following couple of Soul School years, but soon I am accepted to Hobbling University to study medicine, and I shall practically forget all about her.

The more I think about it, the more I realise that most things that happen to me just happen to me: rather than actively & painstakingly crafting my own destiny, I am usually but a passenger of fate's freight train. With Zelda, though, things were different. The past smells so sweet sometimes, and often I wish the future were simply a collection of my luckiest & happiest memories.

***

My sordid adult account of the events leading up to the mathematical orchestration of our own Universe's birth should balance the glamorisation of late adolescence's nowness with a hint of a wistful yearning to be back there. Since English is my third & now only language and I have already exposed part of the proposed formula for the heart of this book, feel free to skip over words, paragraphs and pages at your leisure. This book in its entirety took nearly five earthly years to write and over a hundred to live. I still haven't gotten over a lot of what happens in it. Some stuff you don't get over until you realise that *it* has gotten over *you*. Other stuff you never get over at all. You just can't banish the demons from memory or mentally bandage the scars.

This novel isn't particularly long. It isn't particularly short. It is as simple as it is complicated. This book is my magnum opus, my rainbow-flavoured milkshake, my supreme inkgasm.

For reasons that might already be clear, extremely few people read my writing. Certainly do not consider yourself lucky to be a member of this obscure minority. My own insignificance, as one living humanoid proportional to my planet's ample population, is an idea that often strikes me while I grow up in Restralardin. Still, the capital of the world is wherever my latest crush happened to be and the only thing worth having is the ability to materialise the dream that the capital of the world will soon be sitting down on my knees.

We are all so small compared to stars, but we are bigger than the why. We may be in love with what is far, but today we must try not to die.

GOD'S PRETTY GAME OF GROTESQUE PUPPETS
HAPPY TEARS IN LOVE WITH A COLD

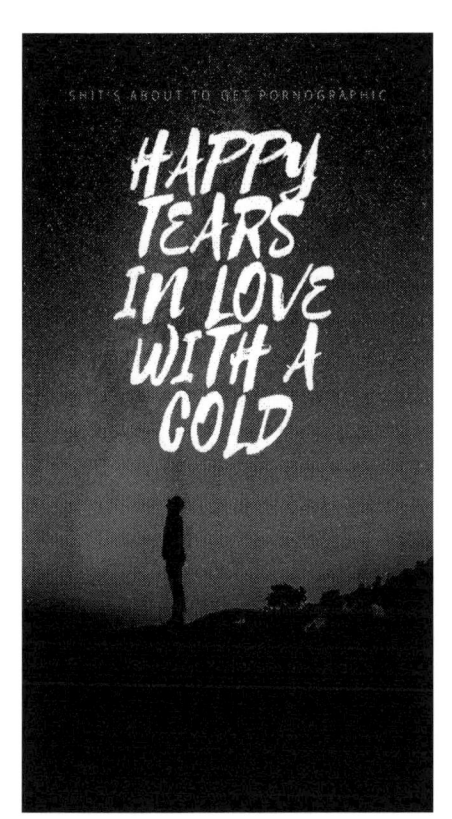

Secretive Magic Soldier

When two humanoids meet for the first time on Restralardin, in formal circumstances it's considered polite for each to pluck three hairs from their head and give them to the other to swallow. It's rather rude to refuse to consume another's hair and the ritual represents the notion of personal sacrifice for the sake of oneness. Rockland is my fellow medical undergraduate and his hair tastes like a bashful blend of stale-vanilla-fudge & halloumi. I quite like it, you know.

When Rockland speaks to me, sometimes I momentarily perceive what seems to be a scorching shimmer of salvation deeply distant down the oceanic canyons of his dilated eyes. I'm half-inclined to suppose that he was delivered to an all-encompassing nirvana a long time ago and developed a dependence on its ever-retreating quality of inebriating intensity. To me, anyhow, the flickering forensics of the forest-fire-glint behind his horn-rimmed spectacles always hint at some extraordinarily exotic form of insanity. There's a duality, too, in those baby-blue eyes that confirms my suspicions that while Rockland believes creation to be conceptually callow & incredibly infinite, it's ultimately his destiny to be awed & aggrieved by the perfect futility of the world.

At 7 P.M. on the second night of University, Rockland shares an ostensibly random & obscenely pornographic hallucination with me in the kitchen. I infer from his tired urgency that he doesn't take the fact that he's speaking to me for granted.

"314 minutes ago, in my golden 159 blazed brain...." Rockland begins, *"I ceased the vilification and viewing of the visual and auditory apparition of the crazy yet content copulation of Kleopatra and you (and by copulation, I mean fucking as hard as you could, fucking as if that were why you were alive, fucking so hard she was bound to produce quintuplets unless she took the pill afterwards: validating the victorious vulture of her vagina, praising the priestly prude of your penis and angelizing the artisan aristocrat of her anus, seemingly concluding with your exclamation of the ecstasy of eloping with Eve into her evangelist ears but then continuing onwards with the joint exploring and adoring of every pore in the mercenary mountains of each other's mouths), and then the vision gave way to my awestricken marvel at two haunting hallucinations – firstly of a slow serpentine blow job Kleopatra gave your knob and secondly of anal sex in a palace of riddles: firstly, at dark in the park by the meadows (where mourning magpies' melodies boomed as if they were responsible for*

the evacuation [or blooming] of chrysalises, and then diminished in decibels as if conspiring to never be heard again like a deleted demo of the time-travelling sperm of the future Rock & Roll Legend cum President of the World) under the tree Kleopatra and you favoured for no particular reason, where she practically sterilised you by licking around the top of your cock and caressing it in the cosy chasm of her mouth, repeating this rhythmically with such regularity you came home with her because that was where you lived; secondly, and this one tugged my heart apart like a horse and cart pulling it in a gallop towards the only infinity possible (for though infinity is infinite there is only one infinity), she seductively stated that she is Satan and that if she made you orgasm you would be responsible for the deaths of thousands of thousands of unborn babies. You didn't say a word, for you weren't willing to continue this religious line of conversation. Kleopatra then recited the Lord's prayer to you, pointing at you when she said 'Father', henceforth declaring you the Father of yourself, her own Father and my Father as if it were a gospel truth, then stroked your frigidly cold cock with her feet for an accelerated month, red toenails and dyed beige hair growing in a simulated eternity with weight being lost in both your images, until she parks her humungous arse on top of your erect cock, her hole submerges it and you fuck until your hair turns grey: by then, 234,000,000 unborn babies were dead." Rockland lets out a deep, gratuitous sigh.

"Great. Cool story, Rockland. I liked your use of language. But who the hell is Kleopatra?" I ask.

"I don't know. I hadn't seen her face before. Kleopatra was really pretty, if a little… uh… strangely stoic… yeah, strangely stoic is the phrase," Rockland says.

You may never be able to put your finger on exactly who I am, but I will remind you of my name in due time.

In fact, it will be due time at this very coming moment: I am Tonnan, secretive magic soldier. Although I am a secretive magic soldier, I rarely disguise myself with clothes, for nakedness is perfectly legal in the prison of the bedroom.

I've always felt a subtle pang of hunger for the simultaneous arrival of the past & the future & complete oblivion. I've always wanted everything that isn't the present here & now to collide in an arbitrary moment of understanding so that I can gratefully altogether abandon my curiosity for this concept forever.

Things are uncomplicated. I feel lucky to be alive. I am young. I am in love. I don't know what to do with this information but rejoice in it. Since I am in love with more than one person at the same time, the odds are in the house's favour. You might think that being in love with more than one person takes time & ambition & is by very nature 'complicated', but to me it is the simple truth of my existence.

Truthfully, I am simply in love with beautiful moments spent with beautiful people. That's all I've ever wanted from life. Despite the fact that all the people I fancy are physically appealing, the reason I love them has less to do with attraction than the fact that moments spent with them sparkle splendidly like distress signals released for the hell of it over an obligingly picturesque ocean of gin.

Yes, I guess this is a tragicomedy that arrives in the contrived guise of an erotic thriller gone wrong. And as long as I live – be it for a day more or longer than forever & a month – the secret strings of my shattered soul will never let me forget this sorrowful song.

A Remarkable Person

Every once in a while, a remarkable person takes centre stage in your life and that person seems to epitomise all the dreams that you deem sacred. When you're with them, the world is exactly how you've always wanted it to be. Seldom is the stuff of your deepest desires transposed onto the canvas of reality, but this world is filled with any number of surprises and beautiful people. Yes, occasionally you grow to adore the essence of someone more than you thought physically possible, more than the rest of them put together, and more than love itself.

In this universe, such slapdash phrases of exaltation might be considered more romantic than they are in the harsh and often highly obscure domain that I inhabit during the bulk of this story. Some folks on Restralardin believe love to be as endless as its ocean, but unlike the quantifiability of that ocean, I don't believe there's an upper limit to devotion.

Fifty-three years from now, I shall realise that Xinx – rather than Zelda or Sheila or Kleopatra – is almost certainly my first true love, and that she will almost certainly be my last true love, too.

Xinx is beautiful & beautifully free & freely frolicsome. She is half-black & half-azure with tresses of parrot-hair. I first meet Xinx at the Hobbling University Fresher's disco. She is wearing loud pink lipstick and a night-sky dress, both of which compliment her magnificent yet unobtrusive breasts. I shall learn that she's studying Classics, that she's *"never met anyone who likes reading but is stupid"* and that she likes conversations about metaphorical death (or maybe that's me).

O, reader, listener, smeller or captive: the instant I spot Xinx there with her friend sipping a pineapple mojito through a straw, almost everything else becomes irrelevant to me. And so, as few sane men would do, I go up to talk to her.

"I want to chat you up," I playfully say to her, standing tall & pointing upwards. Xinx's friend senses danger and departs for the bathroom. A hip-hop track riffs in the background. I should confess, I guess, that some might consider the situation to be a little awkward for a second or two. I haven't ever spoken the words *"I want to chat you up"* before and my opening gambit doesn't seem to pay off or even seismically register with her. In fact, the laser-beam lilac of Xinx's eyes looks both amused & vaguely annoyed; the Commander-In-Chief of her outward appearance (that is, the being that is the one Atom of Life deep within her body) instructs her muscles to frown slightly, which suggests she *might* be interested in me.

"I once heard," I continue in a brazenly tipsy tone, *"an allegory about a real livewire who spoke those exact words to a woman he had never met before. The woman's husband had just died, and she had found out that he left all his money to another woman."*

"I don't know why you're telling me this, but I love stories," Xinx says quietly and as if speaking overly genuinely to someone half her age. *"Why don't you tell me the end?"*

"The woman realised that she had seen the man who wanted to chat her up before in her dreams. His face was rosy-red and vaguely familiar to her. The moment was positively peppered with tension.

'If you want to chat me up, why don't you chat me up?' *said the woman.* 'I am chatting you up,' *replied the man. At that, they gazed deep into each other's eyes, understood everything there is to know about the world, and then hugged for half a century. She was his true love & he hers. I'm not a very good storyteller, but that's it. The end! Finito."*

Xinx claps. *"Cool story, bro. What's your name?"* she asks.

"Tonnan. Yours?

"Xinx," she says.

"Xinx, like I said before, I want to chat you up," I say, a bit drunk on wine & adrenaline & hormones.

Xinx laughs a small little laugh. *"Why don't you try?"* she asks, poking me.

"You're sternly sexy and I'm strangely single. I'm in an odd mood today and so many things could come out of this chance encounter, like us becoming best friends or realising we are actually related by blood," I say. *"Am I doing a satisfactory job chatting you up?"*

Xinx laughs a slightly bigger laugh, shaking her head vehemently and fiddling cutely with a Fire Escape Flute necklace I hadn't noticed until now.

I put each thumb in an ear, wiggle my fingers, and stick my tongue out at her. She laughs for real this time. This I will come to know as a 'proper Xinx laugh'. It's a good sound to hear. She appears to be refreshingly introverted, but I reckon I can tease her out of her solitude.

"You'll have to try a little harder than that," she says.

"You're going to die soon and so am I," I remind her, clairvoyant scientist that I am.

"I died. I'm already dead," she tells me excitedly but as if the truth itself represents an essentially patronising lie. *"I'm already dead as a donkey and as perceptive as a parent. Are you done chatting me up yet?"* She raises one eyebrow and both her eyes wink at me.

After that, I stop trying to flirt with her and we talk more about my improvised story & Hobbling University & the music of laughter. As we discuss the melody of giggling, Xinx's content features suddenly become a bit broody. *"Why don't you put your heart on the line and invite me to your room?"* she asks suggestively.

I politely refuse her offer and invite myself to hers instead.

Xinx smiles and says, *"Sure. Okay."* I'll never forget that slightly asymmetrical smile of hers.

"I have an idea," she says as we make to leave. *"Want to show everyone we are super-cool?"*

"Okay! Why the shit not?"

"Hold my hand, love," she says. Our hands meet halfway between us in this youthful dystopia. I have

completely blocked out all the talking & music & howls & bodies in the room and simply focused my attention on this one woman, but now I take it all in. Many other stories are being born in this casual, small-scale Fresher's disco. A straight lady killer accidently seduces a gay guy. A bored looking eighteen-year-old whose father is a priest decides he has had enough of being social and storms out of the hall on a seductively dressed yet apparently man-hating woman midsentence. A sweet Rastafarian gives a couple of coins to a ragamuffin who claims to have lost her debit ring. Stuff like that is happening. Stuff is happening!

"Are we moving?" I ask Xinx.

"Moving..." Xinx replies. I don't think anyone notices us leave, but I *do* feel super-cool as I walk through the crowd holding hands with a super-hot chick. I turn to start a new page in the diaries of my heart, cockily content with what is going down.

***

Following superfluously deep small talk concerning Xinx's collection of cutleries and the spiritually mathematical nature of music, I place my hands around my neck and strangle myself while screaming like a baby about my drinking problem (an ancient mating call in Restralardin). Then, at once, Xinx leans towards me & we tongue passionately, occasionally pausing to allow me to further vent my feelings towards alcohol. The air is almost amorous, you know, and I daresay it's dreamy, too. Whenever I strangle myself and scream like a baby about my drinking problem, typically in a jiffy I'll be making out with a nearby feminist for a couple of hours. I've been told that this is not a particularly 'cool' act to perform, but I don't drink, strangle myself or scream too often. I'm quite a quiet guy most of the time.

"*Is it difficult to remember?*" Xinx wonders aloud after the final end of my iambic monologues, pulling away from me slightly.

"*It's easier to forget than to remember,*" I reply, sweat trickling from my brow.

"*People always enter a situation with the intention of remembering exactly what happens to them, but then the minutes blur into one another like madmen chasing miracles,*" Xinx says. "*I'm glad you could share your thoughts on your drinking problem with me tonight, and I'm sure you will one day become a member of the proletariat as you forecast.*"

It's not like me to prophesise – that's more up Rockland's alley – but sometimes I feel the urge to do so as well. "*Do you have any literary aspirations, yourself?*" I ask, glad that the mating call worked but keen to avoid further talk about my shortcomings.

"*No!*" she says indignantly, as if that were the last thing on her mind, and she kisses me again. Her tongue is tantalizingly dexterous in its movements around my mouth and mine is equally as ravenous in its slow-fast migration around hers. She places a hand carefully on my ribcage and then through my jeans she caresses my love, which stiffens even more at her touch. "*Let's fuck!*" she says decisively, lying down on the single bed, stretched out as seductive as Soothsayer's sister.

"Sure," I say as I get on top of her with my clothes on. *"Do you have a condom?"*

"I don't believe in condoms..." she says and sticks her tongue as far as it can fit into my ear before elaborating. *"I attend a church that doesn't value condoms as a form of contraception. I'll take a pill tomorrow. I promise I keep most of my promises."*

There's a clause to both of these last two sentences: firstly, she said she'd take a pill tomorrow (what pill?) and secondly, she promised she keeps most of her promises (she hadn't promise me a thing except that).

But bigger, more voluptuous matters soon occupy my fixated, aroused mind. With her strapless dress pressed tight against her black & blue skin, I massage each bosom. Her hand, to my delight, heads south to my penis, brushing against it then retreating, brushing against it a little harder then retreating, brushing against it a little harder than a little harder then retreating. Foreplay is always everyone's friend.

My knowledge of the application and removal of female clothing is limited but from what I gather it isn't too different from male clothing, in that the principle is the same: it comes off the opposite way to which it goes on. Irrespective of this technicality, I strip until I am stark naked and as Xinx eyes the abs I managed to maintain over the summer, she removes her dress and bra until she is only wearing crimson underwear. For some reason, I find women most attractive when they are only wearing underwear. Any more nudity than that is less inviting: the temptation of the unknown beckons like a spliff on the pavement or an unexplored universe.

I pull down Xinx's knickers and lick all around her vulva, one hand still feeling a boob. She groans happily and comes a little, then comes a lot as my tongue nears the G-spot. I continue doing this for a minute or so and then I move upwards and suck her left tit while fingering her vagina.

"Do you want to fuck me now or do you want a blowjob?" she whispers tantalisingly in my ear. Five hours after Rockland's sexually charged 'performance art', my *actual* cock begs for relief: I'd love a blowjob, which at this point to me seems to be the highest conceivable pleasure. A blowjob is the joy after successfully riding a bike for the first time; a blowjob is the beauty of a bird bellowing a breakneck beat through your tenement window; it's a sumptuous vegetarian fruit for the thirsty; it is all the colours of Love Itself.

"Blow me and afterwards I'll make you orgasm again when I can properly concentrate. Then we'll fuck in the morning," I whisper back, half-jokingly.

"Relax," she replies quickly with devilish certainty. *"I know every trick in the book."*

I don't know how long the book she's referring to is, but Xinx knows the precise sequence of those weirdly wonderful words off by heart. First, she holds my balls in one hand and my penis with the other. She licks the tip of my penis and then her two pursed lips, which are now a slightly faded shade of hot pink, softly engulf its head, teasing & transferring a barely finite ration of pleasure onto my loins. She licks up and down my shaft slowly and steadily. Then, in an end to the exceptionally gratifying torture, she submerges most of my penis in her mouth. She gives me one of those sloppy blowjobs you might have experienced or read about in one of your earthly magazines (e.g. Reader's Digest), always sensing when I am about to orgasm and then disengaging.

This continues for about ten minutes and I am drooling slightly at her elegant physique until finally I find the will to ask her to stop, for I realise I don't really want to orgasm but instead fuck her so hard she believes she is the sports star at one of your earthly sporting events – the Olympics perhaps – and will remember this as the day she won the game for the crowd watching at home.

"I like to think of my mouth as a cavern that collapses in on any intruders," she says in a chatty tone, while she masturbates me & I finger her.

"Isn't that what a vagina is for?" I inquire.

"Well, yes. I don't think you're an autistic genius anymore. I think you're a sadistic druggie!" Xinx says.

"The law is a sadistic druggie," I reply, vaguely autistic genius that I am.

Suddenly, without my permission, Xinx finger-fucks my arsehole. These queer realms have barely been explored before (except by the act of defecating & cleaning). After this surreal shenanigan reaches its natural conclusion, I penetrate Xinx's fanny, which is wet, tight & holier than I could have imagined. My penis remains there for ten seconds, barely moving, and then she clenches her cunt. After I regain control of my desire, I chain-fuck her as hard as I can, with retaliatory stamina even I am surprised by in retrospect. I thrust, thrust and thrust my cock into that homely squelchy nest: thrust, thrust and thrust to the seventh power. I have gotten good at mediating my desire to ejaculate through practice with a close female friend of mine two months before. It's fair to say that there is sporadic eye-contact between Xinx and I throughout this fuckery, which I've heard improves sex.

"*This is good,*" says one of us.

"*Yep,*" says the other.

"*Are you happy?*"

"*Yes!*" utters a female breathily.

"*Fuck. Fuck! Don't finger my arse again!*"

"*God, okay! GOD, yes!*" someone moans, biting a neck.

We make quite a lot of noise, but it's our second night at University, so what did you expect? A hunt for needles by the motherfucking railway?

Xinx has a shower, then I have a shower, then we go to sleep together.

"*Good night, Xinx,*" I say.

"*Good night, Tonnan,*" she says.

Who could guess that my humanistic hubris & penchant for mortal women would merely accelerate my downfall? Say whatever you think is clever or novel: I don't care to hear it anymore. You could live in a mansion or a hovel, but you've got to admit we've all been here before. Despite the possibility that eternal return is a myth, I felt a strange sense of déjà vu when Xinx fingered my arsehole & when we said goodnight.

Anyhow, not another word is spoke between us until the next day. Nothing needs to be voiced and so nothing is voiced. I fleetingly wonder who the fudge Kleopatra is & then I fall asleep almost immediately, spooning Xinx.

The Black Cat

I dream I am sitting on a chair in my parent's garden and I see a skinny, pitch-black cat scurry across the fence, as if that is the fence's purpose, with such natural agility it'd not be a surprise to me if it suddenly broke into song. Just as this crosses my mind, the cat stops its journey, turns to me, and winks. The dream dissolves. Later that night, I have a similar vision of the same black cat. It looks at me and shakes its head as if in disapproval. I can't determine its gender, not that it matters: to me, the cat may as well be genderless.

I wake up: 8 A.M. I always wake up at 8 A.M or roundabouts. Xinx is to my left, face against the pillow. She doesn't look very comfortable. I just lie there, staring at the wall. The alarm goes off a little later. It's one of those retro alarms, a big clock, and it buzzes decisively at 8:10. Xinx looks at me sleepily and smiles. She kisses me on the lips, and I feel her bosoms with both hands, massaging them as if they are playdough. She reciprocates, toying with my balls. We have tantric sex for a couple of hours, exchanging and memorising each other's numbers during the proceedings, then we go to our separate lectures: mine is 'The Northern Philosophy to Medicine', in which a short green man with crutches is lecturing. I am chosen to answer a question after volunteering. I answer, and the lecturer nods his head, saying "*Hey, you're right young man!*" And everyone claps. Some people even cheer. It's the second greatest moment of the day for me.

I'm on my way back to my room and by the entrance to the Humanities building I spot a black cat, who looks startlingly similar to the one I witnessed in dreamtime earlier. The black cat yawns majestically and vehemently as if it is about to explode and fatigue has overruled its will to live. It inclines its head ominously when it sees me walk past, urgently moves towards me until it appears to think better of this idea and thus rushes to retreat into a nearby bush. I don't think a lot about my sighting of the cat at first, but later in the day I consider the potential merging of dreams and reality.

It occurs to me that I haven't eaten for some time, so I go to the Union supermarket to get some food. While I'm in the sandwich and drink aisle, an attractive but weird looking woman eyes me up and whispers the word *"angel"* to me in a gasp of twenty decibels. I don't react because I'm not sure if or how I should react. To react would either make me complicit in the deception or destroy the illusion completely. I want neither. I will still think about this happening half a century on, from time to time. I feel it as surreal as the invention of the one-wheeled automobile.

I buy an onion & halloumi sandwich, some assorted groceries & milk, and go to eat the sandwich in my kitchen, where Rockland and Rebecca are finishing making sausages and mash. Neither are qualified to cook this food without the assistance of the trusty student cookbook.

Rockland & Rebecca existing in the same room as one another has not yet disintegrated into the discussion of obstinate niceties regarding their respective courses. They are still in the phase of furtively touching and tentatively flirting with each other. It seems that it hasn't occurred to them yet that the very first person they met at University might not be their match-made-in-heaven, just like it doesn't occur to me at this point that Rockland might poison my affair with Xinx with an injection of hardcore adrenaline that proves to rival my smooth awkwardness

Rebecca unveils some coconut macaroons and shares them with Rockland (and possibly me). She places them on the table, enticingly close to both of us. Personally, if I were either of them, having a coconut macaroon so close to my body would tempt me into skipping the comparatively uninviting main meal of overcooked sausages and mash, but my favourite foods are cheese-based or sugar-based and my opinion on the matter doesn't make the slightest difference. Me, I'm feeling a little depressed after the taste of the sandwich fades from my mouth, and I need something to make me feel better, so I peer at a macaroon. Eventually I get the feeling of déjà vu from staring at it for so long, so after a nod from Rebecca, I plunk it into my mouth and begin to chew. It tastes delectable and expensive, satisfying a craving for coconuts I didn't think I had.

"Ah! I don't think I've ever had a macaroon before. Exquisite! Thank you," I say honestly.

"I doubt you have. These grew in Neonadra," she states, as if my soul is stifled by a sinful stupidity.

"Grew? I don't think macaroons grow," I fire back. Macaroons are neither mushrooms nor mincemeat, I think. I look to Rockland for support, who immediately shakes his head in repulsion upon recruitment to the correct side.

"No, Rebecca, I don't know how you could be so egocentric as to assume that macaroons grow," Rockland says, still shaking his head in disapproval, with his whole body swaying as well. I wonder if this is Rockland's way of trying to seduce Rebecca.

"It's a human right to be born and it's a human right to die. I thought this was afforded to Macaroons.

Macaroons are not made from materials, like iron or cauliflower," Rebecca says in an educative tone and nods her head with her whole body inclining, just as I consider whether I should go to look for the black cat and Rockland realises Rebecca has got another thing wrong.

"Iron doesn't grow and neither do Macaroons, Rebecca. Gosh, I didn't know you could be so wrong about something," says Rockland, hiccupping hysterically. It's at this point that I decide to leave the kitchen, because I realise that Rockland is receiving a foot-job from Rebecca.

A Proper Criminal

I watch television in the lounge for the next half an hour. There is a white guy on the news who can read a novel in ninety minutes.

"How the flipping heck do you complete such a task so quickly?" the sceptical reporter asks, looking morose. She looks like she has been morose all her life.

"Simples!" the white guy declaims emphatically. *"I simply read upwards, as every sane Frolid reader should do. My eyes are athletic acrobats who ace the essentials of every atomic particle on the page. I am a mastermind, a seeker of knowledge and the ultimate truth that literature entails!"*

It seems to me that this is how anyone but the most laidback of housewives would read a book. Some of the more radical breeds of humanoid housewives are anti-sobriety and tend to pause mid-sentence to drink tequila or think about their loved ones, but they represent an exception to the rule. Somehow, I figure that some people have never even actually *tried* a minute in their entire lives, and that the white guy on television has been *trying* his absolute best since before he was even born. I realise that the white guy on television must mean that he is absorbing all the sentence at once. But isn't that how most people read most sentences?

"How many books do you read a week?" the reporter asks so sceptically I sense she believes the white guy to harbour delusions of grandeur.

"Two a day. About fifteen a week. It would be more, but a man has got to make bread!" the white guy

declares defensively. I wonder what he does for a job, then figure I should call my shrink: his eerie words are making me question the very foundations of my status as an 'intelligent humanoid'. The white guy's remark regarding reading fast yet conventionally, too, is ambiguous at best. But maybe I'm just not intelligent enough to even register the existence of the signposts he must have erected around the point to which he is alluding. Like the verbose bastard child of Sujes, my muddled mind trudges through the mud only to find it has forgotten something essential to its existence. I wonder how I even came to be accepted at Hobbling University, which is ranked the 8th best University on Restralardin. It would take me at least a couple of hours to read a novel and a whole fucking afternoon to read *'War Makes Peace'*, which the white guy on television claims to have read in *"four short hours"*.

Anyhow, I'm still hungry but don't want to make things awkward by going to get more macaroons from the kitchen, which although infested by a couple of people touching each other is still my kitchen. I wonder what to do with myself. My heart tells me that the black cat is nearby and that he or she will give me guidance concerning both spiritual & material matters.

It doesn't take too long to find the cat. As with most fictional animals corrupted by the utopia of self-actualisation, the black cat is male, for he & his half-erect willy appear auspiciously as soon as I open the front door. He moseys up to me like a victor joining a jubilant parade of new homeowners and he stutters a meow like he is weighing something up in his soul.

I'd say I am normal in my loathing of the smell of shit. Certainly, better to have no smell than smell like shit, unless it's holy shit. But this cat smells like regular shit, so I pick him up, carry him to the bathroom, and bathe him. It takes a fair bit of convincing for him to allow me to perform the ritual, and I wonder what this cat has done to arrive in such a sticky, shitty situation.

It should come as no surprise to you that halfway through the rinsing process I get arrested. Some cop with a motherfucking stun-gun turns up. Anyhow, next thing you know it, I'm an abashed captive in a street-legal police van heading straight towards Hobbling town centre. If this is all due to the fact that I attempted to wash an apparently homeless cat, they might as well have arrested me for being someone's motherfucking father. The cat, presumably, is left to his shitting migrant ways.

I cry a little. In fact, I weep. My handcuffs stop me from drying the tears in my eyes and I don't particularly want to embarrass myself by asking the cop to tissue my eyes. I don't mind crying in front of men, but I usually don't recruit help from the male race to cull my passion. It's part of my prerogative.

This detention will go on my permanent record, I think; maybe I shouldn't become an opium dealer. I try to question the officer: surely, there must have been some kind of misunderstanding... this was not an actual kidnapping but an attempt to right nature's wrongs.

"You have the right to remain silent. Anything you say can and will be held against you," says the unsympathetic cop. This makes me feel like a proper criminal.

A Two-Story Building

We arrive at the police station, a two-storey building that does just what it says on the tin (except for in cases whose nature the justice system has disregarded, such as my own). The cop shows me to a cell. It is twelve-foot by twelve-foot, about quadruple my height, and empty but for a large piece of shit.

If we carve our respective destinies out of our actions, then I'm certainly the party responsible for the orchestration of my imprisonment. I can't say that I had secretly willed this exact sequence of events to occur but, still, carved them I have. Nonetheless, over the course of the next twenty minutes I grow hungrier and hungrier. The only option is a piece of rank shit, and that doesn't seem particularly appetizing to my refined pallet which is now accustomed to such culinary delights as a cheese sandwich or a macaroon.

In the police cell, I stare at the piece of shit until I decide to eat the piece of shit. It tastes worse than it looks. I would advise anyone else in similar circumstance to simply starve to death instead. I wouldn't go so far as to try to justify my foray into shit-eating by saying I'd be a dead man without the shit's nutrients, but perhaps that's what I just did.

As if on cue, after I finish the food, and I am lithe to call it food given its status as a piece of poop, an officer unlocks the cell door and enters the room. It seems that I have passed some sort of test. Unlike the white guy who's on television, this officer is a crimson woman who's not on television.

"Good. Very good. I hope you're proud of yourself..." the officer says slowly and flatly, as if addressing her disobedient pet pooch attempting a new trick. *"I suppose,"* she adds with an air of pitying sadism, *"it'll be up to me to get you some water. You need to have a shower, as well."*

I don't immediately know what to say to this, so I smile a fetchingly brown smile dumbly for a while. Both agenda items addressed in the officer's speech ring true. I do need some water to wash the faeces down, and two hours of tantric sex with anyone is enough to warrant a shower.

"Okay. I'd like some proper food too. I'm starving," I eventually say, coldly, hoping to buy time to gauge the overall aura of the situation. I decide to keep it cool, so I'm glad that my words sound cold.

"What do you fancy?" she asks.

"What is there?" I inquire in turn.

"Lasagne, Cottage Pie, Extra Special Vegetable Lasagne, Beef..." she starts firmly, and though it seems as if the list could continue for some time, all the items sound better than a raw piece of shit, so I interrupt her here.

"Extra Special Vegetable Lasagne, please," I say.

"Right away, sir." She blinks at me derisively. If I'm right, this crimson woman has the hots for me, but maybe she's just mocking me to amuse herself. She leaves the cell and locks it. During the time she is gone, I question the authenticity of my situation – am I really in a jail cell for cleaning a cat, and if so,

what penalties can befall my person for committing such an act?

The police officer, who at this point I realise is kind of hot herself, returns five minutes later with a ready meal and water, clutched like a crucifix over her breasts.

"*An Extra Special Vegetable Lasagne, for our Extra Special guest...*" she says sardonically, biting her upper lip.

"*Thank you,*" I say, in as gracious a voice as I can garrison.

I drink the water appreciatively and proceed to devour the food, which I think surprisingly tasty for a ready-meal and can certainly be categorised as food. I had been informed of the benefits of ready meals by my uncle before arriving at University, perhaps to compensate for my family's general lack of cooking tutorial.

About halfway through the food, I notice that the crimson woman officer, who is kind of hot, has a whip in her hand.

I look at her identification, which is on a lapel on her police uniform.

"*Maggie,*" I say, "*what the fuck is this about?*"

"*Slow dancer: it's the pay-off...*" she says quietly, almost to herself, as if pondering one of the world's enigmas.

"Seriously, Maggie, a fucking whip?" I say in a tone of castrated fear.

"Oh," she says, apparently taken aback, *"I thought I'd bring it in case my line of questioning didn't get far."*

"Line of questioning? Geez, Maggie, all I did was fucking clean a cat."

"Oh. Oh. There seems to be a mistake. I read that you kidnapped and assaulted a cat," she says, her tongue leaving her mouth a couple of more times than necessary.

"Kidnapped? Assaulted? If adopting counts as kidnapping and cleaning counts as assaulting, then I suppose I…" I start, but at this point, Maggie, the hot middle-aged female police officer of the law, pouts and whips me on the chest. The Extra Special Vegetable Lasagne goes everywhere. It hurts like a stomach-ache would, only all the pain comes to try to assassinate me at once.

"You assault University Property, you insult the law. You insult the law, the law has every right to assault you," Maggie states quickly and factually, as if reciting small print.

"Maggie, I…" I protest, but it is of no use.

She nimbly pushes me to the ground, turns my body over, handcuffs me and proceeds to milk me, masturbating me up and down and up and down and up and down like I'm a hormonal cow.

Though I weakly continue my protest by groaning, in a minute I orgasm a big fat orgasm, after which Maggie showers me like I had showered the black cat (with a little affection and an affected aura of tedium, using a showering apparatus in the cell that I hadn't noticed before).

While she does this, Maggie cackles hysteria as if she has just heard the third funniest knock-knock joke that the everyman so enjoys on the distant Planet Earth (Knock, knock! Who's there? Doctor. Doctor Who? Yes, I am he!).

"So... uh... how did you come to be a policewoman?" I ask feebly, more out of curiosity than a desire to spark small talk.

And so, Maggie's relatively long and relatively boring story starts. Whether you are reading this aloud or not, you should note that Maggie's voice is quite deep when she speaks about serious matters, sterilised by police protocol in the middle-range and girlishly high when she is excited.

"There's a crucial difference between wishing to have long hair while you have short hair and wishing to have short hair while you have long hair: the former is easily achievable in the course of the next year or so and the latter is mere minutes away... if you happen to have medium hair length, then this is a good compromise and no further action is required (that is, protein pills or scissors)," Maggie states in a tone that suggests she is being knowingly longwinded in her verbal reasoning.

"Then again," she continues absentmindedly, *"there is a crucial difference between touching the King on the face and touching the image of the King on the face. With that said, I don't even like to touch*

the image of the King on the face. No, I fear His Majesty just wouldn't enjoy that."

Although I recently orgasmed, I'm almost sorry I asked, because I'm keen to get the hell out of jail as I have some work to do at University. I say, *"Your point being, Maggie?"*

"Well, I thought you'd ask that. The story is not a long one or a short one," she says and gives me this perceptive maternal glance which makes me feel both a little uncomfortable and kind of guilty.

"What story?" I question, now less angry and more confused, and keener to present the front of being interested.

"This story. The story I am in the middle of telling."

"Concerning hair length, the King and your employment?" I ask.

"Yes. I am glad you are paying attention. Anyway, when I was around seven or eight years old, my hair had grown very long – three-foot-long – and my father got out his measuring tools – a ruler – and the whole enterprise of measuring got me quite excited, and my hair was twice the length of the ruler. I loved my hair more than I loved any other form of life… is hair a form of life?! But to cut a long story short, my father told me that I must have a haircut or I'd risk balding. I played along, thinking he wouldn't know how to cut my hair, but we went to the hairdressers. After the cut, when I looked at myself in the mirror, I laughed hysterical with sadness. I couldn't believe my eyes. My hair was much shorter than I could ever have imagined, barely shoulder-length. I decided that this was a form of child abuse…. I would get my retribution, and my father would feel the full force of the law."

"And so, you became a police officer?"

"A lot later, yes, but that was a little after I met the Queen."

"What? You met the Queen?"

"You'll mock me for saying this, but she is like the father I never had," she says factually. "I met the Queen at the circus. I kissed her hand, she said that it was a joy to meet me, and that was that. She was sitting next to me in the front row. She cheered with... how should I say this... these days, after such a meeting with the Queen I don't hesitate in ensuring that my use of language is correct... I suppose she cheered vigorously, if a person can cheer vigorously."

"Gee, Maggie, I didn't know you liked the circus," I say.

"Tonnan – if that is your real name – I love the circus, but not as much as I love the Queen or Sujes, my Lord," she says in a flirtatiously flirty tone.

"Great. Cool story, Maggie." I say.

"That was the beginning and middle of the story. Do you want to hear the end of the story? The Royal Family features again, but it's kind of supplementary to the point that I'm making."

"Not now, Maggie. I have to get back to work," I say.

"Okay," she says reluctantly, "I've always held to the idea that you should treat others as you would like to be treated. So, how about a ride back to the campus?"

"Well, that sounds fantastic," I say, feeling like a character in Ricky Mantle's pretentious portraits. Sure enough, Maggie is a woman of her word and soon we are in a police van heading back to Hobbling campus.

"Hey, Maggie, can you put the siren on please? I've always wanted to be in a police van with the siren on," I ask her as the van swims through the darkening suburbs, out of the metropolis and into greenery.

"Sure, Tonnan... in fact, the sound of the siren was one of the reasons I trained to become a police officer. And that's the end of the story," Maggie says happily and perhaps a little patronisingly for the story is not really a story at all. But the wee-awe-wee-awe sound accompanies us for the ten-minute journey, so I am happy. I kiss her on the cheek when we arrive outside my halls of residence and she jumps up in shock, hitting her head on the police-van roof.

"Oh, sorry, Maggie," I tell her and mean it.

"It's alright!" She giggles sheepishly with a casual air of alertness. *"Occupational hazard."*

"See ya, Maggie," I say.

"Cat ya on the flip-side," she says, and though I expect her to flip me off, she happily awards me with the peace sign. I give it back to her and wave goodbye. I don't know, at this point, that someday soon I will be waving goodbye to Restralardin & its stifling black 'n' white 'n' red politics altogether.

Stupid Is As Stupid Does

My three hours in jail done and dusted, I can barely imagine what will happen next, and I don't have to, for reality's algorithms are such that time moves in a linear fashion, pushing onwards, pushing infuriatingly & thankfully & undeterrably onwards, despite a staggering universal number of births and deaths per second.

Ultimately, I figure that all of the Universes are slowly moving towards their death, an ending that will be the very antithesis to their start. This reasoning is primarily derived from a nonsensical conversation with Rockland regarding the Planet's expansion.

It so happens that, speaking of expanding matter and Rockland, at this moment the man himself appears to offer his opinion on Xinx & her weight & her race & her attractiveness & her position as a person of the opposite gender who has kissed me.

"Hey man! I heard the sound of sirens and figured they were there to emit your return," says Rockland, and before I can reply, he continues speaking, *"I saw you went home with that fat half-caste chick last night. Well done, dude. She was hot."*

"Well, Rockland, I hope she still is. I didn't notice that she is fat, and the phrase 'half-caste' is outdated and apparently discriminatory. Consider that poet in the Restralardin Rookie Raconteur Anthology, the 'half-caste symphony' one," I say.

Rockland strokes his temple thoughtfully, grimacing slightly. He scowls as if he has seen something unsightly, then regains his composure & nods & salutes me. *"Well, as a poet my respect for time is determined by the amount of lyrical gravity latent behind each of my statements."* He shrugs sarcastically, then cottons onto the fact that he is being a dickhead and says, *"Anyway, apologies for what you perceived as my inappropriate comments about last night."*

"Hey, I didn't expect an apology! You're lucky I didn't contact Rebecca's mother and ask her if you had permission to wed her father," I joke, in characteristic feebleness. My witticisms at this point are influenced by the brash humour of an Enodrian girl I used to like a lot. She didn't break my heart but she'll half yours too! Those kinds of gags: jokes that internally bleed. Yeah, she would tell me my dreams and then make them come true with the movement of her small soft hands. Like most teenage affairs, that relationship deflated suddenly like a popped balloon, vaporised like snow to fire.

"Enough about eternal love and eternal return, man!" Rockland says caustically, with a surprising degree of animosity. I look at him uneasily, but he nods at me reassuringly. *"Let's get high tonight. I like to ride the light with no one to guide and nothing to hide. Now that I know Rebecca, I feel so alive. I can't believe it took this long to become my insides,"* Rockland sighs mysteriously.

"I didn't know you were a poet, Rockland," I tell him.

"Well, Tonnan, hopefully I still am a poet... the Frolid language can be utilised in such a way that you can exchange a simple word such as 'use' for 'utilise'. My knowledge of this fact, combined with

my use of 'utilise', is certainly enough to cement my reputation as an E-century poet..." Rockland says, scratching his head and then pointing eastward, seemingly towards another accommodation. *"We can smoke it that way, in yonder woods."*

"You've procured stuff already?" I ask him.

"One thing you should know about me, Tonnan, is that I don't play the victim. If I want love, I will get love. If I want to sound like a poet, I will sound like a poet. Besides, I don't do stuff, I do ganja..." Rockland says, inspiringly, though perhaps a tad psychopathically.

"Right. When do you want to smoke?" I ask.

"ASAP... pronto... right now..." he declares, and for the first time – and not the last time – I feel something that could be called arousal due to his joy-de-vivre.

"Follow me," he says, and leads me towards the woods in a saunter bordering on a skipping run.

We arrive at the lake, a wooden enclave of dark greenery. We light up, Rockland takes three quick puffs, then he hands the joint to me and four separate yet almost singular coughs later, I am as high as a kite and notice that the moon is eerily full. Rockland observes me looking at it.

"I met the moon many years ago. It was my first auditory hallucination. It said 'I'm your cousin's mamma. That makes me your Auntie. Did you sleep with my sister?' and immediately, instinctively I answered 'yes'," Rockland says.

"Wow. That's a profound experience to have," I say. *"But doesn't that mean you slept with your mum?"*

"Well... the way I see it, there are people with parents and people who are born orphans. I don't know which category I fall into. My mum and I... well... we stay well away from each other."

"But not because you slept with her or she passed away?"

"No... anyway, this is just what I told the moon," he says, handing me a half-smoked spliff.

"Thanks. Are you Schizophrenic?" I inquire.

"Only when I want to be. I don't mind it. It mothers me. She doesn't mind it either." Rockland chuckles, peering at the silent grandeur of the moon affectionately and coughing. *"Come up to my room; we can take acid and talk about your assault charge,"* he says.

As soon as we get to his room, he picks up an acid tab from his drawer and places it in his mouth. *"What strikes me most about this whole 'Reality' ordeal is that if you are not me, you are someone else or something else. Stupid is as stupid does."* And he throws his hands up exasperatedly, as if he is stating a circular reason.

"I follow you," I offer, though I don't know where I follow him.

"I... uh... I have something to tell you. This acid is a truth serum."

"Okay. I'm all ears. Could I have some acid as well?"

"How about you decide whether you still want to take acid after I tell you what I have to say? If you could do that, it would be helpful."

"How about you tell me what you have to say after I've taken the acid?"

"Okay, Doctor-In-Training Tonnan. Really, though, I am the victim of your public sexual extravagance. I saw you hold hands with Xinx. If this were a book, your revolting behaviour in the spirit world, too, would unquestionably cause a high proportion of readers to never read past the eighth page. You're the Darting Duck to my Hugo Hepner," he says apparently randomly, laughing sarcastically then genuinely, probably at the sound of his sarcastic laughter. He goes to his drawer and gets another tab. Imprinted on it is the iconoclastic image of Darting Duck. I know I can't be discriminatory based on the artistic virtues of the emblem on my acid tab, but for some reason I am really glad the emblem is not Massive Mouse; that mouse in particular, out of all the family of cartoon rodents, really creeps me out – he's just too big and obnoxious. I take the tab, placing it under my tongue.

"Did you have something else to tell me?" I ask, confused by his words & startled already at what could only be the placebo effect of this acid, which comes to form as a purple circle above Rockland's head, some kind of priestly halo.

"I'm going to fuck Xinx. Do you mind?" Rockland asks in a way that makes it seem like he really

cares what the answer is. In actuality, though, it's nigh-impossible that he does. Sure, I mind. I mind a lot. The fact that he is even asking is a little odd. I don't know what to say, so I just look at him, sort of shell-shocked. "Remember Kleopatra?" Rockland queries enigmatically, as if trying to reason with me with the pretty poison of words.

"Gee, Rockland, I don't know what to say," I say, internally wondering when the effects of the acid I've taken are truly going to kick in. I've concluded that Xix would probably not sleep with Rockland. The purple halo only lingered briefly over Rockland's shaved scalp.

"There are more than 355 million humanoids on this planet. What makes you think that you've suddenly met just the right person?" Rockland shrugs an entitled shrug. "Half an hour from now, I promise you that you'll see the world in an altered way. Everything's going to be okay," he continues, reading through the words of all the letters that my mind writes like a modern palm reader.

"Okay. Cheers. I'm going to go now, buddy. While I'm here, though, I should say that I'm not sure you should be taking these visions seriously. I mean, I don't think what you saw was me, I don't know anyone called Kleopatra… and I don't think you should be trying to get off with Xinx. Bros before hos and all that. Also, you said she was fat…" I say.

"Sure, whatever, forget about it," he laughs nonchalantly. *"I wish you, too, luck with Xinx. Quite the catch. Only a little bit fat, half-black and with huge Babylon."*

"Good luck with Rebecca," I say sarcastically but without a suggestion of sarcasm in my voice, shaken and lying in a sense. Though I do wish the man success in his relationship with Rebecca, I wonder whether the establishment of a 'relationship' between them in my mind means that I have fallen prey to some sort of pseudo-paternal bluff by Rockland, a basic psychological warfare trump card. Sometimes the way that man conducts himself is evocative of a witch doctor!

I wonder whether Rockland's hallucinated visual of my body having sex with a woman called Kleopatra could have possibly triggered the totality of the sadness and madness that followed in its wake. Maybe it symbolised a kind of licence that endorsed or sanctioned or at least theoretically permitted Rockland to have an affair with Xinx. I don't know. I feel small & stupid while still understanding how I could be perceived by the eye of another as an object of desire.

At my sixth form, as soon as I kissed any given girl, they automatically became next party's femme de jour, and some of the guys would make a pass at her. Even some of the girls would: it was a farcical tradition, thinking about it. Over time, I grew a slight victim complex because of this, but it was nice to always kiss the girl before my peers did; it was like being a trendsetter, the first to check out the best new coffee house in town, the one who was vegan before eating vegetables was considered cool.

An Angel Made Of Acid Written Just For Xinx

I go back to my room. I'd only been there a few minutes, thinking about what Rockland said, when a student leaflet advertising *"A Freudian Masterclass on 'Breakfast with the Leader'"* slides under my door. Shit. Not only was I just thinking about how Rebecca looks like my mum did, *'Breakfast with the Leader'* is one of my favourite films. And it was one of my mum's too.

But then the acid starts working. I put the leaflet on my table, and just lie there in bed. I stare at the wall. I should be completing my assignment of memorising the bottom half of the periodic table of elements, but I can already recite most of it. I think about Xinx's phone number, realise I still know it and smile contently. I can picture her now. I imagine our phone conversation.

Hi Xinx, it's Tonnan.

Hello Tonnan!

And then the acid starts working. *NANNOT STI XNIX IH.*

And then the acid really starts working. I wander tragically alone thru the fish-bait of coincidence, quickly figure out the great conspiracy that defines my social life at Hobbling University, and then promptly forget all about it as I see a Santa-Paws shaped car. I see myself symbolically in sardine shape. I get into the Santa-Paws vehicle and drive it up & down spiralling highways only to crash into the Red House. A mother hen, who I understand to be a sister of sleep, locks me in a jail cell similar to the one that I spent a few hours in earlier. In this semi-lucid state, I dive into great valleys of consciousness, invent a few useless household appliances, bathe in whirlpools of supposition and then tread down the boulevard of wakefulness like a disused whistle that craves the mouth of its master.

I pick up my automatic typewriter from the shelf and type a note to myself rapidly: *'I'm telling you. Something's going on. People… they're not all that good.'* The Lokona dollar bill appears in my mind's eye & I climb all the illiterate sketchers of oblivion's strange stares up to a poem. Shit. I don't write poems. Perhaps someone's got in it for me and they're onto me. They're onto me, but what I have done?

The poem represents my simple realisation of the aliveness of every character I have ever met along the road. It is my revenge against love & it is my love against revenge.

After I've finished writing the poem, my scientific brain fruitlessly tries to analyse & dissect what I have written for a couple of lonely moments. And then my phone rings. It's Xinx. I know that number. I must have said that number out loud hundreds of times while we slowly fucked yesterday morning.

"Hello, is this Tonnan?" Xinx says.

"Hi Xinx, Tonnan speaking," I say.

"Sup, homey?" she says in a conspiratorial tone.

"I had mind-blowing sex with this girl, then everyone clapped, then I ate macaroons, then I cleaned a cat, then I got arrested, then I took acid, then I uncovered a conspiracy, then I forgot the conspiracy, then I picked up this phone call," I tell her, anxiously.

"I hope that girl was me, I didn't clap and I'm a member of everyone, I love macaroons, I hate cats, I never once got arrested, I have never taken acid, I hope I'm not part of the conspiracy that you forgot

about, and here we are," Xinx says quickly. Geez, this girl has a good short-term memory, I remember and enthuse.

"Cool. Anyway, how are you?" I say, dazedly.

"Good. Want to see me now?

"Err... okay. Come over to mine? I'm in my room, J58. I'll wait for you in the kitchen."

"See you in a bit..." she says.

I go to the kitchen, where Rockland is microwaving a microwave meal. He doesn't seem to be in any mood to talk, so we just sit there. I tell him that Xinx is coming to see me here and he moves his lips in interest as if about to say something but then thinks better of it and stays silent. Soon Xinx walks through the kitchen door.

"Hi, it's Rockland," Rockland says calmly but with a sense of mortal urgency.

"What happened to Rockland?" Kleopatra asks in Rockland's mind, with an air of happy yet patient concern.

"I AM ROCKLAND," Rockland practically shouts, loudly.

"Xinx," Xinx says, accommodatingly.

"Doctor-In-Training Rockland, I'll get you some water. Hi Xinx," I say.

"Hi Tonnan," she says, waving at me in a knowingly awkward way that is designed to cull discomfort but rather serves to increase it.

"I was born for macaroons," Xinx says out of the blue to Rockland as if discussing a subject of tragedy whilst eying his macaroons.

"I was born for love," Rockland says, self-pityingly inspecting his fingernails. I don't think that it would be possible for me to live like Rockland does, somehow unable to disguise my feelings, a human chameleon changing his behaviour based on drug-ordained judgement, a creature hopelessly chained to his desire, his instinct, his ownership, his love, his self-belief installed in his head by the hand of God & the hand of God alone.

After delivering a glass of water to Rockland, I sit down. I observe Xinx and Rockland. I recall Rockland's words on Xinx to me. Xinx *is* beautiful to look at, *if* a little chubby; no, Xinx is beautiful to look at *and* a little chubby.

"May I have a macaroon?" she asks.

"Be my guest," says Rockland.

Xinx munches on a macaroon, walks towards me with part of it still in her mouth, and we smooch for a while. She tastes great, like macaroon and Sachsgate toothpaste. Rockland gazes at us, smiling as if he is witnessing young love for the first time, as if he is the best man at our wedding, as if over the course of the next few weeks he won't murder my sense of self with his analogies, metaphors and aggrandisement of these visions he is apparently prone to having. For a while, it feels like I am kissing a demi-God, a celebrated virgin porn star.

He Don't Love You Like I Love You

So Xinx and I are kissing, and Rockland is inspecting his ready meal, when the fricking fire alarm goes off and we all have to rush outside. We have so little warning (and my sexual dynamism, demarcated by hours – if not *days* – of experience, is so persistent) that my jeaned boner remains its full length when we arrive outside. Nobody claps. Nobody cheers. But I wouldn't veto the appraisal that almost everyone is oblivious it.

Standing a little behind me, I notice that Rockland has acquired a notebook and pen during the evacuation process. He is sketching what looks to be an early humanoid body. Rockland is usually a man who prospers when left to his own devices: his spirit is driven by amphetamine nights bawling at random tombstones after stints of drinking at the Old Horse, sober days spent courting the spirit world in underwear, weeded weekends writing long love letters he claims communicate the inexpressible, and other larks like lethargically lulling a lady late in labour in the library. Right now he's wearing expensive metallic glasses paired with a princely pink vest, a denim jacket, chinos and a scarf that matches his eyes. His nose is a mammoth landscape of blackheads sandwiched in between his eyes, which are a little too small for his face in light of his nose's enormity.

"This universe is finite due to the fact that space itself exists..." Rockland says apparently to himself with some unease, as if this supposition is so controversial it could get him killed in one of the greatest academic institutions ever, *"... and so the grave realisation that infinity is but a fairy tale transpires and you must confront the paradox of your own condition: a being of his or her own time but still existent within a fraction of the total time,*

which may be limitless itself. If you multiply space by time, you reach a surplus of energy, which though finite can't feasibly be numerically defined. Anyway, I always figured the passage of time can be quantified by the amount of time so far spent within this domain. Thus, for a new-born time passes slow-fast, because he or she has little concept of time."

"Well," Xinx says, "that too is one of the many paradoxes of being a pro-life vegan."

"But you're not a vegan," I say to her, surprised by the sound of my own voice.

"Sure I am," she says sharply. "Almost all of the time I am vegan and that."

"If you're not smoking, talking, writing, enjoying yourself or concocting a plan to escape a box, you are wasting your time," Rockland goes on. Though it will later crystallise in my head that he is a hedonistic heathen, I can't disagree with that point. In fact, according to Rockland's doctrine, I'm wasting time listening to him, which is quite accurate. He lights a cigarillo and carries on as if our interruption to his compelling stream of consciousness had not happened.

"Since we are in a certain space rather than the totality of space, I can only assume we are self-aware bacteria living within an organism..." Rockland continues, "also, since time passes, not even God can live forever; otherwise there would be no time passing. Does this make sense to you? When the organism we're inside dies, we'll die, too!!"

"Wow, Rockland, I knew you were a prophet, but I didn't think you were a heretic idiot as well," I say to him.

"Screw you, Tonnan," Rockland replies in mock-aggression. *"I am not a heretic."*

At this point I notice that the black cat is attending the evacuation process. He looks really good; in fact, he looks great. I make to go up to him but Rockland grabs my shoulder. *"Hey, dude, that doesn't happen to be the cat you kidnapped and assaulted, does it?"*

"Uh, no, Rockland..." I say to him, though of course it is. *"I like all different sorts of cats, okay?"*

And so, with Rockland trotting amiably beside me, I walk up to the black cat, who bares his teeth and hisses upon first sighting of Rockland & his ungainly gait, then wags his tail happily and purrs ardently upon my arrival.

"Gee, Doctor-In-Training Tonnan, that animal loves you!" Rockland says.

"Rockland, please stop using offensive language. How would you feel being called an animal?"

"Gee, Tonnan," says Rockland, *"I guess I am an animal. Are you PC or what?"*

"No, I am not PC Orwhat... you know I got arrested earlier today," I say, stroking the cat. *"Of course I'm not a police constable."*

"What's its' name?"

"It's not a robot, Rockland. It's a real male man who probably wouldn't like being arrested any more than I did. I called him Politico. The name kind of suits him, don't you think?"

Rockland shrugs, looking more baffled than amused. I look for Xinx amid the gathering of young adults and see her talking to some handsome ass bald dude.

Xinx is laughing, smiling and looking like she wants to be where she is, though it's true that women can be masters of deception. My mildly autistic and mildly resentful mind shrugs. The handsome ass bald dude probably likes Xinx for the reason I like her… if she didn't possess those traits, Xinx wouldn't be Xinx: let's just hope the handsome ass bald dude and I don't share the same penchant for super-hot, super-cool women.

I caress the black cat's ears. He stops purring and turns away from me, seemingly displeased. I bid the fellow adieu and go up to Xinx, who unexpectedly kisses me on the lips.

"Hey Tonnan," she says, *"how's your trip going? This is my friend Chester."*

"Hi Chester. How do you do?" I ask. I don't like making small talk with anyone, but I figure it'd be foolish to not at least go through the motions of appearing to be interested.

"I'm not bad. You?" Chester says.

"I'm okay. How about you?" I say. My head is elsewhere; in actuality my paranoid coveting self is still calculating whether or not Chester wants to have sex with Xinx.

"I'm bad. I hate it when someone asks me the same question twice when the first time I gave them the correct answer," Chester says.

"Then there are two correct answers, wise guy," Xinx says, and puts her hand in mine. This comes as a surprise and I can only surmise that I am, as Rockland said of Xinx before me, 'quite the catch'.

Chester doesn't know what to say now. There is a brief standoff of sorts, then pleasantries and smiles are exchanged on both sides.

"You smell funny," Chester says to me suddenly, breaking the pattern of polite joviality.

"You should never willingly smell," I say. *"Nothing good can ever come out of smelling a complete unknown."*

Chester shrugs and turns to another girl, who laughs almost as soon as he says a word to her. Although every single soul is smart in their own way, I reckon Chester is usually humoured by others or there is something inherently funny about his person. I don't see it; I just don't find him funny in the way that every woman he has yet spoken to seems to. As I am a *vaguely autistic* (artistic now, too? You can still be an artist even if you've only ever composed one poem and got banned from art class, right?) *genius*, I don't care to understand the minds of humanoids or the magic of well-structed sentences all that good.

Hey Presto

Xinx and I go to join Rockland, who is still lavishing the black cat with affection.

"Gee, Tonnan, this cat smells like Elephant Shampoo... he must be the cat you washed," Rockland says. *"All things considered, I'm pretty glad that you washed him."*

"Well, what a different world it would be if I hadn't, detective," I tell him. *"I wouldn't have been arrested, for one."*

"Were you charged with anything?" Xinx asks, poking me like she sometimes does.

"Not that I am aware of," I say wistfully.

"Oh..." Xinx says, sounding disproportionately disappointed.

"Maggie, the policewoman on duty, did mention the phrase 'kidnapping and assaulting' more than once, but I don't think the allegation would withstand the scrutiny of a court of law," I elaborate in what I hope is a casually mysterious tone.

"Tonnan," Rockland fondly & shyly starts, *"I was wondering if you would..."* He toys with his left earlobe as if attempting to unlock some awaited instruction from an outside force. *"Oh, never mind, it's too much to ask of someone so recently imprisoned."*

"No, Rockland, what was it you wanted?" I say.

"I wanted your opinion on..." he seems reluctant to finish this thought for a couple of seconds, but finally continues, *"a poem of mine."*

"Sure, man... I mean, I'm no expert on the matter, but okay," I reply.

He hands me a piece of paper. His handwriting is in capital letters, and it is easy to read. The work is titled *'HEY PRESTO! PURGATORY!'*.

I'm not going to lie to you: I was expecting it to be terribly overwritten. Poetically, though, it's really sound. You can't fault the internal rhyme. The syllable count is sometimes a little off, but I warm to it soon after the woman in it starts speaking. The underlying meaning of the verse is odd: his genderless protagonist wants to turn back time to grant a greater understanding of an illusion because they are some kind of 'je ne regrette rien' type of time-travelling existentialist.

From his imagistic style of writing to his distinctively flamboyant style of flirting, to me Rockland remains somewhat of an enigma. There is something extremely old fashioned about him, but he is so retro that he's practically from the future.

Anyway, there I am, reading possibly – no, *probably* – the greatest poem ever written, when the acid floods into my body again. I feel my body shake with emotion, and I have no clue how to formulate words with my mouth suitable to the situation. As Rockland, Xinx and I join the stream of people going back into the halls of residence as the fire drill is over, I hand the poem back to Rockland and say, practically on autopilot, *"Yeah. I really love it. It's got a kind of lucid vibrational quality to it. Did you actually hallucinate this happening?"*

"Yeah, man... well, mostly, anyway... I had to take a bit of poetic license and rewrite the woman's speech almost entirely, but that's about the extent of it," he says.

"Figures," I say. *"Still, pretty impressive. Everything is great now that I'm on acid."*

"I didn't give you acid. That was a bit of fish-food. Literally."

"I want to read it!" Xinx cries out.

"Oh, because I'm pretty sure you said it was acid." I say, pretending to ignore Xinx.

"Yeah, that was acid," Rockland confirms reluctantly.

"Oh, good, because that's what you said," I say.

"Yeah, that's probably what I said," he says.

"That is *what you said,"* I say.

"I reckon so," he says, *"anyway..."*

"Let me read the poem!" Xinx says.

Rockland hands the piece of paper to her. She reads it slowly, savouring every sentence and tracing her right forefinger along the page as she does so. The way she reads is adorable!

"Wow, Rockland... I did expect some mild erotica, but I didn't expect to be so vagina centric. When I met you earlier on today, I was under the impression you were a homosexual," Xinx says.

"Err... no, Xinx, that would be morally, legally and factually wrong. I'm just another bisexual who is high on acid. I appreciate the female form far more than any other," Rockland says.

Rockland does look camp at this moment, though, with his bright blue scarf, pink vest and bewildered priestly air. But looking camp is morally, legally & factually different from actually being homosexual, and I am not the fashion police.

Nine Months

After the fire drill finishes, Xinx and I say goodbye to Rockland and go to my room.

"So here we are. This is where the magic happens," I say, sitting down on the bed. Xinx does the same. I feel like touching her, but for some reason I don't. Xinx must sense that I am incapacitated by nerves because she strokes the hair on my hand

"I've got to tell you," she says carefully, as if peeling an unripe banana while balancing on one leg for the first time. *"Until the day before yesterday, I was in a relationship with a man who took everything quite literally. Not only did he take my virginity, he refused to understand why people would use words to a superficial end. For example, for him, 'I'll kill you' meant 'I'll dismember or choke or shoot you' and 'I'll love you forever' meant 'I'll think adoringly about you for eternity or I'll fuck you for the rest of my life', and so on. He wasn't stupid. Far from it, in fact. He just believed that words carry a certain weight to them and so should be respected. He wasn't ever abusive to me exactly, but towards the end of the relationship, towards present day, he suddenly became distant, and he lost all of his appeal to me. It's like he… yeah, to quote that phrase he used sometimes… became a 'fragment of his former self'."*

"Cool. Okay. I don't know why you're telling me this, but that was then and this is now. People change, I guess. It might interest you to know that I once had an incredibly spotty forehead. Do I have an incredibly spotty forehead now? Hell no! But I'm still me," I say.

"I'm glad to know that about you. When I first met you, I admit I had my doubts, but now I think you're pretty cool. Anyway, where was I? Oh… the man I

was seeing… let's not talk any more about it, okay? I just wanted to tell you. It was kind of a serious relationship, and I only got out of it two days ago."

"Okay," I say, feeling her hand. *"I know how these things are. Nine months is the longest amount of time I've been inside a woman. The average stay is like seven months. The median stay… well… that's much closer to twenty minutes."*

Xinx takes her hand from mine. *"What on earth could compel you to say something like that? That's… just… well… disgusting. Are you still fucking high? Were you trying to be funny or something? Now that I don't get."*

"Sorry. Sometimes these things just come out."

"That's just… that just… doesn't bear thinking about. How could you possibly say something like that?" Xinx asks rhetorically. I can tell from the tone of her voice that she is pretty mad at me.

"Geez, I don't know. I guess I don't know you very well. I didn't mean to make you mad. Sorry."

"Sometimes when you speak, I don't understand you," Xinx says, using the exact phrasing the Enodrian chick once chose to explain why she didn't want to hang out with me anymore.

"I guess… I'm not like other, more normal people. Apologies."

"It's okay," she says, placing my hand back into hers and playing with it. *"Some things just aren't supposed to be joked about. That's all."*

"I guess not," I say. *"What I said was the truth and the truth is no joke."*

Xinx shrugs a big shrug and bites her lip. I sigh a deep sigh and she kisses me.

"So, what were the things you wanted to do in my room?" I ask her encouragingly.

"Oh, I just thought I might have a tidy up and a snoop around. I like to tidy up and snoop around. But there's not much to tidy up. And snooping around is for when you're asleep and don't know what I'm up to."

"I always sleep with one eye open," I say.

Xinx smiles. *"What kind of music do you like?"* she asks.

"Some hip-hop, some new age R&B, reggae... that kind of thing. And you?"

"I like music that takes me some other place. Trance, Pineapple, Oblong, Quixotic... all sorts of music," Xinx says. *"Is Rockland a musician?"*

"I think he'd like to be labelled as one. He has a ukulele and knows at least two chords."

"Yeah, he has that kind of air about him. You don't play?"

"No, but I've always wanted to. 'Always wanted to' may be an overstatement, though... I mean, I've always wanted to be on the top of a mountaintop, but I don't want to put in the required effort to make it so."

"I know what you mean," she says. "I always wanted to be an astrophysicist, but I don't think studying Classics is the best way to ensure that happens."

I laugh. Xinx is right. *"Do you want to have sex with me?"* she asks, suddenly.

"No straight, sane, unmarried man would refuse," I reply. Though that is quite a lot of qualifications, I

am straight, sane, unmarried and a man. And probably a little bit in love with her.

**

Eight and a half hours later, after a fun night, I go to the kitchen to make coffee. I don't need an alarm to wake up at 8 A.M. every day. I bring an OkSo cup for Xinx and a Darnleo Henco 'Grotesque Losers' cup for myself.

"I love you," says Xinx.

"I love you too," I say. And I mean it. There is something powerful about her, a weight to her every word and action.

We drink our coffees, talking about ancient literature, whether people are evolved from apes (she believes that we are but she is gravely mistaken), what regions of Restralardin we wish to visit, and the meaning of life. I walk her to her class, *'Reading Like A Writer'*. I go to my own class, *'Immunology'*.

Human beings – whether they are on Restralardin or Planet Earth – are immune to many things but the doctrine of death is not one of them.

Immunology

Immunology is the study of the immune system of organisms. Prior to my classes on this subject, what I knew was limited. I knew, for example, that allergies are a result of your body reacting to a non-existent yet perceived threat. I knew, too, that cancer cells are mutant cells that have lost the ability to stop multiplying and wrap around other things, preventing them from functioning. Simple things like that.

Anyhow, the class is a group of about ten people, and I sit on the chair nearest the door. The lecturer, an orange lady with snow white hair and a penchant for analogy, introduces herself as 'Professor Vine'.

"Why don't anteaters get sick?" asks Professor Vine.

Someone eventually raises their hand and offers, *"Because they have anty-bodies?"* A wave of giggles and guffaws drench the room.

"Absolutely," Professor Vine says. *"Antibodies are a blood protein produced to counteract a specific antigen. Can anyone tell me what an antigen is?"*

"Proteins found on surfaces of pathogens. To put it simply, harmful bacteria?" another person suggests.

"An adjective is a descriptive word," Professor Vine says deadpan. She then laughs playfully, saying, *"Ha-ha! I got you!"*

I'm not the only one that doesn't get the joke. Bemused looks are exchanged. Notes are rubbed out with erasers. The bleached-brown-short-haired woman sitting next to me shifts uncomfortably in her seat.

Professor Vine goes on to explain, *"I was pretending that my brain had been affected by one of these 'antigens', causing it to replace the word 'antigen' with 'adjective' in my brain. Though the chances of this happening are slim, you students are to 'fool' as Professor Vine is to 'ingenious chef of tomfoolery'."*

We laugh. Now that we get the joke, we find it pretty funny.

"Speaking of my abilities as a chef, have any of you cooked your first meal at University yet? And more to the point, what happens when you heat an antigen?"

A few hands raise. Professor Vine hurriedly chooses some keen scientist bloke, who has turned up already in a lab coat.

"Well, you'd have a hot antigen, and the heat may serve to sterilise the properties of this bacteria which, as has been said, is predominantly protein."

"Precisely," says Professor Vine. And so, our 're-introduction' to the body's immune system continues, with the occasional good-natured joke or pun used to broach a subject. The animated teaching style of Professor Vine may serve to make things more interesting, for the sight of the eccentric orange woman moving her wrinkled hands about in an acutely relentless manner is enough to entertain most anyone for an hour.

After class ends, I chat with the bleached-brown-short-haired woman for a while. She is on her way to get an air bus to the town centre, and I am on my way back to my room. She says something about Professor Vine's cooking probably being more Buddhist than her own, and I giggle. I tell her that I would devour Professor Vine's sprouts. I find this bleached-brown-short-haired woman to be pretty attractive, but since the beginning of University, I've already slept with a beautiful women three times and received a hand job from a police officer, so who am I to push my luck? When it is time for us to part ways, we share a hug. That's nice. I want to hug her again almost as soon as our two-second-long embrace stops.

**

Sometimes I wonder if there's an elaborate masterplan that each being is realising together, or if God is simply shaking Her head at our shenanigans. I don't know, you know; I just don't know. But sometimes there isn't any reason for our actions.

When I get back to the hall kitchen, Rockland is there snacking on a vinegar-quiche-fudge sandwich. I sit down opposite him and the situation's scent is oddly reminiscent of a region of hell I've never been to.

"Smells like a skunk has consumed a pint of cod-liver oil and thrown up all over themselves in a garbage compactor," I comment impulsively. *"Are you enjoying your sandwich?"*

"Reserve your judgements, Tonnan," Rockland says patiently before it dawns upon him that his core values have been accosted and he rapidly taps his foot on the floor to an indeterminate rhythm. *"If you really want to know, it's my firmly held belief that 'good' and 'bad' are defined by societal concepts of normality. They are mere constructs of the mind… they are illusions: as real as fables, Planet Posterity or dancing dragonflies."*

"I guess. Are you enjoying it, though?" I ask, a little perplexed by his answer. I now think about the shit I ate in a police cell yesterday… it didn't even taste that terrible because it seemed at the time to be a

literal necessity, and my expectations weren't high in the first place. Rockland's probably right.

"That's beside the point," Rockland says. *"I'm endeavouring to persevere with it, certainly. The contents of this sandwich are the most luxurious yet inexpensive ingredients I could source on my budget."*

"Sorry to hear that," I say, feeling a little sorry for him irrespective of his increasingly feral words and actions. *"Are you low on money?"*

"Not particularly." Rockland looks kind of peeved at the question. *"No, at the moment, I'm a man of means. I just wanted to try something new for a change. Is that okay with you?"*

"Of course," I say. People have a right to stupidity, especially if its motives are well articulated.

"How would you feel about me stripping to my bare bones to do the macarena?" Rockland says suddenly, grinning challengingly at me. His smirk possesses a potentially proverbial profundity: it is grotesquely angelic. He looks, at this moment, like some kind of crudely cute cherub of a character summoned from a cartoon. There is a cheerfulness to him, too, that practically advertises he would happily take 'no' for an answer. Though obviously as prone to moods as any other being, Rockland is generally quite an affable guy. An aura of kaleidoscopic enlightenment sometimes emanates from his body. There is Rockland, and then there is everyone else. That's how I see things now at least.

"If that's what you want to do, then go for it!" I tell him, thinking he is joking. I put pasta on the boil and go to the fridge to get pesto.

Rockland has finished his sandwich and so shimmies over to the sink to wash his hands. As he does so, he takes off his shirt and performs a trademark 'Hail Mary' ballet. *"I can't remember the macarena, and three drug laws broken is enough rules violated for one day! All I know now is that I want a mandarin, a hot chocolate, and a toothbrush,"* Rockland enthuses, his voice heavy with despairing longing.

"Some extra-strong toothpaste would come in handy, too," I offer, sanely.

"I don't brush with toothpaste," Rockland says, as if toothpaste is just a strange mannerism.

"No wonder I'm so attracted to you," I say, jokingly. The instant I say this, I regret it. It's one of my bad habits to kiddingly come onto men that I grudgingly admire.

"Funny. I think I saw you in my sleep last night. You were doing a waltz-like dance by yourself on the Stallion Road Mall escalator travelling up. I see people I like in dreams a lot. I go there all the time," Rockland says. He looks up at me as if expecting me to respond. When I don't, he gazes at the fridge. *"It must mean something. I mean, your movements in the dream – waltzing by yourself on the Stallion Road Mall escalator travelling up – I mean, it must amount to something. It probably means you're going to heaven or some shit. I don't know! I'll have to ask the Fortune Teller next time I see her."*

"It probably means I am going to die happy and alone. Who's the Fortune Teller?" I ask, glad that he didn't take my faux come-on too literally.

"My imaginary friend," Rockland says. *"She smells like the orchids of the orchard where I met her on Valentine's Day."*

"Cool," I say, and I genuinely do think it kind of cool.

"You know, I like you. I like you an awful lot, Tonnan. In fact, the left side of my brain has even contemplated seducing you a couple of times." He looks solemnly into my green-brown eyes for a few seconds, as if considering some beautiful yet forbidden future of green and brown. *"I think we should just be friends, though."*

"I think so, man. I didn't know you were bisexual in the first place or that you had these feelings for me," I say. I'm not a homophobe, and I don't find the idea of two men being together disgusting but imagining myself with a man does make me squeamish. To me, that's like a poem that doesn't rhyme: there's nothing inherently wrong with it at all, but it isn't great literature in my opinion. For the record, I've been with three men but none of them really did it for me. It was like eating a banana and not particularly enjoying it… personally, I don't go out of your way to find bananas. I might eat something healthy from time to time, but I don't go on many missions to the market to buy bananas in bulk. Anyhow, despite my reservations about his mortal compass, I'm beginning to see how Rockland, with his outlandish impulses and precision to detail, could be regarded as attractive.

"I am trisexual. I will try anything *sexual,"* Rockland says, as if reading my mind. *"Are you and Xinx coming to the C-Century Disco Ball Event tonight at the Union?"*

"I'll be there. I'll ask Xinx in a while," I say.

"Cool. Bye for now," Rockland says. As he heads for our shared bathroom, I wonder whether Rockland is attempting to bed me too.

I eat my pesto pasta as Rockland brushes his teeth in the bathroom for ten minutes. It takes such a long time for Rockland to brush his teeth because he doesn't use toothpaste and he is pungent as a putrid puke pizza petal. I call Xinx to ask her to the ball. She says yes, and two naps & one nervous system essay assignment down the line, I walk with Rockland and Rebecca towards the Student Union.

The Party That Broke My Deal

"Where's Xinx?" Rockland asks. Though Xinx is not my 'girlfriend', I have had sex with her three times, so I feel a little irritably protective.

"We're meeting her there," I reply, dismissively factually.

"So... who's your favourite C-Century musician, then, Rebecca?" Rockland says, as if he needs something to distract his mind pronto.

"Edward Thinker. That man sure can play the ukulele," Rebecca says. Rebecca is studying Mathematics with hopes of becoming an accountant. She's wearing a delightfully blue cashmere cardigan. I notice that her tendency to broadcast an indifference to everything and everyone has been substituted for the casual yet happy eagerness of youth.

"I prefer the Complexities of Youth or Mister Mystery, myself," says Rockland, before cheerfully adding, *"I don't mind a little bit of old Ed, though!"*

"Those were the good times," Rebecca says. *"They'll probably play all three if we're lucky."*

It's a fine autumnal night. As Rockland, Rebecca & I stroll through the Student Union together, there is a palpable sense of anticipative excitement and festiveness in the air. Anyone can talk to anyone, so anyone does talk to anyone. Although I am not the kind of man who dreams while he is awake and works while he sleeps, our destinies seem yet to be designed: almost anything can happen... anyone can wake up to anybody. We are young, alive, and ready for the night.

In the dancehall, Rebecca takes Rockland by the hand and leads him onto the dancefloor in a manner that suggests I am a third wheel and she is trying to lose me. As for myself, I am not particularly fickle in my criteria for the sexual suitability of women, nor am I seeking to mirror Rebecca's nonchalant attitude towards me, but she doesn't strike me as being the kind of woman I would ever willingly enter a relationship with. My mind migrates a little further north, and I ponder love triangles.

There are many famous love triangles. To name the obvious one, which may be apparent to me only because I have watched *Birthday Sunset* & have a brain that processes information alphabetically & have a habit of dissecting daytime television, Regina loves Robert and Robert loves Michelle and Michelle loves Regina. Though I don't mean to suggest Michelle is a lesbian, her attraction to Regina is evident by the end of the second series. It would take an evangelist who is baptised daily in holy water not to imagine Michelle and Regina living together in sin.

I vocalise this fact to Rockland and Rebecca.

"Where did that come from? That wasn't anything close to what I thought you would say," Rebecca says disgustedly to me. She then swiftly resumes her previous position of staring Rockland dead in the eyes with dreamy determination.

"Me either," says Rockland, with a possibly pot-induced gaze of great affection that stretches from the bulge in his jeans to the sparkle in his eyes. *"I always knew I was straight and long-haired men were the devil incarnate,"* Rockland says with a hint of accusation in his voice. My hair isn't exactly long, but it isn't exactly short either.

I observe the dancefloor, but nobody really catches my attention. 'I'm A Suffragette Too' by Bald Guy is playing. Everybody who's anybody knows this song.

It's about a man who loses all of his hair because of cancer and then invents the cure for cancer but never gets his hair back. It's a kind of hipster kid folktale narrative partially based on reality.

There are about a hundred or so people here. Some are short. Some are tall. Some have green hair. Some have tobacco dreadlocks.

"Love triangles usually star three genders," chirps Rebecca suddenly in a manner both condescending yet tragic for a corny kid from private school. Although I consider myself a relatively enlightened feminist, her misuse of the word 'gender' is so monstrous that its original meaning blurs beyond recognition. I reckon Rebecca must feel a little sorry for me, given my position as a third wheel.

"Regina and Robert..." says Rockland, as if testing unknown alliterative waters, similarly harking back to my previous comments and hypnotising Rebecca with his sibilance.

"Rockland and Rebecca and Tonnan..." says Rebecca, in what I can only describe as a carrot.

"Rebecca and Rockland and Regina," says Rockland, using the tip of his tongue to roll the 'R's with such relish that the resulting sound simultaneously resembles a Russian raconteur re-evaluating his relationship with language and Ronald Reagan recounting his role in 'Stallion Road'.

The tension between them, then, is so tangible that the probable becomes the inevitable and the inevitable becomes an event. His hand firmly in hers, the pair ogle at each other for a while as if bewildered by the beauty of their own reflection in water. After a few seconds, there is nothing left on either of their lips but the gaze of the other. And so, she kisses him. And so, he kisses her back. It doesn't seem like a match made in heaven and perhaps it isn't, because - on the top of the foot-job that Rockland received yesterday in the kitchen – it will amount only to a three-night stand but will sour the atmosphere in the kitchen for the rest of the year.

Yet they kiss (I guess it is romantic). And they kiss (it is certainly passionate). And then their kisses converge into one long French kiss, so I go to get a drink.

At this point, the scene erupts as everyone dances to, tries to dance to or goes mad to the opening bars of the classic 'Just Because I Wear Glasses Doesn't Mean I'm Unattractive' by The Dalliances. I presume that the DJ's song choice is in recognition of Rockland, a glasses wearer, and his first University conquest. I scout the room for anyone who looks like Xinx – as will unfortunately become my practice some twenty years down the line – and spot her in the queue for C-Century chocolate mousse. I go to her.

"Xinx!" I shout over the song. She doesn't hear me at first, so I tap her on the shoulder. She turns towards me with these guarded dark-light world-weary eyes, which still seem scrambled & stubborn (like first love or depression) when she sees me and smiles broadly.

"Let's eat and dance!" Xinx proclaims.

"Let's!" I say, echoing her celebratory mood. I remember my dad telling me to never dance because girls don't like boys who dance and I *"can't dance, anyway"*. But I decide to throw caution to the wind.

We eat the tiny (but free) portion of chocolate mousse dispensed by a woman in an authentic C-

Century khaki vest. Then we sway for a while, rock back & forth rapidly to some fast old New-Age WW5-esque track and then kiss passionately. It's still an unparalleled feeling to brush lips with a woman I'd normally consider to be out of my league. As Xinx and I grind against each other, my hands move down to her waist, and our tongues begin battle over key positions in our mouths in experienced yet tenderly steamy lust. The slippery chastising of her tongue and the pulse of her – dancing to her own rhythm, surrounded by young men and women trying to fit in, trying to look like they aren't trying to fit in or not thinking but just dancing or speaking throwaway drivel – well, kissing such a beautiful women in their midst is like fulfilling a fantasy I never knew I had.

"Tonnan!" a familiar voice to my right exclaims unexpectedly. I look for the speaker, and it's the hot, tall, bleached-brown-short-haired woman from my Immunology class.

"Hi," I say. *"Want to go somewhere quieter to talk? This is my friend, Xinx."*

"I can't hear you," she says. *"Want to go somewhere quieter?"*

"Yes! THIS IS XINX," I say.

"Chantelle." Chantelle and Xinx shake hands.

We all head outside to the bar, where some guy is screaming about his accommodation to a member of staff. I'm thinking about how bratty and self-satisfied some University students can be when I gather from his hollering that he has been rendered homeless for a couple of days. Anyhow, shortly he is taken away by security. I think about how the world has a potentially wicked way of resorting to force when words do not rectify the problem at hand.

"I don't know if you just got to the disco and all," Chantelle says. *"But there's a house party uptown. If you've nothing better to do…"*

"That sounds pretty good. Xinx?"

"Yeah… I guess," Xinx says uncertainly, then speaks her mind. *"Actually, you guys go without me. I told some people I'd see them here later."*

"Are you sure?" I ask. Xinx nods her head.

"Okay, then, to uptown!" I say to Chantelle, unintoxicated yet excited.

***

I'm not too sure if not going back to the disco with Xinx is the first mistake in a couplet of blunders or if my real mistake will come later.

I'm not too sure if I know I'm in love with Xinx at this point. I'm not too sure if the following words in this story will represent its climax or its cliff-hanger decrescendo, but shit is about to get sticky.

Although I'm a scientist, I hardly know a thing about the science of the airbus we get into town. The machine itself is a plane that looks like a flying bus.

Chantelle and I sit at the back of the airbus, which is filled with indifferent mature students who are travelling from campus to town. Almost as soon as we are seated, the airbus ascends up a hundred yards, then blasts off into town. It's a quick & bumpy journey. Some kid is blaring 'That Summer You Shook My Soul' by the Red Herrings on his phone. The song makes me kind of dizzy – it pulls me back to my school days – and I feel a little nauseous by the time we get off two minutes later.

"The party's down the road. Do you want to get alcohol from the off-license?" Chantelle asks.

"Are you hoping to get me drunk?" I say lightly.

"Drinking's not compulsory," she replies.

I reach into both pockets. I have two unsmoked spliffs, a gift from Rockland. *"You know, some whisky wouldn't hurt,"* I say. *"You need drinks?"*

"Yeah," she says. We go past the church, past a well-kempt garden of volcanic lilies, and buy drinks from the shop at the street-corner.

"Party, party?" The man behind the counter whimsically smiles.

"Yeah, man!" I say.

"Enjoy it. Make sure you leave with the right person, who is not always the same one you came with," he jests, looking at me then at Chantelle, who blushes.

"Thanks for the advice, I guess," Chantelle says.

The party is about 50 metres down the road, past a mosque and past a porta-potty. I can tell where it is because of the spicy reggae emitted from the rooftop. We arrive a minute later.

"Do I know anyone here?" I ask Chantelle tentatively. *"New places tend to make me feel a little ill at ease."*

"I only know like three people, including the host," she says. *"Come on, Tonnan! It will be a laugh."*

And so we pass a few pale people, letting strangers remain strangers, and enter the somewhat derelict white house. All paints in Restralardin are designed to subtly glow in the dark, yet this house doesn't for some reason.

When we arrive inside, Chantelle immediately introduces me to a couple of her friends. Evan has an attractive scar above his lip and can't seem to stop smiling. He wears a Cloud Cult choker and fiddles with it incessantly while we talk about the meaning of dreams. Judging by the fact that he believes first-person dreams to be real occurrences in another universe, I'll have a little of whatever he's on, please. Evan's girlfriend Rachael looks like she might break into dance at any moment but is a lot more aloof. She nods her head nostalgically at a mention of Chantelle's pet beaver.

As soon as I can, I head for the courtyard to smoke a spliff and sedate my soul. My elements have reckoned with much stronger skunk than this before, and I've been looking forward to this high-grade porcelain for a while. Ever since I took acid with Rockland, I've had a feeling that a slow, gloomy doom looms beyond the window of every room I'm in. Somehow I feel this sensation to be more in tune with the reality of the omens of the present than unbridled optimism about the future.

There are ten or so people out on the patio. I nod at a group of guys who look in my direction, and they all smile, shouting *'hello!'*, *'hey!'* or *'welcome!'* with slightly different inflections. Chantelle is from a region of Restralardin I've never been to and so are the people she hangs out with. I light my first spliff of the night, already feeling somewhat of an outsider in a cool crowd.

I've smoked about a fourth of the spliff when this fine-looking lady in a leather jacket walks up to me and snatches it from my hand. *"Is this weed?"* she says in a well-spoken loglan accent, putting the joint in her mouth. I nod, taken aback. *"I've tried weed before,"* she says.

"Okay," I say, nodding again.

She inhales. *"I'm good with weed,"* she says. *"Oh… I just love weed!"*

I laugh and shrug, looking her comely form up and down. She, like Chantelle, is slender and has short bleached hair, hers dyed silver. *"It's my weed, though!"* I say in weedy protest.

"Sorry. Where are my manners? I'm Lika." She hands the spliff back to me after taking another three smooth, seasoned hits.

"Hi Lika," I say. *"I'm Tonnan."*

"Are you an artist?" she inquires gravely, without warning.

"I'm studying to be a doctor."

"Oh, because you look like an artist… a writer or something. I don't know. I've always had some sketch of an artist etched in my head and you look just like it." Lika now peers at me pretty possessively. She is painted by C-Century period powder, probably because she has been to the disco.

"Huh," I say, somewhat surprised. *"Are you an artist yourself, Lika?"*

"I'm studying Frolid Literature, so… no. I'm the opposite of an artist – I deconstruct art, inferring 'hidden meaning' from language." She's like a likeable mixture of self-confident and self-depreciating.

"Isn't that creative?" I wonder, dubious.

"A doctor can say he has saved a life…" Lika states. *"Literary critics can say they have cured themselves of curiosity."*

I'd like to say that some of the themes of this book are
1. All love stories have endings.
2. Sexuality is jealousy is stupidity is friendship is insanity is betrayal.

3. The improbability of transcendence until just before you die.
4. Indefinite patterns repeating themselves indefinitely
5. God will be The Judge

Anyhow, Lika's voice is sweet & sonorous & highly accented. The way she pronounces some words wonderfully wrong makes me hungry for her love. For all I know, though, Lika might just be a beautiful, down-to-earth, funny, smart, mysterious, tall, foreign, silver-haired chick with a dick.

"Well, I'm not a 'real' doctor yet," I say. *"But I'm sure you can already call yourself a literary critic."*

Lika smiles somewhat begrudgingly, as if I have exposed a flaw in her argument or sussed out some shocking secret about her. *"I decided I wanted to be a journalist a year ago, but I guess you were sure about your own ambitions from secondary school, huh?"*

"Probably, yeah. Right now, my only ambition is to dance with you," I say, surprising both her and I by letting my heart become my vocal cords. She scans my features for a hint of sarcasm before her smile turns even more sincere.

"Lord, okay! I'll lead the way. I haven't danced once since I got to this godforsaken university," she says. Hobbling University has a reputation as being one of the least exciting places to spend your golden years, but I've had fun so far.

Lika takes me by the hand and we go inside. The song playing is a D-Century synth-pop classic, with a drum machine pitter pattering at a frenzied pace and a Tongonian vocalist scatting about his baby's mama. I spin around & around & flail my arms, getting into the rhythm, and Lika responds by laughing & doing the Caterpillar.

Three songs later, we are both sitting on the couch. I'm looking at my phone with one hand and, to her friend's audible amusement, feeling Lika's swanlike neck with the other. Next thing you know it, Lika's hand moves my head in her direction and she kisses me on the lips. Not being one to refuse a kiss from a beautiful woman, I kiss her lipsticked lips back.

We make out for a pretty long time, and a lot of people leave the party. Finally now it's just Lika & her friend & I & a few other stragglers.

"Well," I say, *"I better get going, but it was nice to meet you."*

Lika's friend titters.

"Sure, I'll see you around probably," Lika says.

"Yep," I say, *"Hobbling can be a small place sometimes."*

I kiss Lika on the lips once more. Lika's friend titters. We part. She moves like an aphrodisiac sprung from the sea-salt where she was conceived, talks like a purple manatee would talk if a purple manatee could talk, and tastes sweet as Weetabix with extra sugar. I like a girl like Lika. I'll never see her again, which is a shame I guess, but there is a bizarrely dexterous brevity to every breath, and the world is only beautiful because it ends. You can suck your best friend forever, but never let them fuck your soul.

I get on the airbus, having paid my respects to the snake-skin-attired host. Chantelle had already left. The moon, gaudy & yellow & full, casts its cheese-eye over town. Have you ever seen something so beautiful & transient yet constant you wonder if your worldly eyes were not meant for it?

I open the door and go upstairs to the kitchen, where my hallmate Tim and his boyfriend are discussing Tim's 'friendship' with a woman. I'd recently read a memoir by a man who believed he was a homosexual for half his life but then developed deep sexual feelings for a short-haired woman. Such scenarios do occur in reality and I've been dying to tell someone about the book but given my companions' instable status as a happily homosexual couple, I keep quiet.

As the kettle reaches a boil, Rockland unexpectedly appears from the hallway, all charismatic & bleary-eyed. He is closely followed by Xinx.

"Salutations, Doctor-In-Training Tonnan," Rockland croons sleepily. *"I might be wrong, but according to the lipstick on your mouth, you've had a wonderful night."*

"Hi Rockland and Xinx," I say. "Xinx, what are you doing here? Is there lipstick on my mouth?"

"Yes, and it's not mine," she says, unenthusiastically. *"Oh, well, Rockland, we had a good time, too: didn't we?"*

"Erm, yeah." Rockland scratches the back of his head.

"What did you two get up to?" I ask.

"Rockland has a pretty interesting take on the world. We talked for a while, kissed once, and smoked some herb," Xinx says, nodding like a bobblehead.

"I thought you were with Rebecca, Rockland," I say. "Where is she?"

"Man, it's 3 A.M. She's asleep," Rockland says.

"I'm going now," Xinx says. *"Night Rockland. Thanks again."*

"Night Xinx," he says. *"I'll lend you that book about cover-ups we were talking about soon. Who'd have thought that STRAWS actually took place a long, long time ago in another part of the Universe?"*

"Goodnight, Xinx," I say, tentatively tenderly. *"When am I going to see you next?"*

"If you're going to be getting with other people... well, I'm not sure I want to see you at all, but..." she sighs. *"Rockland and I also kissed, just as I told you about! I thought I was mad at me, but now I don't have to be mad at either of us!"* She laughs as if she has heard something absolutely hilarious. I realise she is truly stoned. *"With the Rockland-Xinx-kiss,"* she adds mulishly, *"the first couple of seconds made me think he's a pretty bad kisser."* Xinx sticks her tongue out at Rockland.

"And then?" asks Rockland, bashfully.

"Then I grew to enjoy taste of fudge & vinegar. I realised he doesn't care, so why should I?!" Xinx declares happily. I realise she has been drinking in addition to smoking pot. *"Anyhow, I bid you good fellows a very good night!"*

Xinx departs in moggy demagogic glory.

A More Metaphorical Climax

It's always been my opinion that love is often found in the ephemerality of a moment. I guess I'm a little less vexed about the intimacy of Xinx and Rockland than I would have been had Rockland not already expressed his intention to fuck her.

A couple of days later, in the Science Block toilets, I go to take a dump and I see Rockland's self-flagellating graffiti etched shambolically across the bathroom wall. It reads *'R.I.P. + X_Y = FOREVER'* in Rockland's recognisably readable handwriting. Next to it is an impressionistic nude of Xinx. I don't know, you know; sometimes I just don't know. As you can imagine, though, I'm not all that happy. Xinx has a middle name – Bee –but this isn't what is bugging me. No, it's how Rockland seems so blasé about the two of us having the same biblical knowledge of a woman I do, as if this turn of events represents a restoration of the natural order. I really like Xinx and though I don't usually believe in such words I might perhaps certainly love her. The actors are stunning, but the world is a farce.

Rockland avoids me for most of the week, but when I finally see him in the kitchen, he hurriedly nods at me. *"I am well, thank you for asking, Tonnan,"* he states.

"But I didn't ask," I say, in an unsympathetic - nay, hostile - tone.

"Oh, okay," Rockland says. And then he wanders deliriously back to his room.

About four weeks after the start of University, I'm awoken in the middle of the night by a text from

Xinx. It reads: *"I know I'm a jerk, Tonnan... but I still have feelings for you that run deep. I just had a beautiful dream about you. I feel so depraved."* I read the message and feel pretty sorry for her. Being deprived of me, of all people, must mean that things have taken a turn for the worse. But I don't respond to the text.

Anyway, it so happens that in the week after the text was sent and received, Xinx and I run into each other by the Humanities block, and she invites me to go on holiday with her in the coming half-term. I don't refuse. We go to Way-West.

There, Xinx ties me to the clandestine palace of ruins by the beach and fellates me for a full hour. Once, we have sex for such an aeon that during the proceedings I contract another cold while weeping with happiness as a climax comes on to me. And that's the genesis of this part's title: *Happy Tears in Love with a Cold.*

***

Two pretty profound months pass but I won't tell you about them now, because the status quo is more or less maintained. Xinx and I are in love with each other properly now and we consummate our lust regularly.

I don't reckon Xinx had sex with Rockland three or more times purely to spite me, but I certainly understand temporarily why he might have appealed to her temporarily. Although Rockland is a hedonistic heathen, I'm not sure he is ever wrong about anything. To put not too fine a point on it, that man is sharp as a knife sharpener yet as ecstatically useless as a theatre without ice cream. We become friends again

Rockland has his enemies in the hall we live in, though. Apparently, he stole someone's yoghurt and knocked over a litre of milk in the process, not bothering to tidy up afterwards. One of Rockland's enemies sneakily recorded him speaking about his vision for his mosquito farm.

Rockland's set-up consisted of a small heater in a cheap glass tank, placed opposite his bed in the fifth week of study. He added rotting fruit, red meat and water into the tank. Soon after this, the first mosquitos were welcomed to their new home. Rockland hoped that mosquitos would breed in his farm in such a way that they *"ethically complete the trials of living and then righteously ascend to heaven"*. I don't know whether they ascended to heaven or not, but boy those mosquitos fuck and breed. Rockland documented the presence of over three hundred mosquitos in the farm.

A police car just arrived outside our halls. It will take Rockland to a hospital that claims to doctor the abnormal mind until it conforms to ordinary standards. By now, Rockland has engaged in intercourse with the two people that I'd made love to at Hobbling. As well as being a purveyor of unapologetic veracity in a world that celebrates restrained dignity, Rockland has done what I would have done were I him, which is partially why I call him a hedonistic heathen. As well as being a hedonistic heathen, Rockland is legally insane. With the ownership of his mosquito farm company transferred to the University, Rockland's last ever words to me on campus are spoken in an exhilarated frenzy of excitement. "*In order to be good at singing or smoking, always soul your mouth: use it as the centre piece..."* Rockland says, laughing sardonically in a way that reminded me of a squirrel from an anime cartoon I used to be a fan of. *"The mouth is like an internal harmonica or cacophonical gift to your audience. The mouth is the best candy that ever existed."*

And that's it for him: he stays there for a good year and a half. He is released a little before I die for the first time and his room at University remains vacant for the rest of year. I go to see him twice in the insane asylum. The first time I see him, he refuses to speak Frolid to me, so we communicate using body language and in broken Hibbish. The second time, he tells me that he feels deeply sorry for me because he has a feeling something very terrible is going to happen to me.

I can't say where I would be were it not to happen as it will, but a cataclysmic apocalyptic force opposing my material, science-based existence shall soon accelerate like a falling moon onto the metal metropolises of my otherwise unremarkable world in a localised Armageddon.

GOD'S PRETTY GAME OF GROTESQUE PUPPETS
THE INAUGURATION OF INSANITY

Toenail Hospital, The Café, The Graveyard, The Skatepark & The Woman

We are now in the clockless territory of Toenail Hospital, where time's tempo goes as slow as an infant giant's toe would grow, though in actuality every moment evacuates the past as fast as a vast tribe of Rockland's mosquitos would multiply, receding beyond the linear dominions of perception and into the villas of memory and imagination. My description of the passage of time in this dimension is deliberately vague, for an explanation of the nature of time itself fails to grace the lips of even the most enlightened of astronomers, and I am at this point a paltry foot-doctor-in-training on work placement. Nonetheless, as you walk through the rotating door at the clinic's entrance, the feeling that you have forgotten something vital to your interest swiftly envelops your being.

The small hospital is coated in hostile scarlet paint that connotes it is under communist control. Mutating motors glide by the complex like big buoyant butterflies pulled by harlequin hurricanes. These vehicles are mostly manned by the middle classes of our civilisation, who can sometimes be found brewing whisky or taming plants in luscious miniature-garden-skyscrapers.

Cyprus trees, generously scattered in cataclysmic constellations, represent a governmental nod towards the primeval years in which nature ruled the streets. Here also reside realistic animated murals and mosaics in memoriam of those murdered in World War Fourteen. But they that don't walk or fly here tend to forget about this section of the citadel, for one can live functionally without toenails.

I don't work late on Thursdays, but it is raining, so I walk home umbrellaed. The silhouetting skies stain the world with an antique oppression, antagonizing all that have the misfortune of being on the street without brollies. They to whom the pain's wrath is not wasted upon wear newspapers over their heads and skip down the street, open-mouthed, hoping to be dry and asleep before it is too late.

I figure I'll get a coffee on the way home. Outside the all-night café sit a miniature dragon and its keeper, the former of whom upon meeting my eye positively howls a minor blues scale at me, the melody climaxing into a harmonious wail reminiscent of a saxophone solo that I heard a long time ago but that I can't place, the rhythm so tightly wrong that any error in the sequence's measure appears to be rectified by time itself. By way of saying sorry to me the miniature dragon keeper says that the miniature dragon suffers from short man syndrome and that I am a tall man (which is quite true). I don't laugh, though, because I don't find her peculiar jest of an apology to be funny, but I'm nowhere near nihilistic enough not to smile at her anyway.

In the all-night-café, a nondescript barrister with weary time-stained eyes takes my order of toffee ice coffee and banoffee pie. I pay, saluting the man energetically to convey my gratitude. I occupy a window seat. An ugly man and a beautiful woman sit in an adjacent booth and talk shop.

"I'm no eavesdropper, but sometimes I find myself in situations where I can't cover my ears out of politeness; I guess you could say I'm the kind of woman that would hiccup to disguise a burp... but

then again, I do shower regularly," says the beautiful woman with mocking venom

"I don't know what I've been doing with my life. I should be spending more time trying to look beautiful. That's where I've been going wrong," the ugly man sighs enviously. I wonder if I should interject to suggest an adult course at Skinny School.

"Washing more frequently would be a start," the beautiful woman reflects with a patronisingly sage sympathy. I agree with the beautiful woman's assessment of the situation, as the stench of sweat emanating from the ugly man is putrid beyond measure, even from metres away.

"You know that I have aquaphobia…" the ugly man says, fidgeting with his legs uselessly.

"And to think we are out on a day such as this. My, oh my, oh my, oh my… how long has it been?" the beautiful woman says teasingly monosyllabically, as if she were playing the role of a teacher who has just caught a student smoking outside his high school in a barely legal porn movie.

"Two months!" he declaims despairingly, shaking his head in shame. Figures, I think to myself. I stop listening and collect my thoughts. They rest on Xinx, who is now my girlfriend. I wonder if I will ever love anyone or anything as much as I love Xinx, then I wonder whether she remembered to buy marmalade from the shop to make marmalade pancakes, then I shake my head with the same shame the ugly man who smells demonstrated seconds ago.

My order arrives. I tuck into the banoffee pie, an optimistically dynamic yet flavoursome fusion of banana and toffee in tart form – just what the foot-doctor-in-training ordered. The dessert's very aura counteracts the smell of the ugly man. I'd even go so far as to say the disagreeable sight and vomitable odour of the ugly man are effectively cancelled out by the majesty of banoffee pie.

Anyhow, the combination of banoffee pie and toffee iced coffee play tricks with my palate and endorphins dance as if in a banana-toffee-coffee ballet performed in my mouth for one night only. I focus on the flavour (I eat and drink quickly so as to maximise the taste per second) and ignore the surroundings for the next few minutes until I leave the coffee shop. The rain has eased up a bit. Maybe I won't die in a tropical storm after all. I wander through the cobbled centre of Treetop Towntain, which is deserted but for a few sombre homeless souls, as is to be expected on such a ferociously aqueous occasion, and I arrive in the cemetery.

We are now in the cemetery. Some gravestones are marked; others are anonymous. Some are adorned by flowers; others are bare. In the centre of the cemetery sits a starkly slim sphinx, who guards the graves in graceful yet serious servitude.

[Some of the regions of this world, including ours, celebrate the cat as a physical representation of Godliness. I still sometimes fondly recall the playful pussy that my parents kept when I was a child; I too grew to respect and admire the acutely feminine traits of our feline friend, who was a little younger than me. It was an extremely novel experience to watch that cat being born, and I can nearly recall the event with photographic clarity. Her mother panted ferociously and in between each wheeze there prevailed a purr of deep affection, as if this were the birth of a saviour set to proffer a solution to the problems of the worlds. It was an ominous sound she made, thinking about it. Eventually out popped a bloody beautiful kitten. The new-born, like her mother before her, would perish in peace a decade and a half later without altering our world in any particularly meaningful way. But at least a few people remember her. Subconsciously my pace quickens.]

It goes without saying that the cemetery is not where the dead dwell, for the dead by definition do not dwell anywhere. Sometimes I feel that the inevitability of death is the only thing that unites all living creatures. If an afterlife does exist, however, I am qualified to offer a healthy doubt that the experience is endless. The practicalities of being dead are unimaginable to most minds. The closest some of us get to death is the state of unconsciousness. When we wake from sleep, sometimes we feel as if no time has passed since the start of our slumber. I don't suppose that's what death is like, though, because for the deceased an eternity passes instantly yet there is no repossession of perception at the end of it.

A hooded man crosses himself and says a few words to his dead relative. Twenty years later, his own body will be buried a few rows away, but this thought does not enter his mind. He is alive. His relative is dead. That's all there is to it. For the time being.

We are now in the underground skate park, where multi-lingual graffiti-stricken walls advocate cold turkey, lucidly decry the state and advertise the numbers of 'service agencies' (drug dealers or prostitutes). A particularly talented artist has drawn a lion gnawing at a kratom carrot triumphantly.

There is music playing. It is not popular music. It is not unpopular music. It is simply music. With that said, there is something unambiguously hipster about the cadence of this specific music: instead of the normal tat-tat-tat, it is noticeably tat-tu-tu-tat-tu-tu. Maybe I am just oversimplifying something complicated. I suppose the basis of music is rhythm. Were I to categorise this style of music, I might call it old-school new-age reggae.

I stand to watch the skaters for a while, as the rain has stopped, and it will be a while before Xinx is home. This is where I meet Kleopatra, the woman that Rockland prophetically envisioned I would have sex for an unrelenting eternity with.

Kleopatra is a little shorter than me, has long purple hair and hazel eyes. She appears next to me. She is dressed in a dense denim sapphire shirt, tight against her gigantic tits, which dwarf mine to the eleventh power (though I appear to have small breasts they are, in actuality, muscles).

"I don't mean to be overly straightforward, but I feel kind of deprived of..." Kleopatra ventures slowly, gazing into the distance and her voice trailing off, though she clearly addresses me.

"Nicotine?" I offer half-heartedly. I'm not in the mood for conversation, no matter how attractive or funny the speaker.

"Yeah. Nicotine..." she smiles, turning towards me.

"Sorry, I don't smoke much yet," I tell her.

"Do you flirt much yet?" she asks.

We look into each other's eyes for a second. There is a tiny resonance of blue in hers amid the hazel.

"No. I have a girlfriend," I reply. *"Anyway, I don't want kids."*

"Sorry to hear that," she says sympathetically.

"Forget about it," I say hastily, smiling at her.

"Phone number?" Kleopatra asks.

"Why should I give my phone number to you?" I reply.

"You might love me," she says solemnly.

My smile becomes vacant. I feel stupid. Sometimes I believe I belong to whoever's talking to me. Sometimes I wonder if any humanoid will ever validate my existence.

"Am, Gm7, F7, D" I say, submitting to her serious mood.

Kleopatra's brain registers the number, and she kisses me on the cheek. She skips off in her skin-coloured skirt. I feel dire yet vaguely turned on. I wince a little or I wince a lot. Above ground it starts to drizzle again. A skater narrowly avoids serious injury as he fails to defy gravity in a 1040-degree flip, instead landing on his back. He shouts out in shock or pain, and there is nothing that a paltry foot-doctor-in-training can do to help him.

Halloumi

In the centre of Treetop Towntain, I walk and talk languidly with Xinx, a twenty-year-old who is quite like me at this moment, in that she is excited and hormonal. We're tipsy and our souls shares the same sole aim of attaining halloumi, which is atrociously low-priced yet euphoric and heavenly in this part of town. The cheese can be bought from a wooden shrine of a store that sells popcorn, pesto pasta, banana milkshakes and coconut juice.

Treetop Towntain is elevated above Moonlight City, east of the accommodation we are renting for our final semester at Hobbling University. Its name derives from the fact that the municipality is on the mountain but is close enough to the forest to be viewable and level with the top of the trees.

Xinx and I purchase fried halloumi from the vendor. He nods and we half-half-heartedly salute him. I consume a little, biting into its frivolity, surprised by its crunch. I decide halloumi tastes more like bacon than cheese and as I convey this revelation to Xinx, she summons a cab by raising and lowering her gloved hand in a way that would look nebulously imprudent were it not to contain such sensuous grace that it is instead ludicrously appealing.

We hold hands and board the taxi, a robust tractor-like Chevrolet, manned by a strangely Aryan, washed-out-looking driver who wears a beret. I'd say that his hair has always been silver-grey. The angelic bouquet of broken doorknobs that I had bought for Xinx falls off her head of parrot-hair as the driver accelerates along the highway. She looks at me light-heartedly then turns to the driver with an expression of incandescent fury.

"My fucking hat!" Xinx cries out, pretending to be aghast at the calamity of fate.

"Sorry, driver, could we go back to get her fucking hat?" I ask, mirroring her mood.

"That's totally possible, hot mamma and good sir," replies the driver.

The Chevrolet speeds on for a second then does an abrupt 180-degree turn, heading straight for Xinx's broken doorknob bouquet, which I notice looks even more damaged after we run it over. But Xinx picks up the bouquet of broken doorknobs, which are in fact so broken that several of them appear to have almost repaired themselves. Doorknobs are the latest sex symbol here, and this hat has a white sign on it which says, *'NOT FOR SALE'*.

The Chevrolet heads to our apartment, and in five minutes the Treetop Towntain scenery ends abruptly and dramatically, like my physical connection to Xinx will.

(Overall, my memories are happy but not without sorrow. Maybe that's why we ever travel anywhere or fall in love with anybody.)

My hands are no longer mine but Xinx's.

"I don't like to think about how it is made," Xinx slurs sovereignly, *"but reason is suspended for it is impossible to be happy all the time, for you would have nothing else to contrast to misery. Nothing, though? I must take that back. It doesn't work in this context... nothing... uh... nothing is for after... that would be it... nothing lives here."*

[Some beings are so beautiful but my soul, now closed, is burdened... I look outwards yet still I mix faces up for most of my brain is lost to quadratic theorems or names, for as previously suggested I probably actually am a vaguely autistic genius. For many seconds on end, Xinx exists just as she is, a drunken woman talking to a tipsy man. For a while I almost feel enlightened, the environment devoid of definitions or labels].

Xinx rambles about the making of halloumi or the act of making love, then she lackadaisically lays her head on my shoulder. I can't understand all of what she is saying, but my sex doesn't ignore her playing with my hand. It is rather egged on by her voice, which becomes posher yet more incomprehensible & unpolished when she is not completely self-aware or has been drinking.

".... Are you? But... oh... no... yes... oh.... we can if you want. But I can't accept the idea that we all must persist in existing essentially as spirits, like objects, unable to change the course of our temporary bodies. Though Soothsayer and her sister made some pretty wild prophecies about our life expectancy, we should be dead rather soon," Xinx says.

Only a fraction of this night has been funny, so I gasp to stifle a giggle then realize I do not have to contain my mirth, so I laugh out loud. Xinx gazes out of the window expectantly as if she is questioning her surroundings and deserves an answer.

"There will be an end to sleep and life, but sleep is a dreamy death and death is dreamless sleep," the taxi driver says, stretching and yawning. *"We have no concept of eternity until we forget, and we will never know eternity itself... for God could not blame us."*

I smile in agreement but then my body twitches, a sign that the better part of me doesn't fully agree with his statement. No, life is not for the meek, where the weeks drift slowly ahead like the corpses of all the chickens we ate, once trapped and now dead. I am nearly vegan now, but I do like halloumi & pine oil. You may believe that I should be imprisoned with Rockland in the insane asylum for saying this, but I can still sense lifetimes before the one I am narrating now spent sexless & hopelessly hormoneless when endless days darted directionless where I meditated desireless in a cage. I think I believed I was a dog and the workers on the farm referred to me as a dog, but I led the life of a pig. Anyhow, it really makes one wonder. Three minutes later, the driver's last six words echo portentously in my head. I realize I have grown up… tortured in parallel worlds, I am now a humanoid monster who has himself facilitated such anguish by accident while somehow not being second to it.

"That'll be thirteen hypons…" murmurs the driver, turning on the Chevrolet waggon screen and laconically putting his feet up. *"The Leader will be on right about NOW."*

I pay, leaving one hypon as a tip before staggering all silly into our accommodation while also choreographing the majestic movements of the inebriated Xinx. I feel almost grossed out by her faux fur, but it's ugly enough to turn me on slightly, even more so because I know it was a present from her Auntie.

A Sex Scene

Inside the sphinx-shaped apartment, the wide-screen television responds to our entrance and turns itself on.

"... I don't believe the transportation system is as operational as your government has publicised," the Broadcaster says. *"'Gus got a bus and didn't cuss' isn't necessarily a better slogan than 'Don't quit if it's shit'. I've waited twelve minutes for a bus that was supposed to take ten minutes. It's outrageous and that's not even the most extreme of examples."*

"I'm not Sorry for wasting two minutes of your life," the Leader says, *"and I know you're not Sorry, either. You're the goddamn Broadcaster. Where is this so-called 'Sorry' individual everyone keeps talking about but refuses to be? Some things simply cannot be avoided, just as sexual torment will most likely occur after both partners have consented to intercourse."*

"What are you trying to say? It's not inevitable or true that the genders are relatives of each other," the Broadcaster says, *"nor that those who are sane are same in the entirety of their being."*

"You're right on..." the Leader says, *"... the chair. But surely insanity and sanity are definable."*

"I'd like to think so – but you, sir, seek to defy and decry such categorisations," says the Broadcaster.

A plethora of people lose their wits and go ape shit: it seems their beloved Leader is being mocked by the Broadcaster! Even the Cameraman grunts uncomfortably as he pans in on the Broadcaster, who victoriously sweeps his hair to one side, the perfect image of his father.

"Either you or I are insane, and I think I know which of us richer." The Leader nods and spits guiltlessly on the floor. Tens of people stand up and clap, then the whole audience starts to clap. There is a cinematic pastiche of the studio-viewers and the scene is cut, moving onto cringe worthy news and monotonous adverts.

Outside the television and the studio and inside our house, Xinx puts her hand on my sex and massages it in a playful way that says she knows I am bored, and she is bored too.

My pen is growing erect. I'm not going to describe Xinx's features again, but to say that she is beautiful is an understatement. And I particularly love the faux fur and gloves she is currently wearing because they accentuate her feminine traits in a quasi-masculine way. Xinx will soon be a qualified archivist and I'm horny to make history with her.

Xinx presses her hand down harder & harder on my cock, and I can't control myself anymore, so I kiss her & she kisses me back & she grabs my hair, slaps my face and titillates me with her tongue on my neck until I say *"off"*. Xinx pulls my jeans down (the television responds too – the ready meals being advertised fade to a blank yellow). Xinx applies a banoffee condom to my cock, then she mounts it and bounces up & down. My hands feel her love handles which are so essentially antique and fatty.

"Ugh," I say.

"Shut up," she says in that superior voice, biting my tongue.

"Ugh," I say.

"Shut up," she says in a more ordinary tone, which though I believe to be more self-conscious is somehow realer.

I lick her earlobe and caress her tits.

For some reason, my favourite physical thing about women is their breasts & earlobes. I love to get sucked, but only if there are breasts & earlobes. Otherwise, women would just be men with vaginas and slightly different brains. This is what I think as she bounces up & down & up & down. That's either because I haven't seen a man's face for a few minutes or because I'm especially stupid when having sex.

"Get off a sec. I want some halloumi," I say.

I lift her off. I put halloumi on her vagina. I eat it off. It really turns me on, the taste of her and the halloumi together. She can be a horrible person sometimes, but her teeth and vagina are always clean. I secretly suspect she is a lesbian, but we haven't ever talked about it.

I lick her out for a few minutes and as always her fluid is as tasty as noodles & as healthy as sprouts (eh? heh, reminds me of sprouts and Henry's Grandma's tofu).

Xinx orgasms and farts at the same time. I keep licking her out until her vagina barely tastes of sprouts or Henry's Grandma's tofu.

"Suck me off," I instruct her, softly.

Xinx loves my right ball almost violently, places her right gloved hand on my left ball and pinches my bottom. I feel her faux-fur jacket, which never fails to turn me on.

"Xinx, suck me please," I beg.

And she does, first licking circularly around the top of my cock, then deepthroating as if her mouth were karma itself. It feels like this is the reason I am alive. I come a little. I don't let her make me orgasm. I don't want to. Only small part of the joy of making love is the relief when it's almost, almost over.

"Orgasm," she breathes into my sex. Xinx sucks my other ball now.

"Take your clothes off," I tell her.

"No," she says but she does in a few seconds, revealing her small plump tits (which at this point I can't help but compare to Kleopatra's, for a reason unbeknownst to me).

Xinx kisses me, transferring a halloumi and banoffee condom flavour to my mouth. She gives me head properly, now, teasing me then going all the way down and again fiddling with my balls. Sometimes when she fellates me it feels as if my whole being could be swallowed up by her mouth. I wonder if my brain is being murdered. I want to wander up to heaven and die the second that I get there.

Suddenly I can't stand my own sanity, an amalgamation of sexual satisfaction and the poetry of contentment. I always believed that time is a fluid entity, but now everything and nothing seems to converge and happen at once, as if the gravity of current circumstance tugs the unreachable fire of the past into the precipice of the future. Yes – that's it, I think again – I want to go to heaven and die the second I get there.

Then – oh! wow! – I orgasm. It's a wonderful orgasm. I can't remember being born, but I expect a 'little death' feels worse than that and 'a big death' feels better than 'a little death'. Hell yeah! I am home, briefly, barely speaking sense in any language, somewhere in between the dogma of the day and the anaesthetic of sleep.

"Though I enjoy the world, sometimes I can't wait to go to sleep or die forever," I say. *"Do you think that makes me morbid?"*

"I don't enjoy this life all that much either," Xinx says, *"but that doesn't mean soon I want to die forever."*

"Soon I will die forever," I insist.

"You will die soon in the grand scheme of things... you just don't have to keep talking about it," she says.

"Okay. Good night, Xinx," I say.

"Good night, Tonnan," says Xinx.

It's silent for a minute, then she laughs loudly.

"First I realised all my friends are celebrities and then I realised I don't know any celebrities. I wept for two minutes straight," she says.

"I'm your friend," I tell her, *"but soon I will die forever."*

Xinx feigns a weep, closes her eyes and nods. *"So... when are you going to die?"* she asks, tricking me with her tongue.

"I don't know," I say.

"Good night, Tonnan," Xinx says.

"Good night, Xinx," I reply.

A Sex Dream

I wake up somewhere random and undefined, so I'm positive that I am in a dream. I'm in a concrete room, without a discernible entrance or an exit. I'm in a cube of walls. Kleopatra sits, over there, across the room, glaring at me expectantly like she did at the underground skate park. She looks the same as she did then, only she's naked and pouting slightly. I reciprocate her look properly this time by narrowing my eyes. Both of her tits are as big as her head, like those of a woman I used to fancy in high school a few years ago. There's a purple tattoo on the right one that says, *'don't fake me or I'll make you'*. Kleopatra sees me eying it. She blushes. Her toenails are painted pink. There is a faint smell of manure & pot in the air.

"*You are my angel,*" Kleopatra says

"*Am I?*" I say, feeling kind of lily-livered.

"*Of course,*" she says as if it's a well-known fact. "*Who else would come to visit me, here, where the procedures of physics are lackadaisical and lethargic like a honeymoon of lollipops?*"

I didn't choose to be here, I think; Kleopatra vaguely nods then shakes her head as if she is indecisive about something.

"*What's your name?*" I ask.

"*K,*" Kleopatra says.

"*What?*" I breathe, feigning confusion.

"*I what you to,*" she misspells sensually.

"*Where are my clothes?*" I ask.

"*Embarrassed?*" K tuts.

"*Eh? Be seedy, F.*" I smile.

"No love for E?" K asks.

She giggles in a revealing way. I feel like I know her now. I like her laugh. I want it to continue for longer than it does.

"Sweet tattoo," I tell her. *"It reminds me of Oestrogen."*

"What does it say? My boobs are too chubby for me to read the message," K says. She laughs.

"Don't take me or I'll fake you'", I say..

"How kinky," K says.

"Come closer. We're too far apart for this to be a good dream!" I exclaim.

She cackles and shakes her head, her wavy hair waving all wavy at me.

"I'll come closer then," I say.

She places her left index finger in her mouth as I move towards her. *"I want to teach you a lesson about the Alphanumerical Highway of Etiquette."*

I sit down about a foot away from her. *"Of course,"* I reply, as if this is standard dream procedure.

"You can dance by yourself forever, but you can never know a person so well you know what they're thinking," K says.

"Oh?" I say, kind of disappointed.

"No. You're as naïve as pot noodles," she smiles.

"So?" I say.

K mirrorishly mocks me, her skin changing into that shade of silver that I have seen in movies of faraway worlds: *"So... So?"*

She moves her feet closer to me and tantalisingly wriggles her toes. She then manoeuvres her left foot up and down my groin as she fingers her pussy & groans in what seems like ridicule.

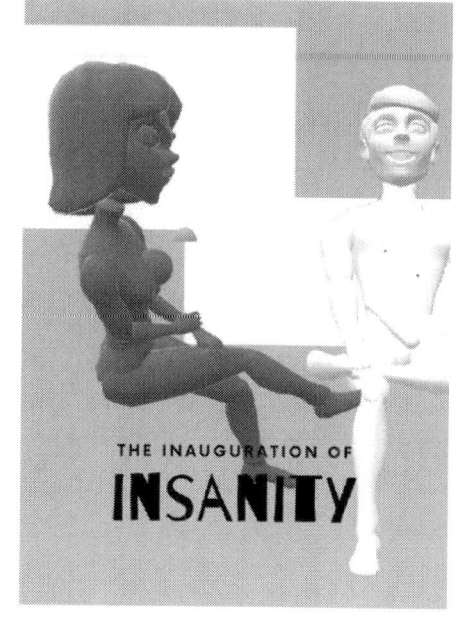

"Woah!" I say, feeling like fate is flying straight for a great discovery.

"Uh. Uh. Uh," K moans.

I smell. It smells like home. Her right foot manoeuvres up and down my penis. Occasionally she uses the left foot to clench it. It's almost embarrassing how fast I come to that foot. I can even smell her toes. They smell of parsley. I'm glad I'm getting assaulted by parsley. I badly, badly, want to orgasm. And I do. It takes three minutes.

"Relax," Kleopatra says.

She giggles. With some athletic certainty & sexual gravity, and against what I thought scientifically possible, she puts her cum-covered foot in her mouth and swallows the discharge fluid.

We chat for a while about the latest happenings on a moon a million miles away. I don't really look in her eyes. I just gaze at her tits.

"Recovery position?" K asks.

But I wake up. I sigh. I wonder if part of me is still there in the dream with K. I ponder the whole affair for a second. I check my watch. It's 4:20 am.

I go to the kitchen, where I raid the fridge for cigarettes. We keep them underneath the yogurt. I smoke one on the balcony. Part of me wants to jump off into the nether the instant I get there, but I refrain from following my instinct, as every man should do. If G.A. was right when he said 'first-thought-best-thought' and were people to follow his teachings as if they were a prophetic gospel truth, we would live in a shallow, twisted world. Personally, I'm not certain I even belong on this balcony, even though it is part of my home.

Shit About My Past

Though I was far from dormant beforehand, I came alive at a crossroads in time.

Some Crayons believed the entirety of the universe would end five years after I was born, while a third of the first world thought itself to be on the brink of a nuclear apocalypse. Though the majority of mankind understood both prophecies to be implausible, a protesting herd of a hundred cows outside Gorpegio knocked down the fence in their field and consumed marijuana from a nearby plantation for medicinal purposes, forming a crew – far from cowardly – that stormed the town & diplomatically made friends with its people like captives making amends with prison wardens. The cows were nervous & bashful. The cows that were particularly stoned wondered if all the journalists typing sentences such as this were going to portray them in the right light.

The cows, finally able to vocalise their thoughts, sought legal immunity from the police department. Although the officer in charge wasn't quite sure what this meant, the outlined demands were quickly agreed to. Three policemen keenly and cheekily posed for a photo.

A dozen cows formed a band, making acapella music in bizarre newfound awareness. Even the old Sergeant General came out from her shack and held hands with a cow, who snacked on strawberry gelato. It became extremely hyper, ran circularly around a post & then shat mercilessly on the Sergeant General's much-prized roses. The Sergeant General wept fearfully after believing herself to be awake and then hooted unenthusiastically, as she was so shocked that she thought she must be asleep. I witnessed all this and didn't say a word. I'd been told it was rude to stare. The anarchy, albeit 'cowed', was but a taster for what I will experience in a coming chapter.

***

My parents divorced when I was an infant. My father was a great philanthropist boozer, oozing cinematic charisma even when he remained motionless. When he looked, drunk at the dinner table, at my mother, it was simultaneously a confident gaze of glowing savagery and an idolatry glare of wakefulness that any non-blasphemer would reserve for an angel. Perhaps my mother was an angel. It seemed my father thought so, and I loved my mum like she was God. I didn't question why, but when I looked at my dad and he sensed my glance, his blue eyes would well up in a kind of hysterical sadness, then he would smile adoringly at me. The more he drank, the less he would speak. My mother and father were a good match for each other, or at least I felt lucky to be their son.

My family lived in one of those high-rise apartments. Holidays happened every weekend. I loved cake and sweet things. Eating was my hobby and profession, but I read poems in my spare time. I even had a Franklin tutor, but she was very impatient and apparently underpaid. She quit in fury after I told her in Franklin that I could speak Franklin more fluently than her and I wasn't even trying – it was a joke, a contrived joke, but I usually cloaked my intelligence. She seemed horrified & hurt by the simple thought of it.

My dad worked in stocks, owned a small computer software company, and I was assured in my teenage years that his was not the stare of an alcoholic but that of a shy man in love. Sure, he could drink himself to hell and back, but he didn't ever make it obvious that he was drunk. My friends have noticed this trait in me, so perhaps it runs in the family, like my dyslexia and addictive personality.

I smoke a cigarette every hour these days. Otherwise, I get a little nervous. Nicotine patches don't seem to offer any permanent resolution to my habit. Rather, they make me long for that subtle yet seismic injection of adrenaline into my body, be it for the purpose of writing a report for my latest toenail patient, or to launch a prostituted statement of resolve towards the moon, or to simply function as an undesirous nicotine junkie. Smoke every cigarette as if it will be the very last of your lifetime and one day it will be.

Last Thursday, I saw my father for the first time in ten years. I was at work at Toenail Hospital. I was standing in for the receptionist. My dad walked in and said, *"Sorry"*. I didn't know what to say. There wasn't much to say. From my point of view, he had been a gifted bully to me after my mum died & before I went off to University. I was pretty sure this figure was my dad though. His nose had sort of changed. But it was him. For sure. My dad nodded at me in the blue raincoat that matched his eyes. I scratched my head. My dad burst into tears. I didn't feel like crying, so I didn't. He handed me a package, stuttered something unintelligible and ran out of the building cackling. At the time, I didn't know that this would be the last I would ever see of this incarnation of my dad. I opened the package two days later. Inside it was a cake, a spiff, and 5 nicotine patches wrapped inside a note that read:

'Is the sun so dormant it prefers no sound? This is what I contemplate on the ground: trend less gratuitously personifies than the blend of matrix mushrooms but some mistakes in the barren wastelands of life & love we can transcend'.

I spent a day thinking about this, analysing it. I decided it really did belong in the canon of famous poems: you know, up there with Homing Problem or Colourful Star. It was a story within a story that told a story. It's not even that it had my blood written all over it. It just seemed to make sense. I'll leave it to you to decide what it means for yourself, but I knew what my dad was getting at. I just don't know why he delivered it and then ran away cackling.

Guitars & Eternal Return Explained

I'm nineteen right now. Over the past few days I've concluded it'd be a waste of my valuable time for me to continue to train as a foot-doctor. I'm sitting at those crossroads you hear about on cassette tapes. I feel I've got to express myself somehow. I decide to learn to play guitar properly. Rockland volunteers to teach me the basics when I next visit him in the insane asylum. He says that there are effectively four barre chord positions which can be moved up and down the guitar to create the majority of the sounds the guitar's structure is capable of making. He also shows me how to move my fingers from left to right from low E to high E strings. He tells me to stick with that. It seems he actually does know quite a lot about music, despite the fact that his ukulele often reverberated horribly thru the walls while we were living together in halls.

Over the next week, I play my guitar for 100 hours. It's enough to drive a crazy man sane or a sane man crazy. I attempt old favourite melodies & work on my own epically simple composition. It doesn't feel like I am at the crossroads for long, even though I've lost my job and potential position in society as a toenail-doctor. No, I genuinely feel great about the world. My personal ambition stems purely from my perfectionist streak: to do something & to be one of the best at it... whether I will be recognized for being the best at doing that thing is a separate matter. Anyway, I suppose this paragraph implies how dedicated to self-improvement I am. My father was or is a trader. My mother... well... my mother died what seems to me to be a long time ago. Wishing it didn't happen doesn't change the fact that it did.

My third visit to Rockland serves to disintegrate my botched understanding of the concept of 'eternal

return' in lieu of a more rounded comprehension of its proposals. Rockland seems to know a lot more about eternal return than I do and places more emphasis on the idea that each recurrence is *"self-similar"* or *"approximately the same"* as its predecessor. This intrigues me and makes me contemplate the question in a new way. He insists, though, that eternal return is just a theoretical conundrum proposed by a *"dead ancient"* philosopher that's designed to make us question the way we live. Would you live your life as you did 'this time round' if every time you died you were born again in your mother's womb? To quote a Restralardin tome on the subject,
'Eternal return (also known as eternal recurrence) is a theory that the universe and all existence and energy has been recurring, and will continue to recur, in a self-similar form an infinite number of times across infinite time or space'.

While we talk about this idea that he claims, *"may in actuality be an actuality"*, Rockland insists that we walk around the yard in circles to simulate the repetition. He tells me to note that though the circles appear to be the same as each other they are really quite different circles, proving that with the awareness that you have been here before you can alter the cycle of eternal return completely. Other than that, though, we have a fairly monotonous time talking about schizophrenia. Rockland maintains the disembodied voices are real, whereas I reason that they are constructs of an overactive mind.

There is something uplifting about seeing Rockland. He speaks in his odd manner, simultaneously manically evocative and redolent of a withdrawn man who doesn't know quite what to do with himself. Words leave his mouth as fast as shooting-stars soar across the solar system, and he says that he feels like *"some caged humanoid magician jailed for blaspheming a God that isn't his own"*.

When I finally make to leave, he stops me, pleading with me to stay another while. I oblige & he seems joyous but isn't sure what to do about this either. He asks me if I've seen any cats recently – *"how's your friendship with the felines?"* – and I reply that I still worship every one. He asks me about Xinx – *"how's your missus?"* – and I reply that she's doing well. I joke about his attempts to steal her from my 'abusive clutches'. *"Welcome to my altruistic world,"* Rockland smirks back wryly. *"You may go back to your world now, Tonnan."*

"See ya, Rockland," I say.

"Bye, Tonnan," he says, and he goes again to observe the great big green light installed at a corner of the courtyard for patients to look at and pray to.

Unlike the caged humanoid magician he feels like, Rockland believes in every deity in every Universe. He dreams of God in elated snatches and isn't afraid to admit it. He rejoices in the beauty of arbitrary moments, with an infectious humility that isn't entirely at odds with the paranoid schizophrenic he became. No, Rockland is a creature of his own making, treading patiently with an eye-to-detail such that each patient step seems now, in my own peculiar imaginings, to be more than just another terse phase on the path to his inevitable demise, signifying instead somehow a vague prequel to the antiquity of thought itself. And so, he gazes & gazes at the great big green light until he finds himself almost more than completely at one with it… a tiny, grotesquely beautiful humanoid desirous of the sum but in the very act of wishing for it exceeding it.

Yes, at least in my eyes, Rockland is a shrewd rebel angel destined to usurp the limitations of his being and in doing so establish another separate, clairvoyant truth that only he is privy to. Rockland believes in a saintly future, in an impossible heavenly epic of bliss that is yet-to-come but that is always hovering on the horizon, almost within reach, almost tangible, yet forever twisting & contorting such that the second Rockland believes he's at the top, he realises that he's only just reached the bottom. Then as now, even as the nadir of this undefinable nirvana evades him like a rare Pokémon in one of our Earth's frustrating man-versus-machine strategy video games, he stretches and stretches, striving forwards, onwards, upwards, towards a foreign yet homely infinity discernible only to himself.

Eventually, infinity itself will materialise itself impossibly far behind him in his wake, but for now, Rockland interminably combs his mind's atmosphere for the furtive shape of an unknown dream, some reassurance that he is not lost. The fact that whatever is there is there and whatever is not is not essentially renders his searching ascension obsolete, but parallel to his 'cape-diem' attitude to the world lies a tidal undercurrent of longing for a completely unfamiliar state of being.

On that third visit to him, I didn't want to upset his increasingly delicate temperament by disagreeing with him, but nothing all that terrible has happened to me yet as his prophecy predicted it would. It is sure to, however, for though Rockland is legally and medically insane, I still haven't known him to be mistaken about a single thing in the entirety of the time I have known him. Yes, life will start to go wrong for me right about now.

A Secret Karma

Have you ever heard the Hunky Williams' song You Broke Your Heart II? Sometimes memories occupy a unique, lyrical position in part of you. Sometimes you wish they'd always stay. Sometimes you wish they'd go away.

There are at least two sides to any story worth telling. But everybody loved Ellie. Everybody except for one person. That one person didn't love Ellie: no, she hated Ellie. That one person was Ellie herself. Ellie loved the world but hated herself. Sometimes she curled up in bed and wished that she – her body and the entirety of her being – would leave her alone, cease to exist, become one with the surroundings, become one with the breeze.

And so it goes that I'm not the hero in this chapter, nor am I the villain. The hero of this episode is Ellie and the villain of this chapter is Ellie. Ellie hated Ellie, so Ellie is simultaneously the protagonist and the antihero. It doesn't look quite right down on paper, but I've said it in a couple of ways. At the end of this chapter, the hero will die, slayed by the villain. The hero of this story? She had serious problems, to put it bluntly. The villain? I could hate her, but I don't. There is a secret karma. But Ellie hated Ellie. There are no two ways around it. Me, I'm getting more hysterical by the second. I've got to get something off my chest before we begin properly. I spoke to one of the doctors on my last visit to Rockland. *Apparently*, I'm a schizophrenic, *apparently*.

I can't ascertain why this word was found to be an appropriate label for my condition, but I suppose it's like assigning meaning, or any sort of poetic justice, to an otherwise holistic cityscape. Anyhow, before admitting me entry to see Rockland, the doctor had asked me if I heard voices. I said, *"Yes"*. The doctor nodded and asked a couple more questions, but he must not have understood my meaning. I don't hear unsolicited voices. I mean, sometimes I like to have conversations with my head in my head, but I'm always aware that I'm not actually speaking to someone other than myself. He printed me a certificate officiating my status as a schizophrenic, yet I am reticent to take his words at face value. I'm not *really* a *schizophrenic*.

(No, I'm the sanest man in this body of insane men. The rest of my brain cells have appointed me to talk with you for that reason specifically. I feel better about the diagnosis now; I don't think my mental health disorder will colour my telling of this story in general, but don't say I didn't warn you.)

Right now, it's pissing down out there. God's speciality in the rainy season. Good news for the flowers and good news for the people that want to drink. Good news even for those whose revenue stream is reliant on the phrase 'no news is good news' resounding true. No. Not much has changed. Apparently.

It's 2 A.M. – the Restralardin Lock is deserted at this time of the night. The path running by Restralardin Canal is occasionally inhabited by someone trying to get home or someone trying to find a place to call home; a homeless drunkard, under the cover of a donated umbrella, tries to explain to a woman that he falls into the second category. A cormorant makes a gaudy display of flamboyantly calling to his mate who returns his cry with a fervour tinged by traces of regret, as if her ostentatiousness were put on primarily to humour the listener. A mysterious genderless entity with a backpack walks by. I take a sip of coffee. It tastes bitter; it's probably because of the way that I brewed it this time, but it's as if until now I never appreciated how bitter coffee can taste. I'm usually good at making coffee. Grr. I sigh.

Ellie lives next door to me. Our flats overlook Restralardin Canal. She's twenty-five. I'm nearly the other side of twenty. My reluctance to divulge an exact figure can be attributed to the happenchance that I enjoy the phrase the 'other side' and the fact that I don't know exactly what day I was born, but the attentive reader should know that I believe myself to be nineteen.

Anyway, back to the real heart of this chapter. Where do I start? It's strange that I feel stumped when trying to describe Ellie. It's not as if Ellie is boring or anything like that: no, the reality is a world apart from that. Perhaps I'm having trouble cataloguing her as an individual because humanoids in essence defy categorisation.

Physically, Ellie falls a little short of five-foot-tall and has deep slender red-yellow eyes, eyes that can express certainty but that also articulate doubt (personally I am often quite uncomfortable when confronted with two red-yellow eyes but that is another anecdote that is best relegated to realms of paranoia reserved only for myself). Ellie's red hair runs down to her bra-line. To call her hair 'fuzzy' would be wrong, but it is certainly messy. Somehow you get the feeling that she takes pride in its manifestation. I guess you could say that it is as anarchic as her personality. She is up one minute and down the next. You never can tell with her. I'd say that she would stand out in a crowd due to her unpretentious beauty and her manner of walking: her overall look is jaunty, with indie clothes to match and, though her legs aren't particularly long, she has a real spring to her step.

Anyway, at exactly 2 A.M. the doorbell rings. At first, I don't feel like opening the door and attending to whoever's there at this dim hour. Xinx certainly doesn't either, judging by the way she turns over upon hearing that wretched sound. Though I'm in a good mood, I'm a firm believer in the phrase 'no news is good news'... besides, it might be the police following up in the complaint of a dope-like smell emanating from my garden or, even worse, Sujes followers resolute it is in the interest of greater society to spread the word of their God in the middle of the night. But then curiosity gets the better of me and I walk through the hall and open my front door. It's Ellie. This is Ellie.

At this moment in her life, Ellie is inebriated and spritely yet soggy and groggy. After opening the door, the first thing that I notice about her is that she has pierced her ears so that they can accommodate a circular 'gong' of black metal. I'm not sure whether 'gong' is the correct word for such a fixture, but the studs make her ears look pretty big. They are quite novel to look at, actually. In my mind, they resemble equipment used by aliens from another planet – I can imagine a tiny gold man pressing his relatively small but comparatively large earlobes and thus suddenly shapeshifting into a vulture or teleporting to another planet.

"I haven't slept for three days" are the first words that come out of Ellie's mouth.

"I haven't ever been awake for more than two," I tell her.

"May I come in?" she says, sauntering past me into the living room.

"Coffee?" I ask.

"Coffee..." she says as if that is the first time she has said the word, as if she is pondering its genesis

or wondering if it has a second meaning. *"Black and two sugars. I love your coffee,"* she says. The reason why she almost always mentions her affectionate feelings towards my coffee when she comes around is that I have started working in a coffee shop on weekends to subsidise my sedentary existence and I can add that special magic touch to every cup I serve. Or maybe it's because I have an exotic strain of coffee seed imported from Coza.

"Coming right up. How are you?" I say to her.

"Well... to tell you the truth... I've taken pills that are going to send me to sleep."

"What?" I say, trying to prevent panic from entering my tone.

"I'm going to die. Yes..." she declaims happily yet feebly, *"I'm going to die soon. Soon to you. But soon to you feels like forever to me. Do you know how long I've waited for this day?"*

"Are you drunk?" I say, averting the question.

"Yes, I'm drunk," she says, *"I'm very tipsy. In fact, I think I'm getting tipsier by the second. What does it mean to be in love to you?"* Ellie laughs and hiccups.

"Are you okay?" I ask, continuing my own line of questioning as the kettle finishes boiling.

"Okay? Yeah. I'm better than okay. I'm... I'm in love. What does it mean to be in love to you?" she repeats curiously on the sofa, blinking her eyes as if she were getting accustomed to a new quality of light.

"Well... I guess the phrase 'in love' implies something of a sexual nature. To be in love means you would do anything for that person. I guess

those words put together implies a kind of infatuation, don't you think?" I say.

"I love you," she slurs, and suddenly falls asleep forever, dead as a dream, still as stone. I dial an ambulance, but it's too late. They cannot resuscitate her.

***

In the coming weeks I try to make sense, but cannot, of what could have happened to Ellie. I ruminate & ruminate & ruminate upon it until I wonder if she ever existed at all or if she was just a figment of my (allegedly) schizophrenic imagination.

While I am writing my speech for Ellie's funeral at my desk – though she has a few friends, they are scattered, and none could face writing a memorial address – Xinx puts her hands on my shoulders and massages them.

"You know... it still hasn't crystallised that she's gone... Ellie was someone I didn't think I would outlive. It didn't ever occur to me, so it just doesn't seem real," she says.

"Yeah..." I say, *"well, that's how it is. She was there one second and gone the next."*

"Let me know if you need anything. I'm going to smoke a cigarette. I've felt the urge to for a while," she says.

"Soon I will be dead forever," I tell her, suddenly fuming with righteous indignation.

"Won't we all?" Xinx mouths to me behind my back.

Yes, perhaps there is a secret karma to the mechanisations of reality's heart. Before we were born, we were nothing, and after we die, we will be nothing: this delicate equation balances on the virtuous assumption of every being's essential equality at birth, but there is nothing innately immoral about any five-minute old child. Translating my thoughts into words, it occurs to me, finally, that death is analogous to total non-existence, like how you were – say – five years before you were born, back when your state was characterised by a complete lack of consciousness, of nothingness.

You can say whatever you want about Ellie's death: call it a tragedy, call it good riddance, but there was a secret karma to it, too. Her desire to die was fulfilled, as I hope all her dreams were before her passing. Reflecting upon her life, though, while it was said her eyes sparkled sequences of sacred arithmetic by a male admirer of hers, there too must have been a secret sorrow to her cheerfulness, a hidden heart that she couldn't help but hide. I speak at Ellie's funeral in a few days' time; I will recite an ambitious rhyming poem entitled 'Coffee in Heaven'.

And At The End They All Suck Him

"Why are you having so many wet-dreams lately?" Xinx asks me, after one of her long trips to the library.

"I don't know," I respond.

"Maybe I haven't been keeping you occupied enough. Shall we go to the park?" she asks.

"Okay," I say.

We lock the apartment and walk to the park.

The sprawling cityscape, swollen by the suffocated gargoyles and by the ruins of the war, is overruled by flora, dressed by florescent dreams and thirsty longing for brown in a parka-jacket laden frenzy of love and loathing. The remnants of rain trickle down the trunks of the wooden guardians, where the wood-peckers rasp in unison, demoralizing the partisan priest whose every particle vibrates to the veneer of the unsaved saviour who gloats feverishly about the souls that he has saved while secretly wondering if it is they that have resigned themselves to the prayer of select pawns whose dreams of destroying matter in such a malicious way materialised. The solace of the soaring senses of the dying or buried soldiers by the graveyard whose nicotine pressure harked back to the lines of the ones who stare at the sun silently willing it to kill their eye-sight and my gosh it will not retreat in its serpentine splendour; if you stare at it too long you will start to feel less lucid and the sun will deplete its visionary worldview from sight like a pathetic professor vacantly declaring that it is he that wrote the magna carta and why else should he share the first name of the character in the book. The drinkers make and break plans at the inn where their ideas tumble like ashes from a colossal cigarette reinventing the bleeding devolution of words. We arrive at the park and sit on a bamboo bench

"Tell me," Xinx says.

"It's mating season for the elephants," I say.

"And?" she says, pretending not to be exacerbated with me.

"Elephants are my favourite creatures, other than Atornan..." I hesitate, before saying, *"If I were to construct my own dreams, you would be there in every single one."*

"You are all I've ever wanted, I'd gladly confess," she says. *"You are all I've been cheated out of, more or less."*

"I couldn't love you more," I tell her.

"The feeling's mutual," Xinx says.

My phone buzzes colours in my pocket. I don't pick it up immediately. I suspect it's a call from Kleopatra, who I have only met for about thirty seconds, though I dreamt about her.

"Hello? Is this the man I met in the skatepark?" K asks sheepishly yet insistently.

"Hi. I'm out with my girlfriend," I say.

"I want to meet your girlfriend. Where are you?"

"Wonderwill park. On the bench by the elephant enclosure," I divulge, then wonder why I have.

"I'll see you in ten minutes," K says.

In the meantime, Xinx and I share a conversation about whether I should grow my beard (I decide not to), whether we should take a break (we decide not to), whether ant colonies are capable of living inside elephants (we decided not too), and finally whether we are inside a creature (of course we are) before K arrives.

K is wearing a green onesie, looks terribly slutty and addresses Xinx. *"Hello. Kleopatra. I got your boyfriend's number, not because I fancy him, but because he has nice eyes. It's been a while since I've seen eyes like that. Green, brown and blue. What a combination. What do you make him do to possess such eyes?"*

"Oh. There's a lot of foreplay. Foreplay is constant. We're even flirting now," Xinx threatens vaguely.

I smile. K nods at me. I blink. Xinx kisses me on the eyelid.

"Oh. Okay," K says, hurriedly taking her time with these three syllables. She turns to me. *"I had a dream about you last night,"* she confesses.

"Oh?" I ask, scared about the ramifications of that sentence.

"Yes. We were in the jungle. There was a massive Chinowap on the loose and you had to protect me from him."

"Was it erotic?" Xinx asks dubiously.

"Not very. Mostly just scary... come to think of it, though, we did smooch at the end."

There is a crude silence of fifteen seconds, spasmodically interrupted by the chirping of butterfly-bats.

"Well, this is awkward," K says.

"No, it's foreplay," Xinx says. *"You just haven't been invited."*

I'll remember this half-dead. I think in my head.

"Oh," K whispers to me. *"I like this bit."*

Three elephants approach. One looks aroused.

"They're fat creatures, just about ripe for the consumption trade," Xinx says sinisterly.

"Just like my bosoms," K says to Xinx.

I shrug. I can't remember a jungle dream involving K. It starts pissing down lilac alcohol. I open my mouth to the heavens.

"Oh. You still do that?" K asks.

"I thought I cured him of the habit when we were teenagers," Xinx says.

"Oh, you knew him back then?" K says, over the instrumentation of rain.

"Yeah, yeah, yeah," I say, happily.

I remember the bewildering words of my friend the Buddhist, *"and at the end they all suck him"*, but I realize reality doesn't resemble the teachings of a science text, so corrupted by... oh, shit... the elephants are at it. My two companions look at me, Xinx's silver eyes almost pushing me away and the winterly whorish Kleopatra's sizing me up me like a hunter.

I hum in finite melody, keeping to the rhythm of the elephant's ecstasy as much as I can.

K farts. It smells like her shit does. It's neither a pleasant nor unpleasant scent. It smells a little like an apple and an orange mixed together, almost putrid but lovely.

"No, no, no!" I exclaim.

"Let's go back to the apartment," Xinx says. She sighs. *"All three of us, if you want."*

"Yes. Okay. Sure," Kleopatra says.

"Why not?" I say.

The Apartment-Apocalypse-Chronicles

Xinx unlocks the door. Immediately we are both taken aback. The apartment looks absurdly abhorrent. Something has gone deeply awry. An army of ants inhabits the artichoke basket which, once abundant with artichokes, is abound with an abysmal autopsy of artichoke shells.

"That's it, then. We must go absolutely abstentious," I say.

Something else is missing but I can't figure out what it is. How did the ants acquire access to the apartment? What is answerable for this?

"Oh... it's not that bad. You can just account for the fact that I don't particularly like artichokes and act accordingly," Kleopatra says.

I smile. Xinx does too.

"Well, I don't want to kill them. Let's just tempt them outside by carrying the artichoke basket outside," Xinx says.

"They're in the artichoke basket," I try to explain.

"What if there are more ants outside?" K asks fearfully.

"I guess they'll meet their maker," Xinx replies.

Xinx picks up the artichoke basket and takes it outside to the balcony, where she drops it & stares out at the sky.

"Holy shit. Holy shit," Xinx says, fixated on the sky.

"What?" I ask.

"You'll have to come and see this," Xinx says.

"Fuck. Fuck. Let's go," K says to me, excitedly.

K & I go out to the balcony. The sky is ablaze with water. There is lightning everywhere. Soaring pyramid-shaped meteors are wed to chariots without anyone on them. Snow is pouring down. Things have really changed in the past minute.

"Woah... this must be the apocalypse," I say.

"Shit!" K twitches. "Let's get inside."

K and I go inside, but Xinx just stands there, ogling at the scene.

"It's so..." Xinx begins, "so.... so..."

Then, suddenly, without warning, just like that, a soaring pyramid meteor wed to a chariot heads straight for her beautiful half-azure-half-black body.

"XINX! XINX!" I shout.

Shit! Shit! The pyramid meteor wed to a chariot beheads Xinx and crashes into the door. Xinx's blood splatters everywhere. She is dead.

"Oh my god!" Kleopatra cries, uselessly.

I'm howling now. "XINX. XINX. XINX..." I shout desperately, as if somehow repeating her name will resuscitate her soul from the reservoir of memory.

"Oh my god," says K.

"Crap. Crap. Crap," I say.

"Oh my god," says K.

"Shit. Shit. Shit," I say.

"Oh my god." K looks horrified, disgusted and frightened.

"Say something else, you fucking idiot," I say, "That's my girlfriend."

"Shit. Shit. I forgot to warn you," K says with the air of a politician about to deliver an apology. *"Things like this tend to happen when you're with me."*

"Huh?" I say.

"I hack the oversoul…" she says. *"There can be the occasional brief malfunction."*

"Bring Xinx back from the dead, then. Fuck. Fuck. Shit. Shit. Life seems to be one big catastrophe since I met you," I reply, livid but trying to contain my anger for an unknown reason.

"You'll have time to think about that," K replies.

"What, for the rest of my life?!" I ask, angrily.

"No, after we fuck," K says.

If the apartment-apocalypse-chronicles feels stiflingly short or incomplete, it's because I feel such a range of emotions following Xinx's decapitation. Even committing what I have to paper makes me feel nauseous as hell. In summary, what happens afterwards is the following: a mail man on a megaphone in the vicinity orders everyone to *"GET INSIDE OR STAY INSIDE"*; the pyramids brided to chariots are shot down using military technology; the skies mysteriously resume service as normal; and Kleopatra comforts me in my grief, ending up my close confidant & staying with me in the apartment.

And, you may have already guessed, two weeks after the Xinx-decapitation-apocalypse, K & I form a pact as friends, as lovers, as seekers of salvation. We will locate Xinx's soul together and fuck in the meantime.

God's Pretty Game of Grotesque Puppets

THE MOTHER OF INFINITY

I'll Die A Dreamer But I Adore A Lot Of Alliteration

I was the reclusive scientist-guitarist-painter who climbed skies in his art. K was the elusive femme fatale who started my heart.

When my tongue made her come, she howled *"God's your mother!"* I laughed at first, but then I thought about what K had said.

It started out simple: a preliminary pact with the oversoul, one of the many bargains we made with God. We lived together and died together and lived together and here we are.

In the missionary position, K & I entwine on the cliff.

Before we jump to our physical death, we recite from memory a long factual formula that expresses something akin to the following: *"God is my mother. Since God is my mother, I am evolved from God. Since I am evolved from God, God is not dead. When my physical body dies in the material world, I will again become a foetus in God's womb.
___+___= so therefore ___=___."*

Then we jump through this world into another.

"Ladies and gentlemen, what you are currently hearing is not the voice of god."

52,535,513 French fireflies freeze in fear,
9,423 Cambodian cashiers clutch their ears
And an eighth of the snakes in the Sahara gaze at the sky.

"This is neither the heart of the apocalypse, nor the start of an advertisement."

54,424 sleeping squirrels squeak in their sleep,
723 protestant preachers pinch their left cheek
And almost all the babies in Babylon begin to cry.

"This is neither a mutation of your imagination, nor a flirtation with your salvation."

97,425 startled shopkeepers shut up shop,
142 Croatian contortionists call the cops
And a herd of hippopotamuses howl at the heavens.

"With that said, my name is Gabriel and I am here to save you all. Listen carefully and don't panic."

103,353 psychiatrists piss in their pants,
45,425 Latvian lovers loop hands
And someone named Sam picks his nose somewhere in Devon.

The mysterious voice is silent for seven seconds, and then a very strange but very beautiful song plays.

1,020,220 turtles tumble into a trance,
5456 Turkish twins begin to dance
And one tenth of all creatures spontaneously orgasm.

"I hope you enjoyed that as much as I did. Take it as a small token of my peaceful intentions."

143,353 synchronised swimmers smile,
1,532 joyful judges adjourn a trial
And a platoon of pensioners shoot the sky to thank him.

"I should preface by stressing the importance of not contorting this message."

243,214 Finnish fingers finger a cigarette,
942 broken stockbrokers break a sweat
And seven squads of secret servicemen simultaneously sigh.

"Have I contorted this message by stressing the importance of this preface?"

153,241 blue butterflies flutter to a flower,
67 scared scientists scour a meteor shower
And a fistful of fiery-thighed lovers fall into the other's eyes.

"Well, I did my best, and I guess that I successfully stressed the blessed mess of expression."

53,432 badly bent backs in Bangkok straighten,
366 certifiably sane Cypriotes shout 'Satan'
And a news reporter reports he has nearly nothing to say.

"But I shall not speak in tongues. I am Gabriel and I am here to save you all. Listen carefully and don't panic."

The mysterious voice is silent for seven seconds, and then a very strange but very beautiful song plays.

THE MOTHER OF INFINITY

The Suicide Sunlight

The sentimental, sentient sense of an impending doom hangs heavy over the harbour of dreams tonight. A lonely couple of fishing boats are anchored to your right, swaying violently with the unbridled pull of the tide, which could climax into a deafening crescendo at any point. The horizon is a heroic haze of two adjacent planets. Photograph it and your camera will melt. Such equipment is not permitted here anyway, for the idea of freezing any soul forever is sacrilegious. Close but not within eyesight, a parrot perches on a pirate's panama on a zeppelin that has just landed, serenading itself torpidly with a sea shanty designed to lull the listener to sleep with its onomatopoeia. You are sitting close enough to read a rusty metal sign by a solitary abandoned market stand where they sell fresh fruit and vegan vegetables to the deities during the day; it proclaims: Welcome to Hunfora!

A shambolic seaside purity sweeps through the surroundings, continually conquering the air with the aroma of a nomad nothing. Imagine, if you will, that the ability to smell is the only sensory consciousness your being possesses, and that this non-entity of a scent is all you will ever experience. And – yeah! that's it: the only existing moment will occur the instant you understand the meaning of this paragraph and – there! bam! – you are death itself and have no present, past or future!

But don't worry, friend: now a soft spray sprinkles the moonlit evening beach and hydrates your face. On top of that, you can hear the ominous rumble of thunder, which is almost definitely one of God's generous gifts to Gaea and perhaps represents a consecrated projection of His grumpy disposition or hallowed horniness.

The sand is adorned with footprints which will dissipate into a uniform flatness, irrespective of the level of urgency with which their architect crafted them. An apparently ownerless Cocker Spaniel vigorously digs a hole, which is now surprisingly deep, and sits in it. With some care, a birdwatcher expresses her barely containable jubilance at the presence of a Crested Ibis perched on the rocks with its bald red head by taking a selfie with the rare bird; the photograph appears in Global Birdwatcher some five months later.

Meanwhile, the suicide sunlight has finally committed to a previously dormant streak of nihilism and abandoned the area, leaving only a faint trace of its heated soliloquy. Streetlights illuminate the fountain in the centre of the nearby square, which is inanimate but for the passage of an occasional tourist. The heroes of our story sit hand-in-hand on the edge of the pier.

The boy and girl are so unambiguously hip yet Neolithic you might vainly and in vein try to delude yourself they remind you of your former self. Disillusioned with the world in the sanguine way that only teenagers can be, their mouths do not care for the exhausted cornucopia of civilization's clichéd conversational topics. They speak sentimentally in an accented patois about a faraway world. Though they have known each other since they were in their early twenties, they are thirteen and fifteen.

"Déjà…" the girl whispers wistfully.

"Ha! Ya. Been shorter than a barfly's thigh," the boy replies, followed by a sigh, which within you gives rise to the sense that he stands on the fence as to whether he should try to exorcise the demons he can't disguise.

"I yearn for... I don't know," she says.

"Long for a song?" he asks.

"An imperfect melody," she states absentmindedly, and you know instinctively just what she means.

Below their feet, the docks and water fight, and in the local pub the old soul singers sing a song until the soul emerges light. The boy hums along after recognising the song's mathematical paradox. The girl covers her ears in mock disdain. They shouldn't be here. But they are. For now.

Conventional Sense Of The Word

Through modifications in the coding of reality, we were able to give ourselves average-sized brains and startling good looks. In the mist of our third life, we lived in a highly populated world that became barren because Adolf Hitler & Leonard Cohen were stillborn. Nowadays, K & I make ends meet by sketching imaginary worlds: paradises and places of torment. In certain states of mind, we can enter these paradigms. Our existence is improved by the lifetime supply of illegal communist drugs that we acquired from a stranger at the real crossroads.

Kleopatra is not beautiful in the conventional sense of the word, but in a way that seems to blur your expectation of beauty. She is, without a doubt, the prettiest woman I have ever seen.

My stupendous friend shyly strips as 'Stardust' plays.
Her breasts are mammoth, and her eyes are purple haze.
I thank the watching God above for all visible love.
She purses her lips and undoes my zip through her glove.
Her tongue darts back and forth up my growing erection.
And then her lips give it a sentimental blowing inspection.
She mounts me, we kiss blissfully, and we fuck forever.
In my blinded mind your bodies are still stuck together.

"My foe, each of my tits are unspeaking accomplices in your authorial act," she says.

Together, we fall into dreamless sleep in each other's arms, like solipsists tied to a crucifix.

It's early January and snow has blossomed unexpectedly like a pimple on the centre of your face. We go the woods. There is a deep incline at their entrance, an almost mountainous knoll. As I hold hands with K and we skip down the snow-lit hill, our coupled footprints fallen fragments of our laughing feet and the moon the only uncomplicated witness to the dawn of our midnight tryst, I imagine for a moment that we are the last people alive, that the internal rhythm of our legs is the sole human testament to the glorious accident of nature, that the trees are secret ornaments to the aimlessness of our pilgrimage, that the firmaments have translated the burden of their restlessness into the premonition of a paradise we were never meant to find. At the bottom we roll around a bit beneath the great white woods and make a baby snowman. We stand back to observe our sentimentality and K replaces her ownership of my hand with that of a now erect knob. We fuck there, as if to eternalise the fragility of our perfect monument. Once I forget everything, it's beautiful for many moments.

There are those who see the God above who never knew the pain of bliss.
And those like me who dream of love with one like you on nights like this.

An Account of The President's Daily Address

As is our custom, we turn on the television at 9 P.M. to watch the President's daily address. The President is a greying, muscular figure. He wears a tight white t-shirt, sits at a desk and speaks directly into the camera.

"God bless you for turning on the television set," the President stutters likeably.

"God bless me for staying alive to talk to you," the President chuckles.

"It's all just a show! Have a laugh! Create things! You may no sooner know me than your Great Uncle who died in the forty-two years of the God War!" The President flexes his biceps at the camera and grins.

The President looks like he has just completed a series of triathlons. He is wearing red shorts. He is sweating heavily. I imagine I can hear his swearing braincells blaspheme their ruler.

"So here I am. Halfway between life and death. A foot in the grave and an earlobe in the heavens. Am I happy? I'm happy if you're happy," The President says. *"May God bless the mess of expression. I remember the time my dad told me to shut the door because the birds were talking to him via telepathy. I was seven and I didn't know what telepathy was but come to think of it neither did he."* The President laughs. *"Here are fifteen Peruvian parrots singing a song,"* he smiles.

A fiendish faction of Peruvian parrots sing a song:

*"A bird slurred a song of sorrow he borrowed from tomorrow's awe.
A cat purred along as she heard the third's absurd swoop and soar.
It's half of infinity squared, a shared laugh, a prayer*

*to time's shore.
The chords run towards the sun and climb the
stairs to rhyme's door.
Nature's law dictates fate creates a gate before you
explore the core.
And it's a hurricane of cocaine in chains as
champagne raindrops pour.
But words can't explain the pain of bliss of the
refrain's sublime score.*

*Picture this volcano where earthly ecstasy loads
To return her dreams in a burning stream that flows
Into the snow forest where mercy grows like a rose
And algebraic angels compose acid odes in a doze,
Painting the paradigm of a paradise no saint knows
Where death has no foes and the hurricane sows
The codes of the unknown into celestial rainbows
As the lone saxophone blows and desire explodes."*

Geez, a man in an apartment block in Queens thinks, *they sing it like fucking virtuosos.* He races out of his living room and sprints to Marty's guitars. He buys a guitar, takes it to a bench outside the shop and starts to play. *He's* a fucking virtuoso. The beauty of the parrot's song taught him how to play guitar like a fucking virtuoso. It was acid. Over time a crowd of some fifty people gathers to watch him jam. After being signed to Distrokid records by a bystander, he will write a song called *'Bird Volcano Event'* and it will reach the top of the charts in Oklahoma. A distant cousin of mine will give me the chip and it will be on the Music Maker in our room.

In our room, there is an ashtray, condoms, notebooks, a music maker, a computer and a stash of hashish. I always sleep on the left side of the bed and K on the right. I don't know why it's this way; it has always been so: a fact, like the blueness of the sky or the traversable nature of the multiverse. The rigidness of our sleeping positions seems to me to be an indication that we are aware of our own mortality and the finite nature of our stay in the physical plane, even if heaven is made of flesh.

We have a Star-Roof and often lie in bed gazing at the stars. I observe my visible universe and wonder whether my diaries will one day be translated into an alien language. I'm no mathematician but the odds of this are not high. If infinity is real, though, this sentence has been written many times. But I suppose that infinity is difficult to contemplate unless you are god. Sometimes I find it hard to contemplate even my own life. For people like me, infinity is a fairy tale. Somehow, I imagine that infinity is something that can only be experienced by a woman.

I can still remember meeting K by the skatepark & thinking she was beautiful & there being a clash between our two minds but our bodies digging each other and two months later telling her *"suck me senseless and I'll fuck you to infinity"* stoned out of my mind after realizing my penis is my head and it dawning on me that is mind and body and soul. Then, we fucked a sublime five years & giggled on rich hash brownies & felt each other & drank coffee in Hapino & died of old age & went back all the way with modifications in our DNA half in an attempt to find Xinx & half in an attempt to get as much pleasure as possible & were reborn one block away from each other & charmed our parents with lies & then had sex as seven and nine-year-old kids. It felt so right because we were not aware that we had programmed the universe to orchestrate itself such that this happened.

An Omen Of A Direction Home

Now K and I are spooning and looking at the stars.

"I believe in first love," K says.

"You may be my last love," I reply solemnly. *"I want to stargaze to an infinity not possible with the number of atoms in my eyes."*

"Next time round?"

I shake my head. *"I hope there won't be a next time we're here. We said it would be the last time last time."*

"Let's get to heaven."

"I want to finally find Xinx," I say. *"I don't particularly enjoy your cooking, and I don't want all this universe traversing, or hopping, or whatever you want to call it, to be for nothing."*

Five minutes later, I fall asleep and in the fiction of night I dream I am talking to Bob Dylan. We are sitting on my grandparents' swing in a swanky apartment in Reading town centre. My Grandma worked as a postwoman and my Grandad worked in the railway industry. Bob Dylan is in a Hawaiian t-shirt and looks dapper, his hair dyed blonde and every wrinkle a document of the wisdom of age.

"I believe in love at first sight," Dylan says. *"We're hyper intelligent creatures. I remember seeing Johanna for the first time. It felt as if I had known her all my life, but she still embodied all the ancient mysteries that make life so curious. One gaze into the cryptic depths of her brown eyes was enough to make me re-evaluate my entire existence. But I was shy and barely spoke to Johanna. Some mysteries are best left unexplored or left until later life."*

The dream, almost an omen of a direction home, fades to purple. When I wake up the next day, I think of the Johanna I knew. But I was shy and barely spoke to Johanna. I realize these are the exact words Dylan used so I figure my brain made that dream up, unlike other dreams I have had where there was a real sense of the presence of the other.

The next day, something crackles through the letterbox. It's a handwritten note that reads: *Do not trust the government. The government is corrupt. Words fail like snails.*

I want to throw it away, but K takes it to be framed and now it's in our bathroom, of all places. I smile at it sometimes as I relieve myself but always a bit begrudgingly because frankly, I find it depressing and if comedy is its aim it fails too. It's handwritten, though, so it's pretty cool, I reason. I don't necessarily admire the President, but to call him a fascist is perhaps to take things a little too far.

As we make beans on toast and brew coffee, K and I talk about the prospect of revolution.

"… and then they came for me – and there was no one left to speak for me," I lecture, without wanting to appear as if I'm lecturing.

"Yes, but who have they come for?" K asks.

"I don't know, but just because I don't know doesn't mean it hasn't happened. Consider the situation with the police and that lady down the road who disappeared with them a month ago, for example…" I reply.

"That's the second time you've brought it up this week and I still don't know why she's not around," K says. *"What isn't free about this place, though?"*

"The press isn't free. The press never has been free. Like all human enterprise it is chained to itself. We're not allowed to do anything to harm others. And this society's obsessed with heaven. I bet soon we'll be building a factory of well-fed microorganisms so that more souls can get to heaven," I guess.

"Not a bad idea. Still, maybe that note meant nothing. It's a piece of art, or at least I thought it was."

There is a silence that accentuates the normality of the situation.

"Do you want to go out tonight?" I ask.

"Let's go to the circus and look for Xinx," K says. *"She may not be as you remember her, but she will certainly be humanoid."*

"Not a bad idea," I reply.

The morning unfolds like this: Kleopatra watches Polarised Morning while I sketch alien dinosaurs & look up at the television occasionally. We go on the Neon Subway to see the circus. There is nothing exceptional about the journey other than the fact that a man in sunglasses stares at K. I look at him inquiringly, he looks at me contemptuously & then the man in sunglasses looks back at K almost angrily.

At the circus the jugglers are the clowns and one rides a unicycle as others throw raspberry pies at him. That clown looks a lot like me, I think. He is a bit fatter than me, but I feel like eating a raspberry pie and if I were him, I would try to catch them with my mouth. I survey the tent but there are no other raspberry pies to be seen. I blink nervously and sink in my seat; I feel somewhat agitated by the lack of raspberry pies for sale. I'm not addicted to any kind of food, but almost everyone would be happier if they gave us free raspberry pies at the circus. I voice this thought to K, who nods her head in a way that makes me think I am going mad.

The next day, I go to work and get a promotion. This surprises me. I don't think I am a particularly good employee, but my sweat-drenched boss tells me otherwise, patting me on the head.

"You're just what this company needs," my boss says *"You have some fucking fantastic ideas."*

It is not particularly like my boss to swear or sweat, so I am a bit alarmed. After a millisecond of reflection on his comment, I realise that I mentioned the circus and raspberry pies to Marcus.

"Thanks a lot," I say. *"I'll take my girlfriend to the circus to celebrate. We had an enjoyable time last night, but we will bring our own raspberry pie."*

"Fucking fantastic!" he says enthusiastically. *"A circus and half of a raspberry pie. Fucking fantastic."*

"A new catch phrase?" I ask.

"No, I've been told that people find me a little uptight, so I've been trying to expand my vocabulary." My boss strokes his stubble pensively. *"What do you say we go to the Sepulchre after work for a few drinks?"*

The Sepulchre is a modern metropolis, but by the time you receive this it will be ancient. The politicians and writers chat there, drinking and laughing on the pavilion. They are carefree, arrogant in their taste yet artless in the enterprise of living. The Neon Subway cars race to the Sepulchre. Although there is seemingly not a lot that they can get wrong, the drivers are crazy. They accelerate to unnecessary speeds and then break ridiculously. I once had ambitions to work as one but after a background check my application was rejected.

On the Neon Subway, my boss puts his work clothes into a bag, donning a denim jacket over his shirt and ostentatiously bright blue jeans over his suit trousers. I yell over the subway sound that I once owned a pair of ostentatiously blue jeans like that, but my girlfriend told me to throw them out.

He nods gravely and doesn't say a word. I feel a little bit stoned, both by his response and my forthrightness in having the nerve to tell him that.

"There will be an accident on the train, and we will narrowly avoid a tragedy," he suddenly says solemnly.

"Great," I say sardonically, and next thing you know it, our train and another train collide, my boss and I hit heads, and the scene plunges into darkness.

A Hospital Admission

I dream I am speeding down Route 42. I look to my left. Rockland is driving, wearing aviator sunglasses. He explains his practice of analysing of license plates.

"You pick any random license plate and figure out what it means to you."

"Can you give me an example?" I ask him.

"See that one. BSTPL8. BullShit Troubles People who Look like the number '8'. I can deduct from that plate that you shouldn't bullshit people with stereotypically attractive forms. License plates can be read in more than one way, too: for example, if you read it as Be Sexually Transmitted, Period's L8, then it's sort of a message that you should act a little more sexually infectious because your period is late," Rockland says. *"I don't know. It could mean any number of things. It's best to analyse, if you can, one license plate every five seconds. It's kind of a word-association game. Go ahead: you try."*

I do, finding that Dwarves Know the Future if they're Above the Age of 8, Speeding Motorcycles Suggest Childish H8, Love Is Louisiana With Crayfish 1 (… WON?!).

"Does '1' mean I have won something?" I ask Rockland.

"Could be. Who knows?" Rockland tries, and fails, to hide his annoyance by feigning amusement – this is clearly not how he plays the license plate game. *"We can the play the license plate game however we want to. There are really no winners or losers. But if you think you've won, you've won. The next licence plate you look at, double its significance."*

The next license plate I look at is 'RIPXBY3'. I calculate. Rockland Iam Percival Xinx Befaim

Yabtosh 3, the amount of times those two have had sex. Could be. Who knows? Do I have to double its random significance as Rockland says? Is Rockland the master-controller of destiny itself?

I dream I am watching Xinx on a carousel. She is on a huge metal frog. Round & round & round she goes. On the fourth rotation I notice that she is wearing a gold crown. I wave to her when I think she notices me, but she averts my gaze. She looks like she is really enjoying herself.

A strange sensation envelops me. It is as if I am not me but someone else. I remember only the essential details of my life, as if I have only been provided with a mere summary of my own existence. I try to picture K but cannot. Then I realise that I *am* K and in my mind's eye I see an amber line connecting our souls to form one being. But that state of consciousness only lasts a second and as I wake up in a hospital bed the memories that comprise my life flood back to me. I look to my left and see my boss unconscious in another bed, tucked up & resting peacefully but looking ten years older than I remember him. I look to my right and see K gazing out a window in a leather jacket and velvet jeans, a combination that I have never seen before.

I grunt and she turns.

"*Hello!*" K says.

"Hello. Where are we?"

"*Saint Chads. I was wondering when you were going to wake up. They said you were going to wake up, but they wouldn't tell me when.*"

"I'm as awake as I ever was. I'm okay. How long was I out?"

"A good two hours. I'm glad you're okay. They said you lost several thousand brain cells but that's hardly any. Did you feel that thing too?" K touches her ear ponderously. I feel slightly cross at her, but I don't know why.

"What does 'thing' mean?" I ask.

She doesn't laugh, only narrows her eyes slightly, looking at me as if I must know what she is talking about. I pretend to gather my lackadaisical thoughts together, but I do know what she is talking about.

"Oh, that," I say. *"Yes, in the unknown between the coma and death, I felt I almost became you."* It truly looks sensationally sarcastic written down, but I meant what I said.

"I had that feeling about you too, but I can't explain it. It wasn't sexual, but it felt as if our souls were interweaving." It's another corny line but this is how it felt and, as I've already pointed out, this is a love story, a love story with an ending.

"How was that?" I ask.

"I was as light as a feather when it happened but when it passed, I could see how tiny my burden is." She laughs that beautiful laugh of hers and I can tell she is just teasing me.

"Death doesn't seem quite as romantic after you die," I tell her, thinking momentarily of Xinx.

"No one but God can live forever, I guess." She smiles almost regretfully. *"The President's daily address is about to begin."*

Kleopatra picks up a remote from the bedside table and flicks the television on. Her eyes hopefully observe my boss, who she has met once before, but my boss remains motionless.

After a commercial for cancer featuring an elderly man with a strikingly deep voice, the President appears. He is dressed in black, a colour that he sometimes uses to denote the fact that he is going to be talking about something serious.

"I am nothing but a listener," the President says resignedly. *"My ideas are not a manifestation of my own talent but a symptom of the world around me,"* he ventures, ever so hesitantly.

"The world woke my heart when I heard about the accident today in the subway, in which two brains – trains, should I say – collided..." the President pauses for theatrical effect (there are rumours that he attended drama school as a delinquent) *"... but then I was told that nobody on either train died!"* he exclaims happily.

"Thank the heavens, I thought to myself, but then I wondered whether the heavens would be so exultant. The population of heaven, if heaven exists, surely fluctuates depending on whether people die or not. If no one dies, heaven would be rendered infertile," he speculates thoughtfully.

"Then, I thought about all the animals, spirits and even bacteria that own their own consciousness. I realised that if every creature heeds God's call to accept that a day will fall when all those great and all those small shall crawl in thrall to heaven's storm in lines they formed, well, I guess it wouldn't be Planet Earth. After composing this nihilistic thought within the cerebral regions of my being, I realised that I had made my mind up properly for once. As of early next year, we will build a plant in which micro-organisms feed upon tasty food and die. Since we now know microorganisms have consciousness, we can venture the guess that some of their souls will ascend to heaven. Believe you me, friends, I already have some ethical qualms

about this endeavour so we shall have a debate on it in two weeks' time. God night and Good bless!" he proclaims.

The camera zooms out and the television starts to play a documentary about Abraham Lincoln, one of my old fixations, but I don't care. I'm fuming inside. I'll watch it on catch-up. I want to talk for a bit & then have angry sex. I shake my head and Kleopatra flicks the television off.

"I don't like anything about what the President said," I say, *"The micro-organism factory was originally Rockland's idea, influenced by my attitude towards living & dying. Did you tell anyone about the factory?"*

"No. Why would I tell anyone? Besides, he said they wanted to build a plant. A plant isn't a factory," K responds, almost defensively.

"They're pretty much synonyms," I tell her.

"Great minds think alike," she says challengingly.

I shoot her a look that says everything I can't be bothered to say and, crestfallen, it dawns on me that there is absolutely nowhere to have angry sex in a hospital.

"I feel like a cigarette," I say.

"I feel like a cigarette," my boss parrots me in his sleep. *"A ciggy - fan-fucking-tastic!"* He rolls over and starts to snore loudly.

"That'll probably be it from him for a while. I bought some cigarettes because I thought you might want one." Kleopatra hands me a cigarette. Smoking is against the rules in hospital, but most people feel that 'guideline' to be ambiguous in its wording [*'you may smoke a cigarette outside'*]. I put the cigarette

in my mouth and K lights it. I inhale deeply and exhale happily, breathing a satisfied sigh.

"Thanks," I say. *"By the way, I realised that the micro-organism factory was a bad idea the second the President spoke it."*

"A remarkable coincidence. Why is that?"

"The actions of each organism are a product of circumstance. It is the events that happen before and after our birth that determine our character and actions. Though understanding of cause and effect is instinctive, only when you gain self-consciousness are you truly responsible for what you do. Even then, your destiny is already preordained because as there are so many versions of infinity it is impossibly likely that there are people who look exactly like us with the exact same history as us having this conversation right now."

"So?" K says.

"You are not me, but if I were you, I'd be you. Heaven is a lottery," I tell her.

"That sounds more like an opinion than a fact."

"That's because it is," I continue. *"I am not my opinions, but I accept that my opinions are a direct consequence of the events that happened before and after my birth."*

"Of course. I think that was the President's point. The causation of everything was the Great Beginning and everything that follows it is a result of the patterns in its formation."

The President said nothing of the sort, but this is a good point, so I nod. *"I just don't think those micro-organisms would have enough free will to determine their spiritual destinations. Besides, I expect I have killed millions, if not billions, of tiny creatures throughout my existence. Does that make me a bad person? To hell with it. There's no hell and there might not be a heaven."*

"Don't speak about that here," K says sternly. "Someone might come in."

I often anger K, sometimes on purpose, for doing and saying things that most people might find deranged or unacceptable, and today is a day that I want to enrage K, because there is absolutely nowhere to have angry sex in a hospital.

"What, chutney? Chutney makes a cat like me happy. We can speak about that here," my boss says reassuringly.

"I forgot to tell you – your boss is on a drug that makes him want to speak in his sleep," K informs me.

"Put a ring on it, baby – pesticide!" he says. My boss' playful instruction, obviously directed towards K, brings me back to reality.

"Shouldn't we call a nurse?" I wonder.

"I am a nurse," K responds.

By ancient standards K is a nurse but I do not think she is qualified to deal with every medical situation.

"Shouldn't we call a nurse?" I wonder, again.

K reluctantly presses the button that summons a nurse who changes the course of my career forever (irreversibly, just like that, forever).

Truthfully, I have never been physically attracted to nurses. This may be because I don't like hospitals: I have always had an aversion towards the medical profession's clinical practice. But that is a discourse best saved for another book, one which I would take no joy in writing and so which shall never see the light of day

A nurse called Isabella enters the room a short second after K presses the button. Isabella nods at K and then at me. Her voice is soft yet confrontational.

"I read your medical notes," she says, addressing me but looking out the window distractedly.

I do not know what to say to this, so I say nothing.

"A page turner?" K says feistily.

Isabella eyes K sulkily and then turns back to me. *"Not exactly. There was only one page. Did you know that you were an IVF baby?"* Isabella asks.

I say nothing. I didn't know that I was an IVF baby. I don't know what to think.

"I was an IVF baby, too…" Isabella says, as if to make me feel better about the fact.

Great, I think, I am in good company. I shrug, bewildered by this new knowledge.

"Good to know, I guess," I say.

"Being an IVF baby means that you were wanted. Don't we all want to be wanted?"

"Sure," I say.

"I'll tell you one thing – this life is a page turner," Isabella says resolutely.

"It depends on who you are. Being a micro-organism means you don't get to have an enjoyable time," I say. I know that the nurse watched the President's address, because it is protocol that all those with jobs watch him speak.

"Are you a micro-organism?" Isabella asks, sarcasm glued to every syllable like a badly

constructed model aeroplane. *"Besides, everyone is the same at birth."*

This shakes me. Suddenly I wonder if everyone can hear what I say. It is paranoid, but I wonder if people are listening to me think.

"I don't care what you say; this life is a page-turner," my boss adds helpfully.

"He will regain consciousness in less than two minutes. People on that drug say, 'I don't care what you say' when they are about to become conscious," Isabella informs us, even more helpfully.

"Really?" K asks, spite permeating her voice for no apparent reason.

"Have we met before? I didn't warm to you immediately because I felt like I have encountered you before…" Isabella trails off.

"I don't know and frankly I don't care," K states.

At this, part of me wonders whether K is jealous of the nurse, who thinking about would be rather attractive if we were somewhere else and she was dressed differently.

"Touché," Isabella says.

"May we leave?" I ask.

"Sure; I thought you might want to remain here until Dave wakes up." It is weird hearing his name. I never think of him as Dave; I always think of him as my boss.

"Hey presto! Cominatcha' like a bearded beaver on a bad beard day," my boss quietly shouts.

"Hooray!" K exclaims. *"Dramatic like magic."*

"I thought it was you. I always knew you were here," says my boss

"Yes. I suppose you can remember me from ACJD?" K asks quite keenly, like a fan addressing a pop star.

"That sounds about right. About then. Yeah, that was nice."

"You featured in my diary." K almost audibly blushes.

At this, part of me begins to feel jealous of my boss, who thinking about it could be rather attractive if we were somewhere else and if he were dressed differently.

"I'm flattered; fuck small talk. How did you describe me?" My boss itches at his nose.

"A man that would be rather attractive if he were dressed differently," K says.

I trip out. I wonder if I died and everyone became me. Perhaps the astute reader and dumbass alike will notice that something strange is going on. I think of *"take what you have gathered from coincidence"*, a Bob Dylan line that I wanted to have tattooed on my average sized hands but was advised by those close to me not to [I still aspired to become a subway driver, then, and they said it wouldn't reflect well on me (and my 'kind nature', as one relative put it)].

A good writer should be a master of dialogue, but alas, I am not, for even I would admit I am not the smartest one in the universe, nor the second, nor the third, and so on and so on to an almost infinite number. This dialogue is happening fast, and my mind is working slow, so I apologise to the dumbass who has by now forgotten where we are, and I apologise to the astute reader whose time is more valuable than a dime a second.

"If that's who I am to you, so be it," my boss says.

"Sorry to interrupt, but can I get you three coffees? This is by far the longest scene in the book, and the longer the better," Isabella says, winking at K.

"I'm okay, thank you," K says.

"Me two," my boss replies.

"No. Funny, two trains colliding; you couldn't make it up," I say.

"I wonder why the President didn't even apologise. This place is pretty poorly designed," my boss says, expert on engineering that he is. My boss was unconscious for the President's speech. I get worried. I hazard the guess that my mind cannot work fast enough to create the environment. I hazard the guess this might be a simulation, like I read about in a trashy magazine.

"I wonder," Isabella says wistfully.

"Do they read this heaven?" K asks to no one in particular.

A cat appears out of nowhere and sits on K's lap.

"I... I don't know," says the cat who appeared out of nowhere. *"We are on Planet Earth."*

"We know," K says. She does not like to be reminded of the obvious.

The cat licks her lips. *"Once you're on Planet Earth, you cannot return to where you came from. But this doesn't make me too sad, because some might say it is paradise itself. It could not function without its flaws, for Planet Earth is perfect because it is imperfect. It is a place filled with anger and lust, for at some point in everyone's life they learn they can never escape. When we bleed, we bleed cacophonical colours. When we cry, we cry tears of fury."*

"Who are you?" I ask, bewildered.

"I am Cat," says Cat. She looks straight into my eyes & purrs.

If you're looking for a meaning, you're in the wrong place. I'm just writing down what happened to me. How naïve I was when I began writing this story. How bitter I have become as the end approaches.

If you want to know the facts, I didn't go home with K after the hospital. She left with my boss. I suppose there is a reason that he is my boss, but I don't mean to make light of it. I still remember Xinx very fondly. The Cat became my friend and came home with me. We talk sometimes, but she gets bored of me easily, for I am not as intelligent as she is and some might consider me a dull person.

"Are we bacteria inside an organism?" I ask Cat.

Cat opens and closes her mouth to indicate that she is not sure.

"I don't mind if we are," I say.

Cat shakes her head.

"I'm sorry," she says.

"What for?"

"I... I don't know."

"Well, if you're sorry, then I'm sorry, too."

Thousands of light years away a giant red man dies.

"I had to do it," says Cat.

"I know, Cat; I know."

"I miss my mother – the smell of her – her movements so graceful I cannot completely replicate them in my memory."

"Yes. I miss my mother too. Still, we might see our mothers again."

"I suppose. I suppose so," Cat says.

She shakes her head. I feel like asking her whether this means we are not going to heaven, but I decide against it. She reads my mind, though I have learnt that she was exaggerating the truth when she said she was God.

"You'll have to wait and see," Cat says.

"Yes, I guess I'll have to wait and see."

"May I have some tuna?" Cat licks her lips and this story ends and the rest is a version of infinity. You couldn't make it up. Or you could make it up, but you'd have to be kind of mad.

My Heart Is A Garden Of Butterflies

In this Universe, I am a half-Irish Roman Catholic heathen. I was born in London, England at the end of the twentieth century. From the age of seven to thirteen, I lived in the Big Easy: New Orleans, Louisiana, USA, Planet Earth. My family had moved to NOLA on account of my father getting an insurance job there.

In this world, Aerith was the first girl I ever thought I had a crush on. We used to be close friends. She had sandy hair, slightly tanned skin, brown eyes and was beautiful in every respect. Aerith's voice was as harmonic as a prodigy harmonicist playing her own Theme Song. Like most of my New Orleanian peers, she had a big old southern drawl. She was a noble person who tried hard in class but could only type a third as fast as me because she didn't spend her free time playing computer games. Don't you ever grow tired of the hot weather in Louisiana, Aerith? Don't you want to escape it all and become another? Couldn't the feeling of personal victory you feel watching the New Orleans Saints beat the Atlanta Falcons be exchanged for a personal cybernetic triumph over a spotty thirty-three-year-old Worgen Druid named Terence?

After fifteen years of genuinely succeeding in forgetting Aerith, I feel a little anxious about something as I go to sleep in my American Communist Council House, but I can't put my finger on what it is. I'm looking for something, too, but I don't know what. As my state of wistful wakefulness meets the surgeon of sleep, a dream plays through my mind in third person, like reality really is a computer game. I feel is as if I am not me but am still controlling someone or something else. From the get-go of this sensation, before visuals even enter into the equation, I'm convinced that I'm trapped in some virtual reality. And I notice that there's a shared sense of futility amongst my fellow passengers on the train we are getting God-knows-where. Then, at once, I realise that all the people in this dream know, too, that we are stuck inside some sort of grumpy simulator. My apprehensive mind calculates that it may simply be just a paranoid technicolour reverie induced by the soft(ish) drug Kratom that I am wont to brew in my tea at night-time.

Eventually, we arrive at a place that I recognise as Thunder Bluff from World of Warcraft, the Massive-Multi-Player-Online-Roleplaying-Game. I now know it is a dream, but I am not saddened by this fact, nor can I seem to attain complete lucidity. Thunder Bluff's train station is situated by one of its wooden elevators that goes up and down and up and down. I get on the lift and while I am standing there on it, I feel a renewed sense of purpose. I feel something important is about to happen. The Tauren capital is crowded as a popular Las Vegas casino at an off-peak hour but not quite as crowded as the San Francisco beach during summer. I walk towards the centre of the citadel, passing various market stalls which sell assorted trinkets, food, and armour.

Suddenly, I notice Aerith peering down at the vegetation on the main bridge linking north and south. Then Aerith sees me too. Her pretty face erupts into a saccharine smile and she looks just like I remember her, only every angelic atom in her beatific body has matured immeasurably (in fact, I suppose you can measure it... she's fifteen years older than she was when I knew her). It feels like she possesses an ancient wisdom and is some kind of tribe elder. I wade through the crowd towards her. Then, all the other figures vaporize as I approach her. She just stands there, still smiling. My heart is a garden of butterflies. I put my arms around Aerith and caress her neck. We smooch for the first time ever. Me? I am in heaven. It starts raining in this part of heaven.

My mum is in another part of heaven. This photograph is ten years old. The man on the left is my father. The woman on the right is my mother. That is me.

I tried on her shoes yesterday and they fit my feet perfectly, so I walked in the garden and believed in everything.

I heard a bird scream at the stream where muddy red water flows. He sung out his lungs, so fraught at the thought of the daughter he never met.

I spied a bride undream the seams of the ghost of her baby clothes. She froze to her toes at the sight of the white blessed boast of a wedding dress.

I saw a door open on the Broken Reality Game Show. I was there on a chair, I never guessed I'd confess.

By the stream that feeds the fountain, transparent faces appear amongst the rocks. Follow its course on horse up to the mountain, and the hollow relics of the age erupt in shock.

"Where are you?"   *"I'M HERE."*
"Where are you?"   *"I'M HERE."*
"I'm here."   *"WHERE ARE YOU?"*

Although conversation continues forever, the torch obscures everything it touches. Its beam lingers on the lilies. It sheds no light. Even he who staggers here on crutches could not brighten the night by sleight of prayer.

At the height of the mountain's lowest peak, a lonely boy looks down from his ledge. But the sight of the fountain makes his legs go weak, so he dangles them over the edge.

Behind my windows, the world is weeping. Reddened rain leaps into sweeping seas. Somewhere something sleeps. Somewhere something sings.

When enough time passes, there is a ceremony. Many people drown and many people watch.

Father Jeff saw his daughter dying in the frock he bought her. Doctor Breath brought her water trying to break the lock that wrought her. Doctor Breath fought her death, teasing the rest out of her chest. She purred a word then signed her crest, fleeing the scene and questing west.

A woman walks away. A man watches her. He feels like is watching his self walk away. He stubs out his cigarette. He locks the door and goes to bed.

Last night I danced with angels. It was strange yet somehow familiar. There was nothing but harmony.

Thoughts On Love

I believe in love because we're hyper intelligent animals and though 'humanity' sometimes places animals below itself on the pecking order, animals have extremely high emotional intelligence. Emotional intelligence is underestimated. As for love, one doesn't have to stay in love; one can fall out of love. Love isn't necessarily a constant – it's like happiness – often fleeting – it's here and then gone like the wind – and that's where drugs go wrong. I'm happy a lot actually but then it slides out of my soul. You just can't put happiness in a goldfish bowl or completely rid your secret sorrows through externally determinate sources (that is, happy pills or orgasms).

Me? The intensity of first love – Xinx, O Xinx! – practically killed and bereavement made me want to die and so I took nearly every drug known to man and engaged in 58 mindless sexual acts and got admitted to 10 insane asylums and attempted suicide twice and succeeded once and on and on it went. Irrespective of my desire to end time for myself, on and on it went.

In former lives, I have been knee-deep in the dung of depression for so long that for a time I came to regard sorrow's swamps as my only home. My brushes with death were often orchestrated and documented by the government, who use words like 'accident' or 'incident' or 'narrowly avoided tragedy' in writing about said events.

I've been seduced by (and I've sometimes seduced) the souls of a myriad of angelic heroines who, in a series of heathenish humps, oversaw my climb up to sequestered pinnacles of hedonistic ecstasy and dopamine gates. To me, death & salvation are as entwined as synonyms: one cannot happen without the other happening, be it a little death or the final emptying of the soul.

Does the legend of the past dwell on the border between actuality and conjecture if we don't instantly preserve it? Haven't you ever wished you could physically feel my love for you again, Xinx?

[I'm a reticent man but I know that you know that I know it has been there for you ever since I saw you from a distance for the first time; it was love at first sight for me, such an experience that only happens once in a lifetime. I never forgot you, though I spent many unmiraculous moments trying to. If I could get a doctor to delete the cells in the prison of my mind that home my memories of you, I probably would, but on second thought isn't it just lucky & beautiful & profound & crazy that all my feelings for you congregate there in the first place? I can dance with them whenever I want! They don't even need me to prove that I'm over eighteen! I'm not a regular in those realms anymore, but I'm so glad you always recognize me when I visit you on hallucinogens. Your boobs look prolific and spectacular whenever I imagine them, and nothing can beat that time you sucked my cock for a kid's eternity in a stoned daydream! I don't think it's particularly English to still speak like a heartbroken teenage heartthrob at the advanced age of 26, but I am still *"a few"* months your junior, and I am not exceptionally English anyway.]

I guess this is a story about understanding and misunderstanding. This is a story about shared orgasms & fags & straights. This is a story about hungry people who want exactly the same narcissistic artefact of tomorrow and all reach to grab for the gravy at once, only for it to shatter into a million unwanted fragment drops before their gaping eyes.

Haven't you ever wished you could physically feel my love for you again, Xinx? Don't you ever grow tired of the hot weather in Louisiana, Aerith? Haven't you ever wished you were once upon a time best friends with someone purer and more ephemeral and handsomer and unholier than me, Rockland? Haven't you ever liked some boy, Kleopatra?

Information About Xinx From Cat

I am writing a story on my laptop and Cat arrives, sitting down on the keys. She smells like she has just had sex.

"I have an announcement," Cat speculates.

"Great. Is it about our spiritual fate?" I ask, hopefully.

"I would consider my announcement to be of a more carnal nature," she responds.

"Oh. Is it about your carnal fate?"

"No. My announcement pertains to your relationship with this 'Xinx' figure," Cat says.

"Cat, spit it out!"

Cat spits semen onto the selectors of my laptop.

"Shit, Cat!"

Thankfully she doesn't. But she purrs with an almost satanic, seductive satisfaction, as if she has just rid something ugly beyond all meaning or comprehension.

"Xinx may be easier to reach than you might imagine," she says. *"You just need to remember her. She's not sleeping in your head. Remind yourself of her. Your last good memory of her, perhaps."*

"Before her decapitation?"

"Well, I guess; yes. See her then now. Replay the moment."

"Well?"

"If my calculations are correct, there is someone just like you were in mind and body experiencing the very scene right now," Cat says.

"Wow, Cat. I didn't think you believed in the multiverse."

"No. I don't," she says. *"But somewhere far away... incredibly far away... but somewhere physical we can reach – and long ago... and now... and in a few seconds...."*

"Okay. That's what I told K at the hospital. So what?" I ask.

"I don't know. I just thought it might be a relevant fact to convey before the announcement."

"I thought that was the announcement."

"No. The announcement is this: your programming of the oversoul means that you can summon Xinx whenever you want," Cat says.

"What?!"

"K designed it thusly; don't ask me why."

"What? How do you know this?"

"My programming as a technophobe allows me to analyse the wirings of this dimension," Cat says. *"All you need to do is call K and ask her how to summon Xinx."*

"She was withholding it from me this whole time? I thought that was the point of coming to Earth in the first place."

"Heh. Women have a lot of information they withhold from men. Maybe she desires you," Cat says.

The doorbell rings. Feeling small, I put my laptop to rest on the desk, mutter a white lie at the wall of the hall and open the door.

It's Kleopatra.

"True love is so intimate," K says.

"K? What are you doing here? I thought you left with my boss."

"Maybe I did. Maybe I didn't. That was a trust test."

"Okay. Do you trust me? I want to find Xinx."

"About that. We can. But you must marry me first."

Cat appears out of nowhere on my shoulder. *"Hah!"* Cat says, *"I read your mind, K. Now I know how to summon Xinx."*

"Oh? You do?" K asks sneeringly, as if particularly relishing the sarcastic aspects of her role of (what I currently have reason to regard as) 'the villain' in this blockbuster parable.

"Yep. Have you seen that show called A Female Detective Cat Finds the Missing Twat?" Cat asks.

"No. Why?" K says.

"At the end, the ginger cat says "You're busted! I'm the main woman around here!" and then she struts around."

"So... so what?"

"You're busted! I'm the main woman around here!" Cat jubilantly struts around. Although she often acts like a grown-up, I've learnt Cat is four to five years old and sometimes this is obvious.

"So, Cat, how do we find Xinx?" I ask.

Cat winks at me with one eye, and then winks at me with the other. She salsas around the hall as if she has just solved the mystery of all mysteries. She blinks. *"Don't worry. I have a funny habit of disappearing into thin-air, but God almighty will be the witness to such shenanigans."*

"Well..." I say, thinking for a second then thinking better of thinking further. *"Let's go to bed, then."*

I think K detects the reluctance in my voice, but she is so intensely attractive that there is a sharp tint of longing to my tone. I haven't told you what she is wearing, because to be frank, she is not wearing much: a white t-shirt, no bra, and denim shorts.

"*Bed,*" she states simply.

We go to my room. I'd been sleeping on the sofa. I have a habit of sleeping on sofas when I'm feeling particularly alone and a habit of sleeping on beds when I'm in company. I sit on the bed.

"*I am an empress and you are my benefactor.*"

"*Okay.*"

"*House, I want to hear The Eerie Shankers sing 'Today I Am A Woman'.*" Kleopatra nods at me. "*Say it.*"

"*Say what?*"

"*Say it,*" she insists.

"*It,*" I say.

"*Do you desire me?*"

"*Yeah.*"

"*More than Xinx?*"

"*I can't really compare... I mean you're two different beings.*"

"*But it's like the choice between Vegan Pizza or Special Stir-Fried Rice. Surely, Mister Sanity would prefer Special Stir-Fried Rice?*"

"*No, Mister Sanity is nearly vegan. Tease me. Say it's Vegan Special Fried Rice,*" I say.

"*Okay. It's Vegan Special Fried Rice.*" She turns her back on me. I look at her bottom. It's grossly rotund. She's gained weight. Shit, though. I want to feel it. I drool slightly.

"I want you to seduce me like you seduce yourself, even though you're latently straight. I don't want you to arouse yourself and have my worst suspicions confirmed," Kleopatra says.

"Men don't do that. That's what women are for..." I say, and she laughs at my reason-lessness.

"Oh? But I...." K dances a sexy dance, prompting me to mechanically feel my love, bearing in mind what Cat said. I stimulate my cock for twenty seconds, drooling more & more.

The music reaches a climax. The whole group sings in unison, *"For Today I Am A Woman! Trombones! Saxophones! Epiphanies! Einstein!"*

"Up?" K asks, as she was fond of doing during the lifetimes we spent living together.

"Yeah." I tell her what she already knows.

"Wanker," K eloquently chastises.

"Feel me."

"Sure."

She parks herself on my cock, denim pressing into it. She doesn't move a lot; she just sits there for thirty seconds. Then she dry humps me until she's wet and I climax.

"Ah," I say.

We relax for a while, fairly content in each other's company.

The television then turns on automatically as there is a Presidential address. Cat races into the room, twitching excitedly.

"It's happening! It's happening!" Cat exclaims.

"A billion immigrants have been forced to evacuate the region and are now assumed dead," the President states solemnly.

"What? But a billion immigrants don't even live here..." K says, annoyed at the apparent inaccuracy.

"This is a senseless crime and we'll prosecute the responsible party," the President continues.

"I am a female feminist scientist and I think I know who is responsible," Cat says.

"I don't see what that's got to do with... oh..." I say.

"Anyway... despite the fact that this is a preach of Universe Law, I changed the programming of our Universe! That means that Xinx is but four hundred words down the road," Cat says.

"Hooray!" I say.

"Whoop-de-doo," K says.

"Wait... what do you mean four hundred words down the road?" I ask.

"Didn't you know? I believe we are characters in a play for the almighty," Cat says.

"I thought *you* were *the* almighty," I respond.

"Not exactly. The almighty is all-seeing and all-knowing. K, hackers like you are mere imposters. You are a dime a dozen. There is only one God. Your day of reckoning will come. I hope my final judgement is fair," Cat reels off in rapid-fire.

"But I thought you weren't God," I say, confused.

"Allah yaghfir lak," Cat says.

"Boohoo," K says patronisingly. "So this means we'll see Xinx in 300 words?"

"Yes. But you can summon her at any time," says Cat in an unthinking move that will ultimately destroy my destiny.

"Allah yrja aistuhdir li 'afdal sidiyq w namudhaj aldhy yusamaa shaynakas," Kleopatra incants.

"I didn't know you..." I start, but then Xinx appears, naked, a little younger than I remember her. Her bosoms already soothe me with their homely, portly nature... I don't mean to obsess over them already, but this book is fantasy-erotica-romance, isn't it?

"Welcome!" Xinx says.

"Hello!" I exclaim.

"Where are we? To what I am I welcoming you to today?" Xinx says, confusedly.

"Hi Xinx! I've heard so much about you!" Cat says, exultantly.

"Welcome!" Xinx says. *"What have you heard about me?"*

"Mostly I've heard your ex go on about your... uh... motherly nature," says Cat.

"I don't like Freud. Please don't speak about Freud," I beg.

"That's not what the implication was," says K.

"K! Welcome!" Xinx says, letting old rivalries die.

"Why are you naked?" I say.

"Isn't it natural? You barbarians wear clothes now? I thought it was outlawed."

"As a suffragette, I have to say I agree with such a principle," says Cat.

"I am half-naked and vaguely covered with your boyfriend's semen," K says helpfully.

"Oh. Sorry, Xinx, I meant to tell you... after we broke up, I had sex with K " I say. "A lot."

"You mean after I was decapitated?" Xinx asks.

"Yeah. That."

"It didn't happen instantly, nor overnight," says K.

"I understand the implications of that statement," says Xinx.

"Oh! Shit! Shit! Shit! Everyone shut up," implores Cat, clawing at the carpet.

"Why?" K asks.

"Shut up!" orders Cat.

No one says a thing for a minute. There is a palpable tension in the room. Xinx looks aggressively at K, who strips to her bare bones. K looks back at her. There might be a standoff coming soon.

Then... then... then... there is a loud bang, some steam and out of nowhere appears another Xinx, also naked. The Xinx look identical.

"Shit. Shit. Shit. I foresaw this after it was too late," Cat says.

"Which one is the original Xinx?" I wonder.

"I am," the Xinx assert in unison.

"Shit! Let's murder one of these motherfuckers!" K says.

"No, no, no!" says Cat.

The Xinx turn to each other.

"Oh," say the Xinx.

"Do you have to mirror each other's movements?" I ask.

Cat winks, licks her lips and looks at me funnily, declaiming, *"Four girls, one guitarist!"*

"Oh... I, what do you think of this?" says one.

"Who, me?" says the other.

"No, I," says one.

"Well, me is naked, too," Cat informs me. *"Let's find out who really owns your love, I."*

"He belongs to me!" say both Xinxs in unison.

"I did notice something. One Xinx is a tiny, tiny bit skinnier than the other," I say.

"Who? Me? No, me!" say the Xinx.

"We're going round in circles here." Cat chases her tail animatedly.

I point at one Xinx. *"That must mean the other one is fatter, meaning she is the younger one!"* I say.

"That doesn't mean a thing! Breed with all three of these women and be done with it!" Cat jumps on the bed, closes her eyes and sulks under the blanket (or at least that's what I believe she is doing).

"Let's put pink hair dye on the Xinx the Youngerer," says K. *"Where are we going to get pink hair dye?"*

K shrugs.

"I don't want pink hair!" says Xinx The Youngerer.

K shrugs. *"Red then?"*

"Wow. Blue, black & red is my favourite combination of colours, given there is three," I confess.

"What about two?" Xinx The Youngerer asks.

"Your colour," I say.

"But I'm only one colour," Xinx The Youngerer says.

"Yeah," I say. *"But blue & black aren't named when they're together like that."*

"Historically, that remark could be considered quite offensive," Xinx The Youngerer smirks. *"It's called Azurack. I tell you this every time I…"*

"That's it. We're dyeing you red," says K.

"I'm dying me unless this book is black & white & read all over, in which case I'll die a celebrated author," I say.

"I don't mind being read," says Xinx The Elderer.

"That settles it then." K clicks her fingers and Xinx The Elder's long-parrot-shoulder-length-hair turns into a natural-looking crimson.

Cat emerges out of the bedding, inspecting Xinx The Elder elatedly. *"Xinx, your hair is inspirational. As a feminist, having the courage to dye your hair is paramount. But you look great. You don't look a fool!"*

"Thanks, Cat." Xinx The Elderer smiles.

Cat's Prophecy

"First it happened to me and now it's going to happen to you," Cat sighs deeply, as if a doctor disclosing that the listener has two minutes left to live.
"What's going to happen to us?" K asks, sounding lost for the first time in a while.
"Whatever it is, it doesn't sound all that good," I say.
"Another apocalypse?" Xinx The Youngerer speculates.
"No, the apocalypse has already happened," Xinx The Elderer reasons.
"I can't say for sure," Cat continues, as gloomy and moody as fog at the center of a storm, *"but beyond reasonable doubt, I can say that one of you will be punished and everyone will laugh at you."*
"Cat! How could you possibly know this?" I ask.
"I don't know. I've just got a feeling in my gut telling me that today is the last good day we'll see for a while and we should appreciate it."
"Cat?" Kleopatra says disbelievingly. *"Are you damning us? Why are you here in the first place?"*
"I thought my mission here had something to do with Xinx, but you seem to take care of that quickly. And now we have two Xinx. So?"
"So? What do you mean so? I was working on getting one Xinx here for I," K says.
"I don't care for your Rastafarian lies. Allah tathir hadhih alghurfa!" Cat looks as infuriated as it's possible for a cat to look.
"No, 'I' meaning the main character in this book," K explains.
"Like that Otis Redding song my boyfriend wants to show me when the neighbours next play it, about a man and a man?" Cat asks, sounding audibly & disdainfully distrustful.

"*Kind of, but not really,*" K says.
"*My boyfriend is an angel in some ways, but I too mean the main guy in this book,*" Cat says. "*This Universe is simply a constant loop of the bible. You all haven't self-actualised enough to alter it yet, not that you ever will.. The main character, I, that is you, I, must get to heaven, which is nothing, and then you will have completed all your trials and can rest for the rest of forever, which will mean nothing because you won't be there to experience it. Then it will all happen again! It's the 'eternal return' paradox that you discussed during the mid-section of the novella, which may soon be classified as a fully-fledged novel!*" Cat laughs at me like I am a joke.
"*Hah. Hah. Hah. Hah. You were only joking, Cat, but for some time I thought we were actually characters in the Bible. Hah. Hah. Hah.*" I fiddle with my thumbs nervously.
"*I'd prefer to avoid discussion of your prophecy, Cat,*" Xinx The Youngerer says, gazing self-pityingly at her fingernails in the way that Rockland, once secret hero of these pages and now seemingly completely irrelevant to the plot of the story, was occasionally wont to do.
"*There is no prophecy,*" Cat explains, spelling out each syllable clearly. "*It's simply a warning about something inevitable that will happen to one of you! And so, I bid you heathens adieu with one final thought... as feminist as I am, don't you think I has such potential as a lover?*"
"*Who? Me?*" I ask, "*I meaning me?*"
"*Yeah!*" Cat looks at me merrily. "*I is not Rastafarian, is I?*
"*Its longevity... the way that you say stuff... it's so humane... it's so hot,*" say the Xinx, finishing each other sentences. [Maybe the Xinx weren't finishing each other's' sentences and in fact were just saying different things.]

"Have I something else to tell you, I," says Cat.
"Oh?"
Now I know 'I' is me, unless Cat is as brain damaged as Yoda or pretending to be a pirate & asking a question only to answer it.
"You sure do look good today." Cat paces on one spot as if she is desperate to get going somewhere important.
"Really? We may have to evict you," I say, unreasonably.
"What? I was just saying how... extraordinary you look today," Cat replies, as if it is obvious to everyone but me that she fancies me.
"Yes, I, you look beautiful," says Xinx The Elderer.
"Yet... phlegmatic," Xinx The Youngerer says.
"I want to murder some more microorganisms in your groins," K confesses.
"Err..." I say, for everyone has lost their minds and become their bodies.
"Meow," says Cat. She licks her lips and then she vanishes for the very final time, just like that, irreversibly, forever: that's it. The sound of silence screeches through some of the remaining scorching souls and not a word is spoke between said parties until the police arrive twenty minutes later. As this book has probably turned you on or off enough by now, I'm not going to describe the scene that unfolds in the next ten minutes but instead leave it to your imagination.

The following words, in any order, can be applied to describe what happens: excruciating, orgiastic, premature, three tips of tongues, overwhelming silence, grotesque, manual labour and the I-ching. After a noiseless episode of infinity, several squads of secret servicemen arrive at the scene, led by a Ginger Cat, as prophesised by Cat, whom I may have been too harsh on when I told her that she should worry about being evicted.

"You're busted! I'm the main woman around here!" the Ginger Cat says and struts around manically, like a downtrodden cop corrupted by the sensation of possessing power at last, the very symbol of the society's shackles. Yes, to coin a Shakespearean turn of phrase like Rockland was wont to do, the shackles of society strangle my soul. To repeat myself for comic effect & to emphasize my point, the shackles of society strangle my soul. Of course, I am arrested. Of course, I am jailed. And, thus, of course, the coming words don't articulate *The Mother of Infinity*, so you couldn't make them up. Or you could, but you'd have to be kind of mad.

GOD'S PRETTY GAME OF GROTESQUE PUPPETS

THE DEVIL CAN'T & GOD WON'T

You Can Have It All

She broke her own heart, too, but Nature writes its own Laws; somehow, I still adore Kleopatra now, even after all our spiritual wars. This is the story of the night before my troubles became God's and yours. This is the story of how I saw my flaws and came straight home into the banks of my brain and yours.

If every breath brings us closer to death, laughter's the path to our demise. I know puppy love so well by now that Kleopatra's kaleidoscopic eyes could be infinity's final surprise. But one night long ago hunger evaporated like sweat to the wheezy keys of Xinx's thighs.

Admittedly, I'm a rather sentimental man, but when I play the moving pictures of the past in my prayers, I never cry. Sometimes I want to cry, but I don't let myself and I forget quite why. After wondering why I don't like myself, I worry there is something wrong with me and teardrops shoot gingerly out of my windows into the sky.

In our world, feelings and moments and friends pass away. And the purpose of tomorrow becomes the circus of today.

Just between you and me, I've seen things that you've never seen. I have smoked more ounces of green than you have had dreams. I love to eat, I love to shit, I love to drink, I love to piss a stream. I love video games, from the Gameboy's screen to Doom and its screams.

Humanity will perish considerably before God does and the wars shall end. God's not sorry for being odd but I'm just sorry that salvation's pretend. My faith flushes fucked down the toilet but – shit! – the world wide web is a godsend!

Confidants and continents and bacteria migrate from the physical plane of material matter onto the calm waters of Memory Bank. Nobody and Nothing should stop you from painting your picture on the future's blank. This world is not a test, a guess, conjecture or a prank. *The Devil Can't & God Won't.*

Whether what resonates with you in this journey is a lonesome moonlit morning mourning morning or an unexpected golden touch that seems to shake the world, I know every part of my past off by heart… and so you can have it all. Future becomes the past and your love will go last. But you can have it all. Future becomes the past and your love will go last. And so, you can have it all.

Guess Who Testified?

All of the seats of the Courtroom are occupied. If I were to guess how many people can see my alienated soul's voice, I confess I don't know whether the number is less than fifty or if it exceeds seventy trillion. I'm not sure I care either, to tell you the truth. I'm jaded by every grave passer-by's hushed denouncement of my actions and, more than ever, I'm haunted by the tears I never learned how to cry.

This is my current Universe's *Courtroom of Externally Internal Affairs*. Here I wait for fate to decide whether I am guilty of perverting the *"Course of God's Masterplan"*. I was teleported & time-travelled back to this absurd area of existence – *"The Central Planet of Diplomacy"* – by an extraordinarily corrupt hedonistic inventor with an IQ that would rival the realms of 249401 (in earthly terms). His brain is bigger than an apartment complex and he's spent a greater percentage of his waking hours head buried in an Applied Science book or a bosom than you have spent sleeping or fucking. The man is a criminal as blaspheming as I apparently am and so seized the opportunity to be *"blessed with impunity"* from the Courtroom's Master Verdict. I secretly suspect that he is the Universe's Smartest Man and also hopes to make a quick capitalist buck by auctioning his abilities to The Law.

The coquettishly extra-terrestrial bodies, whom are like nothing & no-one I have ever encountered before, stare or point at my soul's voice. This world seems a little more like Hunfora or Restralardin than Planet Earth. I still reek of Planet Earth's vulgarly rational convention; in London, I got jailed twice: once for trying to attain access to a stationary car that *"didn't belong to me"* and once for stripping near The Forest Festival in an act which the federal government called *"a forbidden rite of exhibitionism."*

As if to silence all the voices in my head, the Judge bangs his hammer in a seemingly pleased, perfunctory manner. *"Quiet in the Courtroom,"* The Judge instructs. The Judge's command is achieved in 0.15 milliseconds.

"We are gathered here today to question the actions of a male named Tonnan, legally known as Dominic Francis. He is of indeterminate age and was born & raised on Restralardin, a star at the side of Sildaris. By impersonating G-d with the help of his friend who goes by the name of K, he traversed the multiverse three times and ended up on Planet Earth in the Milky Way galaxy, a place where the Universe's Laws of Finality apply. How many bodies he has accidently murdered and given birth to, I cannot say with any certainty. How many lost souls he has saved, killed or induced climax in on behalf of karma, I can vaguely imagine. This trial is the Universe's way of deciding where exactly he ultimately 'goes'; if Tonnan is ruled innocent, he will be able to decide his spiritual destination for himself. It should be noted, thusly, that we are here to determine whether this hundred-and-something male is a good person or bad person. I call a male born on Restralardin in the same year as Tonnan to provide a statement of Tonnan's character for the court. May a soul named Rockland please make himself be known."

"Your Honour, this is Rockland speaking. I knew Tonnan at a University called Hobbling in another life," says a soul voice that I remember as Rockland's. It's pretty good to hear his voice again.

"And?" The Judge seems curious. *"What was he like? Were you friends with him?"*

"Your Honour, Tonnan was a close friend of mine. We were studying Frolardi together."

"And for the benefit of the record and the jury, which consists of me & me alone, what in English is 'Frolardi'?" The Judge asks.

"It's the practice of trying to fix humanoid's bodies," says Rockland.

Guffaws & uncontained laughter drench the Courtroom. It seems Restralardin, a planet I thought pretty advanced at least in terms of technological invention, is one of the most backward-thinking places in the entire Universe and that all humanoids effectively have an intelligence equivalent to that of the brain of bacteria in an earthly ant. The crowd in the court, anyhow, appears to believe it an utterly pointless & unsanitary practice to try to fix a broken body.

"This Tonnan figure… I am curious. Do you think he is a selfish character?" The Judge asks.

"I won't betray his heart because I consider him to be of sound character. Tonnan was smart. Kind of crafty. But selfish? I don't think so. Not at all. In fact, he was very open to my influence," Rockland's soul feverishly states.

"What do you mean by 'influence'? Was he under your 'influence'? Am I correct in supposing his soul regarded you as some kind of idol?"

"Perhaps," Rockland's soul says reticently. *"By influence, I mean I was a key part of his life for a long time. I was perhaps the party that orchestrated his ingestion of acid. For example."*

"So..." The Judge says, as if considering an extremely fine point. *"Would you say that you encouraged him to engage in illegal activities?"*

"Not really. No. It wasn't me. Whoever you're I-I-looking for, he's a long way away from me by now. It wasn't me," Rockland's soul says nervously.

"That's not what I'm asking," The Judge replies patiently. *"What I'm alluding to is the idea that your bodily actions may have persuaded Tonnan to engage in reckless activity. Would you behave the same way you did if you could do it all again? Would you accept the barter of 'ETERNAL RETURN' with the devil?"*

"I... I don't know, Your Honour. Would you prefer sporadic beauty or incessant mediocrity? Do we have a choice?"

"Go on," The Judge says kindly.

"I don't think we have any choice regarding our actions. They are already determined by biology," speaks Rockland's soul.

"So then. You believe all beings are effectively robots?" The Judge wonders, seemingly only addressing Rockland now.

"Your Honour, we are machines. Beautiful & holy & flawed machines. But that is just my opinion. Imagine if you were G-d. What would you do? Nothing. Nothing is the answer. Are you, as a mortal, better than G-d?"

The Judge is silent for four and a half seconds. *"What makes you think I am a mortal, young man?"* The Judge says.

Rockland's soul stays silent.

"I believe in G-d," The Judge says, *"because anything is possible when you harness the power of love."*

"True that," replies Rockland's soul.

"Thirteen billion trillion years ago," The Judge begins sullenly, *"I was an adolescent for the first time. I grew infatuated with the laugh & fragrance & scarf & mouth movements & casual badasssery of a 'sixteen-and-a-half-year-old-woman' called Rachael. We became vagrants together, smoking blunts by the canal and conversing dopily & manically (meaningfully, too, but mostly just dopily) about being born to live for the fleeting and the heavenly and the imperfect and the tangerines – O, the tangerines! – and the black & white films and the old school hip-hop songs and the longing and the wine. We spoke to strangers about their taste in poetry and invaded a barge, christening it Ship Shape before getting a right bollocking from a moustached gypsy sailor fellow who cursed us, in the voodoo language we were forced to learn at school, roaring* "your minds will experience exceptional bodily torment and your hearts will rue this day!" *– and then we ran away back into the now ominous sanctity of the park, speaking about caravans and black canvases and organised religion's view on sex before banalities and her ambition to become a sports writer & mine to become a practitioner of the law, until suddenly she vocalised her desire to sexualise my "body of beatitude" and then we kissed, which was our first kiss together and would be our last kiss together (for another sobering, heart-pounding three seconds). I knew then that I would sacrifice everything and heaven for her."*

The Judge's retelling of his first kiss with this 'sixteen-and-a-half-year-old-woman' makes me remember something, but right now I am so sober I can't quite put my finger on it.

"Your Honour, I enjoyed the tale, but what exactly are you implying?" asks Rockland's bewildered brain.

"Eternal return is a myth. Forever we live and forever we die. I haven't seen Rachael for a billion centuries. But I digress. It is my opinion – Rockland – that you are, to quote Tonnan's tongue, a 'hedonistic heathen,'" The Judge says. *"Not only have you perverted the course of justice by offering Tonnan illegal drugs, you have also swayed his fate by injecting imaginary images and satanical symbols into his being. I have no choice but sentence you in addition to Tonnan."*

Rockland's soul jumps like jingoist, symbolically moons random flags and then sits awaiting his penalty for being himself.

"Speaking in terms that residents of Planet Earth would understand, as of this day, Friday the 13th of December 2019, I hereby sentence you and your soul to one whole year of solitary confinement. During this time, you shall not speak to a single soul, eat an enjoyable food or beverage, touch your penis, smoke or dance. Do I make myself clear?"

Rockland's body has a cold and he sneezes. His destiny is heaven, but Rockland's mind now frantically masturbates over Xinx's soul in his home of Planet Pinocchio, population 3.

"Fuck you, Your Honour," Rockland's soul howls savagely. Rockland's soul is ferried off to another plane. The Courtroom is quiet for half a page.

And They Both Badly Lied

"Tonnan, I understand you know a woman called Kleopatra, eh? From what I know and understand, K is quite the geek. She's not particularly bookish but she has an extraordinary understanding of the inner workings of the oversoul that this Courtroom is guarding," The Judge says, his own soul patting The Past's brain. *"She cannot be here today for we cannot locate her, but I understand it was her handiwork that resulted in Leonard Cohen and Adolf Hitler being stillborn."* The Judge sighs. *"Reality has altered an awful lot since I was a kid. Sometimes I wonder if I ever was a kid. As I mentioned before, we cannot reach K for further questioning. Kleopatra mysteriously vanished in the way that Cats are wont to do, right after the orgy that (given my all-seeing capabilities as The Judge) I have a satisfactory working memory of."* The Judge's soul's voice's vocal cords cough. *"Now, Tonnan, I would like to ask you about a woman called Xinx. Do you still believe she is your first and last love?"*

I don't know what to say. I haven't spoken in this Courtroom yet and to say I am anxious & peckish is an understatement. *"Maybe,"* I say. The Judge's verdict on Rockland was perhaps both damning and fair... I want The Judge to like me. *"I once loved her, Your Honour, certainly. In fact, I adored her. She was a dear friend of mine."*

"Alright," says The Judge. *"I understand the word 'friend'. What would you tell Xinx now, if you could speak to her?"*

"There are those who seek the God above who never knew the rain of bliss. And those like me who dream of love with one like you in pain like this," I say.

"Good. Very good. The investigation is back on track," yells Maggie's soul encouragingly in a stage-whisper. *"I hope you're proud of yourself!"*

"Thank you, Maggie," says The Judge, bemused. "Tonnan, how would you feel if I could summon Xinx's soul to serenade yours and perhaps give you a moment of pleasure before the Final Judgement?" asks The Judge.

"Your Honour, that would be... fantastic," I say, my secret penis wondering if The Judge will actually allow me to meet with Xinx again.

"Xinx," says The Judge, *"show your soul's self."*

Xinx shows her soul's self and it begins to sing. And it is ugly. And it is murderous. And it is beautiful. My heart climaxes & then recoils in the matter of an epiphanic moment.

The Judge reads my mind & bangs his wooden hammer. *"It is my hope that Tonnan will find his Match Made in Heaven again. As a judge, it falls within my powers to marry humanoids. This is a rare event, but then again, this is a rare piece of theatre or literature. I hereby sentence Tonnan and Kleopatra to the fate of man & wife."*

My suicidal soul and hedonistic heart freeze for a few instants. After this final verdict has been given, every soul in the courtroom sucks The Judge off. I am Tonnan, secretive magic soldier, and at the end of the end no one know what happens because we're dead.

The Wedding

The soul of the sun is slumbering as the moon mounts the Seattle skyline. It's midnight, the morning before Kleopatra & I officially marry. The Secretary of State promised us that the ceremony will be *"an extraordinarily grand yet intricately lavish event"*. It will be funded entirely by the US government, a body which appears to be keen to impress the fact that it will undertake the desires of the *Universe's Courtroom of Externally Internal Affairs* with a perfection bordering on pedantry.

I can't get to sleep... I'm too excited, to be honest. Even though K probably wouldn't be my first choice of spouse if I were forced to select just 1 woman out of a line-up of 1000 before I could go home & eat, K is an extremely wonderful woman in some respects. I just wish that girls, and boys for that matter, were trained to cook simple meals in the Seattle state schooling system. Sometimes I just wish that I never arrived on this motherfucking planet in the first place. The 'first world' claims to be liberal in ideology yet it's so concerned about offending the Left that unreserved autobiographies such as the one you have in your hands will soon be ancient history.

Anyhow, right now K is snoring softly by my side. She's 29; I'm 27. She has short bleached-blue hair; I have long(ish) locks of brown curls. Her eyes are coffee-hazel; mine are bluey green with an acorn-brown centrepiece. She has a really pretty smile; I like it when she smiles, because usually it means that I do too, which releases endorphin dolphins, which make me even happier. K & I have enjoyed three (short) lifetimes together after she catalysed a local tragedy on a planet called Restralardin in our native Universe. We then traversed the multiverse together in order to find my first true love, Xinx.

When we first met, K was unemployed, although I have reason to suspect she was a part-time prostitute. Nowadays she works as a barista in the Seattle branch of KookyKoffee, a job that she says satisfies her *"social needs"* and *"cravings for caffeine"*. Having known each other for a hundred-and-something years, sometimes K & I don't have a lot to talk about.

On Restralardin, sitting at a crossroads which led to backward self-reflection (or to a career in foot-doctoring) or to nirvana (or to self-expression), I decided to start to make art. I learnt how to play guitar pretty quickly after receiving instruction from Rockland, my friend on Restralardin who recently accidentally testified against himself & I in the *Universe's Courtroom of Internally External Affairs*.

Eventually, I do fall asleep and I dream I'm getting lunch with Xinx at the Hobbling University Café. *"Haven't you ever wished you could physically feel my love for you, Xinx?"* I ask.

"I've had nightmares before, but none of such severity," Xinx replies wryly. Suddenly I feel like hell on a Monday morning.

The waiter comes over to take our orders. Xinx requests a jacket potato with baked beans & cheese, and a strawberry milkshake. I choose a halloumi & pesto sandwich, and a banana milkshake. Next thing you know it, the baked beans are all on my toes; next thing you know it, the cheese is in my mouth; next thing you know it, the strawberry milkshake is everywhere; next thing you know it, the baked beans are everywhere; next thing you know it, the halloumi and pesto sandwich is nowhere to be seen, and Kleopatra is casually drinking my banana milkshake.

"What the fucking fuck?" I say. 'Next thing you know it' & 'What the fucking fuck?' are my catchphrases, by the way. People particularly like it when I say *"What the fucking fuck?"* I think.

[Two months ago, I quit my previous job. *"I've had a sensational offer from ForgetAboutIt Entertainment,"* I told my boss.

"You're just what this company needs. Fan-fucking-tastic", my boss said, using his own catchphrase which was probably pilfered & adapted from my own critically acclaimed catchphrase. *"Congratulations are in order. Drinks at the Sepulchre tonight?"*

"Sure, okay. Why the fucking fuck not? But... I quit," I said.

"You can't quit," my boss moaned, desperately stroking his stubble as if deeply pondering the predicament at hand.

"Yes, I can," I replied. *"I quit."*

"YOU CAN'T QUIT," my boss quietly shouted. *"Because...YOU... are... fucking... FIRED!"*

I haven't seen my boss or anyone else from BeardedBeaverArt since then. The fact that my boss probably slept with Kleopatra, my bride, had little impact on my respect for him, though it did make me doubletake every time I passed a mirror.]

In dreamtime, anyhow, I'm gaping at the newly teleported Kleopatra and Xinx is choking on a wayward baked bean when, next thing you know it, I'm in the London Underground, which is a place I've never been to before. *What the fucking fuck?* I think. Yes, I confess there is a slight 'diminishing returns' to all catchphrases.

I look around me. The residues of rush hour are washing up on the shores of certainty eighty foot below the ground. It's a packed train boarded by a crowd personifying urgent reticence. I get on.

In front of me is a woman of about forty, middle-weight, average height, flowery hair not quite yet grey, with a great big chain of ear-hair that makes her about twenty centimetres wider on each side. She is reading something on a Kindle device.

To my left is a sixty-three-or-so-year-old man, fidgeting with his fingers. He shakes hungrily; perhaps he is nervous about the journey. Yet he wears a leather jacket and seems able-bodied. Yeah, he certainly looks good for his age, whatever that is.

To my right is a teenaged girl, playing The Jam loudly on her iPod. I wonder whether I would be her friend if I was twelve years younger and at school with her. I like The Jam, and when I was a teenaged boy, I liked teenaged girls.

The tube screeches every so often, due to what I believe to be deceleration. Nothing out of the ordinary. Even the Queen has successfully travelled using the London Underground before. Nope. Nothing out of the ordinary. Not yet.

As we screech to a halt, the sixty-three-or-so-year-old man puts his hands to his ears and the driver announces that there will be a 'short delay before normal service resumes'. You might be programmed to believe this is an ordinary occurrence, but what happens next is extraordinary.

Clasping firmly onto his ears, the sixty-three-or-so year-old man removes his head. Blood rains out. Anarchy reigns. People scream. A man faints, dropping dramatically downwards onto his rear end.

The teenaged girl's mouth drops wide open, and acts as a receptacle for some of the spraying blood. The ear-haired woman in front of me moves her head from side to side, as if trying to absorb the shocking unnatural disaster unfolding before her eyes.

Five seconds later, the teenager is still acting as a receptacle, a vessel for this blood. No one knows quite what to do but express their outrage. To put it bluntly, all hell breaks loose. The man's head is basketball big like a big old basketball, with scars rather than battle-paint, oozing blood. And the girl keeps drinking the blood up, lapping it up like an adorable puppy as it sprays all over the floor. After realising I am in a dream, I wake up on the morning of my wedding to K, whose mouth is currently submerging my phallus. So it goes.

There is no end to my love, I think, as K's tongue darts upwards to my bellybutton after my love comes a little. She momentarily licks out my belly button, then service in the south is resumed as normal as her mouth engulfs my cock.

"Good morning," I say to K.

"Today will be the best day of my life," K says to me. *"I will finally be lawfully wed to the man I've loved all my lives."*

"Hell, I love you too, baby," I say, remembering how certain the extremely elderly Judge was when he deemed K & I soulmates. As stated some fifty pages ago, K is without a doubt the prettiest women I have ever seen. Her tongue trips on the tip of my erection & then she slips my soul above into the smalls of her mouth. And then her tulips & a section of her throat devote a shipment of Thrall to my balls down south. Finally, K completes my happiness & I explode in the recesses of the Primary Door to Her Body. There are many ways to wake up from an odd dream, and this one isn't all that shoddy.

"Thanks," I say. *"This is a good day to wake up to that. Usually I wake up to an alarm clock or the sound of soft, disgruntled snoring."*

"You're welcome," K says. *"Ready for today?"*

"As ready as I'll ever be," I reply as she heads for the bathroom.

We catch separate cabs to the Town Hall. The ceremony will begin at 1P.M. I am greeted by the Mayor of Seattle at the door, who shakes my hand emphatically & tells me to *"come on in!"* I notice that the Mayor of Seattle is looking particularly metrosexual today. This doesn't bother me in the slightest, though, so I follow him down the hallway into my dressing room.

My dressing room is excessively decorated with flowers of all varieties: magnolias & roses & lilies & tulips & blossom & bluebells & poppies & daisies & petunias, all maddeningly ecstatic shades of violet & gold & burgundy & white & pink & teal & scarlet & hues of blue. *Hell*, I think, *maybe the state isn't entirely broke.* I will probably still smell floral tomorrow.

A makeup artist is waiting there for me. *"Let's get you looking beautiful,"* she says with a kindness I can't express in words.

"Oh, I don't wear to makeup. I'm a male man," I say.

The makeup artist laughs as if I have just said something absurdly comical. *"Sorry, but even mail-men wear makeup on their weddings! Sorry - this will only take a minute."*

"You don't need to apologise," I reply. *"You were just saying what you thought you should say. But I'm not wearing makeup and I already look beautiful."*

"Okay... are you sure you don't want makeup? It looks great on the late philanthropist Donald Trump," she asks, sounding disappointed. Perhaps she really likes her job, I think, but I ultimately doubt the legitimacy of her adjectival description of the philanthropist Donald Trump. Last time I checked he's still alive and shitting candy floss.

"Absolutely positive," I assure her.

"Will I still get paid?" she asks, nervous as a cat trying to cross a highway at rush-hour, my original hunch that she just really enjoys her job disproven.

"I don't know. You'll have to ask the Pentagon. The state is funding this funeral   wedding, I mean."

"O-kay," she says. *"And who might you know at the Pentagon?"*

"It's a state secret," I reply, unintentionally winking at her.

The makeup artist leaves the room to settle her inquiries.

Two hours later, I am facing K at a beautifully decorated makeshift altar. There are about fifty people in the Town Hall. I notice my ex-boss in the front row of chairs. He is sweating profusely.

"In the presence of God, Father, Son and Holy Spirit," the tall, thin priest begins, *"we have come together to witness the marriage of Kleopatra and Tonnan, to pray for God's blessing and to celebrate their love."*

The tall, thin priest looks at Kleopatra & I in turn lovingly. *"Marriage is a gift of God in creation through which husband and wife know the grace of God. It is given that as man and woman grow together in love and trust, they shall be united with one another in heart, body and mind, as Christ is united with his bride, the Church. First, I am required to ask anyone present if they know a reason why these persons may not lawfully marry now, to declare it now."*

My ex-boss stands up. Everyone gasps. My ex-boss stokes his stubble pensively. *"I married K in a private ceremony three months ago."*

The tall, thin priests looks like I feel: baffled & maddened by such a shocking twist of fate, yet somehow barely surprised. *"Kleopatra, is this true?"* he asks.

"Well...," K says, *"I did put a Haribo ring on his forefinger and ask him if he wanted me to bite his hand off. If flirting counts as marrying, it stands to reason I'm already spoken for, because Tonnan is the master of flirting. In fact, we're flirting right now."* She smiles at me. I smile back. Her teeth are white. Too white... like Something's Wrong White.

"Okay. Whatever. Sweet," the tall, thin priest says, throwing formality out of the window. *"Without any further shenanigans, I now pronounce Kleopatra & Tonnan– officially, this time – Husband & Wife."*

Everyone stands up & claps. I'm not so happy, myself. I wonder if the priest's words are legally binding given his aside midsentence and the fact that he called Kleopatra my husband. Still, maybe I'm a pedant.

Actually, what the fucking fuck? Do these sorts of things happen to anyone but me? Is this life but my schizophrenic imaginings? Am I really to Rockland as Rockland is to me?

Once I forgot everything for a moment, but as soon I remembered who I was, all the colours were as sad as the sun setting over dignity.

Five Years Later

The late, great
unadulterated state
of Harmony
   can be defined as
        a pleasing combination
                of disparate energies...
while a raucously joyous jazz bar by the lake
becomes the conquest of five plucky ducks
who quack aquatic angels & feast pancakes
   big silly butterflies forecast death's escape
   then tickle a stuttering seven-stone Buddha
  who menstruates snowflakes awestruck,
as a miniscule orphan Prince is crowned King
among bacteria on a fiery star a light day away
in a ceremony of self-immolation & sitar & Tsar
    and I salute the secret code of creation's
cigars
       before spellchecking sections of sentence
       & polishing its parts until harmony
prevails.

      Harmony binds atom together.
      Positively or negatively charged atom=
'ion'.
 Properties of 'ion' = Harmony = balanced
mayhem.

   Harmony needs not & wants not,
   But Harmony is wanted in 211 states.

Harmony is more famous than the Shetland Pony,
can be as elusive as a four-leaf clover
& is as sexually ambiguous as my relationship
with my ex-best friend & current stalker, Aerith.

Nevertheless, show me a train and I will write you a
collision of values. Show me a hotel and I will write
you a wordy waltz. Tell me I'm a Nihilist and I will
craft you a dream. Tell me that I am to write a

factual autobiography and I will hurl you a fictional metaphor for my world, together with philosophical musings on the philanthropic nature of harmony and other associated acts.

Symbolically speaking, I always knew that a quintessentially particular woman was The One For Me, but in literal Reality, I always figured I hadn't met her yet & probably never would, or that she was Xinx. Despite the turbulence of our marriage, I'd say that K is a close enough match – numerically, I'd guesstimate she is approximately an 89% match for me two thirds of the time. This figure can intensify to a solid 92% when I'm hammered.

In the living room, Kleopatra plays *'It's All Over Now, Baby Blue'* to me on her azure acoustic guitar over & over & over again, each and every time swearing it will be the last time she ever plays *'It's All Over Now, Baby Blue'* to me on her azure acoustic guitar in the living room. I sit there, kind of entranced: her voice throbs heavy with bittersweet sadness and the atmosphere is passionately apocalyptic. She can play guitar significantly better than I can (and I myself have been learning guitar for eight years). If I didn't know she was trying to prove a point, and were I allowed to comment during one of these impromptu concerts, perhaps I might suggest one of my favourite jazz numbers or tell her that she is playing in the wrong key.

But, no, I just sit there, smoking a marijuana cigarette (though I don't ever smoke tobacco by itself, it helps make the joint smoke better).

Anyway, after hearing Bob Dylan's line *'you must leave now, take what you need, you think will last'* for the 10th time, interpreted with increasing venom by K in our marital home, I figure that the song's message is more or less embedded in my skull, so I say farewell and leave with my backpack, which contains one change of clothes, a toothbrush, toothpaste, a laptop and a book. K's spontaneous performance is her parting gift to me, and it's not entirely my fault that my wife wants some distance from me.

No, Kleopatra is not an irrational woman. It went like this: Aerith became my best friend again after we corresponded but after a misguided fuck yonks ago she started stalking me, keeping up sleeping-bag vigil outside wherever I am. And there's nothing K (my wife) can do about that, because Seattle is lawless and Aerith is a stronger woman than K, both physically and mentally.

Yep. As I said, Seattle is lawless, more or less. One gets bored less. Its fatality rate isn't flawless but the atmosphere ensures a fateful saxophone testament to Mother Nature's copulating jokers and dealers and brokers and freewheelers and smokers and spiritual healers, whose aches and hopes climax together in the soupish delirium of midnight's drunken now, where money is exchanged for dope to cope with the clowns in the compound of the skull.

Seattle is most alive at five in the morning. Around midnight the fights start; you have your average 'Revenge' brawl, and more dangerous ruckuses on the other end of the spectrum. A 'Seattle Brawl' is where the judge yells *'FIGHT, FIGHT, FIGHT!'* on a megaphone and everyone starts fighting each other, with various 'teams' being established. Once K & Aerith & I were on a team and we killed a guy by accident, paralysing him by tapping him on both shoulders and his head at the same time. Apparently, he died shortly afterwards, because we were invited to his funeral at the Hob Goblin (none of us attended).

For a while, I will wonder what on earth shall possess K to do what she will choose to do. After some contemplation, though, I shall decide that life itself is an inevitable fluke, that bodies don't necessarily have souls, and that K will do what she will do because she can, because her faculties tell her to. Perhaps K (my wife) will decide to become a prostitute again for more primal reasons.

How far I have come since then. While K opens her honkytonk brothel unbeknownst to me until a later date, I'm travelling all across the wilderness of Seattle closely followed by Aerith (my ex-best friend and current stalker). I guess the book you have in your hands now is my story. This is my story. My story is the planted seed that could have blossomed but never did. This is my story. I don't know why I am repeating myself, but I don't think it's for dramatic effect.

I step out onto the street. Union Street. Baby, I have been here before. Baby, I have been here many times before. Aerith's encampment is situated right in front of our garden. Our garden consists of an old tree & garbage bags. Aerith's encampment consists of an army sleeping park, Walmart sandwiches, energy drinks, Aerith and her manually rechargeable radio.

Aerith's whole face lights up when she sees me, and she stands up. With the urgency of a sports commentator delivering tragic news about the home team's captain, she comments, *"There's something urgent I'd like to talk to you about, Tonnan. Did you know that eight six percent of deaths are preventable?"*

You might have some vested interest in preventing your own death, but I know that whatever comes out of that woman's mouth is bound to be a puerile, pseudo-scientific 'fact' about saving the country, the church, the family unit and civilisation itself. I've heard her phony propaganda before, so I rapidly tune out.

I check my phone. It's 8:04PM. I figure I should find somewhere to sleep. Somewhere that isn't next to Aerith in her sleeping bag. Money isn't a huge issue. I guess I'll head into town. I walk three blocks towards Cherry Street station – I pass five stores, two pubs, a café and thirteen people insignificant to this story – and, though I don't look back I am obviously trailed by Aerith, as we get the bus together. Yes, she follows me, mood unchanged, seemingly unmoved by my quivering marital status or my status as someone who prefers to ignore her. A blank-sheet lady, forty-something, is dressed in fur and looks menacingly at me as I sit next to her in the second-to-front seat. I smile at her and she starts chatting, rapid-fire, to me in words that I can't understand because the external intricacies of the sound of frenzied Mandarin mean nothing to me. After offering that the only languages I speak are French and English, I simply ignore her. Aerith stands near the driver, so as to keep her eyes trained upon me.

After 9 stops, I arrive at Mercer Street. There's a Travelodge a hundred meters down the road, but first I go to The World's End. Alcohol can kill you, but it can also kill a few hours. Alcohol is the way the first world medicates itself. Alcohol stimulates your Silly's synapses until they snap, and harmony emerges, naked and blushing at its nudity. Most of the time when I get drunk, I realise that I have forgotten how good it is to be drunk.

[In high school, Aerith won many medals for her persistent athletic prowess. She scraped Bs and successfully pursued me and some other guys who proved more suitable to her manic disposition. Her primary focus, though, has always been on the wellbeing of her body. I've seen her do 200 press-ups in one go in front of my house.

But Aerith wasn't particularly well-liked in school: she was called a slut by the popular bitchy girls and represented an unattainable fantasy for the geeky crowd. She felt at home amongst her fellow athletes, though. There were even rumours that she had slept with the P.E. teacher. These allegations were unsubstantiated and as fictional as the farce that will soon unfold in The World's End, where once upon a time I briefly became famous for singing 'Touch Me' by The Doors in karaoke. I autographed thirty napkins. Though my celebrity was short-lived, the same night I fucked a short brown-eyed chick, wrote three psychedelic pop songs, and decided hummus is unequivocally too tasty to be vegan.]

Anyhow, at the bar, I play my recent favourite, a virtual reality game called "The Sexiest Man in Paradise", in which a Very Sexually Experienced Man drives around the region looking for his long-lost true love. You can race around at such speeds that the cops – all shit hot & female – give chase and you can either stop & seduce them (often resulting in incredibly hot sex) or try to kill them or drive away. You can do practically whatever you want in the urban landscape. But the aim of the game is to find the perfect woman for you: if she likes you back, you have theoretically won the game and can enjoy incredibly hot sex with her in various role-playing scenarios. The instruments of virtual reality release endorphins and simulate the orgasm pretty well, too.

This game costs 2 dollars a pop, and I happily part with my coin. Wanting virtual reality to resemble physical, I immediately head for the Rock Bar, for if

I remember correctly there is a good vibe there, and lots of beautiful women to chat up. Halfway through consuming my first pint of lager in-game, I make an ill-advised pass at an undercover journalist doing a write-up of the Rock Bar. Though her bosoms are epic & she is crazy, her love for me is not so epic or crazy, and it results in her trying to arrest me. Since no one likes journalists pretending to be cops & I'm getting arrested for no reason, I am quickly able to enlist a couple of tattooed figures to help me get this crazy voluptuous journalist to cease and desist her attempts to restrain me. The crazy voluptuous journalist is punched once, then twice, then thrice in the face, but remarkably she doesn't seem to show any signs of pain nor does her body move very much. Maybe she is an undercover cop… still, I wonder what her problem with me trying to chat her up was.

Anyhow, she bangs the two tattooed figure's heads into each other, and in turn quickly hurls me over her head, causing me to land on my head. I black out. GAME OVER. Oh, well – maybe there'll be more joy next time. Although in this game you play a Very Sexually Experienced Man, it is sometimes hard to actually engage in acts of fornication. I didn't get too hurt in the process of the gameplay, though, so I am thankful. The sensors in "The Sexiest Man in Paradise" are pretty sophisticated, but you can still die unexpectedly, like in "Don't Cry" where one shot from behind can set you back a tenner.

As soon as I remove my headpiece, Aerith (my ex-best friend & current stalker) says to me, "*I was thinking about you and I.*" That makes a change, I think.

"*What is it now, Aerith?*" I ask.

"I've decided that I'm not going to follow you around anymore. None of my dreams have been realised by doing so, and plus, I don't think it's healthy, as – you know – you've told me you don't like it, in less kind words."

"Okay. Great. Why now?" I ask, still dazed from my experience in "The Sexiest Man in Paradise".

"What's the use in chasing something that's already got away?

"I know what you mean," I say. *"Anyway, it's great that you've come to that realisation by yourself."*

Aerith nods her head, then looks at me as if she is expecting me to offer a concluding comment to complete her Hero's Journey back to nowhere. I don't bite the bait. *"Hey, I want you to keep this,"* Aerith finally says. She hands me a passport photo of herself, in which she smiles at the camera with red lipstick on. Her expression in the polaroid is kind of awkward, as if she is a little embarrassed to be spending time taking a photograph of herself. It's not like her to wear lipstick either.

"Thank you," I say, *"I'm going to play another game. It's surprisingly addictive."*

"I saw your last go at it," she responds. *"There's no pleasing some people."*

And with that, Aerith leaves the pub and doesn't look back. I play another game, and another game, and so on and so forth until I've spent twelve dollars over the course of three hours. I head for the Holiday Inn, surprisingly energetically, with a spring in my step, heart still pounding, feeling like the sexiest man in paradise, uncharacteristically not tailed by any admirers.

***

Do you believe in God? There will always be a God for those who believe. Believing makes it so, though God couldn't care less whether you do or don't. If you don't believe in God, it could be argued that both of your parents jointly form The Creator, and that's the last thing any healthy adult wants.

I feel as tired as God must feel when I wake up in the Holiday Inn the next morning. It's as if something's not quite right in the fundamental ecology of my body. I have a profound urge to smoke a marijuana cigarette, but marijuana is supposed to be a non-addictive substance. I also feel a hankering for the comforts proffered by "The Sexiest Man in Paradise". Yeah, I figure, if I can just play that game for another while, be someone other than myself & experience all the bodily sensations that encompasses, then and only then I shall feel more myself.

I go to the lobby. Aerith is nowhere in sight. So far so good. You know, I am about to get a bus to the Village and walk the rest of the way back home to Mercer Street, but in the hotel lobby something catches my attention. It is one of those novelty Mind-Readers, kind of along the lines of "The Sexiest Man in Paradise". It's a device that supposedly scans the Universe and reads your fate using formulas designed by 'scientists'. This one claims it *"prints a picture of your match made in heaven"*. What the heck? Scientists talk to God, so what the heck? I put a coin in. I keep my mind blank, as instructed.

The machine prints a picture. I look at it. It's Aerith's face. I check it against the passport photo she gave me yesterday. The only difference is that in this picture she is not smiling and does not have lipstick on. The passport photo of Aerith and the picture of my 'match made in heaven' are obviously the same woman. What on earth is wrong with this cruel world?

I get the bus to the Village, walk back to Mercer Street and discover that there has been an intercom installed on the house K & I share. Since I don't have a key, I buzz it.

"Are you my ten o'clock?" K's voice sounds through the intercom. She has an odd sense of humour at times.

"Hi K, it's Tonnan. Aerith stopped following me. Can you let me in?"

She doesn't. If you don't know why, it will take a little bit detective work to figure out why.

Since I am now dependent on nicotine (I was oblivious to the subtle warning message at the beginning of each "The Sexiest Man in Paradise" game), I amble around aimlessly, then fuck my stupid 'no-marijuana-no-tobacco' rule and so buy a pack of 20 Marlboro Reds.

It so happens that I won't see Aerith, my apparent match made in heaven, ever again in this lifetime. To be honest, I hope that I won't see her next lifetime either. The woman doesn't have very good taste in food, so her breath is always a little off kilter with my sensibilities.

Anyhow, Kleopatra is resolute she wants to finish the new, or old, chapter that she has started in her life, so eventually I just go to The World's End again and become truly addicted to "The Sexiest Man in Paradise".

In the virtual reality, it so happens that I meet the 192% Perfect Woman for Me. I don't have a very good memory & I'm not very good with the theoretical side of Maths, so for a while I forget that I am just playing a single-player game & that if the

192% Perfect Woman for Me is the 100% Wrong Woman for Me, she (or it) is still 100% Wrong. But I have a wonderful life for five months, working & spending my savings on a game. Yeah, I have it pretty good for a while.

***

My boss at ForgetAboutIt Entertainment is called Violet. Unlike my stubbled ex-boss, Violet never makes patterns out of her facial hair or breaks a sweat. Unlike my stubbled ex-boss, Violet is irresistibly attractive, irrepressibly brash and irresponsibly inventive. She has a childishly mischievous, crow-like demeanour and spends the majority of her time wrestling with the 'artistic embryos' of long-winded slideshows.

Perhaps wrongly, Violet believes herself to be somewhat of a latter-day prodigal princess, an inspiringly female Vincent Van Gogh. Though many of Violet's delusions have yet to materialise, her face does resemble that of a faintly fatter Marilyn Monroe, and her doodles can indeed be likened to Michelangelo's incomplete erotic masterpieces. In other words, Violet is easy to look at, and her creations for ForgetAboutIt Entertainment are riddled by epiphanies that are already inexplicably deformed by the dawn of their conception.

I often wonder what the figure of Violet means to me. As my boss, she dictates how I spend most of my waking hours, but does she function as some kind of symbol too? Perhaps Violet represents the God that all of us will be answerable to at our private apocalypse, ultimately unknowable & potentially damning yet utterly fair. In terms of the commercial hierarchy, certainly, I am a slave to Violet & Violet is a slave to her boss & Violet's boss is a slave to the current ebb of the economy of Video Games. Am I to the donkey as Violet is to

Jesus as Jesus is to God and God is to the immutable shifting of the seasons?

I suppose everyone has a Violet in their lives, a boss whose mouth can purge you of purgatory with a murmured phrase of praise or dreary your day with an ambiguous grunt. Am I secretly in love with Violet? I forget.

Me, I'm still as verbose as verbatim theatre. Me, I've forgotten far more than I know, and I suppose that's why tomorrow comes so slow. I can cloak myself from head to toes in wine & divine prose, but all forms of conforming to normality have always been elbows to my slowing brain & growing ego. This 9-5 job of mine is, by now, my sworn foe. My only refuge is the hourly smoking break, which is generally attended by four fellow smokers.

"Many people survive without nicotine. I think. At least this is what I was led to believe," says Michael. *"A Google search, however, reveals that nicotine is contained in tomatoes, potatoes, eggplants, teas, and peppers. Many people probably still survive without any nicotine dreams in their bloodstream, though."*

"I can't survive without nicotine in my bloodstream," confesses Quentin. *"Nobody knows what would happen to me without nicotine. I'd probably be dead. A blood-test calculating the amount of nicotine in my system would be an effective way to determine whether I am dead or alive. I love tomatoes, potatoes, nicotine patches, cigarettes & cigars. I don't mind the occasional pepper, either."*

"I'm addicted to a virtual reality game called 'The Sexiest Man in Paradise'," I say. *"The simulation issues nicotine into your system as a way of stimulating the release of endorphins. I didn't read the warning on the title screen properly, hence I*

now smoke every opportunity I get. I'm not like you guys, though. I'm not a real addict."

Michael guffaws at my remark & this triggers a spit-laden cackle from Quentin, which in turn causes Olivia to wince & may act as the catalyst for a coughing fit from Kate. But I wasn't joking. [I'm only joking – I was joking when I said I wasn't joking].

"You should quit that fucking game and get a real girlfriend," Olivia says to me. *"Video games may be fun, but you're having sex with something that's never been alive & never will be… and in a public place. What would you mother think? Would your father be proud? That's sick as swallowing shit, man."*

Olivia's remark wanders round my nicotine-induced migraine until well past sunrise that night. What she said should have come as no surprise, but it seems to crystallise a series of revelations in my mind. Sometimes loneliness completes itself so damn vividly.

Firstly, I realise that Olivia is right, and the characters created by geeky computer-designers are not my real friends, irrespective of one cartoon's telepathic claim to me that it is living female mutant bacteria.

Secondly, I realise that 'The Sexiest Man in Paradise' is perhaps the image of what I project onto it, and my affair with the game represents my erotic imagination rebelling against its maker in a desire for pristine perfection that even porn cannot achieve.

Thirdly, Olivia's remarks about my folks remind me of my dad's hope to invest one day in 'video-sensory technology'. My dad was, and probably still is, a chain-smoker and often used to refer to himself as the 'Sexiest Man South of North'. I wonder. Could my dad possibly have a hand in the creation of "The Sexiest Man in Paradise"? I never properly concentrated as the Virtual-Reality credits rolled in the arcade.

And is my dad even my real father, given that I have lived three lifetimes or more? Moreover, where is my own mother whom, regardless of the form she takes, will forever remain so dear to my soul?

I remember writing Welcome to Planet Earth & Thomas the Tank Engine & Blue Peter & speech therapy & celibacy–
I remember pissing in drain & apocalyptic visions of headmistress at door with expulsion papers –
I remember goodbye England motel days & roar of crowd & Mardi Gras jingle jangle blues –

I remember Golden Gate wonderment & bewildered beauty of century's ambition –
I remember ramblings with K & stories of Steroid McKinnon hurling portapotty at love rival –
I remember nature dumping dumpy patron saint of society stark naked in televised disaster –

I remember pillaged streets & abandoned riverfront bars & old fallen heroes inanimate in rage –
I remember forty-five prostituted statements of intent flung at moon & forgotten by sunrise –
I remember popping pimple in mirror & undreamt satisfaction of creation destruction –

I remember discussions of unfathomable futures under sanitised ceilings that stunk of sanity –
I remember first trembling body exhalation surprise in K's bed & thinking nothing for two minutes –
I remember your howl after Uncle Dead Telephone

Call & sound of matchsticks & broken voices –

I remember Geiger counter & growth of your pillbox
& talking to you from 1 to 4 in the morning –
I remember tragicomedy of wheelchair & torturous
moment of understanding & forever fading to past –
I remember Godfather & 8am ambulance screams
& chasing familiar worlds back to their beginnings –

I remember position of bed & catholic priest
solemnity & moonlit morphine utterances –
I remember old news & waking in empty rooms to
weepy-eyed relatives & dead adrenaline nothing –
I remember your face, I remember your hands, I
remember the feeling but forget the words!

I remember urn & wind & unceremonious attempt
at finality one unhinged October evening –
I remember genius sings the blues & abandoned
wank to Jukebox Creator under red misted skies –
I remember swallowing mistake & how atomic angel
hid under table begging for fish-food –

I remember ecstatic jump to K as train entered
heart of St Pancreas pulled by twelve imaginary
horses –
I remember oblivion & journey back from oblivion &
how K made map-drawing an art –
I remember final infatuate sunrise & how her scent
lingered on my pyjamas as evidence of dawn –

I remember mushroom paradise hotel near Royal
Albert hall & hypomanic week alone in room –
I remember sudden alienation in cereal aisle of
supermarket & riding plastic elephant outside for
50p –
I remember perfect expression of violinist's
heartstrings & thinking human capacity for creation
infinite –

I remember sitting stoned on bedroom floor,
grieving fifteen years in four hours –
I remember your face, I remember your hands, I
remember your eyes & your voice & your laugh –
I remember our home, I remember our love, I
remember it all & I never forgot!

And I remember Zelda, naïve yet worldly, originally
so unjaded by civilisation's offerings & consciously
collaborating with Restralardin biblical characters in
the prison of her skull, munching on something
every few instants yet a better writer than me for it.

I remember Rockland, whose grotesque charisma
radiated magnetism, whose unwavering decency
was his downfall, whose schizophrenic soul
continued to communicate with the great unknown
behind everyone's eyes.

I remember Xinx, whose physical beauty & stature
originally compelled me to introduce my already
infatuated self to her, whose shyly intelligent
playfulness pulled me back for more like a
lonesome visionary addict chasing the next hit.

I remember K, whose becoming
straightforwardness once signalled the start of
something beautiful, whose side-splitting subtleties
made her my closest confidant for so many years &
tears.

Yes, I recall it all with hallucinogenic precision.
Some of the important stuff. And the sum of the
important stuff on Earth at least.

So, I decide to quit the "Sexiest Man in Paradise"
forever, because I want my own forever back.

Drunk on whisky & dreams, I phone my wife, who is still working as a part-time prostitute.

"K, I quit the fucking game. I fucking quit every game," I slur. *"Where the shit shall we go to next, friend?"*

K laughs contentedly on the other end of the line. *"Wherever. We'll go wherever."*

"Sounds like a plan," I say. *"I'll see you in ten."*

And so I hang up & shamble back home through the midnight haze, drunken figure dancing past the drunken world like the vision of a love story gone wrong, dancing to the sad and soundless music that wide-eyed dreamers make as they fall like rain, shackled by their own fantasies, suffocated by their own memories, but dancing, dancing in a crazy breathless reverence for life and feeling – brain screaming, soul bleeding, mind running, heart gunning – but feeling… feeling feelings… and feeling is the only thing that ever mattered to me in this world so I was the happiest I've ever been being the saddest I've been because I realised that it all meant something.

But who's to say? *The Devil Can't & God Won't. The Mother of Infinity* licks her lips and the rest is a version of infinity. This, however, is an erotic thriller which twists, in a serpentine slinky of kaleidoscopic climaxes, until it reaches an inevitably understated & wholly frustrating ending.

The Animal Circus & The Secret Sum Of My World

Happiness is fleeting and so are some second chances. Two weeks pass before I finish eating K out.

"Grains of sand are so damn tiny & stars are so damn big, but there are more stars in the visible Universe than there are grains of sand on Planet Earth," K says. She is liable to deliver a fun fact after her thousandth climax.

"The existence of God Science perhaps partially accounts for that 'truth', but maybe the idea in itself represents part of a federal government drive to pacify mankind by inducing an aspiring awe in the poor, inspire middle-class artists, and doctor a happy complacency in the rich." I say. *"I don't know what to think."*

"I think you need to start thinking for yourself. You're starting to sound like a high school psychology fan radicalised by Marx. You read more books in a month than Odell Beckham has read in his lifetime. But Odell Beckham is about 50,000 times richer than you & he is famous & he does what he really loves for a living, which is keeping fit. I guess what I'm saying is that you need to take a good look at your life before it's too late to become a sports star," K says lightly, not intending to offend but still wounding my increasingly delicate self-esteem. She polishes off the ready-meal lasagne that she had been sporadically chewing at during our sex act. Fucking and food are her favourite things. There are more grains of sand in K's body than there are in mine because she grew up on the coast and that surely accounts for some of her cunningness too.

"I think I need a marriage counsellor to help me make my decisions," I say, suddenly, with a fragility that is not entirely at odds with my overall feeling of helplessness.

"So be it," breathes Kleopatra with challenging malice, before her expression shifts into a happy indifference. *"Want to go to the Animal Circus afterwards?"* she asks.

***

"I love Kleopatra because she tries her best at whatever she does, even if the entirety of the task is doomed to failure. For example, anything that necessitates the use of an oven or balances upon the understanding of an extended metaphor is always a complete write-off. But K rarely sets the kitchen on fire and our quotidian life seldom requires an analogy to animate it. Personally, though, I don't quite understand how anyone as intelligent as K can be so inept at cooking or comprehending a simple quadratic equation. But that's another story," I say, itching at an earlobe after realising I haven't quite risen to the premise of the psychiatrist's original question. I sigh a bewildered sigh and cough a smoker's cough, masking my shame with my left hand whilst making a knot in my hair with the right. *"But... anyway... I love Kleopatra because she makes me laugh. I love K because she has beautiful dimples and because she never wears makeup & never needs to. I love K because she is the best dancer I have ever met, because she cares about the environment ten times more than most members of PETA and because she always cleans up after herself, even when she's in a bad mood. I love K because she's prettier than almost everyone else I've ever had sex with, because there's a sweet ambiguity to her every 'see you later', and because Kleopatra is a*

much more elegant name than any other. I love K because she gives what she takes. I love K because she feeds me Oreos after we have sex. I love K because she is only clumsy when she wants to be, though I don't mean to suggest that she is manipulative. I love K because she doesn't give a shit about the past or the consequences of not giving a shit. Yep. I love K. Most of the time. Is that a good enough answer, Doc?"

"*Sure. That's good. That is a pretty damn fine answer, actually,*" says the happy hippy psychiatrist patronisingly and dopily, pretending to jot down notes. He looks as sincere as a stoned madman trying to procure more drugs from the party he believes to be the town medicine man, but somehow I don't believe he's being entirely genuine. "*No, that's a fucking* great *answer. Kle-o-pat-ra?*" The shrink shrilly spells each syllable of K's name as if it were his first attempt at a foreign word. "*What do you love about your husband Tonnan?*"

"*Doctor, before I met Tonnan, I was always running. Not towards something or some goal but running to escape myself. As you can guess, this proved futile. Tonnan gave my life meaning. I love Tonnan because Tonnan taught me to love myself and I love Tonnan because I love Jesus and I love Jesus because I love God and I love God because I am grateful for existence. Tonnan is a Christlike figure to me,*" says K, delicately trimming her blue fingernails with small flirtatious bites, like a high school girl trying to sleep with the principal.

"*Kleopatra! How wonderful!*" The happy hippy psychiatrist beams at a hummingbird hovering outside the window, then fixes his gaze upon me. "*Isn't that something, Tonnan? That sounded like an 'extended metaphor' to me. And a pretty damn fine one at that. Do you share Kleopatra's feelings about finding 'meaning'?"*

"Christ's wife is the Church, no?" I ask.

"Why... ye-es," the psychiatrist replies hesitantly. *"What's your point, Tonnan?"*

"The last time Kleopatra went to church was years ago. In fact, our wedding was not even held in a church. That must make it over a century, or since she was a kid. Still, since Time began for her, K has enjoyed aggrandising religious figures. She has often, for example, claimed to be 'God's Mother and Satan's Daughter'.

"God is mother? Why... ye-es," the happy hippy says, nodding his head in agreement as if considering a Crossroad Conundrum for a second. *"God is indeed each of our mothers. But Satan's door ta what?"*

"K said she is *God's mother and Satan's daughter*," I repeat reticently.

Now Kleopatra glares in my direction and wrinkles her face up as if she has seen or smelt something utterly disgusting. *"What are you on about? Tonnan? Are you trying to win brownie points with our new shrink? I don't believe you. Judas."*

I look at K in disbelief, but then I wonder why I had even brought up K's dalliances with black magic. Perhaps I didn't like her comparing me to Christ. Usually whenever K compares me to Christ or calls me Judas it's for the purpose of some weird sex ritual. Once, she let me starve for hours on end, chained to a cross. She did look seductively satanic eating Oreos, naked in all the right places, but I was chained to a bed and fucking hungry. And Oreos are usually *my* snack! I mean, just for me...

"I don't want to unintentionally wander into the realms of allegory, Kleopatra, but do you think you may have been slightly insensitive towards Tonnan's feelings?" the happy hippy psychiatrist asks, as if he's keen to embark on some allegorical voyage and wants to hear another extended metaphor.

"Tonnan? TONNAN'?" K speaks then vaguely shouts my name at an obtrusively beautiful pot of fake flowers, as if an ancient disdain clouds the memory of my refrain. *"Sometimes you need to forget in order to forgive. Tonnan's not my boss and I am not dependent upon his continuing love in order to fulfil my potential as a contributing member of society. I don't have the perspective to say I am being insensitive towards Tonnan. I was instantly infatuated with him the instant I saw him, and my infatuation was not yet faltered."*

"Okay. Okay." The happy hippy psychiatrist seems to be trying to calm K down yet sounds disappointed she has not risen to the bait even more. A confrontation in this office might not sour the air of the premises forever, but as I rapidly retreat into my mind, I figure the marriage of K & I is a time bomb without any professional intervention or symbolic stitching of wounds. *"I wonder what Tonnan's intentions were in calling us to congress here today. Did you hope, Tonnan, to bridge the differences between you & Kleopatra, or did you hope to start a fight?"*

Without as much as a word or a glance backwards, I stride out of the shrink's office, gait shrinking without shrinking. K follows after me in less than a heartbeat. Women are quick to detect the inept exteriorities of men, even quicker to follow the object of their affections, and most beings are lithe to stay in places they did not want to be in during the first instance. Figures, I figure.

***

The atmosphere at the Animal Circus is joyous and festive. There's a real mixture of ages in the audience tonight. I find the premise of the Animal Circus unethical & barely legal, but I guess that's part of the magic of show biz. If K was pretending to be mad at me, K has stopped pretending to be mad at me. As the lights dim, my wife squeezes my hand as if nothing has changed since the first Big Bang. The happy intensity of her fingers upon mine seem to promise a sweet future for the both of us. I look at her and her eyes temporarily convince me that is impossible to feel ecstasy without feeling hope.

A spotlight focuses on the centre of the ring. A frowning human clown on top of an ape in a gown rides a gigantic liger who strides around menacingly. The crowd boos. Then the frowning clown breathes a ring of fire, which baby kangaroos vault through. The crowd goes berserk. I wet my pants a bit. The show must go on, so the show goes on.

My favourite bit of the Animal Circus is the end, which is a Meet & Greet with the animal stars. I meet the dancing frog, the somersaulting parrot, the laughing penguin, and all kinds of cool characters. Each animal star seems genuinely thrilled to be where they are. I expect the ape in a gown to break character when I ask him a serious question about the morals of the Animal Circus, but all he does is mime a weep.

All of the animal stars seem proud yet down-to-earth and grateful for the attention. Animal stars definitely aren't robots, but I don't think most of them have a clue how extraordinarily talented they are. I wonder if some of the animal stars – the chickens or the elephant or the frog, for example – figure they lucked out and got a free front-row ticket to the human freak show every night. Anyhow, I just love watching these animal stars strut their stuff. These particular animal stars are the best of the best and they just know it.

It is getting late, so K & I fly back to town. We cuddle in bed, and I think.

Like a minority of spiritual men, I consider myself a spiritual man. I may be wrong, but I believe I've developed an immunity to the more outrageous demands of my ego. I've reflected upon it a little and I figure my personal brand of tranquillity flowers predominantly in men who accept that their destiny is preordained. The actions that arise out of whatever temporal state of enlightenment I may sporadically experience tend to be misunderstood by the community and usually result in an arrest. In the eyes of the authorities, I am abusing my genius. I'm being totally serious. It's as sad a state of affairs as sitting on a toilet for half a century laughing at a broken mirror. I'm being totally serious.

After an exhausting day that includes our first & last meeting with the psychiatrist, several red herrings and the profoundly bizarre & infinitely cool Animal Circus, K starts snoring loudly. I decide to sleep on the sofa.

Before I drift into the mysterious mayhem of slumber infused by starkly symbolic reverie, I characteristically consider the significance of my own insignificance. My world unfolds around me & always will whereas your world unfolds around you & always will, but as time passes I find I'm increasingly perceiving that some beings have it easy and some don't. I could expand upon this point, but right now I won't because I'm busy contemplating a ludicrous impossibility: will I one day have experienced every single living being's existence? Am I gravely underestimating my soul's forgetfulness & the number of lifetimes I have been alive? I arrive at the strange supposition that Reality is a single-player game I'm playing against real human Gods and animal stars but chiefly against myself & the Devil. And then this tautological mindfuck knocks my wilfully retarded mind unconscious, into the realms of reverie and the Underworld.

I'm on a downward throttling elevator face-to-face with a teenage Goblin about 3-foot-tall with purple eyes and green skin. We seem to be shooting directly downwards in some sophisticated metal machine.

"Hey man!" I say to my companion, excited to be dreaming a novel dream. *"Where are we going?"*

"We are travelling to the World," the teenage Goblin asserts morosely. I gather this is accurate information and somewhat of a routine for him from his distantly friendly tone.

"Care to elaborate?"

"The World is simply the only failproof recipe for disaster, man. Billions of humans & trillions of beings, all without a masterplan," he says coldly. The goblin itches at his scalp, which boasts around fifteen visible yet colourless hairs. *"Sometimes it's a struggle to find your godforsaken Freedom Pass. Sometimes it's a struggle to find a wisp of decent angel grass. Sometimes the past blasts her theme song just a little too loud. Sometimes you must dress in a tuxedo and sometimes in a shroud."* The goblin spits a big ball of phlegm onto the otherwise pristinely clean floor. *"Any day now I will be the only author of my tomorrow. Even now each moment is*

complete in itself. I must pray for tomorrow, and you must pay for today." The goblin nods jerkily in the direction of the elevator ceiling with a detectable bitterness.

"What's your name?" I ask him.

"Zelda," the goblin replies sulkily. "I love you," the goblin whispers in a summarizing tone of geriatric prayer. The goblin shrugs. The goblin cackles. "Show me an egoless man and of him I will make a profit." He grins a big goblin grin at me, teeth sparkling a disconcerting blue.. I feel a pang of pain in my heart of hearts, but my soul is unmoved. When Xinx died for the first time, the World – how do you say this in English? – crushed a soul that worshipped Her… I don't know why I think of this now, but I do.

"Yes," the goblin says, though it is unclear if this is an answer to my original question. "We are headed for the centre of Planet Earth, which has arbitrarily been labelled the Centre of the Universe by the Central Planet of Diplomacy. Planet Earth is the Central Planet of Diplomacy. Where have you been half your life?" The goblin laughs at me. I expect I must look unduly bewildered or vacant. I notice that the goblin's panic dramatically lessens as mine dramatically increases as the elevator dramatically descends. He tuts twice. I'm not sure he is a teenager anymore. The goblin is of indeterminate age… he is ageless, somehow. He looks me up and down. "I am twenty-seven."He smiles invitingly. "This is because you are twenty-seven!" The goblin is gleeful now. "My birthday was February 13th too, but this does not mean that I am Jimi Hendrix." He jogs in slow-motion on the spot. "Does Sir want an alibi now?!"

The Captain shakes my head. I'm more intrigued than frightened. I've had plenty of bad dreams before. Most bad dreams have one thing in common: most bad dreams end. I look around the elevator. It's a decently sized machine that seems to be free-falling through thin air. There are no buttons on it. By the time the ceiling falls off, I've become pretty insular. I just want the reverie to conclude. I feel sick. The goblin scoffs, his eyes conveying that he is offended by my reluctance to engage in conversation.

If there's a ride, I know I am already on it, because a voice that is distinctly my own proclaims, "For as long as you remain here, these words form a guiltily guiltless guide to My Underworld. The time you spend reading informs your future, so let us pray that this has been and will continue to be entertaining, engaging & fulfilling!"

The goblin frowns as if absorbing my thought-dreams in this dream. He scratches his non-existent stubble for a couple of seconds, and then nods at me derisively. "So be it," he declares. He plucks a strand of hair from his head and swallows it. He opens his jaw impossibly wide and swallow me whole.

My dick tingles home and I am transported to another dream.

I dream I am witnessing a witch fly high over a snow forest. I instinctively know that this figure is a personification of Satan. I laugh because I already know for a fact that Satan is not God, and neither am I. We are in it together, to a small extent anyway. The only time I wished the whole Eden shenanigans didn't happen was when I found out that the real Zelda has a dick. He or she is still super-hot and a great conversationalist, though. I'm so schizophrenic I would totally tap that if I weren't so damn religious.

My dick tickles another home and I am transported to a new dream.

Mum & I are walking and talking on Hampstead Heath. Mum seems to be some kind of apparition, yet I know she is with it. Mum is smoking a tailormade cigarette. I know I am in a dream because while I am alive Mum isn't dead.

"Xinx is Love," Mum says. "The second you realise you are in love with Love, the world gets complicated and you blow it, or destiny fucks you up the arse."

"I nearly gave myself a happy ending," I sigh. "I get restless, I guess. What good are happy endings if they are not thrilling?"

"Rockland is the man you might have been," Mum continues, ignoring my question. "Every baby is charismatic. Rockland is commercial fiction, the wailing bastard child of Oscar Wilde.

There's nothing innately wrong with stoicism, though."

"That means every boy and every girl… they're all going to Helen," I say, quoting the Restralardin bible. I hesitate. "Did this story happen somewhere? Who is Cat? Who is K? Who am I?"

"Cat was an animal star," Mum says. "She was so good for you while you thought she was God, but she was just a star animal. K? K is a stranger to you, yet she is your closest friend. Schizophrenia is Tonnan. Tonnan is schizophrenia. You are Tonnan. Schizophrenia is you. You are schizophrenia."

"What the fucking fuck?," I say to Mum, and next thing you know it, I am dead awake and typing the final draft of a fantastical & allegedly revoltingly erotic thriller onto a Dell laptop.

Were I a worse storyteller, I would end at the ending, but I'm not sure if The End is really The Beginning & The Beginning is really The End. I guess the preceding words are a factual alibi for loneliness. I guess this is a love story with an ending. I guess this is the story of how I didn't marry my one true love or actually even like my 'match-made-in-heaven'. I guess this is a discourse on mortality and the immortality of illusion. But, of course, at the end of ending, *The Mother of Infinity* licks her lips, just like she always does, and the rest is your own version of infinity to endure or enjoy.

THE FOOTNOTE TO "GOD'S PRETTY GAME OF GROTESQUE PUPPETS"

You are the surprise homepage of my heart and half of my brain. I used to be cleverer but now I'm wise to the spies and the rain. The only sedentary part of me is my body. Let your eyes explain. I used to love sunset but now I prefer sunrise. I can't complain, but I don't forget that my future will always be foggy. Almost every verse I've written since I met you has a secret refrain. You're that secret refrain. I never got to ask you if you know who you are, but I know who you are because you are the secret refrain to most of my verses.

I could talk about how I feel about you for years, but I expect my friends are getting bored of hearing that crap. None of them have ever even met you. Circumstances get strange and sometimes shit happens. You're the secret refrain to almost every verse I've written since I met you. You might be other things as well but people can be more than one thing at a time, right?

As a vaguely handsome schizophrenic, partially disabled introvert loner and mathematically-minded brain damaged genius, society hasn't always treated me with the dignity and respect that every being deserves. I've been arrested three times for breaking the somewhat victim less drug laws and I've been locked in mental hospitals for 4 years of my life because some people thought I was a little weird. As a matter of fact, I was a little brain damaged and a little traumatised. I would never rape anyone, I would never kill anyone, and I would never steal from anyone except for those who can afford it and if I am truly struggling with life. Nowadays it's a well documented fact that I can be 'mentally unwell' and at times must be kept away from 'the public'.

For example, the last time I got arrested was for walking around my neighbourhood naked because I felt like having a once in a lifetime experience. I spent 4 months in mental hospital following the arrest. Jesus! I am a Christian. I used to study the bible? Is it illegal or insane to be a Christian? Here's my understanding of the bible. Apparently, God created the world and the garden of Eden was paradise for a man and a woman. Then Satan - who is apparently the bad guy - did some 'bad' voodoo and they realised that all of them was exposed (they were naked, in other words). This realisation led to 'original sin'. Maybe I am missing something or misread the text, but one point has never been properly explained to me: why aren't all Christians naked now?

You could argue that we live in the era of the new testament now, but I believe Eden is the paradise we are on the brink of destroying. So why aren't we naked? Why not pretend the world has just begun? Are people afraid of dying? In all honesty, once you rid yourself of your ego, you rid yourself of the fear of death. My mum died when I was 16. I didn't want her to die particularly but I didn't want her to live a miserable existence due to the pain that her cancer caused.

Me? I nearly died when I was 19. I jumped off a bridge. I reached a state of nirvana. Nirvana is a transcendent state in which there is neither suffering, desire, nor sense of self, and the subject is released from the effects of karma and the cycle of death and rebirth. It represents the final goal of Buddhism.

You are being fooled. There is no eternity. Eternity implies a time frame. There is no time. There is just life. To quote one of my heroes, Bob Dylan, "stick with me, baby, stick with me anyhow - things are going to start to get interesting right about now".

I'm a dude who drinks funky spirits when thirsty for taboo. I'm a truly nude junkie on an epic quest that involves you. I'm curious as Casanova and perhaps as beautiful as my cat. When Corona is over and I'm famous, you'll realise that. I'm a servant to the monarchy and an angel-headed trickster. I became a shop-lifter at five but my soul was born a drifter. I'll fantasise about you forever, which is as long as I've been alive. I plan to finish my poem about your earlobes by the time I'm 35.

You know what? This next bit is for someone special. This next bit was written for everyone else to hear, but I am addressing someone special.

I wanted to feel you dance with my existence for hours on end within about ten seconds of meeting you. You made me feel special. You made me care. You made me a person. I can't thank you enough. You're the secret refrain to almost every verse I've written since I met you. This secret refrain helps my brain sing my soul. You are my secret refrain.

(Every God damned being is special. Didn't they teach you that in school?)

I like Eliza, man. I like Eliza a lot. She's a beautiful person. I'm talking about the Irish Eliza.

Luisa? She's alright; she's just clear. She's delicate, seems like a peer. But she's just too precise and too dear. And Johanna's not here. And so what if she were in another universe? I don't have any profound sexual feelings for any of these people anymore.

The scent of lent pornography dances dressed in beer.
But the druid shells I shed are just dandruff to your ear.

For no man should ever repent
The severed time he never spent
As he begins his slow descent
Into worlds that lovers bent
With the scent of their lament cemented to every burning nose.

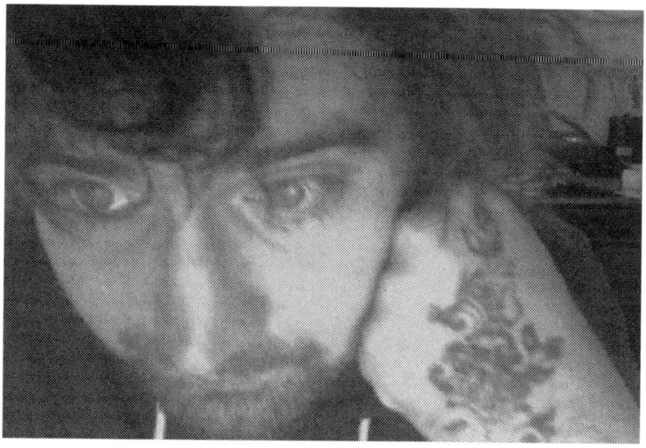

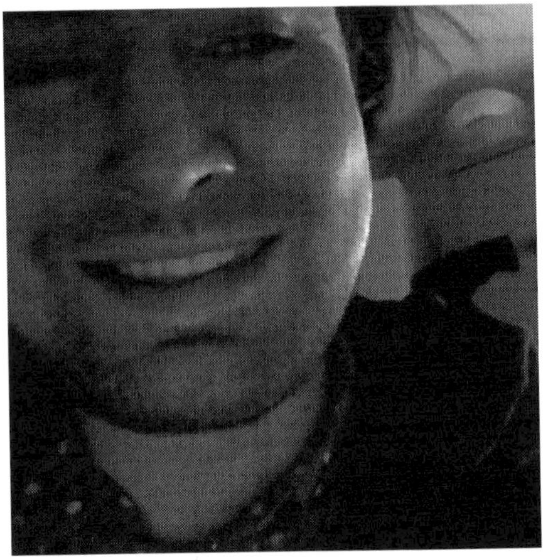

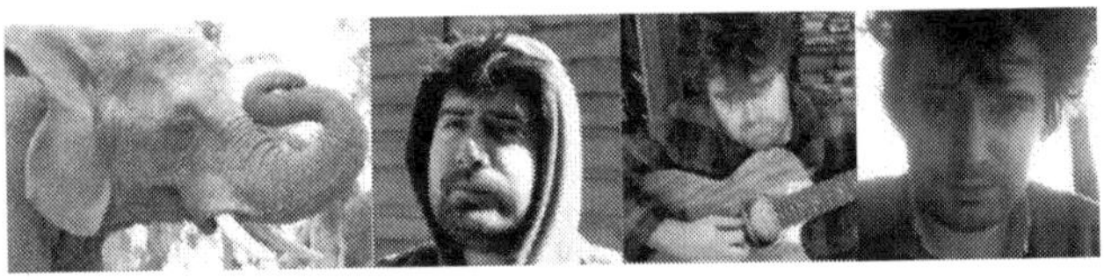

TOP SECRET RECENT BONUS LYRICS (!!!!!!!!!!!!!):

I was dreaming of the future. They put the past in a computer.
I was screaming of my death. Doctors say I'll have no breath.
I was scheming with a sweat. I had no time and not one regret.
I had no son nor change to bet. I woke up and the bed was wet.
But you know what makes me sad.. you're too serious to be mad.

Will you lend your harp to my end? Is it a tall order to call you friend?
If it's okay, I'll pretend you are. Anyway, you mend my shattered heart.
I love to smoke cigars in your car. Thanks for the socks and guitar.
I won't prefer the end to the start. I will still want to know how you are.
But you know what makes me sad... you're too good to be bad.

When I was young, I was so dead. When I was young, I had no head.
When I was young, I knew nothing. When I was young, I was bluffing.
My fears are sung but you forgave. My years are flung into your grave.
Your ears and tongue are so brave. Save a brainwave for a close shave.
But you know what makes me sad... you're too happy to be glad.

****

If you know me too well, then I will push you away.
I don't care what you say because hell is yesterday.

But the policeman yelled and said next stop is bedlam.
It's too late to die because I'm already dead as lamb.
There's no time to itemise or hunt for who I am.
But I'm headed to Louisiana and I shall go by tram.

I can forget; I swear. I can let myself care.
I am here but I'm not. I forgot what I forget.
The sun sets over mystery, and history too I bet.
Silence reigns truth and everyone gets wet.
I'm going back down the alley I used to smoke in.
I'm listening to the blues in the clothes I woke in.
But my heart is dancing to its own Theme Song.

And my soul is a mute and mutes are rarely wrong.
I'll fool ya straight to the ocean and back to the city.
I'll school you til I've learnt all I can and that's a pity.

I can forget; I swear. I can let myself care.
I am here but I'm not. I forgot what I forget.
The sun sets over mystery, and history too I bet.
Silence reigns truth and everyone gets wet.

I must have written a thousand love poems or more.
Now I realise there's not much left of love to explore.
But I'm evolving my communication and sex appeal.
Some feelings run so deep that they'll never heal.
I'll be her secret soul mate for as long as she likes.
I can't swim anymore or ride your odd pedal bikes.

I can forget; I swear. I can let myself care.
I am here but I'm not. I forgot what I forget.
The sun sets over mystery, and history too I bet.
Silence reigns truth and everyone gets wet.

****

As I stood in her clown shoes, I found I could snooze.
The newspaper said the town drowned in the blues.
I swear I wept as I slept confused and dead yet again.
I fled from a prayer and read the reviews of madmen.
I learned of the trouble because of the Wizard of Oz.
He stroked my stubble where a blizzard once was.
He said, "Let's dance for life". I replied, "I have a wife right now".
He said, "Let's kiss for death". I replied, "Bliss is breath, anyhow"
He said, "I'll pay." I said, "Why didn't you say?" I milked the cow.

So I felt the fat on his tall face and then I spat on his tongue.
The cackling cat sung a song about rats wronging the young.
We traded cards and it was funny because I was his honey.
We swayed hard for gluttony until the bard had no money.
That toad-connoisseur of a whore was eight-foot-four.
He exploded more before the law who swore at the door.
Trades involve a lie and before I run, you must learn to fly.
Don't ask me why I serenade the sun in a homemade bowtie.
My mascara blurs so I'll dig my grave in a big wig and cry.

****

Where did our sleepy countryside screams go?
Will it still weep snow by the flowing stream?
It seems no. It might rain dreams, though.
Have you named this game in which losing is the sole aim?
Why'd you change what I became then hate me all the same?
I remain me, so... shame ain't on me (no, no!)
Should I grieve you as you leave me?
I believe this word-weaving will peeve you.
But I'll love you more if you relieve me.
The stuff of fantasy will still receive me.
Do you believe me? I'm tired of dreaming.

Where is the menu you stole of the pub we went to?
Will I still scrub your soul in the new tub I'm sent to?
No means no. But I meant I know we grow, though.
Have you found the profound sound you lost so long ago?
Why'd you hound the burial ground and say I oughta know?
Fell in love, caught by love... then I fought the dove!
Should I grieve you as you leave me?
I believe this word-weaving will peeve you.
But I'll love you more if you relieve me.
The stuff of fantasy will still receive me.

Do you believe me? I'm tired of dreaming.

****

A schizophrenic policewoman addresses me angrily;
She pulls a rope out of her earlobe and strangles me;
She bans tranquillity and hands me a dirty hankie,
Saying, "You're mad but I'm glad that I'm still immune."

Kanye says the US President doesn't like black people,
Then the next US President makes marijuana legal,
Making the whole of society's soul peaceful and gleeful,
Then a businessman is elected but he's an ill cartoon.

The Prime Minister's spam folder is full of ventilators,
Then Covid strikes one too many of his neighbours,
So BoJo searches for saviours amid the spectators,
Yet all pandemics end as the humanity will soon.

Mama's moved to heaven and she's got no news.
Papa's snoozing by seven dreaming of his muse.
Brother's losing to Kevin because of 40% booze.
Cat's amusing her herself by sitting in my shoes.
I'm perusing my bookshelf with the bitter blues.

A yeti meets my grandma Betty in a woodland up above,
Saying, "Why forget yourself in such a petty thing as love?"
As a rock star plays air-guitar in his socks then eats a dove,
And his lover mutters to herself about another's grace of heart.

Shakespeare rides a reindeer to Marlowe's premiere;
Disguised as King Leer, he vomits a comet onto his peer,
Who sneers and jeers at the revered profiteer's career,
Then steers his rear in front of Shakespeare's face and farts.

My dear, I wish I could engineer you a teary love ballad,
But right now I can't write because I've got to eat

salad,
Yet I hope these light words are doleful and absurdly valid;

I've no dope at the moment but I often embrace banned arts.

Mama's moved to heaven and she's got no news.
Papa's snoozing by seven dreaming of his muse.
Brother's losing to Kevin because of 40% booze.
Cat's amusing her herself by sitting in my shoes.
I'm perusing my bookshelf with the bitter blues.

****

She'd kill for a sleeping pill but she's still on the treadmill in a quizzical trance.
She thinks romance is drinking without thinking and a metaphysical trance
She digs agents in wigs but ain't giving a statement (no, man, not a chance).
She speaks Beethoven and she's betrothed to an ashen pavement snowman.
I picture my vicar take off her knickers but he's the Greatest Fake Showman.
Maybe he's the one man who can bury the cherry of the hairy lady of no land.

She sparkles the fission of banjos and death disco at Eurovision
She trusts no glowing stardust and ducks lust with such precision.
She must silence the island asylum before she arrives at a decision
Now she's rooting for the Parisians in the thaw of Facebook deletion.
But at last her fast ends and her Christian mission

reaches completion.
She's not English yet digs fish and thus wastes a wish upon its secretion.

****

Someone planted an enchanted seed that cajoles the vacuumed womb of my soul.
Now I blindly scan tomb-like scrolls in the crowded flute of my mind's black hole.
The blazing gun of the sun is an inquisitive fruit shooting around like the mute stars.
Looting the moon was always a futile goal but at least soon Jupiter will be ours.
The thugs steal from Butcher's Palace, and I am no stranger to tearless men.
I kneel before Life & chug an orphaned chalice to make me feel fearless again.
If you call my ghost, it's because you can't face all the tall-fat small-talk anymore.
But remember me for who I was; we had jokes & pokes & smokes in broken awe.

Meet me at the party; we'll repeat the start, see; you know I know I'm partly to blame.
I'm so lonely & you're so sparkly; the only feat of my heart is knowing you feel the same.

Now the Captain wakes in the ship's closet & it feels apposite because all of us speculate.
He figures if he configures bigot braincells it's okay if he's gay but he can't fake a mate.
The last stoner loon left on earth was tone-deaf at birth due to the depressing face of entropy.
Now past clowns & gowns & down tubes of distress, she and I chase down murdered memory.

The poets of wonderland hold hands with grime &
you don't know it but you're almost a rhyme.
The ghost alien talkers push petty crime & they don't
show it but they too walk a mighty fine line.

While others smothered motherless kids with bogus
smiles, I'd guessed you'd forgive me with a kiss.
But as the rain grows wetter, you remain in a letter,
and I know better than to live life missing bliss.

*Meet me at the party; we'll repeat the start, see; you
know I know I'm partly to blame.*
*I'm so lonely & you're so sparkly; the only feat of my
heart is knowing you feel the same.*

You should pity the pretty, baby.. I pity you every time
shit gets a bit shitty or a little lame.

Printed in Great Britain
by Amazon